THE
ALCHEMIST

also by Kenneth Goddard

BALEFIRE

THE
ALCHEMIST

Kenneth Goddard

BANTAM BOOKS
TORONTO • NEW YORK • LONDON • SYDNEY • AUCKLAND

THE ALCHEMIST
A Bantam Book / August 1985

1-86 BT 1695

Copyright © 1985 by Kenneth Goddard

Book Design by Nicola Mazzella

Library of Congress Cataloging in Publication Data

Goddard, Kenneth W. (Kenneth William)
   The alchemist.

   I. Title.
PS3557.0285A78   1985   813'.54   84-91722
ISBN 0-553-05057-5

Published simultaneously in the United States and Canada

---

*Bantam Books are published by Bantam Books, Inc. Its trade-
mark, consisting of the words "Bantam Books" and the portrayal
of a rooster, is Registered in the United States Patent and Trade-
mark Office and in other countries. Marca Registrada. Bantam
Books, Inc, 666 Fifth Avenue, New York, New York 10103.*

PRINTED IN THE UNITED STATES OF AMERICA

FG   0 9 8 7 6 5 4 3 2 1

In memory of Hazel and Jingles . . .

THE
ALCHEMIST

PROLOGUE

When they went back over it all, in writing the final reports, it was readily apparent that Jamie MacKenzie had been the key, although the whys and wherefores *still* didn't make much sense.

Given his well-documented IQ and brilliant scholastic achievements, it was difficult to believe that an intelligent youth like MacKenzie could have so badly underestimated the cold indifference and the inherent violence of his chosen profession. Yet, in retrospect, it was all too clear that MacKenzie had simply not *understood* either the mind-boggling magnitude nor the inevitable consequences of his foolish error.

Somehow, Jamie MacKenzie had convinced himself that it was all just a gloriously fun and lucrative game; the irony, of course, being that while his part-time vocation was occasionally fun, and certainly lucrative, it was definitely *not* a game.

Thus, when the telephone in Voyager Hall dormitory room 245 at the University of California, San Diego, rang twice, it was a distracted and indifferent—rather than a cautiously alert—MacKenzie who looked up from his calculations and reached across his desk.

"Hello?"

"Hey, Jamie, how's it going?"

MacKenzie immediately recognized the slurred voice of Bobby Lockwood. Alcohol this time; most likely Moosehead beer, he nodded. As Jamie MacKenzie and every other resident on Voyager Hall knew all too well, Bobby Lockwood had inherited more than just brilliant blue eyes, curly black hair, an independent spirit, and some hard-earned money from his late, Alaskan-born father . . . and it wasn't a dedication to his studies. Bobby Lockwood's academic interests were strictly limited to researching the many and varied effects of chemicals on the human mind and body. Ethyl alcohol happened to be one of his favorites.

"Pressure time," MacKenzie responded good-naturedly. "Finals coming up next week. Thinking seriously about hitting a couple of books, or maybe going down to the Center to hustle up some tail. Can't make up my mind."

"That'll be the day," Lockwood laughed. "Hey listen, buddy. I think I've got somethin' nice going with a foxy little chick I just met. Planning on taking her out on a little ski trip this weekend, you know. Trouble is, I can't find any decent snow. Figured I could count on my high-livin' buddy for some help."

MacKenzie did a few quick mental calculations.

"Might be able to do something for you," he hedged. "I'm pretty well booked this month, but I just might be able to squeeze you in for a double. Gonna cost a little extra, though. Quality powder's going at a premium these days."

"Ain't that the truth," Lockwood grunted. "Double'll do us just fine, my man. Just fine. So what's it gonna run me, us being compadres and all that shit?"

"Ordinarily, this time of year, no reservation, I'd have to be getting two bills, minimum," MacKenzie said. "But seeing's how it's you, I'll make it one-fifty even. Fair enough?"

"Knew I could count on you, my man," Lockwood sighed happily. "Come tomorrow evening, that little lady's gonna be feelin' mighty grateful."

"That right?" MacKenzie chuckled, amused because the curly haired, blue-eyed Lockwood had a reputation of needing very little help in scoring with the local coeds. "You sure she knows you come with the package?"

"Scratching outside my door right now," Lockwood laughed. "So how're we gonna work it? Same as usual?"

"Box two-four-five," MacKenzie nodded. "Same old routine."

"Payment's on the way right now, buddy. Hey, listen, thanks again. And don't stay up too late hittin' them . . . books."

MacKenzie smiled, hung up the phone, and then checked his watch. Eight forty-five on a Friday evening. Plenty of time to scan a couple of calculus chapters down at the Student Center while he did a little trolling—see what he could find to play with over the weekend—before he made his evening pick-up.

Grinning in pure, unabashed contentment, Jamie MacKenzie grabbed up the thick, rarely opened calculus textbook, reached for his blue-and-gold windbreaker, and headed for the door.

Given all the benefits of his current lifestyle, there really wasn't much point in trying to encourage Jamie MacKenzie to put more effort into his college education; or, at least, not into his formal college education . . . although a lot of people had certainly tried. People such as his faculty adviser, three of his professors, and several of his freshman classmates; not to mention a few of his very close friends, who really should have known better.

But then, the fact that these people made any effort at all on behalf of Jamie MacKenzie's education was ironic in itself . . . since every one of them, on a day-to-day basis, deliberately provided Jamie MacKenzie with the one incentive that allowed him to remain totally indifferent to such trivial events as semester finals.

That incentive, of course, was money. Or, to be more exact, a great deal of money.

In fact, every time one of these high-minded individuals purchased a gram-bindle of white crystalline powder from Jamie Mac-Kenzie—who was reputed to be the most dependable cocaine dealer on the ocean-edge campus of the University of California at San Diego—they simply reinforced his overall impression that life was a piece of cake that had been baked, sliced and hand-delivered to his door.

As such, at the age of eighteen, Jamie MacKenzie had just about everything he wanted out of life: a steady and sufficient influx of money and dependably high-quality dope; a campus filled with readily accessible young women; a closet filled with expensively stylish clothes; a brand-new English sports car, paid for in cash; and even a reasonably satisfying amount of notoriety and respect, given the inherent necessity of maintaining an extremely low business profile in the course of his daily activities.

Understandably, all of this would have been difficult enough for any eighteen-year-old mind to fully absorb; but the part that really blew Jamie MacKenzie's mind was the fact that he didn't have to work hard at all to maintain his free-wheeling lifestyle. If anything, it was almost too easy. Just a simple weekly routine of pickups, and sales, and money drops. Absolute child's play for a highly intelligent, hustler like MacKenzie.

The routine started off every Sunday morning when MacKenzie opened a locked cash box concealed beneath the lower drawer of an extremely heavy oak dresser in his dorm room, and removed twenty-five hundred dollars (or, on occasion, double or triple that amount) in small bills. After sealing the money in a small envelope, he would lie back on his bed with some easy reading material—preferably a high-class skin magazine—while he waited for a phone call.

At 9:30 A.M., plus or minus five minutes, the phone in his single-resident dorm room would ring. The caller would give the address of a public telephone booth somewhere on campus and an arrival time—usually ten to fifteen minutes after the call, depending upon the walking distance involved.

At the designated phone booth, MacKenzie would receive another call, this time directing him to the drop point, typically a towel dispenser in a public rest room somewhere on or near the campus. There, he would use one of his small universal keys to open the dispenser, slide the envelope somewhere near the top within the stack of towels, and then return directly to the University.

In accordance with specific orders, Jamie MacKenzie did not, ever, loiter around the drop area to try to identify the bag man—who, he assumed, would be arriving soon thereafter. Being a very practical individual, MacKenzie correctly judged that such curiosity would be extremely hazardous, and possibly fatal. No problem, because Mac-Kenzie wasn't especially curious about his "connection" anyway.

So far, a piece of cake.

The subsequent pickup phase of the routine occurred every Tuesday evening following a drop. At 6:45 P.M., after a predictably bland cafeteria meal, Jamie MacKenzie would walk back to his dormitory mailbox, just as he did every other weekday, dial in the four-digit code, and collect his mail. On Tuesday, or occasionally Wednesday, this would include one, or two, or occasionally three ounces of 40% cocaine. Each ounce would be hermetically sealed in several thin, heavy-duty plastic packets distributed within an assortment of mailer envelopes.

Having received his weekly supplies, MacKenzie would very quickly and cautiously walk back to his room; whereupon he would immediately double-lock the door, shut the window, and draw the curtain . . . and wait.

At 7:00 P.M., at the start of the dormitory's strictly enforced three-hour study period, Jamie MacKenzie would open the concealed compartment in his dresser, remove a digitized pan balance, a five-pound jar of lactose, a large mortar and pestle, a box of thick, glossy paper squares, and a small metal spatula, arranging these items neatly on a cleared portion of his desk. Then he would sit down at the desk and spend the rest of the evening cutting and packaging cocaine.

Apart from the minimal dexterity needed to operate the pan balance and to fold paper bindles, cutting dope at the gram-dealer level wasn't the least bit difficult. As a direct result of some careful planning at the pound and ounce distribution levels, the numbers were extremely simple.

The ounces of 40% cocaine that Jamie MacKenzie received each week weighed approximately 28.3 grams. It was MacKenzie's responsibility to weigh out and thoroughly mix from each ounce exactly 25.0 grams of 40% cocaine with exactly 25.0 grams of powdery white lactose; thereby producing 50.0 grams of 20% cocaine, which he would carefully fold into fifty precisely weighed one-gram bindles.

As one of two authorized gram dealers on the University campus, MacKenzie was expected to sell at least fifty of the $60 gram-bindles each week, realizing a weekly gross of $3000 on the ounce. Twenty-five hundred went to his connection—via the drop point—every Sunday morning. Five hundred dollars and the remaining 3.3 grams of 40% cocaine represented MacKenzie's share of the profits on each ounce, which was more than enough money and dope to keep a young man like Jamie MacKenzie in women, clothes and cars for his entire undergraduate career. Just so long as he didn't get careless, greedy or stupid.

But then, in all fairness, Jamie MacKenzie really wasn't the careless type. He religiously followed the prime directives taught to every one of the General's ounce-and-gram dealers: Sell only to those people you know and trust implicitly, preferably on a scheduled X-grams-per-week basis. Never sell to anyone who has just recently been busted. Never admit or even suggest to anyone you haven't checked out that you sell dope. And never ever sell to an absolute stranger. In effect, you were supposed to know your customer before you risked your ass.

And, likewise, Jamie MacKenzie wasn't all *that* greedy. With rare exceptions—as in the case of Bobby Lockwood's emergency request, which had forced the young gram dealer to dip into his private stock—MacKenzie seldom boosted the price on his bindles when the market started running low. Certainly he had no desire, as yet, to move up to the ounce-and-pound distribution levels, figuring he had plenty of time for heavy-weight dealing later on in life. For the moment, Jamie MacKenzie was perfectly content to make do with his moderately handsome looks, and his gradually expanding reputation. Supplemented, of course, by his continuing allotments of dope and money.

No, Jamie MacKenzie was not acting carelessly when he went down to mailbox 245 at ten-thirty that evening to collect his daily assortment of envelopes, one of which contained one hundred and fifty dollars in ten dollar bills. Nor was he being excessively greedy when he dropped a sealed envelope containing two folded paper bindles into the drop slot of Bobby Lockwood's mailbox approximately thirty seconds later.

He was simply making an unforgivably stupid mistake.

At 9:15 the following Saturday morning, Bobby Lockwood stopped by his dorm mailbox and picked up the sealed letter from MacKenzie containing the two folded paper bindles. He made a quick detour into a nearby bathroom stall, spending enough time behind the locked door to confirm the presence of white crystalline powder in each bindle. Then he hurried out to the back parking lot, got in his car, drove off-campus to the Highway 5 junction, and then headed south toward San Diego.

Contrary to the story he'd fed MacKenzie, Lockwood had no intention of using the two grams of cocaine to properly seduce an imaginary young lady on an equally fictitious ski trip. While the idea might have been appealing to Lockwood; it definitely wasn't an appropriate use for valuable evidence in a highly sensitive investigation; a polite way of saying that Bobby Lockwood wasn't about to blow the proceeds of a successfully concluded undercover buy on a casual piece of ass.

And then, too, the buy-operation wasn't quite finished yet. Lockwood still had to get the powder analyzed, to find out exactly what he had purchased for one hundred and fifty of Jimmy Pilgrim's highly accountable dollars. And for that, Lockwood had to deliver the bindles to someone who knew a lot more about chemistry than he did—to a professional chemist like Simon Drobeck.

Twenty-five minutes later, Drobeck met Lockwood at the back

door to his well-isolated laboratory and took the envelope out of his hand.

"It's about time you brought me something interesting," Drobeck grumbled as he waddled back to his workbench, slit open the envelope, carefully unfolded the bindles, and reached for two glassine weighing papers. "I'm getting tired of doing all the routine shit."

Typical Drobeck, Lockwood nodded as he watched the elderly chemist manipulate a fancy electronic balance. Sullen, withdrawn, and sarcastic. Must be what happens when you spend your entire life playing with test tubes, not even knowing you're getting old and senile, Lockwood thought, shuddering. In spite of the stipulation in his father's will that he obtain a degree in biology or chemistry before inheriting the balance of the Alaskan-based estate, Lockwood couldn't imagine a life spent inside a confining laboratory. Especially in a laboratory like Drobeck's.

"This should turn out to be a lot more interesting if we're guessing right," Lockwood said, visibly distracted, his eyes flickering nervously around the room at the numerous cages, aquariums and plastic garbage cans sharing bench and floor space with a wide assortment of chromed instruments, sinks and gas tanks. He could feel the muscles in his stomach tense up. The palms of his hands were beginning to sweat noticeably.

Goddamn senile old fart, Lockwood thought, uneasily aware of his involuntary reactions to the contents of the distinctly odorous laboratory.

Lockwood didn't like being in Drobeck's lab; mostly because he couldn't stand to be around Drobeck and his obscene personal research projects. In fact, if Lockwood had had any say in the matter, which he hadn't, Jamie MacKenzie's dope would have been delivered to Simon Drobeck by U.S. Mail, or parcel post, or by fucking camels, for all he cared. Just so long as *he* didn't have to do it.

But he did.

Jimmy Pilgrim had made it very clear that there was a time factor tied to the MacKenzie buy. He wanted the results back this afternoon; which meant that Bobby Lockwood was going to have to stay in the same room with Drobeck and his goddamned slimy zoo until the fat, bald and wrinkled scientist came up with a couple of answers.

"Have a seat," Drobeck muttered as he made some notations on a sheet of paper, motioning Lockwood toward a chair on the opposite side of his lab bench. "Got a name on this one?"

"Yeah, thanks," Lockwood nodded, moving around Drobeck to reach for the back of the chair. "MacKenzie. M-a-c-K-e-n-z-i-e. First name Jamie, spelled with a—SHIT!" Lockwood screamed, jerking his hand back as his fingers came into contact with cold, smooth and scaly skin.

"Spelled with a what?" Drobeck asked, his thin lips curling slightly into what might have been a smile. It was hard to tell with Drobeck. He hadn't even bothered to flinch when Lockwood screamed.

"You goddamned *asshole* . . ." Lockwood whispered furiously as he backed away from the lab bench, moving around behind Drobeck cautiously so that he could see what he had touched; this time from a much safer distance.

It was big. Lockwood couldn't tell how big. He didn't even want to think about how big. It was wrapped around the chair seat in about five loops. The head was about the size of Lockwood's hand, attached to a neck about the diameter of his wrist. One of the middle loops looked about as thick as his thigh. It appeared to be asleep; not that Lockwood had any intention of getting close enough again to find out.

"She won't bother you," Drobeck said, his attention back on the analysis of the powder in the first bindle. He had already mixed a small portion of the powder into a vial of solvent, and was in the process of injecting the mixture into one of his multi-dialed instruments.

"Yeah, you gonna guarantee that?" Lockwood glared, trying to bring his breathing under control. He continued to back away from Drobeck's bench, to put some distance between himself and the huge lethargic snake . . . and backed right into a large, covered metal trashcan that immediately erupted into a chorus of hissing and scuffling noises that spread from cage to cage across the lab.

Lockwood jerked away from the trashcan as though he'd been bitten, then stood there—immobilized—in the middle of the floor, his arms and legs trembling, his eyes and nostrils widened, and his fists clenched impotently as he searched desperately for the point of maximum distance from every one of the cages and metal cans.

Drobeck seemed to think about Lockwood's question for a few moments, his back still turned to the enraged and nearly panicked dope buyer.

"No," he said, turning around slowly and staring directly at Lockwood's paled face, "Come to think of it, I wouldn't. Perhaps you'd care to wait in the other room?" Drobeck suggested, motioning with his head toward the door at the far end of the lab. The one with the

sign reading "DANGER, HOT REPTILES! ENTER WITH CAU-
TION!"

Lockwood didn't even bother to look. He'd heard all about the
other room. There was no fucking way in the world he was going in
there. "I'm fine," he growled, his youthful face twisted with anger and
fear. "You just let me know when you're finished."

Twenty-five unreasonably long minutes later, Drobeck finally
turned away from his instruments and faced Lockwood.

"The weights are very consistent," he said. "One-point-zero-
two and zero-point-nine-nine. Legitimate one-gram bindles. Both
contain cocaine hydrochloride, of course . . . as I'm sure you expected. The relevant numbers are fifteen-point-nine and sixteen-
point-zero."

"Sixteen percent coke," Lockwood translated. "Just like the
first ones. You could testify to that?"

Simon Drobeck looked up at Lockwood, and for the first time
displayed an expression of what might actually have been amusement.
"Yes," he said, his thin lips spreading out into a perfect replica of a
smile as he nodded his bald, wrinkled head, "as a matter of fact, I
suppose that I could."

In compliance with the guidelines directing all maintenance
personnel not to disturb the resident students during study hours, the
schedule for changing burned-out light bulbs and making other minor
repairs at the residence halls on the University of California, San Diego campus, was strictly limited to the hours between one and four
P.M. on Tuesdays and Thursdays.

This schedule happened to be very convenient for one of the
graduate students in the Philosophy Department, who needed a part-
time job to make monthly payments on a new 1000cc Honda motorcycle that his otherwise supportive parents knew nothing about. Coincidentally, it also fit quite nicely with the plans of several other people
who had far more substantial financial interest in the U.C.S.D. dormitories.

At precisely 1:10 on the Thursday afternoon following Jamie
MacKenzie's two-gram sale to Bobby Lockwood, a muscular young
man with wildly curly blond hair, pale blue eyes, white overalls and a
baseball cap used a stolen master key to enter the rear basement door
of Voyager Hall. He was carrying a wooden ladder and a cardboard box
labeled "BULBS," and had a hefty tool kit strapped to his waist.

The full-time philosophy major and part-time maintenance assistant who as supposed to be changing light bulbs in Voyager Hall that

afternoon didn't know that his key had been stolen; nor did he know that he was already ten minutes late for work. In fact, he didn't know much of anything, because he was still face down, unconscious and snoring on his disheveled apartment bed—the victim of an aggressively friendly young woman named Skylight, whom he had met at the Pub yesterday evening, and too much alcohol; a great deal of strenuous sexual activity; and a professionally dispensed dose of chloral hydrate, after the vodka and sex had sufficiently weakened the budding philosopher's basic sense of caution.

From 1:10 to 1:45 P.M., the frizzy blond young man who answered to the name of Roy Schultzheimer diligently replaced light bulbs and made other minor repairs on the first floor of Voyager Hall. With the exception of a couple of mildly interested coeds, the few students who happened to be in the dorm hall paid no attention to the white-overalled figure. They all had far more important concerns, such as due dates on unfinished term papers and final exams that started the next day.

At 1:46 P.M., Schultzheimer was standing on his ladder in the main hallway, examining a perfectly functional overhead light, when he observed Jamie MacKenzie exit the elevator and go out the door in the direction of the main campus, presumably enroute to his two o'clock Western Civilization lecture. Schultzheimer then made a quick trip out to his car for a heavily taped box labeled "PARTS," and then returned to his ladder and waited for the last of the disorganized and late-for-class residents to come running down the stairs.

At 2:07 P.M., the box-burdened Schultzheimer took the elevator up to the second floor, walked down the hallway to 245, knocked on the door, waited approximately five seconds, and then used the stolen master key once again.

Then, after taking a few moments to put on a pair of heavy work gloves, secure the door, and close the curtains, Schultzeimer quickly went to work. Starting with the bookcase, he removed selected volumes and replaced them with books from the "BULBS" box.

A crumpled receipt went into the top drawer of the single desk.

Several other items in the room were added, removed or replaced.

At 2:14 P.M., Schultzheimer moved the second, heavily taped cardboard box labeled "PARTS" over to the floor next to the solid oak dresser, and then went to work with considerably more caution, his pale, cold eyes glittering with amusement as he carried out Jimmy Pilgrim's precise instructions.

Thirty minutes later, Roy Schultzheimer cautiously stepped out

into the hallway again, closed and locked the door to room 245, took
the elevator to the basement, placed the ladder, boxes and tool kit into
the back of his van, and drove away.

There were still several room numbers remaining on the re-
quested-repairs list for Voyager Hall, but they would have to wait until
a much wiser and chastened philosopher returned to work the following Tuesday.

At 6:15 on that same Thursday evening, a mildly aroused Jamie
MacKenzie reluctantly decided to excuse himself from the company of
two seemingly fun-loving coeds in the Resident Dining Hall.

MacKenzie hated to leave the two young women—who had
spent the entire dinner hour making casual suggestions about a
friendly *ménage à trois* in his dorm room later that evening; but, unfortunately their comments had reminded Jamie that he had a job to do.
A job that necessarily took priority over a pair of horny young women.

That was the one major problem with the dope business, Mac-
Kenzie told himself once again. Never enough time to really enjoy all
the built-in fringe benefits—which happened to include a hell of a lot
of friendly young coeds who normally wouldn't have given an eighteen-year-old freshman like MacKenzie more than a casual glance in
the hallway. And also included, to MacKenzie's continuing amazement, a considerable number of juniors, seniors, and graduate students, not to mention a couple of dependably grateful faculty
members.

In fact, MacKenzie suddenly remembered, he had promised to
meet two of those friendly female-type grad students "after work" this
evening. He tried to remember their names. Kaaren, he nodded with
a sudden smile. Couldn't forget Kaaren . . . an absolute knockout who
looked a hell of a lot more like a *Penthouse* Pet than a Visual Arts
major. Yeah, MacKenzie definitely remembered Kaaren; but he
couldn't recall the name of her less attractive but still interesting
friend. The computer nut. Sharon? No. Susan? Or was it . . . yeah,
Sandy, he nodded, that was it. Kaaren and Sandy. Somehow, he was
going to *have* to work those two into his very tight schedule, no doubt
about it. Especially Kaaren. Maybe even this weekend, he shrugged.
Never knew how these things were going to work out.

Distracted by the necessity of watching his immediate surroundings very carefully (a rip-off was always a possibility during the
pick-up phase, even in the relatively benign University environment)
MacKenzie never saw the girls, or their long-lensed camera. Thus
Kaaren Mueller was able to take a total of twelve low-light photographs

in rapid succession, the last four straight through the large open window of the Student Center, as MacKenzie looked around casually once more and then quickly removed a handful of varying-sized envelopes from his mailbox.

Five minutes later, Jamie MacKenzie had securely double-bolted and isolated himself in his room, changed into a comfortable pair of cut-off shorts, and was clearing away some work space on his desk when his telephone rang.

"Hello?" he answered, mildly annoyed at being disturbed during his "study hour".

"MacKenzie?"

"Yeah, that's right." He didn't recognize the cold, emotionless voice.

"You haven't been very smart."

"Huh? What're you talking about? Who the hell is this?" MacKenzie demanded, reacting nervously to the chilling voice in spite of himself.

"Pilgrim," the soulless voice rasped.

Jamie MacKenzie made a whimpering sound deep in his throat.

"Does seven hundred and eighty dollars mean anything to you? Jimmy Pilgrim growled.

"No," MacKenzie whispered weakly, which wasn't true at all. Seven hundred and eighty dollars very definitely meant something to him. He had spent many pleasurable hours calculating and recalculating that specific figure during the past few weeks. He realized that he was starting to feel very sick to his stomach, as though he was going to vomit.

"Seven hundred and eighty dollars, Mr. MacKenzie. Do I have to explain it to you?" If possible the faceless voice had become even more icy and dispassionate—like a call from the dead.

"It's not what you think," MacKenzie whispered pleadingly. "I didn't—I mean, I—I can pay it back," he tried.

"We've already taken care of that."

"What . . . ?" Realization finally crystallized in MacKenzie's numbed mind. "Oh shit, no," he whimpered, dropping the phone down on the desk top and rushing across the room. He knelt down in front of his oak dresser and fumbled with the concealed release-mechanism.

Jamie MacKenzie had less than a half-second to absorb the fact that the cash box, and the pan balance, and several other familiar items were no longer on the bottom of the hidden cabinet and that something else was—an empty cloth sack with a tie string?—when his eyes registered a movement in the back of the cabinet . . . .

"HISSSSSSSSSSSSSSSS!"

MacKenzie screamed and threw himself backward—an instinctive reaction to the inconceivably *loud* reptilian sounds that erupted from the dresser. In that horrible, frozen moment, MacKenzie's eyes bulged and his mouth stretched wide-open in terror as a triangular light-brown head with dark, reddish-brown rings and widely extended fangs lunged with blinding speed out of the concealed cabinet, the blurred head missing his outstretched bare foot by a fraction of an inch.

As MacKenzie desperately twisted away from the savagely hissing creature, scrambling for the relative safety of his bed, his second panic-stricken scream was drowned out by a shrill clanging as the fire alarm in the outer hallway cut loose.

Before MacKenzie could react—other than by voiding his bladder, which he did unknowingly—every light in the dorm hall went out, throwing MacKenzie's room into utter, terrifying blackness.

"NO! NO! NO!"

Jamie MacKenzie had never known such fear in his life. He couldn't even comprehend such fear. All he could do was scream. He was still screaming and clawing his way across his bed, the rational portion of his mind paralyzed by the knowledge that the hideous creature was down on the floor somewhere in the blackened room, when he slammed face-first into the solid cinder-block wall.

Stunned by the impact against the rough brick, bleeding profusely from the mouth and nose, and partially deafened by the loud clanging, a now-whimpering Jamie MacKenzie could only cower down on the unsteady mattress in his urine-soaked pants, his back and shoulders pressed tightly against the unyielding block wall, his hands and arms trembling uncontrollably as he tried to focus his mind . . . .

The door? No, MacKenzie shook his bloodied head, wincing at the pain. The door was double-bolted. It would take too long to find and unlatch the two locks in the dark. Too many fumbling panic-stricken seconds. Besides, he knew he couldn't stay on the floor that long . . . not in this god-awful terrifying darkness . . . not knowing where, or when . . .

MacKenzie shook his head again, unwilling to even imagine such a horror as he felt his limbs grow numb, heard the horribly cold voice of Jimmy Pilgrim echo through his ravaged mind, tried to think . . .

The window?

Then, above the eardrum-pounding din of the fire alarm, the fiercely aggressive snake started to hiss again, somewhere close. To his right?

MacKenzie twisted frantically to his left, crashing into his lamp and nightstand as he tumbled off the bed and onto the floor of the now unbelievably small and confining room.

At the instant his hands came into contact with the tiled floor, Jamie MacKenzie's survival instincts finally came into play. He hesitated one second to brace himself up against the wall, orienting himself. Then he lunged in the direction of the door, taking one leap, then a second—

—his bare right foot coming down solidly on the cold rubbery, writhing midsection of the snake!

MacKenzie began to scream hysterically even before he felt the piercing pain of the long, needle-sharp fangs when the snake struck—its wide reptilian mouth clamping tightly onto his bare foot.

Functioning solely on reflex action, because he was no longer capable of rational thought, Jamie MacKenzie grabbed at the twisting coils, pulling frantically at the thrashing reptile until he finally ripped it loose and away from his burning foot, and then lunged toward the door.

He was still fumbling desperately at the first dead-bolt when he heard the horrible high-pitched hissing again—at his back—and then felt the sudden sharp pain once again as the curved fangs stabbed deep into his lower right leg.

Something in MacKenzie's head snapped. Forgetting the unyielding door lock, he turned and bolted for the window. Driven mindlessly by the creature clamped tightly onto his leg—pumping in venom with every contraction of its jaw muscles—Jamie burst through the curtained window glass and began to fall . . .

Mercifully oblivious to any further pain long before he struck the hard cement walkway, landing less than a dozen yards from a pair of stunned and horrified young women who were working themselves into position to get the critical thirteenth photograph of the youthful gram-dealer cutting his dope.

In an oceanside apartment several miles north of the University of California, San Diego campus, a man who had long used carefully directed fear and violence as tools—to work himself progressively higher in the Organization that Jamie MacKenzie had so foolishly underestimated—did something completely out of character.

For a brief moment, he actually smiled

And in doing so, he nearly startled the living shit out of the ruthless black man who had been the cutting edge of Jimmy Pilgrim's rapid climb into the Organization's corporate management; because as far as Lafayette Beaumont Raynee knew, Jimmy Pilgrim never smiled.

Not ever.

Predictably, the smile quickly faded away—much like a mirage—as Pilgrim replaced the phone on its receiver, nodding in apparent satisfaction as his long-time street partner pressed the STOP button on a cassette tape recorder that was hard-wired to the telephone.

"Excellent," Pilgrim said, his eyes seemingly unfocused. "What did you use?"

"Russell's Viper," Raynee replied casually as he rewound the cassette tape. "One a' Drobeck's play-toys. Man said it's gotta be the meanest snake he ever seen. Once it starts attackin', ain't nothin' gonna stop it. Said it hisses like a banshee, an' Ah guess we can't argue that none, neither," Raynee shook his head, chuckling quietly as he patted the top of the tape recorder.

"I assume the attack will be fatal?" Pilgrim said, shifting his mind back to the problem. He'd been distracted by the pleasure of listening to MacKenzie's screams.

"Gonna know pretty soon," Raynee shrugged. "What old man Drobeck said, them Russell's Viper's be jes' 'bout as deadly as them mean-ass king cobras, 'cept the poison's more slow-acting—he-mah-toxin, or some such shit," the black drug-dealer, pimp and street-killer added, dredging the word up out of his memory. "Bite's gonna screw a man's blood all up. What Ah'm told, ain't much he can do 'bout it neither, 'less'n maybe he cuts off his leg or arm real quick-like."

"So . . .?"

"Figurin' he probably got bit, and he ain't already died goin' out that window . . ." Raynee shrugged. "Ain't likely they're gonna get him the right antidote-shit in time."

"Do we have everything we need out of his room?" Pilgrim demanded with icy indifference. He had already begun to lose interest in Jamie MacKenzie.

"Cash box, notes and cuttin' tools in mah safe," Raynee nodded, pulling the cassette out of the recorder and handing it to Pilgrim. "'Less'n somebody starts looking for powder residue, ain't nothing in that room gonna put MacKenzie down as a user or dealer. Even had Roy-boy put a few snake books in his bookshelf, couple a' burlap bags an' a hook under his bed. Made it look like ol' Jamie MacKenzie's jes' some rep-tile freak what got a little careless," Raynee grinned. "'Sides, ain't likely none a' his customers gonna be too anxious t' give the *po-lice* any help. Know what Ah mean?"

"Excellent," Pilgrim nodded, slowly turning the small, rectangular cassette over and over with his thick, manicured fingers. "Do we know when he started?"

"Looks like 'bout six weeks ago. Cuttin' one a' them forty percent ounces down to sixteen, 'stead of twenty, every week; that works out t' be 'bout an extra thirteen gram-bindles," Raynee shrugged. "Seven-eighty a week. Roy found an envelope in the cash box. Little over forty-five hundred in small bills. Numbers work out right."

Pilgrim's eyes never shifted from their cold, malevolent expression. He handed the cassette back to Raynee. "See to it that everyone listens to this. I don't want any more misunderstandings. Especially not now."

"Ah'll see to it, personal," Raynee nodded, pocketing the cassette. "'Course we ain't 'xactly keepin' up with the big boss man, is we?"

"How's that?" Pilgrim growled.

"Hear tell Locotta caught one a' his people playin' games with the numbers last week."

"Oh?" Pilgrim whispered, his eyebrows rising with suddenly renewed interest.

"Yep. Accordin' t' mah sources, he had Tassio chain the dude by the neck t' 'bout five hundred pounds a' concrete block. Strapped a scuba tank on the man's back an' put him down in 'bout thirty feet a' water off Catalina Island. Hear tell the dude had himself 'bout a' hour t' think over all his troubles 'fore he ran outta air," Raynee smiled widely. "Might hafta 'member that one."

"Nice. Real nice," Pilgrim grunted, his dark eyes glistening with malicious appreciation . . . and hidden amusement. He didn't bother to tell Raynee that a nineteen-year-old enforcer had demonstrated that innovative use of underwater breathing gear to a clearly impressed Jake Locotta and Joe Tassio many years ago. The enforcer's name was Jimmy Pilgrim.

"'Course, thing like that could make a man get down-right suspicious 'bout the rest a' his employ-ees," Raynee added. "Could be that's why we got Lester sniffin' round down here, wantin' t' talk t' people like Theiss."

Jimmy Pilgrim's glaring eyes snapped up. "Did he—"

"Not yet," Raynee shook his head. "Theiss got his ass outta

town real quick-like, soon's he heard Lester was lookin' for him. Said he can stay gone a couple more days, but—"

"I'll take care of Lester," Pilgrim growled. "Anything else?"

"Any objections, we lay out a little bonus to that Lockwood boy?" Raynee asked. "Ah'm figurin' maybe five grand. Boy did a good job, pickin' up on MacKenzie like that. Thinkin' Ah might even move him up a peg or two. Try him out on distribution over the summer."

"Fine," Pilgrim grunted indifferently.

Raynee took out a small gold-embossed notebook and wrote in the word "Lock" and the figure '5.' "Gonna need a decision on our next order to Locotta," he said, looking up from the notebook. "Figure we can move close t' six hundred pounds come March. Gonna run us right close t' twenty-one-point-six mill, wholesale. We okay on that?"

Pilgrim nodded, his eyes still dead cold. "I'll arrange for the transfer."

"Sure do hate to see all that bread goin' Locotta's way," Lafayette Beaumont Raynee shook his head sadly as he replaced the notebook in his suit pocket. "Money like that can't help but tempt a man sometimes. Know what Ah mean?"

This time Raynee saw something flicker behind the glacial expression on Pilgrim's face. Something faintly resembling amusement, possibly even cheerful anticipation.

"Yes," Pilgrim whispered roughly, actually smiling again now, "I know exactly what you mean."

". . . which, of course, begs the obvious question about our alchemist's sex life."

Dr. David Isaac paused for effect, grinning mischievously as he looked out over the podium at the faces of the professors, instructors, students and assorted University of California alumni who had crowded into the five-hundred-seat auditorium of the San Diego campus to enjoy his end-of-the-term symposium on the origins of chemistry. From the oldest emeritus to the youngest undergraduate, they all sat in respectful, attentive silence, clearly enthralled by the topic and the speaker.

"Instead of laboring to satisfy their patrons by trying to convert base metals into gold," Isaac went on, "is it not more likely that the ancient alchemists—our predecessors—were actually diverting much of their time and energy toward a far more compelling goal? That is, the enhancement of their own sexual potency?"

A quiet murmur rose from the audience.

"We are frequently reminded, in the *Physica et Mystica* of Zosimos," Isaac continued, holding up a well-thumbed copy of the ancient text, "that the early chemists were driven to produce unlimited amounts of pure gold—an understandable endeavor, certainly. Yet, as we have seen here tonight, there is ample evidence to suggest that they were also fascinated—and perhaps even preoccupied—with the occult and other more, ah, esoteric aspects of alchemy."

Isaac paused again, savoring the heady sensation of being in complete control of the hushed and attentive scientists.

"So, you see," the youthful, clean-shaven professor leaned out over the podium, his eyes gleaming wickedly, "I simply cannot resist offering three quite reasonable—if somewhat amusing—hypotheses.

"One," he held up a single finger, "that the alchemists were much more interested in trying to produce sexual stimulants than gold.

"Two," a second finger, "that these evasive stimulants were intended for the exclusive use of the male aristocratia, that is the members of royalty, and of course—" he smiled, "—the alchemists themselves."

Isaac allowed himself a final two-second pause.

"And three, that one of the most vocal advocates for this, uh, critical research seems to have been a very outspoken—and possibly self-serving—woman named Maria. Thank you."

A roar of laughter intermixed with a thunderous applause echoed through the auditorium, continuing for almost two minutes before the moderator stood up, signaling for silence.

"Thank *you*, Dr. Isaac, for a most enjoyable, and—if I may say so—most stimulating presentation. If you don't mind, I believe we have time for a few questions from the audience."

"Certainly." Isaac looked out over the auditorium again and motioned at a familiar face. "Allen."

"David," Dr. Allen Bacon rose up from his seat, "on several occasions this evening, you alluded to the possibility that our little 'Maria the Jewess' might be of Asian origin, rather than Syrian or Egyptian. Do you have any new evidence to support this blasphemous contention?"

"Only a few obscure references in the original Greek texts credited to her fellow alchemist, Democritus, a scholar who was, of course, well known for his irrepressibly, uh, 'romantic' nature," Isaac smiled. "Actually, I doubt that we will ever be able to separate fact from fantasy in what remains of his writing. There are simply too many indications of jealousy—both professional and personal—between these two fascinating individuals. And, of course," he added wistfully, "we have only Democritus' side of the story."

Isaac paused to shake his head sadly.

"Thus, regrettably," he went on, "Maria remains an elusive woman of intrigue and uncertain origin. Although I must admit, the idea of a mysterious oriental woman introducing the water-bath retort to early chemistry certainly does reinforce the exotic nature of our historical legacy. Being an incurable romantic myself and a longtime admirer of Maria's, I'm always willing to entertain the possibility."

"Thank you, David," Dr. Bacon grinned happily, "but I still prefer to think of Maria as my little Jewish princess." He sat back down amid the appreciative laughter.

"That is the advantage of worshiping legendary figures, Allen," Isaac said, nodding his head and smiling. "We can always mold them to fit our own fantasies." Isaac looked up and motioned to an unfamiliar face. "A question, sir?"

"Yes, Dr. Isaac." A tall, dark-complexioned man, neatly dressed in a grey three-piece suit, with a carefully trimmed black beard and dark horn-rimmed glasses, stood up in the back row. "Earlier you suggested that the future of pharmaceutical drugs may be in the production of analog compounds. Would you mind expounding on that theory for a few moments?" The tall, bearded man sat back down.

"Not at all," Isaac shrugged. "I'm simply of the opinion that our current stocks of pharmaceutical drugs—aspirin, Valium, Percodan, what have you—will be replaced in the not-so-distant future by analogs: that is, compounds which are very similar to the parent drugs—structurally—but not quite identical.

"For example," Isaac elaborated as he noted the confused expressions in his audience, "let's take sodium acetylsalicylate—a simple twenty-one-atom molecule that we all know much better as aspirin." He started in to explain the analog theory, and then hesitated.

"Do you all really want to sit here and listen to a lecture on chemistry?" Isaac asked skeptically. "I can always answer this gentleman's question after . . ."

A sea of shaking heads and several murmured words of encouragement caused Isaac to shrug agreeably. "All right," he smiled, "but don't say I didn't warn you. Now then, where was I?"

"Headache remedies, David," Dr. Allen Bacon called out helpfully.

"Oh yes," Isaac nodded. "As you may know, we now suspect that only a small part of the aspirin molecule—the part which fits snugly into special receptor sites within our central nervous system—actually triggers its miraculous analgesic effect. So, to make a useful analog of aspirin, we would want to retain the essential, pain-killing part of the molecule, while trying to alter other structural parts which may be producing the less-desirable effects.

"For example, a useful analog of aspirin might be one that soothes minor pain, but doesn't irritate the stomach lining. The trick, of course, is to determine which parts of the molecule we must save—to retain the desired pharmacological effects—and which parts we can safely alter in the hope that we'll come up with something better."

Isaac waited until he observed nods of understanding from several of the non-chemists in the group, and went on.

"So, now, let's assume that we're going to make a test series of ten analogs for aspirin; and, furthermore, that we'll prepare these analogs by removing a specific atom from the aspirin molecule, and substituting ten different atoms or atom groups. We mix ten sets of ingredients, potboil away merrily, and then end up with ten different compounds, the molecules of which all look pretty much like aspirin. Correct?

"Certainly," Isaac nodded, answering his own question. "Ten batches of aspirinlike molecules, each of which is structurally *very similar* to aspirin. But the question is: Do any of these analog compounds *act* like aspirin? And if so," he added meanfully, "do they also possess more desirable side effects? Or side effects which are even more *dangerous*?"

Isaac paused, hesitant for a moment, and then continued.

"One might think that the development of useful drug analogs would simply be a matter of extensive 'potboiling'—that is, just churning out batches of likely analogs and finding out which ones work. Unfortunately," he shook his head, "it's not quite that easy.

"As we all know, there are hundreds—if not thousands—of possible analog structures for any one compound; many of which are difficult to synthesize. So, to be efficient, we need to be able to predict useful analogs on some logical basis—ideally by computer modeling, as we are doing in my lab right now. But then, of course, we rapidly discover that even slight alterations in the molecular structure can result in pharmocological effects which are *absolutely unpredictable*.

"Thus," Isaac added with a sad shake of his head, "I would have to warn any future analog-research chemists in the audience that such projects are horribly time-consuming, outrageously expensive, invariably prone to recurring failure, and otherwise highly frustrating. Fortunately, I suppose, there are many of us who—like Maria—continue to cherish that tiny spark of hope . . . for one reason or another."

The auditorium erupted in a burst of quiet, knowing laughter.

"But that's the part I don't understand," the tall man interrupted as the chuckling died down. "Surely there must be a huge market for some of these useful analogs—certainly enough to justify the expense of producing and testing these thousands of analog compounds."

"With all due respect, sir," Isaac said, smiling, "I can only assume that you have never had to deal with the government agencies that regulate drug testing. Let me assure you that the paperwork involved in trying to comply with the hundreds of often-conflicting rules and regulations governing this type of research is mind-boggling, to say the least, not to mention prohibitively expensive."

There were murmurings of agreement throughout the auditorium.

"But even setting aside the regulatory problems, it just isn't that easy," Isaac emphasized. "You must still face the critical problem that has plagued research chemists for generations: the unavoidable fact that, in order to fully understand the action of *any* analog on a human brain, you *must* eventually test that analog out on human guinea pigs."

"I'll volunteer!" a voice among the undergraduates standing in the back of the auditorium yelled out. There was immediate laughter and some scattered applause.

"A very noble offer," Isaac grinned. "However, perhaps I should warn you about a young man in Los Angeles who made exactly that kind of mistake, a few months ago, when he apparently consumed a drug analog produced by an—uh—underground chemist. Fortunately, or unfortunately, depending upon your point of view, the only organs stimulated by this particular analog were the young man's kidneys. Unknowingly—I think we can safely assume—the chemist had synthesized a very potent forty-eight hour diuretic."

The audience chuckled appreciatively.

"Two days later," Isaac continued, "an extremely dehydrated and disgruntled young man checked out of a hospital and immediately turned himself in to the police, subsequently, I'm told, providing them with the name and address of the chemist . . . and, I assume, teaching them both a very lasting lesson."

"Boy, he must have been *really* pissed-off, to call the cops," a youthful voice in the front stage-whispered, causing another roar from the academicians who were clearly enjoying a welcome respite from their intellectual labors.

"Yes, thank you—I imagine he was," Isaac responded good-naturedly after the laughter had died down again. Then his voice turned sober.

"But the story could have ended quite differently. As I have indicated, the very real problem with testing drug analogs is that you cannot predict with absolute certainty which receptor sites in the brain will accept a particular analog structure.

"And *that* is *dangerous*," Isaac emphasized. "Instead of acting as a diuretic or as a hallucinogen—as was presumably intended—the compound that the unsuspecting young man ingested could have just as easily functioned as a rapid carcinogen, or possibly even as a central nervous system poison. Or, perhaps, with much better luck, it might not have functioned at all—a chemical version of Russian roulette, if you will."

Isaac looked down at his watch and discovered he had far surpassed the time allotted for his lecture.

"If there are no further questions, then I thank you all for being a most gracious and attentive audience." He stepped off the podium to a standing ovation that echoed throughout the auditorium.

As a select group of senior professors and other aggressive underlings gravitated toward the floor surrounding the lecture podium in order to spend a few more enjoyable minutes with the ever-congenial Isaac, the less-imposing or more restive members of the audience gradually worked their way up the aisles and out into the cool night air.

"I think I see why you enjoy his lectures," the diminutive, dark-eyed coed said, smiling contentedly as she and Bobby Lockwood walked slowly in the darkness, hand in hand, following the long, winding asphalt pathway that led to the distant student dormitories. "I didn't understand much of what he said, but he was fun to listen to anyway."

"Yeah, he's really something, isn't he," Lockwood nodded absentmindedly, and then impulsively turned his head down to give the affectionate girl a slow, gentle kiss before returning to his quiet musing.

"Uhmmm, you know, maybe if you studied more . . ." the warm-eyed girl suggested as she tightened her hand around Lockwood's sweatshirt-covered upper arm, leaning her head in against his shoulder as they walked.

"Why? You think I could become a chemistry professor?" Lockwood asked in amused disbelief, the absurdity of the girl's suggestion momentarily jarring him out of his morose state.

"Well—you *do* like chemicals," the girl grinned. "Besides," she added, her voice turning half serious, "we might be needing a good chemist around here now that Jamie MacKenzie's out of business. You hear about what happened to him the other night?"

"Huh—ah, yeah, I did," Lockwood nodded, his voice a raspy whisper.

"Really bizarre, huh? I mean, I bought from the dude all year, and I didn't even know he *liked* snakes," the girl said, shaking her head. "Sure hope he makes it."

"Yeah, me too," Lockwood nodded.

"You know him?"

"Used to score some crystal off him every now and then," Lockwood shrugged. "Seemed like a nice guy. . . ."

"Hey, which reminds me—remember, you said—"

"Oh yeah—hey, don't worry, I've plenty of good blow up in my room," Lockwood winked halfheartedly.

"Uhmm, you *sure* it's good stuff? I mean, you're not planning on giving me some of those analogs like that professor was talking about—trying to get me horny?"

"In *your* case, it'd be a waste of good dope," Lockwood laughed. "Probably oughta give you something to slow you down."

"Oh, I don't know," the girl grinned, "wouldn't you like to?"

"Wouldn't I like to what?" Lockwood asked, his spirits starting to pick up now that he was longer thinking about Jamie MacKenzie.

"You know, be a guinea pig. Try out all the new dope these chemist guys make."

"Yeah, I guess it does sound kinda interesting," Lockwood admitted as he guided the girl toward his nearby dorm hall. "But I don't know. Like Isaac said, that kinda shit could be real dangerous if you don't know what you're taking. Me, I get myself in enough trouble with booze and coke. Not sure I'd want to get involved with anything any *more* dangerous."

"That include me?" the girl asked impishly.

"Oh yeah," Lockwood nodded, grinning opening now. "Well, I don't know, I guess a guy's gotta live a little dangerously every now and then, doesn't he?"

Later that same evening a man who took a certain amount of pleasure in living and working at the edge of danger finally decided that he'd put in enough time on the Pilgrim evaluation for one day.

Having spent the past two days and nights carefully probing the undercurrents of rumor and intrigue within Jimmy Pilgrim's four-county territory that comprised the southernmost portion of Jake Locotta's underworld empire, Lester was almost convinced that he'd found something. It wasn't anything concrete. Nothing he could take back to Locotta that would cause Jimmy Pilgrim to spend a few agonizing hours dangling at the end of a meat hook. But there was something going on, nonetheless. The signs were all there. Lester the head-hunter could almost smell it.

Tomorrow, he told himself as he walked across the border into Tijuana, slid into a waiting taxi and gave the driver specific directions, leaving his three bodyguards to fend for themselves. Tomorrow, he'd track down an investment broker named Michael Thomas Theiss. Then he'd find out what the hell Jimmy Pilgrim was doing with all his excess money.

But tonight he was going to enjoy himself . . . even to the point of adding a little extra touch of danger to his illicit amusement.

Normally, on a covert evaluation like this, Lester wouldn't have even gone to the john without having at least one of his highly trained bodyguards standing at the door. But this was different. From Lester's point of view, Tijuana was like the Free Parking space on a Monopoly board—a safe haven from the normal hazards of life—simply because *nobody* had enough balls to screw around in *federale* territory, where a man's rights specifically did *not* include a speedy trial or a phone call to his lawyer. Not even Jimmy Pilgrim.

A man could spend a *very* long time in a *federale* jail—years, in fact, if you really pissed them off—before he ever *saw* a telephone, Lester reminded himself reassuringly, confident that he was perfectly safe down here. Pilgrim and Rainbow were unquestionably vicious, and exceedingly dangerous to cross, but they weren't stupid.

Which was just as well, Lester shrugged, because he knew his bodyguards didn't care much for his kind of entertainment. Apparently cold-blooded violence was one thing, but violence with sexually sadistic overtones was something else entirely. Not that it really mattered, as far as Lester was concerned. He didn't really mind that his men thought he was a pervert, as long as they did their job. In fact, in all honesty, he kind of liked the idea.

Yes, Theiss was going to be the key, Lester told himself as the taxi driver made several tire-screeching turns that took them progressively deeper into the darkened heart of the notorious border town. Theiss, and a couple of the pound-dealers, Lester nodded to himself. Then maybe Locotta would let him go to work on that nigger Rainbow.

The idea of being allowed to use his special talents on the lean, muscular body of Lafayette Beaumont Raynee was highly appealing to the sadistic and bigoted Lester. So much so that he actually remained sitting in the back of the cab for a few moments, lost in his pleasant thoughts, after the driver had pulled to a sudden stop in front of a darkened alley and began gesturing impatiently for his money.

Suddenly remembering the pleasurable purpose of his journey, Lester quickly paid the cabbie, glanced down at his watch, scrambled out of the rundown vehicle, and then began to walk very quickly down the alley. He was late, and he knew that Angelo wouldn't wait to start. . . .

The hand that came out of the darkness caught Lester at the base of the throat, sending him staggering back into the adobe brick wall.

"Good evening, Lester," the cold voice whispered in the darkness.

Leaning weakly back against the rough brick wall and trying not to vomit as he clutched at his damaged throat with both hands, Lester the headhunter slowly brought his watering eyes up to blink and stare helplessly at the dark shadow-figure. Not that the darkness mattered. Lester knew that voice.

"Jesus Christ, Jimmy," he rasped through his painfully bruised throat, "I wasn't—"

"Of course you were, Lester," Jimmy Pilgrim whispered savagely. "That's your job. And you're very good at it, aren't you? You even enjoy it."

"But—but, the *federales*—!"

This time it was a foot that struck out of the darkness. It caught Lester square in his exposed crotch, causing the helpless headhunter to gurgle a high-pitched scream as he fell forward into Jimmy Pilgrim's strong, waiting hands.

"It's all right, Lester," Pilgrim whispered soothingly as his hands tightened around the man's pulsing neck, "you can talk to the *federales* all you want—later on."

When Lester regained consciousness, his flaccid body having finally neutralized the swarm of barbiturate molecules that Jimmy Pilgrim had thoughtfully injected into his bloodstream, he immediately became aware of four horribly numbing facts:

First, that he had somehow become wedged into the driver's seat of some kind of police car that was tilted forward into a ditch.

Second, that the interior of the vehicle seemed to be filled with the pungent aroma of Mexican whiskey.

Third, that there was a heavy revolver lying on his lap, and some sort of police hat on his head—both of which, he quickly discovered, almost certainly belonged to the man in the back of the vehicle (that is to say, the senior *federale* officer who was lying quietly on the back seat with the back of his head caved in and his pants pulled down around his knees).

And finally, that most of the men who surrounded the car, staring in through the windows in wide-eyed disbelief, seemed to be wearing the same uniform as the man in the back seat of the crashed patrol unit. Not one of them looked as though they'd be terribly interested in listening to Lester's frantic explanations.

The situation was bad enough (unbelievably bad, from Lester's point of view), but it was only as his desperately screaming mind sought to end the agony—before it really began—that Lester the headhunter really understood the sadistic nature of Jimmy Pilgrim . . . and the fate that the underworld dope boss had so carefully and maliciously arranged.

Swiftly bringing the barrel of the revolver up to the side of his head with trembling fingers—an act that truly defined the wretched hopelessness of his situation—Lester closed his eyes and squeezed the trigger, first once, and then five more times in frantic succession as the hammer fell loudly on the empty chambers.

The *federale* officers who now surrounded the crashed police vehicle with drawn guns could have ended Lester's torment at that moment—but, to his horror, anguish and despair, they didn't. Instead, they simply laughed among themselves—a cold, heartless kind of laughter that had very little to do with humor—as they dragged the whimpering headhunter out of the patrol car.

These police officers had other (and certainly more effective) ways of dealing with a cop-killer in their country.

1

IN THE SMALL, suburban city of Fairfax, Virginia, located approximately twenty-four hundred miles east of the university campus where Dr. David Isaac and his colleagues pursued their diverse academic interests, two men with virtually identical professional interests walked purposefully along an asphalt driveway toward a small house glowing brightly within its dark protective cluster of tall oak, maple and ash trees.

In spite of the low-keyed purpose of their visit, both men were visibly cautious in their approach—an instinctive survival response reflecting a long history of dealing with violent individuals, and an ingrained distrust of night-darkened forests. There was no reason to expect anything but a friendly welcome at Tom Fogarty's house. But it was easier and—on a long-range basis—much safer to stay consistent and responsive to well-honed instincts.

The smaller of the pair—slim, sturdy, black-haired—stood openly in the doorway and rang the doorbell while the second visitor—much larger—moved reflexively into the shadows on the door-knob side of the thick, dead-bolted door.

"Good evening, boys," Hazel Fogarty said as she unbolted the back door to her spotlessly clean Northern Virginia home, after checking out the identity of her late-arriving guests through an eye-level peephole in the door. "They're all in the den waiting for you. Beer's in the refrigerator if you're thirsty."

"Hi, Hazel," Benjamin Koda said as he stepped into the kitchen, kissing Hazel Fogarty on the cheek, giving her a lecherous wink and grin, and then heading directly for the refrigerator after giving the glass door to the oven a warm, appreciative look. Charley Shannon stepped into the kitchen behind his partner and carefully locked and bolted the door.

"Offer's still good," Koda said, closing the door and tossing a chilled bottle of beer to Shannon. "Any time you want to leave the old goat out here in D.C. and run off to Hawaii . . . "

"Benjamin, my dear," Mrs. Fogarty said, her eyes twinkling beneath her frosty grey hair as she reached for a pot holder to check the progress of a browning pie, "you are a delightfully gallant, wanton and shameless young man, and the offer is most tempting." She tossed her head to move a stray lock of hair out of her eyes as she quickly shut the oven door, after deliberately allowing a generous waft of warm, cinnamon-laden air to fill the kitchen. Both men inhaled, emitting approving and contented sighs.

"But I'm afraid I'm still very fond of the old goat," she continued. "And I know I could never trust you out on those beaches, constantly being tempted by all of those mischievous young women. Although, if you shaved off that horrible mustache and trimmed your hair, those beautiful oriental ancestors of yours just *might* show through enough . . . "

"Well, ah—"

"There, you see. Besides, how would I ever know if you loved me for my evil ways, or just for my recipe book? Now, on the other hand, Charley here would be much more dependable." Hazel Fogarty turned to pat the hard, muscled stomach of the massive ex-football player who had moved away from the locked door to stand directly in front of the radiating oven. "Isn't that right, Charley?"

"No question about it," Charley Shannon laughed, displaying a wide mouthful of straight teeth gleaming white against the dimpled, dark brown texture of his bearded cheeks. "I like evil women jes' fine, but I do *love* your cookin'." He squatted down on his haunches, bringing his seventy-eight inch, two-hundred-seventy-pound frame closer to the oven window, gazing in sincere reverence at the two browning apple pies as the sweetened juices dripped onto a protective sheet of aluminum foil.

"Sure hope you made something for the rest of them folks, Hazel," Charley said, grinning widely and further defining his almost-hidden dimples as he looked up hopefully at the woman he frequently described as his "honorary honky mama." "Hate to see 'em all go hungry while you and I sit here an' eat these little tarts."

"I've got two more cooling down in the dining room," Hazel Fogarty said reassuringly, "and eight dozen fresh chocolate chip cookies in jars to take home. Now you two get into the den and listen to what Thomas has to say. I'll stay in here and see to it that no one starves."

Koda and Shannon took their opened beer bottles into Tom Fogarty's spacious den, and immediately received the expected greetings from three impatient men.

"Hey look, it's Godzilla and tag-along!" Freddy Sanjanovitch commented in wide-eyed mock horror as he nudged his partner, Bart Harrington, with a silk-jacketed elbow. "Somebody must have found 'em wandering around in the woods and brought 'em home."

"Nah, it'd take those two a couple of days and a compass just to *find* the woods out here, and they don't even know how to read a compass," Harrington chuckled. "Besides, who'd want to bring them ugly bastards home anyway?"

"Beats the shit outta me. Benji's kinda cute though," Sanjanovitch winked at the approaching Koda.

"Glad to see you two could make it," Fogarty commented with barely contained sarcasm from the vantage point of his favorite reclining chair, inwardly relieved and relaxed now that the most aggressive of his paired teams had arrived. "Either of you hit anybody with a beer bottle and you clean it up," he added warningly, eyeing Koda's contemplative glance toward Sanjanovitch.

Ben Koda and Charley Shannon settled themselves into the remaining empty chairs, Shannon patting Freddy Sanjanovitch's grinning and dimpled cheek gently with a meaty hand and muttering something about a "lowlife muthah'. . . ."

Based upon outward appearances alone, a casual observer would have found it difficult to sort out the factors that presumably linked all of these young-to-middle-aged men together. There were simply too many contrasting variables.

Freddy Sanjanovitch was a tall, extroverted prettyboy-type body-builder in his late twenties—with long, light brown hair and green eyes—who looked as though he was ready for an evening of dancing at one of the nearby Georgetown night clubs, which was exactly what he planned on doing after the meeting.

In contrast, Bart Harrington was a deeply tanned, sparsely blond-haired, forty-two-year-old man who preferred comfortable, well-worn deck shoes, a pullover shirt and trousers—clothes not quite right for the Northern Virginia tennis set, but certainly appropriate for life on the thirty-foot sailboat waiting for him back at Newport Beach, California.

And then there was Tom Fogarty himself: a middle-aged Washington, D.C. type, who would have appeared equally at ease sharing his home and beer with government bureaucrats or with a bunch of disreputable hoodlums—which, in this case, wasn't all that far from the truth . . . and made the underlying connection between the five men seem all the more curious.

The presence of the late-arriving Ben Koda and Charley Shannon offered little in the way of additional clues. Aside from Shannon's eye-opening mass and intimidating demeanor, and the subtle Japanese-American features and outwardly irreverent humor of Ben Koda, there was little indication of the feral awareness and the burnished-steel edges that lay hidden beneath the friendly and playful exteriors of the oddly matched pair.

Taking into account the wide disparity in age, size, clothing, demeanor, dialect and racial background, even a practiced observer of law enforcement types might have been excused for not making the connection between the five men. Which was just fine with Special-Agent-in-Charge Thomas Fogarty Jr. of the Federal Drug Enforcement Administration, because that was exactly what he'd had in mind when he selected the Special Agent members of his Task Force team.

"Have trouble getting in?" Fogarty inquired.

"Trouble getting out," Ben Koda said, taking a sip at his beer. "Carson's not real happy about losing people to Special Task Force projects. Especially when nobody tells him what's going down. Want to know what he said you could do with this one?"

"Not particularly. You both clear on your assignments and court dates?"

Koda and Shannon both nodded again.

"Good, because we've got a nice hot one on our hands. Exactly the type of operation we talked about when we set up the Task Force teams. We're going to utilize your real-background covers, leapfrog tactics, the works with this one."

Koda and Shannon looked at each other quickly and then

looked around at the other agents for an answer. Sanjanovitch and Harrington shook their heads and shrugged to suggest their own ignorance as Fogarty went on.

"I've been going over general background with Bart and Freddy. I assume you two have heard of the Locotta family?"

"Southern California?" Koda asked.

"Right."

"Sure. The big boys. Supposed to be heavy into imports from South America and Singapore."

"Don't they share the California action with a couple other organized-crime families?" Shannon asked.

"As of about nine months ago, they don't share shit," Fogarty said, emphasizing his words with his wine glass. "They are it. Sole source for mob-controlled distribution of heroin, cocaine and hashish—which probably covers at least eighty percent of the powder sales south of 'Frisco."

Koda whistled softly. "How many people'd they buy off or kill?"

"We don't know, but it had to be one hell of a power play. Thing is, our informant claims that Jake Locotta's upgrading his operation—using computers to keep track of his dope. He's got a son in the business who's pushing the high-tech angle. Anyway, Locotta apparently got the green light from the big boys to show his stuff on a trial basis. Assuming that they're still a little disorganized, we figure it's a good time to make a penetration."

"So why make this a Task Force operation?" Koda asked. "Why not let the Western Regional Office run the show? Keep everybody happy?"

"'Specially seeing as how this real-background cover business is a onetime shot," Shannon added. "You use all of us up on one operation, you're going to have a hard time finding another clean team when you need one."

"That's exactly what we've been discussing for the last couple of hours," Fogarty nodded. "Approximately nine months ago, the Western Regional Office found itself under a microscope. Increased contacts by the U.S. Attorney's liaison people. Government Accounting Office audit team. Review panel on hiring practices from the Office of Personnel Management. Liaison contacts with three Congressional Oversight Committees. Even had a surprise visit from the governor's staff."

"Any similar activity in the other regions?" Koda asked.

"No."

"Hell of a coincidence," Shannon grumbled.

"Yeah, that's exactly it," Fogarty agreed. "At the moment we have no proof of an internal leak or political control situation developing within the Washington office, but regardless, there's no way we can run an investigation out of the Western Region on the Locotta Family. Even money says Locotta would have a list of the assigned agents—complete with addresses, phone numbers and girl friends—on his desk within a week."

"How's the regional director taking all of this?" Koda asked.

"About the way you'd expect an ex-marine colonel to react," Fogarty commented drily. "Mike's ready to land troops in the San Diego Bay, sweep north, and stop when he hits the Oregon border. But, since he can't get clearance for Marines, we get a blank check in his Region. We'll run the operation covert out of San Diego, and funnel the paperwork through the Special Action Division in D.C. All Mike wants is to be in on the takedown."

"All *right*! Man sounds like a fuckin' gy-rene," Shannon laughed approvingly as he slapped his muscular hands together with a solid whap.

"So what's the action?" Koda asked.

"Very low profile, Ben," Fogarty anwered. "On the presumably remote chance that we have an internal problem, we've decided to operate independent of Agency support at the entry stage. Obviously, that means no Regional backup unless things really go to shit."

"By which time, it just might be a little late," Koda noted.

"Precisely," Fogarty nodded. "And it also means no liaison with any other law enforcement types," he added. "I want clean deep-cover entries into these people. Go slow and easy on this one, and for God's sake, be careful. We want Locotta bad, but we've got plenty of time to do him.

"And regarding our entry," Fogarty went on, "until we can come up with some less-noticeable equipment, I've decided to restrict the use of beepers, transmitters and recorders. Like I said, the penetration has to be deep, and absolutely clean. We'll worry about documentation after we get a couple of the teams set in place."

"No recordings and no panic buttons," Shannon nodded his head thoughtfully. "Could get kinda lonely out there."

"That's why you've got a partner," Harrington said with a barely discernible smile beneath his sun-crinkled eyes. "Somebody to help hold on to your goodies when it gets dark."

"My-oh-my," Shannon drawled, shaking his head in mock sadness.

"Better find yourself an armor-plated jockstrap instead,

Charley. You ain't got shit for a partner," Freddy Sanjanovitch suggested, grinning cheerfully as Ben Koda winked and made an appropriate gesture in his direction.

Tom Fogarty enjoyed an inner sense of optimism and satisfaction as he looked around the room, confident that he had picked good operational teams. If nothing else, their casual bantering confirmed his belief that this group wouldn't be intimidated by either the political or the field hazards of the operation. Now all he had to do was to get his most volatile players, Koda and Shannon, past the next stage. Harrington and Sanjanovitch had already been informed.

"For security reasons, we're going to be running three paired teams, each one operating independently," Fogarty began. "For the first few days, Ben'll function as group leader in the field while I'm busy throwing smoke at the Washington Office."

"Ah take it the D.C. boys ain't gonna know a whole lot about this operation?" Shannon suggested, looking over at Fogarty with raised eyebrows.

Fogarty didn't even blink.

"At the moment, not even the director is fully aware of what we'll be doing. Your transfers were cut on my authority, which, at this point, means—"

"—try not to screw up?" Harrington suggested.

"Yeah, I'd appreciate it," Fogarty nodded. "Anybody want out?"

"Naw, sounds like fun," Charley Shannon grinned.

"You said three teams?" Koda looked around the room. "Aren't we kinda short a couple people?"

"This is the part you're not going to believe, Benji," Freddy Sanjanovitch smiled gleefully.

"Believe what?" Koda looked over at Fogarty.

"I'm extremely limited as to whom I can use for this task force, Ben," Fogarty said, a trace of defensive embarrassment evident in his voice. "I want experience, certainly, but there are other—equally important—factors. First of all, I need people familiar with the Southern California area, but preferably ones who haven't worked cases in the Western Region. Second, I don't want anyone who's been in court recently. Third, I'm not about to use anyone who's worked mob dope during the past few years. Fourth, I need people with good technical backgrounds. And finally, I have to have people who can merge their legitimate past history into a tight cover, because we're expecting a very intense hunt for agent names and IDs during this operation."

"Okay, so Charley and I try to remember what life was like in the goddamned army, Bart sells day-charters to desk jockeys who get seasick at the dock, Freddy goes back to being a gigolo. Figure we all made clean transitions. So . . . ?"

"So there were four experienced agents—namely us heroes— who fit the ticket," Freddy Sanjanovitch finished helpfully. "Four experienced *male* agents—and two, ah, somewhat less experienced females."

"Like as in *rookies*," Bart Harrington added.

"You gotta be shitting me."

"Benjamin, dear. Please stop being such a depressingly male chauvinist," Hazel Fogarty's voice rang out pleasantly from the kitchen.

"I repeat . . ." Ben Koda started, but Fogarty held up his hand.

"Ben, I sympathize with your often-expressed opinion of some of our less effective female agents," Fogarty said, giving the kitchen doorway a dark look, "but I don't have any other reasonable choice, so kindly shut the fuck up so we can get on with this briefing."

Koda rolled his eyes and shuddered but he shut up. Tom Fogarty had long since earned the respect of every one of the men sitting in his home.

"All right," Fogarty went on. "You'll all get a chance to hold hands with your new teammates in San Diego. Their names are Kaaren Mueller and Sandy Mudd."

"Sandy Mudd? Aw come on, Thomas," Sanjanovitch laughed.

"Sounds like a down-to-earth gal to me," Shannon offered.

"All right, enough!" Fogarty growled, slamming his hand on the chair arm. "Mueller's our surveillance specialist. Got a damn good reputation for low-light photography. Supposed to be real good with miniaturized camera equipment."

"Bet I know how—" Sanjanovitch started to whisper to Koda, and then cringed and went silent under Fogarty's smoldering glare.

"Sandy Mudd has an excellent background in electronics," Fogarty continued. "Fact is, I had one hell of a time stealing her away from the Technical Support Unit. She's top-rated in communications and computers—which may turn out to be very useful, seeing as how Locotta's supposed to have transferred his entire record-keeping operation into a protected computer data base."

"Never figured I'd have to learn computers just to buy dope," Charley Shannon muttered, shaking his head morosely.

"I'm glad you mentioned that, Charley, because that's *exactly* what you people have to understand," Fogarty nodded, gesturing with his glass again. "This business used to be just a matter of guts, flash and bullshit, but that kind of action isn't going to cut it anymore. At least not with players like Locotta. You people have to face it: We're in a new ball game. You, me, and the whole fucking Agency. And right now, they got us beat before we even set foot out of the dugout."

Fogarty stopped to take in a deep breath and then let it out slowly before he continued. "Look, what I'm trying to say is—we can't just go out there and buy a pound of coke off one of Locotta's dealers, and then expect him to fall. Not today. Not when his entire operation is protected twenty ways from Sunday with computer codes and electronic cutouts and all that shit."

Fogarty looked around at each of his investigators. "What it comes down to is one simple fact. We want to take out Locotta, we've gotta get into his system. And the only way we're going to do that is to play in their league, which means we need the Muellers and the Mudds and all their hardware, 'cause we're not going to be able to pull it off without 'em."

The silence in Fogarty's den was numbing.

"Kaaren and Sandy are down in San Diego right now, working background intelligence on one of Locotta's middlemen," Fogarty went on. "They've also been probing at a couple of street dealers. Had one real good prospect for us till they lost him."

"Sounds like one hell of a surveillance team—" Koda started in, and then was interrupted by Harrington.

"The kid they were tagging's on a respirator. Somebody nailed his ass—put him out a second-story window with a fucking poisonous snake hooked on his leg."

"Shit," Koda, Shannon and Sanjanovitch whispered, virtually in unison.

"Kid hit the concrete right in front of Kaaren and Sandy," Fogarty went on. "I understand that Kaaren just wiped the blood off her camera lens and kept on shooting—with the goddamned snake thrashing around about by her feet—until Sandy nailed the damn thing with a rock."

"And on top of that, they both managed to get out of the area without being questioned," Harrington added.

Koda, Shannon and Sanjanovitch looked at each other with shrugged expressions of grudging respect.

"They've been down there almost three months," Fogarty continued. "They're good people, so give them a little slack. If necessary, that's an order. Understand?"

All of the men nodded their heads, with varying degrees of enthusiasm.

"Fine. Okay, team assignments. Kaaren will work with Freddy. Sandy goes with Bart on the boat."

"Thank God . . ." Koda muttered, mostly to himself.

"What was that, Koda?" Fogarty demanded.

"Uh, nothing, sir."

"Good. All right, let me give you people the picture on Locotta's Family."

Fogarty hit light switches and turned on his slide projector.

"But first of all, you can have a look at your new partners. Sandy Mudd . . ." Fogarty said, thumbing the advance switch on the projector, ". . . and Kaaren Mueller."

"Jesus Christ," Freddy Sanjanovitch whispered.

"Whooo-eee," Charley whistled softly.

"Hope you picked up a good maternity rider for our insurance plan, boss," Koda said, shaking his head. "Either that, or you'd better get Freddy cut right now."

"We hired her for her brains," Fogarty said pointedly. "Not her face or her body. Kindly keep that in mind."

"Jake Locotta," Fogarty went on as he advanced the slide. "Early fifties. He runs the financial side of the business through an accountant named Al Rosenthal." Fogarty's thumb triggered the slide advance. "Rosenthal's an old family associate. Zero chance of using him to get to Locotta."

"How about the dealers?" Sanjanovitch asked, still distracted by the memory of Kaaren Mueller's face.

"Coming to them. Locotta uses three primary middlemen to run the dope end of his operation. Enrico Nogales." Click, whirr. "Jean Claude LaQue." Click, whirr. "And Jimmy Pilgrim." Click, whirr. "This is another associate of Locotta's—a dangerous one. Joe Tassio, his chief enforcer."

"Looks like a heavy dude," Charley Shannon commented.

"Start taking notes," Fogarty interrupted his slide lecture. "We're going to put Nogales on hold for a while and concentrate on the other two. Right now, I'm planning on putting Bart, Sandy and the boat in on LaQue. From what I hear, the son of a bitch spends every spare minute he's got hustling broads onto a yacht he's got in Newport Harbor, which happens to be docked ten slips down from our slot."

"Man doesn't sound all *that* bad," Harrington shrugged.

"Thought you might take a liking to him," Fogarty nodded.

"Continuing on . . . Freddy, you and Kaaren get to go after the *real* shithead in Locotta's operation—Pilgrim. Okay?"

"Fine by me," Sanjanovitch shrugged.

"Come on, Sanjo, 'fess up," Bart Harrington grinned. "You'd go in on Dracula himself, as long as you get to keep Mueller for a partner."

"Ah, two questions, boss." Koda raised his hand politely.

"Go ahead."

"To start with, what's the deal on Pilgrim? And secondly, what've you got planned for Charley and me?"

"Jimmy Pilgrim is a freak on fear," Fogarty explained. "His street dealers all seem to be scared shitless of him. The ones we've gotten into won't talk much about him at all—apparently for good reasons. Intelligence has him down for at least five murders personally. All strangled, probably with bare hands. Also, there are some unsubstantiated rumors that he was tied into the attempt on a State narc last year where a fairly sophisticated booby trap was used . . . along with three telephone warnings before the hit."

"Ralph Barreno," Harrington muttered bitterly. "The guy ended up with one arm, one eye, partial use of his legs, and another divorce. He was a good field man. Tell you what, I'd really like to find the asshole who made those calls. See how long he lasts in the Santa Barbara channel with a couple bloody stumps for feet after the Makos and Whites start checking in."

"Yeah, nice idea," Fogarty nodded. "But remember, there's no confirmation that Pilgrim was involved. We know he likes to use a rope or bare hands. Lifts weights. *Definitely* likes to play mind games on his people. Far as we know, he's never been seen carrying a weapon. The one thing we do know for sure about Jimmy Pilgrim is that he's a stone-cold madman, period. Doesn't even bother to use a street name when he operates. We've got him down as highly intelligent, gutsy, unpredictable, dangerous on a personal level, indifferent to the idea of killing a federal agent in general, and probably our best shot at Locotta."

"I move we dump the son-of-a-bitch straight out, and then look for the second best shot," Harrington offered.

"And you're putting Sanjo in on this shithead with a *Penthouse* broad like Mueller for a partner?" Koda shook his head. "Kiss your pretty ass good-bye, Freddy. And don't forget to will me that Walther."

"Laugh it off, hotshot," Sanjanovitch grinned. "The man still hasn't told you the best part."

"Huh, what's that?" Koda demanded, turning toward Fogarty.

"Freddy and Kaaren are going to be perfectly safe working Pilgrim," Fogarty said. "Because they are going to have a couple of very dedicated baby-sitters watching every move—"

"Oh Jesus, no!"

"—they make," Fogarty finished.

"Hope you get to like new wave disco music, Benji," Sanjanovitch said, smiling pleasantly. "'Course, we're going to expect you two to be a little discreet later in the evenings . . ."

"Discreet, mah ass . . ." Charley Shannon started in as Koda groaned and closed his eyes.

"Jimmy Pilgrim's primary associate is a gentleman named Lafayette Beaumont Raynee," Fogarty continued. "Black male. Thirty-one. Five-eleven. One-sixty. Goes by the AKA of Rainbow. You can see why."

"Hey, Freddy," Charley Shannon grunted, "you and Rainbow're gonna get along *real* good. Neither one a' you got any fuckin' taste in clothes. Man, just *look* at the dude's colors!"

"Rainbow is a full-time dealer and a part-time pimp who likes to play with knives and razor blades," Tom Fogarty continued. "Certifiable psychopath. Creams over anything sharp. Be careful with him. I repeat, *be careful with him*. He and Pilgrim are a matched set."

"Also, based on what we know about them, it's very possible that either Pilgrim or Rainbow put that kid out the window with the snake, regardless of the fact that he works for them," Fogarty added as he advanced a slide showing Jamie MacKenzie lying facedown on a blood-spattered sidewalk, the thick-bodied viper still visibly attached to his leg by its rock-smashed head.

"Fuck me," Sanjanovitch whispered.

"If that was Pilgrim or Rainbow, then they got themselves one hell of an employee incentive program," Bart Harrington muttered as every man in the room continued to stare at the numbing images on the wall.

"Hey, Tom. How about going to Pilgrim again?" Koda asked softly, his attitude sobering as he began to contemplate the magnitude of the danger that Freddy Sanjanovitch and Kaaren Mueller were going to be facing.

"Certainly." Click, whirr. "This is the only photo of Jimmy Pilgrim that we've got. He doesn't go out in public very often. Too many shadows to show much facial detail. Kaaren's going to try to shoot something better if she spots him out in the open. Our information has it that Pilgrim favors grey three-piece suits. Black beard and hair, usually well-trimmed. Always wears horn-rimmed glasses . . ."

2

IN THE COOL, quiet sanctuary of his University laboratory, Dr. David Isaac methodically went through all the known variables and probabilities in his mind one last time. Then, after a final moment of silent contemplation, he made the irrevocable decision to involve himself with a very imaginative and exceedingly dangerous criminal.

Isaac really didn't see it that way, of course, but then a man of his sheltered background and experience really couldn't be expected to understand all of the necessary and inevitable consequences of such a decision.

From Isaac's point of view (that of a highly intelligent and extensively educated man who had spent the last ten years of his life almost exclusively in a university environment), the offer that he had received from a man named Jimmy Pilgrim was quite simply overwhelming, especially when he considered the motivators . . .

First, and perhaps most persuasive, there would be the opportunity to expand the scope of his treasured research—to actually test his fascinating analog compounds on human subjects—to an extent that only days earlier would have been unimaginable . . . as well as illegal.

And too, of course, there would be the money—equally enticing because the yearly salary of a full professor of organic chemistry at the University of California barely equaled the wages paid to the apprentice union plumber who spent a leisurely work week searching for leaks in the miles of University plumbing. Certainly, the prospect of earning at least ten times that amount each *month* appealed to Isaac, but still, there was more to Jimmy Pilgrim's well-thought-out carrot than simply expanded research opportunities and money.

Much more.

Interwoven among the other factors (which included the unnerving possibility of being discovered by law enforcement specialists on either side of the law, Isaac reminded himself), there was the critical element: the enticing dream of bringing to life the long-buried legend of Maria. It was a fantasy that had haunted the orderly recesses of Isaac's brilliantly logical mind from the early bookworm days of his youth. But now, two weeks after his evening seminar on alchemy, it was a fantasy that had become tightly entangled in stark reality.

Having made his decision, Dr. David Isaac sat in his cramped office with his feet carefully propped up on his paper-strewn desk-top, outwardly absorbed in his lab notebook as he waited patiently for his graduate students to complete their evening research.

It would be a while yet.

Isaac was the youngest, and said by many to be the most gifted, full professor of organic chemistry in the history of the University. It was, without question, an honor to be selected as one of Isaac's four doctoral candidates. But in keeping with that honor, there was also the corresponding obligation to produce a thesis worthy of publication under Isaac's widely respected name. So it was not at all unusual to find all four of his grad students spending every spare hour at their laboratory benches.

At 10:35 P.M., Isaac finally heard the soft, scuffling sound of well-worn tennis shoes approach his office.

"Professor?"

"Yes, Nichole?" Isaac looked up from the draft manuscript of his current article—a comprehensive and fascinating treatise on psychomotor-active compounds that might now (out of necessity) never be published—as the last of his late-working graduate students poked her head through the doorway.

Nichole Faysonnt was an energetic twenty-one-year-old woman who possessed a delightfully inquisitive scientific mind, two undergraduate degrees with honors from France and Switzerland, and an appealing habit of concealing her subtly attractive Eurasian features behind large wire-framed glasses, loose blue jeans and a white lab coat. She was also, Isaac knew with a twinge of guilt, the primary subject of another one of his often recurring fantasies.

"About that new analog series you suggested. I've worked out One through Sixteen . . . and I left Seventeen on the computer disk," the dark-haired girl said, her voice radiating quiet confidence and energy, in spite of the readily apparent fatigue that had reddened her dark, sensitive eyes behind the wire-framed lenses.

"What do you think?" Isaac inquired casually.

"I think the series is very feasible," Nichole shrugged, the gleam in her tired eyes revealing her undiminished enthusiasm for her thesis project. "The spatial geometries look very good, and I believe we've covered most of the known receptor sites. But I also think that the synthesis of Fifteen through Twenty—the most likely ones—will be very difficult. Perhaps not possible. I'll be in by nine tomorrow morning to start work on Eighteen. I promise."

"Fine," Isaac nodded approvingly. He knew she'd be back in the lab at 8:30 sharp. Like her dissertation, and her computer programs, Nichole Faysonnt's life was tightly controlled, efficient, and dependable . . . which made the fantasy even more enticing, he realized.

"Do you want me to shut down the lab? I'm the last one in tonight."

"No, go home and get some sleep," Isaac smiled, shaking his head. "I'll see to it in a few minutes."

"Thank you." A brief, seemingly flirtatious smile crossed her face and then faded away—like a faint remnant of a long-forgotten childhood. "Good night, professor."

"Good night, Nichole."

Isaac waited until he heard the lock on the main door of the laboratory slam shut. Then he sat back in his chair, punched the "PLAY" button on the small tape recorder attached to his office phone, and listened once again to the incredible conversation that would now, irrevocably, alter his sheltered academic life:

"Hello?"

"Dr. Isaac?"

"Speaking."

"Dr. Isaac, this is James Pilgrim, Bio-Action Research Technologies. I called earlier . . ."

"Yes, my secretary took the message. I'm sorry . . ."

"Dr. Isaac, to be very brief, I'm trying to locate an organic chemist capable of synthesizing a fairly complex organic compound for us. As I understand, you do accept consulting work on occasion?"

"Only on rare occasions, Mr. Pilgrim. My spare time is very limited. I usually refer such projects to a private laboratory."

"Yes, I realize you're very busy. Under normal circumstances, I wouldn't presume to bother you. But the thing is, the compound we require for our research is apparently difficult to produce. You were highly recommended to us as a chemist who enjoys intriguing and challenging projects. And too, of course, we're prepared to compensate you very well for your time and materials."

"I'm sorry," Isaac's voice chuckled, "but I—"

"We were thinking of a fee of twenty-five thousand dollars for a test batch of ten grams."

There was a three-second pause.

"I beg your pardon?"

"Twenty-five thousand dollars, Dr. Isaac. With the stipulation, of course, that payment would be made in full upon delivery."

Then a four-second pause.

"Tell me, Mr. Pilgrim. Exactly what type of compound are we talking about?"

"The chemical name is one-one-two-thienyl-cyclohexyl-piperidine. I believe you would call it—"

"—a rather simple thiopene analog of phencyclidine," Isaac's voice interrupted, "which is really not all that challenging a synthesis. Interesting, perhaps . . . but only because the compound is structurally similar to phencyclidine, or PCP. Which, as you may be aware, Mr. Pilgrim, is classified by the Federal Government as a restricted dangerous drug."

"You have a commendable knowledge of the drug laws, Dr. Isaac."

"And you have selected a most 'intriguing' compound for your, uh, research project, Mr. Pilgrim." The sarcasm in Isaac's voice came across clearly on the tape. "Particularly from my perspective, as I'm planning to publish a paper on hallucinogenic analogs of restricted drugs in the near future."

"An amazing coincidence."

"My thought exactly," Isaac snorted derisively. "I suppose you've considered the distinct possibility that your compound will exhibit hallucinogenic properties?"

"Yes, of course."

"Fascinating." Isaac's voice took on a droll tone. "I must confess, Mr. Pilgrim, you have me very curious about a number of things. For example, aren't you just a little bit concerned about your, ah, legal status in all of this? Not to mention the possibility that I might decide to contact the police?"

"Quite the contrary. I'm simply offering you a perfectly legitimate business proposition. If you'll take the time to review the Controlled Substances Act very carefully, you'll note that it's not illegal to produce or sell an *analog* of a restricted drug."

"Very true," Isaac grunted after a moment's hesitation. "Yet, you're still willing to pay me twenty-five thousand dollars to produce ten grams of a 'perfectly legal' analog that shouldn't cost more than a few hundred dollars to synthesize at any one of several private laboratories I could name?"

The amusement in Isaac's voice was again clearly discernible.

"That's correct, Doctor. And as for your concern about the police—did I happen to mention the bonus we're offering for this project?"

"No, you didn't mention a bonus," Isaac chuckled indifferently.

"You *are* interested in the history of alchemy, are you not?"

"One of my few diverting hobbies. I'm surprised you know—"

"Actually, I had the distinct impression that the study of alchemy was more of an obsession in your case. But, be that as it may, we happen to be an international corporation. Coincidentally, one of our financial backers in the Mideast is now in possession of a fascinating artifact. Actually, it's just a piece of very old paper; however, it has been authenticated by experts as being an unrecorded page from the *Cheirokmeta*. Apparently, some sort of experimental notes made by a woman chemist named Maria. I understand that such an artifact would fit very nicely within your—what shall we call it—quasi-legal private collection?"

Now there was a ten-second pause.

"Dr. Isaac?"

"Uh . . . yes?"

"I'm sorry, I thought we'd lost our connection. Tell me, is this thiopene analog really as difficult to synthesize as I am told?"

"What—? Uh, no. No, it wouldn't be all that difficult," Isaac said distractedly. Then more firmly, he added, "I'd like to know who authenticated this artifact you've just described."

"Three certifiable experts, all very familiar to you, I'm sure. Almarian? Cohen? Fauss? But I believe we were discussing the difficulty of producing ten grams of a thiopene analog."

Very clearly, it was now Pilgrim who was amused.

"The synthesis of your analog is trivial, Mr. Pilgrim," Isaac replied with a distinctive edge to his voice. "Well within the capability of
any graduate-level chemist. Certainly not difficult enough to warrant
your fee—to say nothing of your bonus, which, for your information,
happens to be priceless. Assuming, of course, that the artifact actually
exists and that you're serious about all of this."

"The artifact exists, and I am *very* serious, Doctor. Serious
enough to put you into contact with my Mideast representative within
twenty-four hours of your decision. But you don't seem to understand.
If we come to terms in this matter, we would be purchasing more than
just your chemical expertise. You have other—attributes—which fit
our needs precisely."

"I don't understand—"

"You are a full professor of chemistry at a major university," the
deep voice growled coldly. "To be blunt, you aren't paid shit. But you
can come and go as you please. No one questions your selection of
research topics or equipment, as long as you work within your budget.
No one stands over your shoulder while you work. Correct?"

"I suppose that's an accurate appraisal," Isaac said hesitantly,
"but what—"

"Dr. Isaac, you can work in absolute privacy in one of the best-
equipped research chemistry laboratories in the world. We want to
purchase a piece of that privacy, as well as your absolute silence regarding our product research."

"I believe I see . . ." Isaac whispered in sudden understanding.

"I'm not asking for your decision now. Think it over. You have
my phone number, I believe?"

There was silence . . . and then a rustling of papers in the
background.

"Uh—yes."

"Fine. The number connects to a secure answering service. It
will be disconnected if I have not heard from you within one week. I
may contact you once more in the meantime. As an additional consid-
eration, I should note that we will be interested in purchasing more
analogs in the future. For an appropriate fee, of course."

"Fascinating," Isaac whispered.

"We think so. Oh, and by the way, Professor. When you do
make your call, please be sure to use a public phone some distance
from your lab or residence. In our area of research, there is always the

problem of unfriendly competition. I believe you understand the problem."

"Yes, I believe I do."

"Good-bye, Dr. Isaac."

"Uh—yes, good-bye, Mr. Pilgrim."

Shutting off the recorder, Dr. David Isaac walked out of his office and across the lab to Nichole's assigned work area. There, he keyed the access code into her computer console, watched the disk directory come up on the screen, and then typed in a series of commands.

Nichole was right, Isaac thought as he scanned the numbers and the words glowing bright green on the darkened screen. The synthesis for analog seventeen—the most interesting of the "A"-series to date in terms of potential psychomotor activity—would be complex. But certainly not impossible, he smiled as he transferred the relevant information into his notebook and then cleared the screen.

Having made the decision to add an unauthorized twist to Jimmy Pilgrim's project, Dr. David Isaac stood up, stretched contentedly, and then walked back over to his own private laboratory area.

Selecting a spotlessly clean flask from a nearby cabinet, Isaac used a wax pencil to mark the letter and number A-17, his initials, and the date on the smooth glass surface. He filled the flask half full with distilled water. Then, after consulting his notebook once more, he sat down in front of an ultra-precise electronic balance, placed the notebook and the flask within easy reach, took a small vial containing a light brown powdery substance that he'd been working on for several hours now out of his lab coat pocket, and reached for a weighing paper.

The contents of the vial weighed precisely 10.024 grams.

Isaac replaced the powder in the unmarked vial, replaced the cap, and then slipped the vial back into his coat pocket. Phase one—the synthesis of the thiopene analog for Jimmy Pilgrim—was now completed.

The more intriguing work was about to begin.

On a small island resort separated from the Brunswick, Georgia coastline by a narrow river, a man who had been a very imaginative and a very dangerous criminal for most of his fifty-four years sat in the back of a very expensive hotel suite overlooking the Atlantic Ocean, and listened casually as his son presented a thoroughly gratifying financial report to the directors of their reasonably discreet and very well organized "corporation."

Jake Locotta had begun his career in an era when the only thing "organized" about the criminal underworld in the United States was its highly publicized name.

Now, thirty-seven years later, Jake Locotta's "family" controlled the major percentage of all the smuggling, bookmaking, loan-sharking and dope-dealing in and across Southern California. What he did not operate directly, he monitored, controlled, and "taxed" through an interlocking maze of warehousing, transporting and money-laundering enterprises. All in all, a very lucrative operation—especially the narcotics smuggling and sales.

Settling back into his cushioned executive chair, Jake Locotta took a thoughtful glance out at the night-lighted golf course adjoining the Jekyll Island resort, and then turned to Al Rosenthal, his old friend and accountant, who sat with him in the back of the room.

"So whaddaya think, Rosey?" Locotta asked quietly.

"They like the way you handled that runner, Jake," Al Rosenthal said softly in a deep, husky voice—the inevitable result of too many cigarettes and too many late hours poring over several sets of books. "Reminds 'em what kinda business we're in. The air tanks were a nice touch."

"Yeah, somebody gets outta control, you gotta stamp down hard," Locotta nodded grimly. "That way, everybody knows the score. Which reminds me," he added in a growled whisper, "you get any word on Lester?"

"Yeah, I think so," Rosenthal nodded grimly. "Guy matching his description got picked up by the *federales* near that show place Lester likes to hang out at. Word is the guy got drunk and killed a Mexican cop."

"Shit," Locotta snarled, his face contorting in quiet fury. "That fuckin' pervert . . ." Then suspicion suddenly flashed across his mind. "Listen, you sure Pilgrim or Rainbow weren't involved?" he whispered.

"No way to tell," Rosenthal shook his head. "Can't even get confirmation they got Lester in jail. You know how things like that work down there."

"Yeah, kiss the son-of-a-bitch good-bye," Locotta nodded, and then shrugged indifferently. "What the hell, we got other people. So what you think about the finances?"

"Like the kid's saying," Rosenthal rasped, "the fourth quarter . . ."

"Naw, skip all that crap," Locotta gestured with his cigar. "Gimme the nut on the dope."

Al Rosenthal grinned, his watery eyes sparkling in amusement. Like his longtime boss, Rosenthal was slightly distrustful of the way the new computers churned out 100%-accurate numbers in milliseconds. Although in private he willingly admitted to a certain amount of amazement and respect. Jake Locotta's Harvard-educated son had recently designed an account-hiding program for the computers that made Rosenthal's head spin in amazement as the elderly pen-and-paper accountant recognized the possibilities.

"Like we agreed last year," Rosenthal began, talking softly from his sharp memory, "we've limited our narcotics investments to three products: cocaine, heroin and hashish. In round numbers, our sales receipts were eight-sixty-four, one-seventy-five and one-sixty-three, respectively. Total of one-point-one-zero-two gross."

"And the nut?" Jake Locotta asked, seemingly concerned.

"Very consistent with last year," Rosenthal whispered reassuringly. "Purchasing, two-sixty-eight. Operations, just about fifty-three. And our outside consulting has steadied out at nineteen."

"Fucking bribes gonna eat us up some day," Locotta grumbled. "Come on," he urged, "give it to me in numbers I can understand. Bottom line."

"Bottom line," Rosenthal smiled. "On an outlay of approximately three hundred and forty million dollars for drug operations this year, we have taken in just over one-point-one billion. That comes to—

"Two hundred percent profit," Jake Locotta said, grinning now. "Don't need a fucking computer to figure a percentage like that, do we? So whadda ya think?"

"About the dope?" Rosenthal shrugged. "Lotta risk, like always, but good business. *Real* good business."

"That's right," Locotta grunted. "And as long as we pull two-thirds of our profit out of powder and hash, we *stay* in the business. *Nobody* puts us out." Locotta and his longtime advisor exchanged knowing grins. Then they both turned their attention back to the meeting.

As Jake Locotta and Al Rosenthal listened patiently to the reports of the other mob bosses in the meticulously secured meeting room, twenty-six hundred miles away the Creator reached for one of the small bottles of expensive chemicals arranged in an orderly row next to the ultra-sensitive balance.

Carefully controlling his breathing, the Creator methodically weighed out precise amounts of the expensive chemicals onto glassine paper squares. Then, with equal care and precision, he began to transfer the powdery chemicals—paper by paper, in the correct sequence—into the flask of purified water that now contained a rapidly spinning teflon-coated magnet.

Twenty minutes later, after the pH of the liquid had been slightly shifted three times, the last of the swirling crystals finally disappeared into solution. Dr. David Isaac stepped away from his lab bench, satisfied.

Having completed the first stage of the complex synthesis, Isaac carefully placed the now-stoppered flask on the grey bench-top. He made a few notations in his lab notebook, replaced the notebook in the locked drawer of his desk, shut down the lab instruments, shut off the lights, and then walked out of the chemistry building en route to the parking lot, his old Volkswagen bug, and ultimately to a distant public telephone. An increasingly impatient man named Jimmy Pilgrim was waiting for a phone call.

Back in the lab, the mother liquid, now a clear rich broth of free-floating ions bearing the label A-17, rested quietly and alone in the transparent glass enclosure, reflecting the bright moonlight into a faint rainbow pattern on the white wall of the cool, empty laboratory as it waited—contained, homogenous and potent—for its creator to return.

3

IN THE PICTURE-WINDOWED living room of an exclusive hillside home overlooking the beautiful northern San Diego coastline less than five miles due north of the University of California, San Diego campus, a telephone resting on a hand-carved red oak coffee table began to demand attention.

"Rainbow, honey. The phone."

Raynee accepted the phone, motioning the girl out of the room.

"Rainbow."

"Good morning."

"James, my man." Raynee smiled warmly, relieved by the inner knowledge that all must have gone well. Unlike Raynee, Jimmy Pilgrim rarely displayed his emotions openly, but there were subtle indicators that could be detected in his voice if one were alert. To Raynee's hashish-tuned ear, his business partner sounded relatively calm and content. For Jimmy Pilgrim, any deviation from cold indifference was significant.

"Ah been waitin' for your call," Raynee hided gently, testing the waters.

"The wait was worthwhile," Pilgrim said evenly. "We have a new associate on our staff."

"You sure the man understands our needs? *All* our needs?"

"Yes. The product research has been initiated. He will deliver a minimum of ten analog variations each month. We can reasonably expect at least one marketable variation out of each batch."

"We still gonna do the testing?"

"Yes. I assume you're prepared?"

"No problem," Raynee shrugged. "How 'bout them labs? He gonna do that too?"

"He will provide us with the necessary formulations, tooling specifications, lab design and material needs. We provide the raw materials, site and labor."

"An' the dealers," Raynee added cheerfully.

"Yes, of course."

"Then there ain't no way we gonna lose," Raynee laughed.

"We *can* lose, but we won't," Pilgrim corrected, now infusing his words with his characteristic coldness. "Once we begin full distribution, our competitors will be in no position to compete with us."

"'Specially if they can't find us. Ain't that right, Bro?"

"Security is essential in the first few months," Pilgrim agreed, his voice now totally devoid of emotion. "Absolute security."

"What about the new dude? He understand all that? Ah mean, does the man *really understand*?" Raynee pressed, concerned because he knew how bad it was going to get out there on the streets. He had no intention of ending up like Jake Locotta's numbers runner: chained to the ocean floor with a scuba tank rapidly running out of air. Or worse, like Lester.

"We have a mutual desire for secrecy," Pilgrim said. "Aside from the necessary mechanics of transferring products and funds, he desires no contact with us—none whatsoever. I see no need to concern him with the risk elements associated with our competitors, or the details of our strategy. He is intelligent. He will reason them out on his own soon enough."

"An' then . . . ?"

"He has sufficient reason to accept a minimal risk factor. His motivator is very compelling . . . as is yours."

"Can't argue with you on that, my man. So what 'bout that there test sample?"

"It's ready. He's mailing it to box alpha-five. I want you to be sure to use someone expendable to make this first pickup, just in case." Pilgrim paused. "This may be an appropriate time to conduct the initial testing and, at the same time, resolve that special problem you mentioned last week. I assume you're still suspicious?"

"Suspicious ain't 'xactly the word. If'n Ah didn't trust your market research, Ah'd swear our lady friend's burnin' hot. Can't think a' any other reason why she'd be coming on t' a pitiful little dude like Squeek. Boy's a total loss. 'Less, of course, she's doing a little precautionary scoutin' for the Main Man."

"I've been assured that all investigations are being conducted in the routine manner, and we are not a focused target," Pilgrim said. "It's much more likely that she's either a talent scout for our competition or, as you suggested, another one of Locotta's headhunters."

"Tell you what, you don't mind gettin' things off t' an early start, then Ah got jes' the act t' show the little lady," Raynee chuckled.

Jimmy Pilgrim paused for a moment, and then said, "You do that. Let me know when you're ready."

"You got it—" Raynee started, then realized he was he was talking into an empty line.

It took Lafayette Beaumont Raynee all of five seconds to select the most expendable member of his multilayered narcotics distribution team to make the dangerous, first-time, mail-drop retrieval of the thiopene analog sample, which was about four seconds more than he needed, considering the nature of Bylighter's qualifications.

Eugene Bylighter (or "Squeek", as he was called by almost everyone except his parents and certain elements of the California criminal justice system) had been described by his own father as a scrawny, useless, acned, ill-mannered, burned-out and functionally illiterate runaway. Local law enforcement authorities and his street peers were less generous. They had Squeek pegged as a thoroughly incompetent criminal: equally inept as a petty thief, dope dealer, dope addict, residential burglar, rapist, bathroom-wall scrawler, and occasional snitch.

In effect, a dumb shit.

And, as if all that weren't enough of a jacket for an eighteen-year-old-dropout, the Fates had seen fit to provide Eugene Bylighter with yet another albatross to hang around his skinny, blotched neck. In spite of his most determined efforts—which usually degenerated into outright pleading in the front seat of a borrowed automobile (Bylighter had never figured out how to talk a girl into the back seat of a car, much less into a bed)—Squeek was still a virgin in the truest sense of the word.

Understandably, perhaps, this condition had long since developed into an all-encompassing obsession with the ill-fated street youth, who insisted on confiding the luridly imaginative details of his latest plan of attack to the few people he knew who were still willing to listen, a number which grew steadily smaller with each passing month.

But even considering his inherent problems, Eugene Bylighter's bemoaned precoital status shouldn't have been all that difficult to remedy. Given the pathetic nature of his general life-style, and the irrepressible maternal instincts simmering in the glands of his otherwise wary female contemporaries, there should have been any number of impulsive young women anxious—or "at least *willing*, for God's sake", as Bylighter was often heard to comment—to clutch the pathetic Squeek to their bosoms for some sorely needed comfort.

And in truth, the emotionally downtrodden Squeek probably would have gotten laid long ago if it hadn't been for his outwardly wasted and diseased appearance, which inevitably convinced even the most open-minded young women that Squeek's mental and physical condition simply had to be the result of terminal VD. In effect, just another fateful twist in an overwhelmingly disastrous life that made Bylighter's one attempt at rape almost understandable—although nowhere near successful, due to his predictable luck in selecting a victim with a decidedly commercial outlook toward sex, a vicious right knee, and a resolve to *never ever* give it away for free.

As a result of all this misfortune, Eugene Bylighter finally found himself strung out to the point of being obsessively troubled, confused and depressed over his lot in life. Understandably then, he was eagerly receptive when he received the fateful telephone call from the man he almost worshiped: Lafayette Beaumont Raynee, the high-stepping, woman-loving, street warrior he knew only as "Rainbow."

Thus, Eugene Bylighter went out early on a Saturday morning to a post office box at a specified address and picked up a package for Lafayette Beaumont Raynee. No questions asked. Even though Raynee's detailed instructions—which included a three-hour random walk around the San Diego harbor after the pickup—should have alerted even the most naive street youth that he was being used as a sacrificial decoy. Of course, that possibility never occurred to Bylighter, which was why Raynee had selected him in the first place.

But then too, even if Bylighter had realized the nature of his assignment, it wouldn't have mattered. Taking a lesson from his mentor, Jimmy Pilgrim, Lafayette Beaumont Raynee made it a point to know the most effective motivators for his street dealers. Well aware of

Bylighter's difficulties with the ladies, Raynee's second-phase instructions included a motivator that was easily an order of magnitude beyond any of the youth's most vivid wet dreams.

And because the imagery of that all-enticing carrot was still jiggling erotically within the dreamy confines of Eugene Bylighter's relatively vacant skull, he was able to follow the first phase of Raynee's instructions to the letter.

As instructed, Bylighter walked into the post office in downtown San Diego the next morning at 8:00 A.M. sharp, dialed in the correct numbers on a post office box, removed a small brown-paper-wrapped package, placed it in his jacket pocket. He then proceeded to walk the entire perimeter of the San Diego harbor completely and blissfully unaware during the entire three hours that every step he took was being closely monitored by a group of very dangerous men.

As Eugene Bylighter was approaching the end of his mandated three-hour walk along the San Diego harbor, Kaaren Mueller and Sandy Mudd sat in the living room of a rented Chula Vista apartment five miles away and glared at the silent phone.

Unlike Lafayette Beaumont Raynee's $450,000 home in nearby Del Mar—which contained six spacious bedrooms, four elaborately furnished bathrooms, a sunken tub, and a panoramic view of the Pacific Ocean—the apartment Special Agent Kaaren Mueller rented for $345 a month plus utilities in the industrial-based city just south of San Diego had one small bedroom, a single bathroom with a chipped enamel tub, and a distinctly unappetizing view of a trash-ridden alley.

"Admit it," Sandy said finally, breaking the moody silence, "the kid stood you up. He said he'd call you by noon. It's twelve-thirty now. We've got a five-hour drive to the river, and I've still got to pick up my ski at the shop. So . . ."

"So we cruise in empty-handed," Kaaren muttered sullenly. "Just a couple of camp followers ready to party. Just like they expect." She looked up at her ex-Academy roommate for confirmation.

"Kaaren, there's not a whole lot we can do about it," Sandy said reasonably, shrugging her muscular shoulders. "It's just the way the game's played these days. We start out second-class. Maybe we work our way up to first, maybe we don't. A lot of it's luck. We just didn't get lucky today, that's all."

Sandy Mudd's easygoing attitude wasn't as casual as it seemed. Raised with four older brothers, she had learned the hard way to keep her mouth shut on the topic of feminine equality. She had been forced to learn, at a very tender age, that it was much more effective to demonstrate the power of brains and coordination over muscle-mass than to simply talk about it. Sandy Mudd had never had any doubts about her own equality. She had always believed—in spite of a great deal of mental, and, occasionally, physical harassment—that she was perfectly capable of competing with her brothers, or any of their male friends for that matter. It was just a matter of learning how to prove her point.

Sandy learned by the painfully instructive method of trial-and-error, ultimately selecting her fields of battle—which included skiing, sailboating and racquet sports, in addition to her treasured ham radio equipment—with foresight and planning worthy of a military tactician. As a result, her success had gone far beyond her most confident expectations. It had been a long, long time since the Mudd brothers looked upon their determined sister as being anything less than equal.

But then, Sandy mused, she didn't have to deal with the additional handicap of physical beauty in competing with her brothers, boyfriends, and male agents of the Drug Enforcement Administration. At least not to the extent that her stunningly beautiful, red-haired, green-eyed, ex-Basic-Agent-School-roommate, friend, and fellow task force agent faced, Sandy thought with just a twinge of admitted envy.

Which wasn't to suggest that Sandy Mudd was ugly. She was, in fact, a relatively attractive young woman who just happened to have a father with an unfortunate sense of humor when it came to naming his children, and who also happened to be far more interested in athletics, electronics and—more recently—computer programming than in the careful selection of clothes and makeup. The inevitable comparisons of Mueller and Mudd—linked by gender and alphabet from their first day at the DEA's National Training Institute—invariably resulted in descriptions such as "glowing with robust health," and "radiating sex appeal."

Sandy Mudd glowed and Kaaren Mueller radiated, in spite of Kaaren's determined efforts to play down her inherited physical charms as she put in a succession of sixteen-hour days before finally attaining her immediate goal: being a top-ten graduate at NTI.

"Yeah, well I didn't bust my butt getting through Basic to go second class in this outfit," Kaaren replied. "Besides, if I need luck to con an adolescent pervert like Squeek into meeting me for lunch, I might as well give up and shack with Sanjo. At least he'd show up on time."

"Which reminds me . . ." Sandy Mudd said, turning her head and raising her eyes quizzically.

"I told Freddy that if he touched one more button or zipper, I'd cut him ear-to-ear," Kaaren grinned in spite of herself.

"I don't know, " Sandy shook her head in mock sadness. "Business is business, but Sanjo's still got a nice bod. Besides," she said, her eyes lighting up with conspiratorial amusement and curiosity, "you can't tell me you don't get warmed up a little when you two dance."

"Uhmm, maybe a little," Kaaren admitted, displaying a set of deeply creased dimples as she grinned impishly and shrugged. "But I'm not copping to anything else. Freddy's just a little too smooth for my taste. I just get him good and horny, then send him out to pick up something at the local bars."

"Probably a good case of herpes, knowing Sanjo," Sandy chuckled.

"Wouldn't doubt it. Hope I can't catch anything through polyester."

"So, is he still planning on coming out tomorrow afternoon? I can't wait to see him try to keep his hair styled while he's out on a pair of water skis."

"Don't bet on him getting out of bed before noon," Kaaren warned, looking glum again. "Which reminds me—" She looked up at the clock. "Listen, why don't you pick up your ski and head on out? I want to give Bylighter a little more time, just in case."

"Look, Kaaren, the guys aren't going to give a damn—" Sandy started in.

"Yeah, I know, but it's something *I* want to do," Kaaren shook her head stubbornly. "Bylighter's got to be the weakest link in Rainbow's operation. We get Rainbow, then we've got a shot at Pilgrim."

"We've also got a shot at getting our tails in a sling," Sandy warned. "Fogarty was real specific when he talked to us about working without backup. Not to mention you promised Ben we'd stick close together this weekend till we got to the river. He wasn't too keen about leaving us here as it was."

"Even though we'd been working together on this case for over three months without any problems," Kaaren nodded sarcastically. "And remember what else Fogarty said? 'Our best chance to penetrate Locotta is to work Pilgrim's area.' Right?"

"Yeah, well that guy still gives me the creeps," Sandy said softly.

"Who, Pilgrim?"

"Yeah. For once in my life, I'm seriously willing to let the guys do the point work," Sandy Mudd confessed. "What about you? Wouldn't you rather have Ben and Charley make the penetration, instead of you and Sanjo?"

"I wouldn't mind having either one of them for a partner right now," Kaaren admitted quietly. "Freddy's a good agent, in spite of his flash, but . . ."

"Yeah, I know," Sandy agreed. "If you're gonna play around in a snake pit, it's nice bein' in-tight with a mongoose and a bear, instead of a show dog."

"Something like that," Kaaren nodded. "Except in this case, the mongoose and the bear are a couple of thick-headed male chauvinists who don't think we have any business being in that pit in the first place."

"So you're gonna let me drive to the river by myself, just so you can have a chance at Squeek by yourself?"

"That's right," Kaaren nodded. "He's too good to pass up. Besides," she shrugged, "I can use an extra day of rest before I let Bart drag me up and down the river in that day-cruiser. I'll get a ride out with Sanjo tomorrow morning. Give him a chance to catch a couple more hours of sleep if I do the driving."

"Just what he needs, an angel of mercy," Sandy laughed, standing up. "Hey listen. I could stick around for backup, then we'd all drive out tomorrow. Fogarty wasn't just flapping his jaws about safety precautions on this one."

"Come on, mother hen," Kaaren shook her head, leading her partner toward the door. "Go pick up your ski and get on the road. I'm not going to do anything dumb while you're gone. All I want to do is talk with the little cretin, see if I can rig up a preliminary buy to set the stage before Sanjo and I go at Rainbow. I may even do it by phone. And I'm sure as hell not going to get anywhere near Rainbow. If I meet with Squeek, it's going to be in a very public place, and he's going to be alone, or it's no go. Scout's honor. I'll even tell Sanjo before I go anywhere. Okay?"

"Well . . ."

"Besides, this'll give you a free evening out there in the open sky. Good chance to get to know Ben, Charley and Bart a little better. Especially Ben," Kaaren added, and then grinned as Sandy Mudd began to blush.

"Yeah, that's what I thought," Kaaren nodded, gently shoving her partner out the door. "When Freddy and I get up there tomorrow, I expect to see at least one male chauvinist-type special agent lying belly-up on a cot. Think you can handle them all by yourself, partner?" Kaaren Mueller winked suggestively.

"I can handle those three just fine," Sandy Mudd nodded seriously. "You just watch yourself, and make sure Sanjo knows exactly what's going down before you go out on the street by yourself. Fair deal?"

"You got it," Karen agreed, closing the door with a solid, no-nonsense thunk as her partner walked with visible reluctance toward her alley-parked car.

In the phone booth down the street from Eugene Bylighter's low-rent-district room, Roy Schultzheimer, a blond young man with an intimidating expression on his handsome face, was sorting change in his knuckle-scarred hands as he waited for Squeek to end his three-hour marathon by staggering up the steps of his rooming house. Then he dropped the proper amount of change into the phone and called Rainbow.

"Yeah?"

"This is Roy. The kid's clean," the young man with the scarred hands said calmly.

"You sure 'bout that?"

"Yep."

"You ready for the next part? Got everythin' we need?"

"Yeah, sure," Roy said as his pale blue eyes made another routine sweep of the area.

"Then Ah'll meet you right where we planned."

Moments later, Raynee was back on the phone to Pilgrim.

"We're ready," he said. "Anythin' else Ah oughta know?"

"Nothing," Pilgrim said. "Just be sure to check the perimeters. I want you to be *very* cautious on this one."

"Yeah, Ah been thinkin' 'bout that," Raynee said. "Thinkin' maybe you'd wanna be stayin' down low a few more days, 'case we be dealin' with the big man here. Bad time t' be gettin' careless. Know what Ah mean?"

"That's right . . . a *very* bad time," Pilgrim growled coldly. "Do it."

Click.

4

Approximately seventy miles due south from Hoover Dam, where the massive concrete structure holds back the canyon waters to form Lake Mead, the southward-flowing Colorado River begins to form a continuous east-west boundary between the rugged and isolated deserts of California and Arizona.

Following the course of this irregular liquid border for another forty miles, the river suddenly makes a twenty-mile jog to the southeast, and then back to the southwest for another twenty-odd miles before continuing on its southern course. In doing so, it appears to trace the smooth outline of an aroused human female breast.

Appropriately, perhaps, the upper and lower slopes of this geographic mammary provide what is perhaps the most popular vacation spot in Southern California for legions of federal, state and local law enforcement officers. And coincidentally, it is just below the point of the enlarged nipple, among the river-edge resorts between Parker Dam and Big Bend, where some of the most determined law-enforcement-type vacationing takes place.

The available pleasures at this river resort area are fairly basic and primitive. Bone-warming sunshine, outdoors-loving women, a flowing current of cool river water, and every variation of eighteen-to-twenty-two-foot power-boat known to man. Not to mention one hell of a lot of chilled beer. All in all a lawman's dream of nirvana.

Contrary to the opinions of a few embittered river patrons, however, this particular small strip of vacation land is not sectioned off as a "LAW ENFORCEMENT OFFICERS ONLY" preserve. It just so happens that many people, for one reason or another, find it very unnerving to set up camp among a few dozen police officers, sheriffs' deputies, federal and state special agents, and just plain old-fashioned street cops. If nothing else, there were definitely better places to lie out on a river bank and smoke a little grass with a few friends.

But, at the same time, aside from the occasional beer-soaked raceboat driver who decides to bring his twenty-thousand-dollar flat-bottom into shore by the timesaving method of using his chrome-alloy prop as a sand brake, a person couldn't ask for a camping area more attuned to the physical security of wives, girlfriends and assorted children. Although an overly cautious father might stop to consider the wisdom of allowing any daughter over the age of sixteen to wander around loose in this "secure" environment for any extended period of time. Say for more than five minutes, max.

Thus, all in all, the Colorado River was able to offer most reasonably adaptive individuals an increasingly rare opportunity to commune with nature and mingle with strangers without having to be overly concerned about the hazards and fears of the "real" world—such as the occasional roving gangs of bikers who usually had enough aggregated common sense to avoid the cop-infested portions of the river bank.

All of which didn't necessarily explain why three special agents of a DEA Task Force chose to be lying on towel-covered folding lounge chairs in front of two rented corrugated metal cabanas on the California side of the Colorado River just north of Big Bend, and about fifty feet away from the nearest tree-covered campsite.

Aside from being mostly indifferent to the presence or absence of motorcycle gangs, cops, wives, girlfriends, children and ever-foolhardy dope-smokers, all three men were simply waiting. And while they waited, they intended to make the most out of an Agency-paid River trip by savoring the warm sun, the cool flowing water, the enticingly beautiful women, and the ice-chilled beer to the fullest extent possible.

Having made a determined effort to empty one of the nearby

ice chests single-handedly, Charley Shannon was forced to make the first voluntary movement.

"Where you going?" Ben Koda asked sleepily from underneath his wide-brimmed straw hat, hearing the already overstressed aluminum-tube lounge chair protest against the sudden shifting of weight.

"Gonna go check the prop," Charley replied, grunting painfully as he forced himself up on his thickly muscled legs.

"We don't have a prop, ya landlubbing dumb shit," Bart Harrington muttered, his eyes tightly shut as the sun reflected off the oiled surface of his deeply tanned face. "*Spirit of Seventy-six* is a jet boat. Can't check the prop on a jet boat."

"Okay," Charley grunted agreeably as he began to tiptoe cautiously through the rocks and pebbles toward the water edge. "Gonna go check out the jet. See if the motherfucker fell off."

"Better give 'em a warning downstream," Koda advised, still immobile beneath the straw hat. "What do you think, Bart? Fly a yellow flag or something?"

"Nope. Gotta use the proper navy signal. 'Stand by, I am about to discharge my bilges in your area.' Something like that." Harrington lifted one eyelid cautiously and watched Charley Shannon wade precariously into waist-deep water next to the buoy-and-tree-moored red, white and blue day-cruiser. "Can that son of a bitch swim?"

"'Bout like an outboard motor without a boat," Koda mumbled.

"Jesus, maybe we oughta tie a ski line 'round his waist."

"Those two mamas from Atlanta still out there?"

"Uh—" Harrington opened both eyes long enough to check out the entire cabana river front. "You mean them gals Charley disappeared with last night? Yeah, they're both out there. So's their old man. You know, the one who looks like ol' Big Daddy Lipscomb, 'cept twice as mean and ugly. Matter of fact, he still looks kinda pissed."

"They can swim. Anchor-butt gets in trouble out there, they can keep his ears dry and scream till their Daddy thinks about it a while and then rigs up a tow rope to his truck. No problem," Koda said reassuringly as he groped blindly for the latch of the ice chest.

"And speaking of women . . ." Harrington said.

"Wasn't speaking of women," Koda grunted as his hand surfaced from the ice chest clutching a dripping beer can.

"Whaddaya think?"

Koda grunted again noncommittally as he popped the can open one-handed and drew it underneath the straw hat. There was a long gurgling sound, followed by a loud burp and a relaxed sigh.

"I think Sandy's going to be okay," Harrington said. "She's pretty levelheaded, streetwise. Knows how to handle herself on a boat. Sharp as hell on navigation and radios. Only trouble is—"

". . . she ain't Kaaren Mueller," Koda finished helpfully. "Which is probably just as well 'cause you'd probably run that fucking sailboat aground first day out," the lanky, bare-chested agent added, lifting the straw hat up high enough to expose a black handlebar moustache and a grin.

Harrington screwed up his face in momentary contemplation. "Yeah, you're probably right," he nodded agreeably, reaching for another beer.

"Sandy's okay, but that Mueller broad's gonna cause us trouble, I don't care how good they say she is," Koda predicted, sliding his protective hat back down over his face as he settled comfortably into the lounge chair.

"Ah, I don't know . . ." Harrington wrinkled his face. "Maybe it's just a couple of old gonads talking, but I don't think—"

"Exactly," Koda nodded under the hat. "Old buzzards like you get up next to a piece of young tail who thinks she's some kind of a superwoman secret agent, and you go apeshit. Gonads start kicking out testosterone in all directions. Probably start dressing like Freddy, if you don't watch yourself."

Bart Harrington choked on his beer, laughing.

"And while we're on the subject, as the temporary acting honcho of this tag team, how come you let those two stay over in San Diego last night?" Harrington asked, keeping a sailor's eyes on the bobbing head and shoulders of Charley Shannon—who had ventured out into neck-deep water to join his recently found girlfriends, both of whom were hanging on to the stern of their father's flatbottom raceboat, floating easily and giggling at their late-night lover's cautious approach.

"They got a job to do," Koda said, slowly sitting up in his lounge chair and wincing at the sudden exposure to the overhead sun, his voice betraying a trace of uneasiness. "Kaaren's supposed to set up a buy with some dumb-shit kid who works for Raynee. The one they call Squeek. Soon as they do that, they're gonna get their butts in that Toyota and head east. Direct orders."

"And you're not worried about them at all, right?"

"Like you said, they're big girls. They want to be agents, they gotta do the job." Koda took another long sip at his beer can.

"That why you told Sanjo to stick around down there last night?"

"The kid they're working on's not heavy enough to worry about," Koda shrugged. "Sandy could probably rip his arms off one-handed. And if Kaaren can keep Sanjo strung out on a leash this long, well then, shit . . ."

"Long as they stay the hell away from Rainbow and Pilgrim," Harrington suggested, echoing Ben Koda's unspoken worry.

"Yeah," he nodded, his squinted eyes staring out at some distant point over Charley Shannon's dark head and shoulders, "that's exactly fucking right."

Physically drained by his mandated three-hour trek of the San Diego harbor area, Eugene Bylighter allowed himself a ten-minute rest on the dirty, sagging bed of his shared $125-a-month flophouse before forcing his malnourished body back to work.

Had it not been for Lafayette Beaumont Raynee's promised enticement, Bylighter would have never been able to summon up the necessary energy and willpower to complete his assigned tasks. As it was, the erotic images flickering through Bylighter's ever-horny mind were just barely stimulating enough to keep his fatigued body moving.

After first steadying his nerves with a poor-quality joint, Bylighter stumbled into his kitchen to complete the necessary preparations for his call to Kaaren Mueller, and then remembered, in his exhaustion, that he had carelessly left the small brown-paper-wrapped package on the kitchen counter.

Very carelessly, as it turned out, because the package was no longer on the counter. It was, instead, resting at the bottom of a pan of stale water left on the floor for his roommate's pet cat.

"Oh, Jesus Christ," he whispered as he dropped to his knees and fished the thoroughly soaked package out of the water, watching it come apart in his hands. Peeling away the shreds of paper, Bylighter exposed the two small, screw-capped, brown-glass vials, each filled with a tannish powdery substance. After wiping the outside of the vials dry with a dirty dishcloth, he cautiously unscrewed each vial, discovering to his immense relief that the slightly off-white powders seemed to have been protected by the tight-sealing caps.

It was only as he went to throw the soggy remnants of the package into the trashcan that he discovered the two barely legible labels which had evidently been soaked off the vials. Closing his eyes and shaking his head slowly in helpless frustration, Bylighter sat back down on the floor and began to consider his options.

Basically, it boiled down to one of two choices. He could call up

Rainbow and admit to one more screw-up, or he could make up a new pair of labels, and attach them to the vials on the basis of a fifty-fifty guess.

It really wasn't much of a choice, Bylighter told himself as he carefully printed "THIOPENE" and "A-17" on two pieces of white medical tape. And it probably didn't matter anyway, he tried to reassure himself, as he attached the "THIOPENE" label to a randomly picked vial, because the powder in both vials looked identical. Probably just some sort of packaging scheme, he nodded, affixing the "A-17" label to the other vial. Then, having made the fateful decision to try and cover his scrawny ass one more time, Eugene Bylighter began to prepare for his meeting with Kaaren Mueller, praying as he did so that he would never have to tell Rainbow what he'd done.

Fifteen minutes later, having finished his preparations, Bylighter went back down the stairs and out on the street to use the nearby pay phone at the corner Exxon station.

The phone on the other end rang twice.

"Hello?"

"Can I speak to Kaaren, please?" Bylighter asked in a tremulant voice.

"This is Kaaren," the voice answered, maintaining a carefully neutral tone.

"Kaaren, this is Squee—ah—Eugene Bylighter. You probably don't remember me, but I'm the guy you talked to at the donut shop last week. Remember, when I was cleaning up around the tables? You and your girlfriend were sitting at the corner table. The one with the plastic yucca tree." Bylighter stopped and took in a deep, steadying breath. "You said you'd heard around that I might have some connections for some primo grass?"

"Oh, sure. Squeek, the guy who sells donuts with the flaky green icing. Yeah, I remember," Kaaren Mueller answered pleasantly, carefully choosing her words. "You said you might be able to score a lid of premium weed for me. So what's happening?"

"Well, I made the score," Bylighter said proudly. "Genuine Maui Manna. A righteous ounce. And it's only gonna cost you one-fifty, your price. I thought, maybe—well, you know—maybe we could get together—maybe at your place?" he tried hopefully, his voice tightening into a high-pitched breaking squeak, in spite of his concentrated effort to act appropriately cool and calm.

"I don't think my place would be a good idea, Squeek," Kaaren said. "Like I told you the other day, I'm just trying to keep my boss supplied. He wouldn't be too happy if I got popped at my place, seeing as how he's kinda helping with the rent. So I've gotta be careful. You understand."

"Oh, for sure," Bylighter said hurriedly. "Listen, I already knew you were the careful type. Which is good, I mean," he added quickly, suddenly afraid that he might scare her off by admitting he had already tried to find her apartment. "I didn't mean—"

"Hey, no problem," Kaaren said softly, allowing her voice to shift to a more friendly tone. "Listen, maybe we can set up a time to get together next week to do the deal."

"Next week?" Bylighter blurted out. "Ah, but—ah—I really wanted to see—I mean, I really want to get rid of this grass—like as soon as possible, you know. I thought maybe, you know, today—?" he finished pathetically, his slow mind thrashing about in a panic as he tried to save the deteriorating situation.

Kaaren Mueller hesitated. She'd been trying to get hold of Freddy Sanjanovitch, with no success, ever since Sandy Mudd had left her apartment. She had already left a message on his answering machine, advising him that she was on her own and was going to need a ride out tomorrow. Goddamned slider, she thought, and then shook her head, realizing that Freddy wouldn't necessarily check his phone messages, assuming that she and Sandy were already on their way to meet everyone else at the Colorado River.

"I'll tell you what," Kaaren said, making a quick decision. "Why don't I meet you down at the donut shop. Just you and me. Say about one? You can put the grass in one of the take-out bags. How's that?"

"Yeah, that's all right. One o'clock at the shop. I'll be there. You can bet on it," Bylighter said excitedly.

"Bye-bye, Squeek," Kaaren laughed, and hung up the phone.

She tried Freddy Sanjanovitch's number once more, received the "Hey, sorry I'm not in" message again, and then dialed Sandy's apartment, on the unlikely chance her partner hadn't left yet. This time she got a more subdued recorder message. Then she sat there on the couch for a few more minutes, drumming her fingers on the armrest as she tried to rationalize her decision.

Mueller knew that Fogarty was somewhere out in San Diego, trying to set up a clean communication link with the local field office. Probably much too busy to be bothered with a simple backup problem. And besides, she shook her head, suddenly irritated with herself, it wasn't as though she was going to make a pound coke buy from someone heavy like Rainbow. She was only going to hand over a hundred and fifty bucks to a puny teenaged kid with overactive hormones in exchange for an ounce of high-grade marijuana. Hardly enough to qualify for a misdemeanor arrest these days.

Reasonably satisfied with her rationalization, Kaaren Mueller went into her bedroom, slid her hand under her mattress, pulled out a little .25 Baretta automatic lying next to the larger and more potent 9mm Walther, checked the load and safety, and then placed the tiny pistol into the concealed pocket in her purse.

Unlike the larger handgun, which didn't really fit the image of an administrative assistant trying to maintain an office supply of grass, the small Baretta could be explained away as protection against rapists and muggers if necessary. Not that a little twerp like Squeek was going to get anywhere near her purse anyway, Kaaren thought, as she changed into new designer jeans, a work blouse and casual shoes.

After removing three fifty-dollar bills from her concealed cache—the bottom of a half-filled can of coffee—Kaaren Mueller grabbed up her purse and headed for the door, intent upon making a quick check of Freddy Sanjanovitch's favorite haunts, in person, before it was time to meet Bylighter.

On a two-lane country road five miles east of U.S. Highway Five—an eight-lane ribbon of concrete roughly paralleling the western coastline of the United States from Tijuana, Mexico, to Vancouver, Canada—and at least fifteen miles from the condo home of his impatiently waiting Saturday afternoon date, Freddy Sanjanovitch stood beside his rented MGB, in his new four-hundred-dollar suit (special funds for the sports car and the suit having been grudgingly approved by Fogarty), and stared morosely at the nail-flattened tire.

Irritating as it was, the flat tire was only the latest in a series of events which had served to make Freddy Sanjanovitch a very frustrated man that afternoon.

First of all, thanks to an indifferent Federal bureaucrat at the Washington Office headquarters, Fogarty had been unable—as yet—to effect a clean transfer of funds into the personal real-name banking and credit card accounts of their assigned special agents, which meant the agents would be forced to live on the remains of their cash advances and other covert accounts as best they could in the interim.

For agents Shannon and Koda—who were used to operating within lower-income-level covers anyway—the delay was simply a minor inconvenience. Hamburgers, beer, gas, and cheap hotel rooms were relatively inexpensive, and well within the limits of their remaining funds. But for an agent like Freddy Sanjanovitch, who enjoyed his flamboyant lifestyle cover to the fully authorized limit, the sudden spending money restriction amounted to corporal punishment.

Freddy had also discovered that, unlike past occasions when he had been teamed up with a female agent, his new partner was a determined professional who had no interest in playing out a serious boyfriend-girlfriend role. Kaaren Mueller had made one thing very clear at the outset of their first day together. She had rented an apartment with only one bedroom and one single bed, and she was perfectly satisfied with that arrangement. Period.

Normally, separate living arrangements wouldn't have put an unbearable strain on Freddy Sanjanovitch's psyche. In fact, his personal lifestyle was such that having an emotionally involved roommate for a partner usually resulted in a very uncomfortable working relationship by the time the operation was ready to be taken down anyway.

So normally, no problem, except that in this case his new partner happened to be one hell of a looker. She also had a body bordering on irresistible entrapment, and she wasn't at all shy about putting a little something extra into her dancing style—especially during the slow numbers, when the body heat from her well-toned thigh muscles radiated suggestively through her thin nylon dress.

And then, to round out Freddy's frustration, the new team of Sanjanovitch and Mueller suddenly discovered that Jimmy Pilgrim had stopped showing up at San Diego's expensive restaurants and nightclubs with his primary assistant, Rainbow—weekly meetings which had been well documented, from a very safe distance, by Kaaren Mueller and Sandy Mudd for more than three months prior to Sanjo's arrival.

Freddy and Kaaren immediately began hitting the entire list of night spots in rapid sequence, spotting Raynee on several occasions, but never with Pilgrim. They made a couple of carefully casual inquiries. Again, no Pilgrim.

Fogarty was quickly notified of this new development by phone, and he acted immediately. Koda and Shannon were ordered off rotating guard duty and sent out to prowl San Diego's less-sophisticated night haunts.

After six seemingly endless nights of cruising through country, gay, biker, and straight bars, strip joints, porno theaters, and back-room gambling halls, they reported back in with uniformly negative results. From all outward indications, Jimmy Pilgrim was no longer in San Diego.

Thus, all in all, Freddy Sanjanovitch's mental condition was probably best described as "emotionally disrupted," although the phrase "hornier than a zoo monkey" might have been just as accurate, and perhaps even more significcent. It was a condition that Freddy Sanjanovitch had every intention of remedying, prior to joining the other members of Fogarty's task force at a secluded spot on the Colorado River for their emergency skull session.

Now thoroughly irritated and frustrated by the added factor of the flat tire, Freddy Sanjanovitch realized his reasonable options had been reduced to two, the least appealing of which involved the time-consuming dismemberment of the MGB's trunk, followed by an attempt to jack up the car and change tires without covering his pants and shirt with dirt and grease.

The other option involved hitchhiking and/or walking an unknown distance to the nearest telephone, whereupon he would have to try to convince a service station attendant, somewhere, to accept a credit card bearing his old cover name—one that didn't quite match the rest of his current ID—in payment for an undoubtedly expensive road call. Otherwise, he would be forced to use a substantial amount of his remaining cash, which would leave him far short of the funds necessary to properly entertain and ply his newfound lady-friend.

Approximately two long miles down the road, Freddy Sanjanovitch limped into the hoist bay of a two-pump gas station and approached the elderly attendant.

"Excuse me," Sanjo began.

"Looks like you been doin' a bit of walking, young feller," the old man observed, looking down with unconcealed amusement at Freddy's ruined shoes as he rubbed his wrinkled hands on his greasy overalls.

"Uh, yeah. Listen, I need to get someone out to change a tire—"

"Got a flat tire, huh?" the old man cackled gleefully.

"Right," Sanjo nodded, struggling to maintain a pleasant smile on his face. "I'm kinda in a hurry, and I've got a little problem with cash. I was wondering if you'd accept a credit card for another station?"

"Gonna cost you 'bout sixty bucks for a road ree-sponse."

"Fine—"

"But we don't take charges over fifty bucks. Station policy."

"Yes, but—"

"And we don't accept any credit cards 'cept our own."

"How about a personal check, if I—?"

"Don't take personal checks neither," the old man shook his

head. "Too many young fellers running around in fancy duds these days, trying to pass phony checks."

"Sixty bucks, huh," Sanjo muttered, glaring at the grizzled attendant as he began to thumb slowly through the few bills in his wallet.

"Cash money," the old man nodded agreeably. "'Cept I can't help you jes' yet. Gonna be a little dee-lay."

"A dee-lay?"

"Yep. Gotta wait till the boss gets back with the truck. Can't leave the station unattended. Young feller like you might—"

"How much of a delay?" Sanjo demanded, pronouncing each word very slowly and carefully through clenched teeth.

"Oh, I'd say not more'n three or four hours."

"Three or four *hours*?"

"Yep."

Sanjo counted slowly to ten before he could trust himself to speak.

"Do you mind if I use your phone?" he asked.

"Pay phone right across the street," the old man pointed helpfully. "Say," he added, yelling out toward Sanjo's back as the enraged agent turned and started toward the distant phone booth, "young feller like yourself oughta try changing his own tires once in a while. Does a man good to get a little grease in his veins."

Kaaren Mueller rang the buzzer on Freddy Sanjanovitch's door four times before she finally accepted the obvious, checked her watch, discovered she had less that twenty minutes to make her appointment with Bylighter, and then headed back downstairs to her Toyota.

As she pulled into the parking lot of the Hole-in-One Donut Shop, Kaaren spotted Bylighter sitting by himself at one of the back row outdoor tables. After making a slow, cautious check of the area for readily identifiable faces, and finding none, she got out of her small vehicle and approached Bylighter's table.

"Hi, Squeek," she said warmly as she sat down at the metal table across from Bylighter. "How you doing?"

"Pretty good," Bylighter responded shyly. "I didn't think—you know—that you'd show up," he stuttered, his face flushing as his eyes took in the reality of the tight blue jeans and almost-transparent white blouse, re-etched the images stored in his perverted memory, and then blinked away in embarrassment as his eyes met Kaaren's.

"'Course I'd show up," Kaaren smiled cheerfully. "My boss'd be really pissed if I didn't take care of his stash," she added meaningfully as she gingerly patted the top of one of Bylighter's pale, sweating hands.

"Oh, yeah, sure," Bylighter nodded hurriedly, fumbling around in his lap and coming up with a medium-sized white paper bag filled with something about the size of an honest one-ounce lid. "See, I told you I could score for you," he said, smiling brightly as he handed over the sweat-stained bag.

Kaaren casually opened the top of the bag, took a quick look inside, reclosed the bag tightly, and just as casually placed it on the table next to her right hand.

"It looks fine, Squeek," she said, dropping her voice slightly. "Still one-fifty, my price?"

"Oh, sure," Bylighter nodded, grinning nervously. "Even got you a coke. On me," he added hurriedly, pushing one of the plastic-capped waxed paper cups over to Kaaren as she started to reach for her purse. "No extra charge. You know, kinda like a—ah—a date," he finished, stammering helplessly.

"That's very nice of you, Squeek," Kaaren smiled as she casually transferred the tightly folded bills to Bylighter's sweat-moistened hand. "And I'm sure my boyfriend won't mind," she winked as she took a sip of the cool, sweet liquid. "But we'd better not make this too much of a habit. He might not understand, you know."

"Oh, yeah, sure, I understand," Bylighter nodded quickly, trying to regain his self-imagined cool. "Hey, I don't want to cause trouble or anything. But if you need anything else, you know, I'll be glad—"

"You mean you've got connections for some heavier stuff?" Kaaren asked, shifting smoothly into the "startled-curiosity" routine. "Like maybe some real coke," she added, winking conspiratorialy as she took another sip of her drink.

"Oh, yeah, sure. Anything you want," he shrugged manfully. "Rain—I mean my bo—buddy and I," he stammered again, trying to get the right words out, "he and I, we can get just about anything you can imagine. Even some stuff you couldn't imagine," he added softly, his eyes searching around in a quick furtive motion. "We're gonna get some new stuff—"

"Oh, yeah, what's that?" Kaaren asked, taking a deep draw on her drink to combat the smoggy Southern California heat that was starting to make her sweat uncomfortably.

"I can't really talk about it yet," Squeek whispered confidentially. "Strict orders. But it's gonna be the hottest thing on the street. Some kind of analog or something—"

"Boy, it's really getting hot out here, isn't it?" Kaaren interrupted, using one of Bylighter's napkins to wipe the beading sweat off her forehead.

"Oh, yeah, Santa Ana weather always gets to me too," Bylighter nodded. "Anyway, like I was saying—"

"Squeek, excuse me a minute," Kaaren said, feeling an old familiar cramping sensation in the pit of her stomach. A sensation that was starting to make her feel light-headed and more than a little nauseated. "I gotta use the john. . . ."

Jesus, she thought as she stood up weakly, what a hell of a time to get hit with a full-on case of menstrual cramps. Shouldn't be coming on this late though, she told herself, but then the nausea started to come up and she ran for the back of the cinder block building. She reached for the door knob, tried to turn it, and only then saw the tacked-up sign on the door through her blurring vision:

"CLOSED FOR REPAIRS."

"Oh, shit, what a time—" she shook her head dizzily, clenching her teeth as she looked around in a panic for a trashcan, or a tree, or anything—and suddenly saw Bylighter come running up with a key in his hand.

"Here, I'll let you in," he said breathlessly, fumbling to push the key into the lock.

As the door came open, Kaaren pushed past Bylighter and dove for the commode, barely making it to the bowl on her knees before she began to vomit helplessly. She remained on her knees, racked by spasm after spasm, until her stomach muscles refused to cooperate any longer, and she crumbled to the cold, dirty floor. Miserably sick, exhausted, and now beginning to tremble violently, she wasn't aware that another person had entered the small restroom and squatted down beside her until she heard his voice . . .

"What's the matter, sister? Got yourself a little problem?"

. . . and she stared up through the swirling colors into the cold, impassive brown face of Lafayette Beaumont Raynee.

Rainbow.

5

THE COLORS SEEMED to originate from a pinpoint floating in space, expanding outward in irregular three-dimensional ribbons of vivid multichromatic light. But from Kaaren Mueller's frame of reference, the singularly *odd* thing about the light point was that it seemed to be trying to communicate.

She turned her head slowly to stare up at the source point, trying to focus her concentration on the sounds radiating out of the colored swirls . . . to put them into a logical sequence. Finally, she gave up, ultimately realizing that her logic receptors were limited to only three dimensions, and were thus totally insufficient.

So she reached out to caress the shimmering photons, to absorb the soothing radiance of the rapidly shifting hues, and became confused when her hands refused to separate. She tried to remember when and why they had become fused behind her back. The memory datum should be in there, she reasoned. That was the purpose of a memory. Should always be data in her memory . . .

She tried hard to concentrate on her hands, unable to control a sudden flow of emotion that caused her face to become tear-streaked. She could sense the determination of the tears, each struggling desperately to hold on to her clifflike face as gravity dragged them down, screaming . . . .

An inner blackness surged out of the hidden depths of her mind, expanding frighteningly.

"Don't cry, it's okay," the focal point said as the color-saturated ribbons reached out, flowing around her reassuringly.

"Falling," Kaaren mumbled, mind-numbed by the inner fear of emptiness.

"No, you're not falling," the point-source responded, allowing a thick, warm tentacle of reddish-orange light to slide beneath her opened blouse and flow across the smooth geometric perfection of her curved breast, causing the rounded areola to enlarge as it absorbed the chromatic energy. Expanding and absorbing until it could stand the pressure no longer, the engorged nipple released a pair of hot, white, all-color ribbons inward, one leaping upward to fill her brain with a blinding pleasure-awareness, the other thrusting downward, searing . . .

Kaaren Mueller saw her moaned response to the probing white heat as a slowly mounting wave of crimson that surged back over the point source, creating a swell in the continuing river of reddish-orange light which had split off into two separate streams, each surrounding one of her exposed, islandlike breasts with glowing warmth. . . . .

Neither she nor Bylighter was aware that the van had stopped.

"Havin' fun back here?" Lafayette Beaumont Raynee inquired, sticking his head through the middle of a black velvet curtain. The curtain separated the driving compartment from the lushly padded, carpeted and cushioned rear area of a large Dodge van that had been moving steadily along a back road in north San Diego County for the past half hour. The interior of the van was almost completely darkened, the sole illumination being a pair of red 25-watt lights recessed behind the upper molding, adding a slightly eerie tone to an otherwise provocative and sensuous environment.

Startled by the unexpected sound of Rainbow's voice, Bylighter jerked around, quickly pulling his hands out of Kaaren Mueller's blouse in a reflexive guilt response.

"Oh . . . yeah, uh, sure. Yeah, she's really, uh, whacked out, isn't she?" Bylighter nodded wide-eyed, licking his lips nervously as he furtively brushed his hidden hand against the softly moaning girl's blouse, swallowing hard as he felt the swollen nipple respond again. "What'd you—I mean I, uh, give her?"

"Experimental brain food," Raynee chuckled, his white teeth gleaming pink in the dim, reddish light. "Fertilizer. A-number-one shit. Just what that little lady needed to get her bionic motor goin'. All you got to do now is rev her up a bit, boy. You *sure* you know what to do?"

"Oh yeah, I know what to do," Bylighter nodded quickly, embarrassed by his nervously cracking voice, and intimidated by Raynee's intrusion—by the flashing smile and the all-absorbing eyes. "I just never—ever had anyone like this. You know . . ."

The girl moaned again, moving to push her swollen breast up against Bylighter's sweaty, trembling hand.

"Bet you haven't," Raynee nodded knowingly, his street-trained eyes taking in the sight of Kaaren Mueller's partially exposed body. The girl was really something, Raynee thought to himself as he continued to survey the pathetic scene. Hell of a waste, giving a hot piece of ass like that to a little shit like Bylighter.

Momentarily, Raynee considered letting Roy, his martial arts instructor, bodyguard and driver have her. Or even taking her himself. But he immediately shrugged the idea off. Too much involved. Too many things happening too fast. Besides, it appealed to Raynee's perverted sense of humor to let Bylighter continue to enjoy his payoff.

"Better get your act in gear, boy," Raynee gestured with his dark head toward the girl. "Gonna be there pretty soon. And you ain't never gonna get another chance to tear off a piece in the Rainbow Motherfuckin' Box-Wagon again. So, get serious. Get it ON! Grab them tits like you mean it, boy!"

Bylighter obediently slid his other hand back into Mueller's opened blouse. Then, at Rainbow's urging, he slowly began to squeeze both of the silk-smooth, turgid breasts, feeling his entire body tremble in a spasm of nervous anticipation as the girl groaned loudly and strained against her bonds to press herself tightly against his fondling hands.

"That's the way, boy," Raynee nodded approvingly. "Don't they feel good?"

"Yeah," Bylighter whispered, starting to breathe heavily, responding in confused helplessness to the inhibiting presence of Rainbow and the irresistible stimulus of the girl's fevered body.

"God, I always dreamed . . ." he gasped, finally able to forget about Rainbow as the long-repressed eroticism filled his mind. Keeping one hand pressed tightly against one heaving breast, Bylighter tore at his dirty clothes, ripping off his shirt, shoes, socks, pants, and finally his stained shorts, unaware that Rainbow's reddish-tinged Afro had disappeared and that the van's engine had started up again. Then he began to fumble feverishly at the belt and snaps of Kaaren Mueller's tight jeans.

"That's right, get those things off," Raynee laughed loudly from the other side of the curtain as Bylighter fought with the zipper, and then began to whimper with crazed lust as he dug his fingers under the stiff and tight Levi material, tugging the jeans and nylon panties down, inch by inch, over Mueller's unbelievably warm and sensuous hips and thighs and knees. . . .

Then, unable to control himself any longer, Bylighter threw himself onto the still-moaning girl's hot, straining body, his mouth engulfing one of the engorged breasts, his right hand still firmly attached to the other, and his left hand sliding quickly over the tightly smooth and responsive stomach and abdomen.

Kaaren Mueller was tumbling slowly in a churning reddish-orange current, every cell in her body seemingly bathed in a liquidly sensuous warmth, when Bylighter's hand slid across her trembling abdomen and dropped down between her legs.

It was as if Bylighter's two hands had completed an electrical circuit possessing tremendous potential energy. The reddish-orange ribbons disappeared in a shuddering explosion of mind-searing white. In that instant, two things happened simultaneously: Kaaren Mueller became aware that she was tied, naked, and pinned beneath another thrashing nude body, and the point-source dilated outward like a leaf shutter in a camera lens, framing the slobbering, lust-ridden image of Eugene Bylighter before her focusing eyes.

The emotions that suddenly came pouring into Kaaren Mueller's conscious mind were overwhelming. Confused, swirling, color-saturated, three-dimensional streams of monochromatic emotion. She could feel her mind—an incredibly complex profusion of tingling, naked receptors—being buffeted by strong, contradictory, easily distinguishable forces:

Disbelief . . . Shock . . . Anger(!) . . . Desire(?) . . . Love(??) . . . and overwhelmingly, RAGE!

Bylighter never saw the changes of expression flash across Kaaren Mueller's face. He was completely absorbed in frantically positioning himself to satisfy one of his most unlikely fantasies with one deep, mind-blowing stroke, and therefore missed the quick flicker of fear and confusion in her eyes . . . which gave way to shocked and furious rage as she tried to pull her hands free and met unyielding resistance.

Emitting a deep gutteral snarl, Mueller drove her right knee upward with every ounce of force she could generate with her drug-wired muscles, and, at the same time, lunged upward at Bylighter's exposed neck with savagely bared teeth.

Bylighter's high-pitched scream nearly caused Roy Schultzheimer to run the van off the road. By the time he managed to wrestle the wildly fishtailing vehicle back under control and get stopped on a dirt turnoff along the dark road, Bylighter's frantic screaming had degenerated into a continuing series of shrieks, moans and gagging sounds, punctuated by the irregular thudding sounds of thinly padded knee bone impacting against engorged flesh. . . .

When Raynee and Roy dove through the curtain into the back of the van, cussing and yelling, they discovered Mueller with her teeth anchored into Bylighter's thin neck muscles, mindlessly intent upon driving his offending genitals up into his rib cage by slamming her right knee again and again into his thrashing groin. . . .

"SHIT!" Raynee snarled furiously, wrinkling his nose at the pungent odor of vomited bean burrito as he reached in to separate the thrashing bodies. As Roy wrenched Bylighter's ravaged crotch away from Mueller's jackhammering knee, Raynee had to use both hands to slowly force Kaaren's tightly clenched jaw open before finally managing to free his severely injured gofer. Bylighter fell back on the van floor, both hands clutched tightly to his groin, and gratefully proceeded to gag and vomit once again all over the thick van carpet.

"GODDAMN BITCH!" Raynee screamed in outraged frustration, grabbing the still-snarling girl around the neck with both hands and then slashing a fist into the side of her jaw when she spat into his face and lunged at him, wide-eyed, with her bared teeth. Mueller's unconscious body tumbled to the floor alongside Bylighter.

"You watch her, *and keep her quiet*," Raynee snarled at his blond bodyguard. "Understand?"

Roy Schultzheimer nodded his head, then pulled a loose blanket over Mueller's limp body before settling down into a cross-legged position on the horrible-smelling van floor, his pale blue eyes reflecting little interest in the naked woman who lay still within easy reach of his relaxed hands.

Shaking his head and muttering to himself, and still ignoring Bylighter completely, Raynee pulled himself back through the curtain, and put the van into motion again, this time with more purpose and determination.

*   *   *

Raynee made his entrance into Kaaren Mueller's apartment through the side door in the alley, using the keys he had found in her purse.

He had left the van with Roy, parked in the alley, after taking the necessary time to secure Mueller to the floor-bolted rear legs of the front seats with rope. In the unlikely event that the girl regained consciousness before he returned, she wasn't going to cause Lafayette Beaumont Raynee any more trouble this evening. He had other things on his mind.

Raynee wasn't the least bit concerned about Bylighter—who had also lapsed into merciful unconsciousness—but he *was* distracted by the presence of the small .25 automatic he had discovered in the girl's purse. There were any number of possible explanations for the weapon, but one of those possibilities—that the girl was a some kind of federal, state or local narc—could cause a great deal of trouble at an inopportune time. A *very* inopportune time.

Raynee spent a half hour conducting a methodical search of the apartment. He found the 9mm Walther and the remainder of Kaaren's money stash. He noted the presence of the phone-answering machine. And the extent of the girl's personal belongings.

After spending another five minutes in silent, uneasy contemplation, Raynee decided to take the risk of making a necessary phone call.

By the time he finally managed to stagger through the doorway of his apartment, Freddy Sanjanovitch was well entrenched into a frame of mind best described as "pissed."

Discovering that the phone booth across the street from the gas station was out of order hadn't really been unexpected. It was only the knowledge that he would likely be driven to commit a rash act of violence that prevented Sanjo from returning to the station and demanding to use the phone. Instead, he simply muttered something unpleasant, took in a deep sighing breath, and began the long walk back to his crippled vehicle in his now painfully tight shoes, wondering every step of the way why he had ever allowed himself to drift into a career in law enforcement.

After making two wrong turns in the darkness, one causing him to stumble into a still-wet drainage ditch, Sanjanovitch found his way back to the car. He then removed his new coat, and proceeded to change the almost-new tire. In the process, he managed to rip his pants against an unnoticed burr on the edge of the rear fender, split open three of his knuckles when the short angle wrench slipped off of a lug nut, and finally smacked the back of his head solidly against the trunk-lock while working to remove the spare tire, thereby splattering an interesting pattern of blood, grease, and tire-rubber on his new dress shirt when he dropped, dazed and cussing, face-first into the offending trunk space.

Approximately forty-five long, dark minutes after the trunk-lock incident, the traitorous tire was finally replaced with the almost identically new spare. The changing iron had been flung into the darkness, immediately followed by the jack.

To Sanjanovitch's bitter disbelief, the remainder of the trip home took place without incident.

It was only after he had stomped in through the door of his apartment, called his date, received a not-so-polite brush-off, slammed the phone back down on the hook, took a well-deserved bath and put on clean clothes, that Sanjanovitch remembered to check his answering machine.

He hit the button to play back any calls.

". . . Freddy, this is Kaaren. I decided to hang around another day to finish up some paperwork. I sent Sandy on ahead to catch up with the rest of the guys. No sweat on the homework. I'm just going to hang around my place, maybe try to set up a little something with my donut stand buddy. I'll let you know if it works out. Meantime, I'm going to need a ride out tomorrow. Give me a call and let me know when you're going. 'Bye."

"Fucking wonderful," Sanjanovitch muttered to himself. "Just what I need. A four-hour drive in an MGB with that broad."

The rest of Kaaren Mueller's message was just starting to sink in when the answering machine came to life again.

". . . Freddy, this is Sandy. Just in case Kaaren didn't get word to you: she's going to hang around down here this afternoon and try to work a deal with Squeek. She says it's no big thing, but I wanted to make sure you knew. I—ah—thought you might want to give her some backed-off support if you're free. She doesn't want me to help, so I'm going to head on out. See you guys tomorrow."

"Jesus fucking Christ," Sanjanovitch muttered, slamming his fist on the table. Mueller was obviously intent on making a buy from Bylighter. Instead of waiting for her partner, as she'd been told, she was going out by herself. Or had already gone out, Freddy realized, looking down at his watch. Shit! And the goddamned broad hadn't even implied that she was going to try to make a buy. He reached for the phone. If it hadn't been for her little bosom buddy deciding to use her brains . . .

Kaaren Mueller's phone gave out a busy signal.

Shit!

Freddy Sanjanovitch slammed down the phone for the second time that evening, shoved a cocked-and-locked .45 automatic in the side waistband of his pants, and ran for the door.

"This is Rainbow. Connect me with Jimmy. Fast." He read out the number on the receiver and hung up the phone.

Lafayette Beaumont Raynee stood impatiently in Kaaren Mueller's living room, watching out the window for any sign of surveillance activity, as he waited for the man who would have to make a very quick and important decision to call back.

The phone rang and he reached for it quickly.

"Yeah."

"What's wrong?" The voice on the other end of the line was distant and cold.

"We got ourselves a problem." Raynee detailed the situation quickly, his eyes still flickering back and forth to the streets, and to the nearby van. "Way Ah see it," Raynee finished, "we need a confirmation, one way or the other. She's gotta be connected. Question is, with who?"

"Can you stay where you're at?" Pilgrim demanded.

Raynee looked out the window again, uncomfortably aware of the intermittent flow of people strolling up and down the street past the alley. There were better locations, but it would take time to make the shift. Psychopath or not, Raynee wasn't especially interested in doing much more driving with two unconscious people in the back of his foul-smelling van. Particularly when one of them happened to be naked, white, young and female. Very bad karma in conservative North San Diego County where the nighttime cops just loved to make car-stops on suspicious people like Lafayette Beaumont Raynee.

"How long?"

"Ten minutes."

"Yeah, sure."

Eight minutes and twenty seconds later, Raynee reached for the ringing phone.

"Yeah."

"I have been reassured that there are no known federal or state investigations directed at our operation," Pilgrim said calmly. "A local police operation is always a possibility, but they would almost certainly request state money to deal with someone at our level. Agreed?"

"Yeah," Raynee said. "So . . . ?"

"Locotta, however, is a very likely possibility," Pilgrim went on firmly. "Especially in light of Lester's . . . difficulties. Does the girl appear to be a pro?"

"Possible," Raynee nodded again, his eyes continuing to sweep.

"Vegas quality?"

"Easy," Raynee grunted. "But Ah'm tellin' you, it don't read right. Them guns . . ."

Pilgrim was quiet for a moment. "You said she has a boy-friend?"

"Seen her make the rounds with the same dude a couple times," Raynee said. "A night-daddy. Lotta flash, but he ain't no cream puff neither. Thing is," Raynee added, "Ah don't think she's tied in with Locotta. Not the man's style."

"So who then?" Pilgrim demanded.

"Beats the shit outta me," Raynee admitted. "Only thing Ah can figure is one a' our pound-dealers might be lookin' t' expand out . . . or maybe promote up the easy way. Work a littl' kiss-ass with Locotta."

"Anyone in particular?" Pilgrim's voice had turned deadly cold.

"All kinds a' possibilities," Raynee replied, his eyes sweeping the street as he considered his answer. "General comes to mind right off for a lotta reasons, 'specially seein's how we're in his area. Thing is, though, man'd have to be flat-ass *dumb*, playin' games like this in his own backyard."

"Considering the individual, that's exactly right," Pilgrim responded icily. "So this is what you're going to do. . . ."

Freddy Sanjanovitch was still pissed by the time he finally found a parking spot for the MGB around the corner from Kaaren Mueller's apartment, walked quickly around the sidewalk and up the steps to her front door, the .45 caliber autoloading pistol poorly concealed underneath his hastily pulled-out shirttail, which was why he only pounded on the door a couple of times with his fist before he tried the doorknob.

Discovering that it was unlocked, he stomped into the apartment, pulled the door shut behind him, yelled out . . .

"KAAREN, YOU STILL HERE. . . ?"

. . . and had no time to think at all as he saw his partner sprawled bare-ass naked on the living room couch, and the tall, black Afro-haired figure (Rainbow?) coming up to his feet next to the dis-assembled telephone on the coffee table with a small, glistening knife in his hand, and the loose-limbed figure with the pale blue eyes and curly hair coming at him *fast* like some sort of huge cat . . .

Had Sanjanovitch simply reacted out of fear and gone for his gun—wasting the precious seconds necessary to free the lethal .45 from the confining shirttail—Roy Schultzheimer would have been all over him before the weapon ever cleared his waistband. Instead, the startled agent had the presence of mind to kick one of Mueller's dining table chairs directly into the path of the oncoming Schultzheimer . . . and then throw himself backward against the far wall as he reached frantically under his shirt, coming back away from the wall in a crouch with the .45 extended and cocked in a doubled-handed ready position, index finger tight against the sensitive trigger.

"Right there, hold it!" Sanjanovitch barked a warning at the swiftly recovering Schultzheimer, and then quickly shifted the heavy pistol over to standstill the man he now clearly recognized as Rainbow. . . .

"You too, sport . . . and drop the knife, now!"

. . . before centering the weapon back on the broad, muscular chest of Roy Schultzheimer, because the pantherlike bodyguard was still much too close, and therefore seemingly the most dangerous. Rainbow was a good four or five paces away, although he still hadn't dropped the knife.

"Back away slowly, buddy. Yeah, that's it," Sanjanovitch growled at Schultzheimer, nodding approvingly as the fiercely glaring fighter stepped slowly and carefully away from the tangling chair.

According to the "book" that was supposed to guide law enforcement officers in such circumstances, Freddy Sanjanovitch had acted properly from the moment he accidentally stumbled in on the two men and his naked partner. Which was to say, he hadn't maliciously triggered a .45 round into Roy Schultzheimer's chest, nor had he opened up on Rainbow for disobeying the first command to drop the knife, for two perfectly logical reasons. One, because Freddy Sanjanovitch didn't know what the hell was going on. And two, because he truly believed he had the situation—whatever the situation *was*—under control. But there was a significant difference between reacting correctly and reacting properly.

Having little faith in the "book," and being far more inclined to act on street-honed instincts, neither Ben Koda or Charley Shannon would have hesitated to drop the oncoming Schultzheimer with a pair of heart-shattering .45 slugs, and then put the next four into the widest part of Rainbow's body, regardless of what the fearsome street dealer decided to do with the knife. Mostly because they knew the book couldn't even begin to deal with a savagely violent killer like Rainbow. But also because it made a lot more sense to write a Cover-Your-Ass shooting report after the body bags had been removed, as opposed to risking the loss of a special agent—rookie, female, naked or otherwise—in a hostage situation.

But then, too, Ben Koda and Charley Shannon were cynical enough to half-expect an obviously drugged and distractingly naked female agent like Kaaren Mueller to stand up and stagger forward in front of a dangerously alert killer like Roy Schultzheimer and start slurring crazy things like ". . . no, don't hurt him . . ."

Freddy Sanjanovitch was a far more civilized man who expected nothing of the sort. Consequently he made the fatal mistake of reacting to his firearms training by quickly shifting the aim-point of the deadly .45 away from his partner's glassy-eyed face, and slipping his index finger out of the trigger guard.

It was an understandable mistake that lasted little more than a second. But a second was plenty of time for an instinctive street fighter like Rainbow to send the heavy, razor-edged throwing knife into the overlapping pectoral and deltoid muscles of Freddy Sanjanovitch's upper right chest . . . where it glanced off a curved rib to slice through the critical median, ulnar and radial nerves that controlled the agent's gun-wielding right hand.

Whether the shock was caused by the unexpected impact of the heavy knife, the immediate pain, or the sensation of having his entire right arm go numb and limp as the .45 clattered noisily onto the wooden floor, the net effect was the same.

Freddy Sanjanovitch staggered away from the searing impact, gasping in shock as he clutched at the horrifying knife protruding from his shoulder. He was still in that hunched position, staring open-mouthed at his fallen pistol, as Roy Schultzheimer lunged forward, twisted in midair, and slashed the edge of his tennis-shoed foot into the agent's sagging jaw. The impact sent the mercifully unconscious Sanjanovitch crashing against the far wall of the apartment, whereupon he dropped limply to the floor at the bare feet of his partner.

6

IN THE DARKNESS, the water looked like a sheet of rippled black glass, reflecting glary streaks of light and echoing the sounds of enthusiastic partying at the campsites on the Arizona side of the Colorado River across from Big Bend.

"HIT IT!"

Benjamin Koda and Bart Harrington had no intention of getting up from their comfortable lounge chairs and going out into the water again to rescue the hairy-chested behemoth now standing in ankle-deep water with a water ski attached to one unsteadily raised foot and a double-handled ski rope gripped tight in two muscular hands.

"AH SAID HIT IT!" Charley Shannon roared, his booming voice echoing out over the water as he wobbled precariously on one tree-trunklike leg.

"Charley, you dumb asshole, you're gonna drown for sure this time! It's too goddamned dark to ski!" Koda yelled out over a mouthful of steak.

"SHEEEE-IT, AH CAN SEE WHERE I'M GOIN'!" Charley roared back.

"What do you think?" Koda asked, looking over at Bart Harrington.

"Son-bitch ever find a life vest that fits?" Harrington asked, graciously adding an extra shot of Kahlúa to Koda's steaming cup.

Koda squinted out over the dark water.

"I think he's wearing one on his head. Looks like a fucking Zulu warrior."

"Probably wouldn't hold him up anyway," Harrington suggested as he took a tenative sip of the hot coffee.

"Fair enough," Koda nodded. "OKAY GIRLS," he yelled out, "HIT IT!"

The echoing giggles of two fun-loving young women were drowned out by the high-pitched whine of a puny jet-ski motor being given full throttle. The coils of nylon ski rope floating beside Charley Shannon's single supporting leg began to flick out quickly into the darkness. As the last loop disappeared, the rope leaped up out of the water and went taut in Shannon's hands.

The little jet-ski came to a sudden motor-screaming halt at the end of the rope, sending both laughing and shrieking females tumbling into the water and jerking Shannon forward off-balance.

For a long moment, the final outcome was uncertain. Charley Shannon swayed back and forth on one wobbly leg, sending curses echoing against the surrounding bluffs and waving his arms in a frantic attempt to regain his balance. But then, with the slowly gathering momentum of a toppling tree, the law of gravity prevailed.

Charley Shannon dropped face-first into ten inches of cold, sandy shore water just as Sandy Mudd finished maneuvering her small car down the steep, graveled launching ramp and into a section of scrub weed-covered dirt next to the yellow-bulb-lighted cabanas.

"Goddamn, the son-bitch *can* see where he's going," Bart Harrington commented through another juicy mouthful of steak.

"Charley always ski like that?" Sandy Mudd asked as she walked up to the campfire, a duffel bag in one hand and a tightly-rolled sleeping bag in the other.

"Nah, he usually has more trouble with the takeoff," Koda said, looking up and grinning as he raised his coffee cup in greeting. "Decided to try it with a ski this time."

"'Bout time you all got here, partner," Harrington said, reaching into one of the ice chests and throwing three more thick steaks on the sizzling grill. "Throw your bags down and grab a seat. How do you like your steak?"

"Anything I cook usually turns out raw on the inside and black on the outside," Sandy shrugged. "Take anything I can get about now. Medium would be nice."

"You got it."

"How's it going, Sandy?" Koda asked as the girl settled into a web-backed lounge chair with a tired sigh. "Want a beer, or you gonna risk your kidneys on Bart's version of Navy coffee?"

"Beer sounds real good," Sandy said, blinking her eyes sleepily. "Gets kinda dry making that desert run by yourself."

"Absolute truth," Koda nodded, reaching into another ice chest and tossing her a wet bottle. "Start in on this one. We'll keep 'em coming."

"Ahhh, tastes good," Sandy sighed gratefully, twisting the cap and then downing half the can in one deep swallow. Then she looked back down at the shore. "Uh—aren't you guys going to go pull him out?" she asked.

Koda glanced out at his sprawled partner and then back over at Harrington. "How long's he been down this time?"

Bart Harrington checked his watch and shrugged. "Maybe forty seconds."

"We've been letting him go at least a minute," Koda said, grinning at the visibly uncertain Mudd. "Nothing like a little oxygen deprivation to calm a man down. Helps clear the alcohol out of his brain."

"'Course, the longer he stays down, the heavier he gets," Harrington reminded.

"Good point," Koda nodded. He cupped his hands against his mouth and yelled, "HEY LARD-BUTT. GET YOUR UGLY FACE OUTTA THE MUD. WE GOT COMPANY!"

Charley Shannon slowly pushed his frame out of the water and shook his head a couple of times before looking back up at the campsite. Then he stood up and began staggering toward the fire, seemingly unconcerned about the water ski still attached to his foot.

"Hey, Muddy-girl, how they hanging?" Charley winked and grinned drunkenly as he pulled a towel off the clothesline rope and began to rub his head briskly.

"All right," Sandy nodded, her cheeks dimpling into a cheerful smile, grateful that her working relationship with Koda and Shannon had undergone a noticeable shift during the past two weeks.

The first week had been difficult. As both Kaaren Mueller and

Sandy Mudd had been warned to expect, Koda and Shannon were characteristically up-front in expressing their opinions about working a covert operation with a female partner. Opinions, however politely expressed, left no doubt in the minds of Mueller and Mudd as to their status in this particular DEA team, regardless of any special talents they might possess.

Sandy had listened quietly to the objections, some of which, she had to admit, were understandable—assuming that most of the more blatant horror stories could be believed—if not necessarily reasonable. She listened, and then, just as she had done earlier in her life with her brothers and friends, she began a quiet, low-keyed effort to establish herself within the team, using her tried-and-true methods. Hard work . . . tolerance . . . and more hard work. Unlike Kaaren Mueller, Sandy Mudd had learned to be patient in dealing with the built-in prejudices of the thick-headed half of the species.

It was probably the beer, she reminded herself as she accepted a second bottle from the outwardly congenial Ben Koda. Charley Shannon had been relatively easygoing from the start, but this was the first time that Ben had initiated a friendly comment in her direction. Not exactly a sign of back-to-back comradery, to be sure, but not an indifferent brush-off either. Take it for what it's worth, she shrugged internally. Plenty of time.

"Thought I was gonna have to go out there and play lifeguard when I drove up," Sandy said to Shannon after taking a slow sip at the new bottle. "Your buddies here didn't seem too interested."

"Shee-it, couldn't depend on these mothers to save mah beer, much less mah ass," Shannon grumbled beneath the towel. "Already tried three times today. Dragged 'em under every time." His eyes twinkled brightly as he emerged from the towel and kicked the ski off over into a corner.

"Next time we're gonna tie you to the friggin' dock," Koda threatened, reaching over with a fork to poke at the steaks. "Hey," he said, looking up at Mudd as the implications of her earlier comments regarding her solitary desert drive suddenly registered, "what happened to Kaaren?"

Sandy described her conversation with Kaaren Mueller as Harrington began dishing out diced chunks of hot steak and fried potatoes onto thick paper plates. As she talked, she saw Ben toss the spiked contents of his cup into the nearby brush and refill it with straight black coffee. She also realized that Charley Shannon, who had quickly consumed the steaming contents of his plate and reached quietly for seconds, now appeared—unaccountably—to be completely sober. All three men sat in a quiet ring around the fire, slowly consuming their food and coffee, their eyes fixed on her as they listened in total attentive silence.

"So I left a message for Freddy, just in case . . ." she finished, feeling her stomach begin to knot up as she belatedly realized the potential seriousness of her decision to leave Kaaren Mueller on her own. She looked around at all three faces, waiting for someone to speak.

"You think she'd try to make a buy without contacting Freddy?" Koda asked, breaking the uncomfortable silence.

"She might," Sandy nodded. "She's like that. Real hardworking, but kinda . . ."

"Thick-headed?" Shannon offered.

"Yeah," Sandy nodded again. "That's about it. I shouldn't have . . ."

Koda stood up quickly.

"I'll try to contact Sanjo," he said to the two men, reaching for a pair of worn tennis shoes. "You two better get the gear ready, just in case." He turned and glared somberly at Sandy Mudd for a moment. "You'd better come with me."

Koda and Mudd made the quick climb up the steep metal stairway to the upper bluffs in total silence.

As Shannon and Harrington tossed the remains of their dinner plates into the nearby trashcan and began to break down the campsite, Ben Koda began to feed coins into a phone mounted on the outside wall of the small grocery store located just above and behind the cabanas. Sandy Mudd stood next to him, feeling chilled and numb as she waited in spite of the warm summer air.

It took Koda almost five seconds to realize he didn't have a dial tone.

"Shit," he muttered as he quickly traced the problem. Someone—probably a half-drunk camper who didn't want to take any chance of being called back to work—had tried to yank the receiver off the phone box, and almost succeeded. The telephone was still attached by a few thin wires, but the incoming line was completely separated. Koda looked around quickly. There were no other phones. "Can you fix this?" he demanded.

Sandy Mudd stared hopelessly at the irregular lengths of thin, color-coded wire, realizing immediately that the inner mechanism of the phone had to have been damaged.

"No, I don't think—but wait just a minute. Maybe I can do something else," she called out over her shoulder as she ran for the stairway, heading for the trunk of her car. Less than two minutes later she was back upstairs, quietly intent on connecting a partially disassembled Sony tape recorder to the exposed innards of the abused telephone while Ben Koda held a flashlight as directed. After five more minutes, she looked up at Koda and nodded. "It'll work. You can use the phone dial, but you'll have to talk into the recorder."

"Will it still pick up a transponder signal?"

"Uh—yeah, sure," Mudd nodded. "Here, I'll hold it up for you," she added as Koda reached over her arm to dial "O."

"Operator, may I help you?"

"This is a credit card call," Koda spoke loudly into the tape recorder in Sandy Mudd's hands. He recited a series of numbers. The speaker clicked four times, signaling that the connection had been made. As the phone at the other end rang the first time, Koda held a palm-sized metal box up to the recorder and depressed a recessed button. An audible series of tones caused a second relay to connect down-line, activating the answering machine in Freddy Sanjanovitch's apartment.

". . . Freddy, this is Sandy. Just in case . . ."

Koda listened to the entire recording and then signaled for the next message.

". . . Ben, this is Sanjo. Seventeen thirty-five. Can't make dinner tonight. Missed connections with Kaaren. Typical. I'm on my way to her place now, see if she needs a hand with her sale. Give you a call when we get clear . . ."

"He—doesn't sound right," Sandy whispered, swallowing nervously as the recorder clicked off.

"He's pissed," Koda growled absentmindedly. "And in a hurry. Probably at a phone booth." He keyed the transmitter once more. This time there was just the hiss of blank tape running past the play-head in Sanjanovitch's machine.

"He would have erased the messages when he got back. That's standard procedure, isn't it?" Sandy asked quietly.

"Yeah," Koda muttered, looking down at his watch.

Already nine forty-five, Koda realized. Over two hours since Freddy Sanjanovitch had left the message on his recorder. Plenty of time for him to contact Kaaren and leave an all-clear message. Plenty of time for a lot of things to happen.

"What's Kaaren's number?"

"Uh—" Sandy shook her head, trying to clear her numbed mind. "Two-two-five . . . nine-seven-two-one."

Koda dialed "0" again.

"Operator, this is a credit card call," Koda began. "Four-four . . . uh—never mind. What's the cost for a station-to-station call to San Diego?" He listened to the slightly hollow-sounding voice in the Sony recorder for a few moments. "Thank you. I'll be back in a minute." He disconnected the line and then turned to Sandy.

"The coin-box still connected on this thing?"

Mudd checked the wiring in the phone box quickly with the flashlight. "Yeah, it'll work, but I can bypass it."

"How long?"

"Uh, maybe ten minutes or so. I'll need to rewire—"

"How much change do you have?"

"Uh—couple dimes, I think, maybe . . ." She dug into the pockets of her jeans and fished out two dimes and a nickel.

"Go get Charley and Bart. Tell them to bring change for the phone. And hurry," Koda added, his voice tight as his eyes flicked back and forth from the disassembled Sony recorder to the even smaller transmitter he held in his hands.

Shannon and Harrington were standing around the phone within a minute, dumping change on the phone box ledge as Koda confirmed the number with the operator.

"What have we got?" Shannon asked as he fed another quarter into the slot.

"Sanjo left a reverse on his checkout message two hours ago. 'Sale' instead of 'buy.' He was heading out to Kaaren's apartment. Apparently couldn't reach her by phone. No check-in," Koda said, holding a hand over the Sony recorder's speaker.

"Why doesn't he use the credit card number?" Sandy whispered to Charley Shannon as Koda brought the transmitter up to the speaker.

"Possible tap," Shannon said, his eyes focused on the transmitter in Koda's hand. "We use a reverse code as a caution alert. Charge call might cause a problem, since our card number's dirty. Might be traced back to a government billing if someone's got the right connection. Complicate things if she's in trouble."

"Shit," Sandy Mudd whispered.

"Yeah," Shannon nodded in agreement.

Koda triggered the transmitter and held the Sony recorder out so that everyone could hear. All four agents came in close to listen as the phone rang twice. Then Kaaren Mueller's answering machine cut in.

The scream exploded out of the tape recorder speaker. A high-pitched, anguished scream that seemed to echo off of the trees surrounding the darkened store. There was a second scream—this one a longer, more visceral sound of pain that was suddenly cut off.

The four agents stood frozen in shocked silence. Sandy Mudd started to make a choking noise in her throat.

"That was Freddy," Bart Harrington whispered unnecessarily. "Goddamn it—" Then he stopped when Koda waved quickly with his free hand.

Almost ten seconds of hissing silence elapsed before the recorder clicked. Then a silky voice laughed.

"Don't that sound pretty? Surely do, don't it? Yeah. An' don't you know that's not the best part. That's right, baby. Whoever you be, you jes' listen t' this."

The recorder clicked again. This time the sounds coming out of the speaker were less violent. Soft rhythmic moans and screams, punctuated by deep-throated grunts and the sounds of squeaking mattress springs.

"My god, that's Kaaren. I think . . . they're raping her," Sandy whispered in a choked voice.

The sounds continued on for another thirty seconds, then the recorder clicked back to the silky voice.

"Now warn't that nice? Surely was. But don't you be thinkin' no racial jive now, bro'. That be a mean-ass white boy jumpin' that lady's bones. Sure 'nough is." The voice laughed again. A giggly, whispery laugh. "So, *whoever* you be, you jes' back away real nice-like. Unnerstand? 'Cause if'n you don't—" The voice broke into an eerie giggle. "We don't want no trouble, now, but you *know* we ain't gonna back off none. You hear what Ah'm sayin'? Gonna have t' start payin' little more respect t' us folks. Yeah, that's right, you listen up, now, 'cause Ah'm bein' serious. Dig?" A pause. "Yeah, well jes' in case we ain't *communicatin'*, we're gonna give you people little somethin' extra t' think about. Help you *remember* next time."

The speaker gave off three clicking sounds at one-second intervals. Then the silky voice was back.

"You hear them little clicks? All right, now you jes' listen *real* good 'cause your phone call jes' activated a little *present* for your man here. Somethin' he's been waiting for *real bad*. An' jes' so you *understand*, you're gonna get t' listen in . . . see how happy he is." The voice paused, allowing the agents to hear the sound of his rapid, excited breathing.

"You bastard . . ." Koda whispered almost inaudibly. Then the speaker clicked again and Freddy Sanjanovitch's voice, hoarse and panic-stricken, burst out of the recorder.

". . . JESUS GOD! BENJI! THEY TOOK HER . . . TORREY PINES . . . HANG UP THE FUCKING PHONE! FAT MAN'S—"

The explosion that shredded the interior of Kaaren Mueller's apartment echoed in the ears of the four stunned agents milliseconds before the phone connection went dead in Ben Koda's hand.

Professor David Isaac was spending another late night within the clean, orderly confines of his research laboratory, concentrating on the task of devising a simple cookbook procedure for producing pound-quantities of Jimmy Pilgrim's thiopene analog in an underground laboratory (a method necessarily within the skill-capacity of the average undergraduate chemistry student, Isaac reminded himself, wincing inwardly at the thought) when the phone in his office rang loudly.

"Isaac," he said, yawning.

"Good evening, Professor."

"Mr. Pilgrim." Isaac's quasi-motivated analytical mind came fully alert as he recognized the cold, lifeless voice. "It's, uh, good to hear from you again."

"I wanted to let you know that we'll be sending you a computer program, appropriate security codes, and an access telephone number so that you can use your laboratory computer to send and receive messages through our message-switching system," Pilgrim said, ignoring the social amenities. "Once this system is in effect, we will no longer communicate by phone except in the event of an emergency."

"That sounds fine," Isaac nodded, curious as to how Pilgrim knew what type of program would function in his lab computer. He was becoming even more impressed by the constant attention to detail that was apparently characteristic of Jimmy Pilgrim's organization.

"In the meantime, I'm advising you not to call that number I gave you unless it's an absolute emergency. I'm very serious about that," Pilgrim said coldly. "Very serious."

"Yes, I believe I understand," Isaac said.

"Fine. I'm also calling about our procedures manual," Pilgrim went on. "I understand that our thiopene analog produced an acceptable effect on our first test subject. I want you to be ready with the manual as quickly as possible. We want to go into full-scale production as soon as the confirmatory testing is completed."

"There's no problem in getting your cookbook ready, and I'm, uh, glad to hear about the thiopene," Isaac acknowledged, not sure how he was supposed to respond to such noninformative news. "But what about the other compound I sent you?"

"What other compound? What are you talking about?" Pilgrim demanded, immediately alert and suspicious.

"I'm sorry, I assumed you'd receive the package directly," Isaac hurriedly explained. "I included a sample of the A-series—the one we discussed earlier—in with the thiopene. It was marked 'A-seventeen.' I—uh—wanted you to see the comparison between a crude, broad-spectrum hallucinogen such as the thiopene, and an analog that should function on a much more specific basis."

Pilgrim's end of the phone line remained ominously silent.

"And of course," Isaac added nervously, "the test data will be extremely valuable if we are to continue to develop a useful analog series."

"I was not advised that we had received a second sample," Pilgrim finally growled, clearly displeased by the sudden revelation. "But I'll check into the matter immediately and get back to you. In the meantime, the manual . . ."

"I was just finishing up a few minor details," Isaac said reassuringly. "Your stipulations regarding the skills of your, uh, chemists made things a bit more difficult than I anticipated."

"Is there a problem—?" Much to Isaac's surprise, there was a discernible element of concern in Pilgrim's voice.

"No, not at all," Isaac reassured. "Just a matter of taking a longer, but less demanding pathway. The chemical result will be the same."

"Excellent. Then, as to the delivery . . ."

"And the reimbursement," Isaac pointedly reminded him.

". . . since we don't have our message-switching system in operation," Pilgrim said, ignoring the comment, "we'll have to arrange an exchange point. I suggest—"

"Uh, I assume you know where I park my car," Isaac broke in.

Silence.

"Yes, of course," Pilgrim finally answered, making no attempt to conceal the chilled inflections in his voice.

I'll bet you do, Isaac nodded to himself, unaware he was treading a dangerous edge.

"It's nine forty-five right now. I'll place the chapter on the back seat of my vehicle in exactly one hour," Isaac said. "The payment can be left in the same location."

Isaac paused for a moment, waiting in vain for Pilgrim's reaction, and then continued. "I'm assuming that it would be better for us not to be seen together in public."

"Ten forty-five will be fine," Pilgrim said. He hung up the phone with a sharp click.

It took Dr. David Isaac less than thirty seconds to call up the cookbook procedures for the thiopene analog out of his computer's huge hard-disk memory. After consulting his notes, he quickly made a few appropriate corrections in the text, made a rapid check of the format, rememorized the corrected version back onto the disk, and then pulled on a pair of white rubber gloves before placing the first of five pieces of bond paper into the attached printer.

When the computer-guided printer finally stopped chattering, Isaac removed the last page with his gloved hands, made a quick visual scan to confirm that the synthesis steps were in the proper order, folded the sheets of paper, placed them in a plain white envelope, and then headed for the door. It was 10:02 P.M.

Eight minutes later, Dr. David Isaac was back in his darkened office and standing at the edge of his curtained window, staring out through the night blackness at the illuminated parking lot where a small, innocuous Volkswagen Bug sat waiting.

At 10:15 P.M., the first of three dark late-model sedans turned into the University parking lot adjacent to the chemistry building. As Isaac watched with nervous interest, the three vehicles made a slow, methodical sweep of the entire lot and the surrounding area with their headlights, each vehicle stopping and parking at least twice—for two-to-three minute time periods—while the other two cars continued to move from point to point at speeds that were both unhurried and unre-markable.

Impressive, Isaac thought to himself as he watched the silent, predatory ballet. Most impressive, indeed.

At 10:30 P.M., the three vehicles terminated their search. They moved to three predetermined parking positions about a hundred yards apart and shut off their lights with chronological precision, form-ing a large triangle around Isaac's VW. As best Isaac could tell, there was only the driver in each of the parked vehicles.

It was at this moment that Isaac, using a pair of dusty bird-watching binoculars, spotted the slowly rotating circular antenna—approximately the diameter of a dinner plate—partially concealed on top of a camper truck parked at the far corner of the lot.

Dr. David Isaac's calm, analytical mind went numb.

For twenty-five interminable minutes, the three dark vehicles and the camper truck remained fixed in position. His eyes intent on the sodium-vapor-illuminated scene below, Isaac remained at his darkened vantage point, forcing himself to methodically consider the frightening possibilities churning through his mind.

The camper appeared to be a police surveillance vehicle with a transmission source locator. But as Isaac quickly realized, it might just as easily be Pilgrim's camper, listening in for the radio traffic of a routine police surveillance. The figures in the three sedans could be police officers, or they could be Pilgrim's men. No way to tell. Presumably all four vehicles were together, because the headlights of the three sedans had swept across the front of the camper several times, Isaac remembered. It was logical to assume that Pilgrim's men would spot a blatant police surveillance. And yet—

Suddenly, two of the sedans moved out of their parking slots with their lights off, drove up on either side of Isaac's VW, and came to a quick stop. A dark figure carrying something—a manila envelope?—came out of each vehicle. The figures opened both doors of the VW and ducked into the interior. Seconds later, both figures were back in their respective sedans.

On either side of Isaac's VW, pairs of bright headlights suddenly came on. As Isaac watched with growing confusion and concern, the two bracketing vehicles sped off out of the parking lot in two different directions, leaving the third sedan and the camper in their fixed and darkened positions.

Feeling his throat begin to tighten, Isaac checked his watch.

One minute.

Two minutes.

Three minutes.

Four . . .

"Professor Isaac?"

Isaac jerked away from the window and stared wide-eyed at the figure silhouetted in his doorway.

"Is something the matter, Professor?"

"Ah—no. No, nothing's wrong," Isaac shook his head, chuckling with forced amusement, as he tried to still the frantic pounding in his chest. "You startled me. I was just . . . staring out at the parking lot, trying to remember if I'd left some papers out in my car."

"And you make fun of me for working too late," Nichole Faysonnt teased, a brief provocative smile appearing under her tired eyes. "I'm going downstairs for a couple of minutes. I'll go by your car and look for your papers."

"Ah, no—that's all right, Nichole. I—"

"I have to drop a letter in the mailbox anyway," she shook her head. "The keys, if you please, Professor?" She held out her hand, the expression in her eyes flickering perceptibly to some sort of undefined warmth.

"Ah—" Isaac's mind wavered indecisively between an undefined sense of fear and reflexive chivalry, and then surrendered to his awakened survival instincts. "The door's unlocked," he shrugged. "Nothing in there worth stealing."

"I'll be right back," Nichole promised, smiling brightly, and then disappeared around the corner of the doorway.

Isaac ran back to the window in his office. The sedan and the camper hadn't moved. Muttering a curse, Isaac waited with nervous impatience for Nichole to appear on the sidewalk. He followed the rapid progress of the white-coated figure as she walked quickly across the black asphalt, and then reached for his binoculars as she opened the door to the Volkswagen.

Isaac swept the visual field of the binoculars back and forth across the darkened parking lot in the areas surrounding the Volkswagen, the sedan, and the camper. Aside from Nichole, there was no visible movement. Then he focused on Nichole as she backed out of the small car, stood up—empty handed!—and then started walking, much more slowly now, back across the parking lot toward the chemistry building.

Isaac was still trying to puzzle out this new piece of inconsistent data when the headlights of the parked sedan flashed on. As he watched in mind-constricting horror, the sedan surged forward out of its parking place and headed directly toward Nichole, the headlight beams reflecting brightly off the back of her white lab coat.

As Isaac stood immobilized—watching first in helpless rage, then in terror, and finally in confused disbelief—the sedan swept past the girl, turned out of the parking lot, onto the main road, and then disappeared into the darkness.

Moments later, the lights of the camper came on. It also drove out of the parking lot—at a slower, and somehow more sinister rate of speed—under the intense scrutiny of Isaac's binoculars, finally disappearing just as the sound of Nichole's footsteps echoed through the cold, quiet laboratory.

Isaac hastily put away the binoculars, strode out of his office, and almost ran into Nichole.

"Is this what you were looking for, Professor?" She handed a large, thick manila envelope to Isaac, who in turn stared at the block-printed letters on the flap spelling out his name, an envelope that—Isaac was absolutely certain—had *not* been in Nichole's hand when she walked away from the parking lot.

"I—ah—yes, I believe it is. Where did you find it?"

"I told you you'd been working too hard lately," Nichole shrugged, her face dimpling into what Isaac suddenly and irrationally decided was a thoroughly sensuous smile. "It was right here on the counter all the time . . ." She gestured over at a nearby lab counter. ". . . underneath this old scalpel."

Isaac stared at the unfamiliar object, realizing finally that the old-fashioned, one-piece surgical knife had to be several decades old, manufactured long before the era of the individually packaged, sterilized and disposable scalpel blades. He had never seen or handled such a crude instrument in his entire life, especially not in his modern university laboratory.

Isaac took the knife out of Nichole's hand, and only then noticed that the small, spring-steel blade had been honed to a glistening, flesh-splitting edge.

At some inner level of awareness, separate and apart from the brain cells processing the raw data, David Isaac registered amazement that he was no longer capable of outwardly emotional reaction. He was simply filled with a sense of all-encompassing dread, a sensation that caused his mind to go momentarily blank. He suddenly realized that he and Nichole were staring at each other.

"I'm sorry," Isaac shook his head. "I didn't—I mean, I was thinking about something . . ."

The light-hearted expression in Nichole Faysonnt's eyes suddenly shifted to concern. She was accustomed to the occasional absentmindedness of her mentor, but she couldn't begin to comprehend the paled look of shock on his face.

Not knowing what to say, she impulsively reached out and took the heavy surgical knife out of Isaac's hands, placed it on the lab counter, and then wrapped her soft warm hands around his chilled fingers.

Isaac finally blinked, and became aware of their situation. Gently removing his hand from the compelling warmth, he carefully opened the envelope and then slowly removed an inner transparent plastic envelope that a contained a single ragged, water-and-grease-stained piece of ancient parchment covered with compact blocks of faded-ink script, a separate letter typed on modern bond paper with three scrawled signatures at the end of the brief text, and five band-wrapped packets. Hand-printed labels indicated that each packet contained fifty one hundred dollar bills.

Blinking several times, Isaac gingerly carried the protected document over to an optical enlarger that projected a crisply sharp magnified image of the parchment onto an eye-level view screen. The two of them stared wordlessly at the image for several minutes as they both—Isaac more quickly than Nichole—silently translated the Greek symbols.

"Maria?" Nichole finally asked in a quietly curious voice, long aware of Isaac's fascination with the mysteries surrounding the legendary mistress of alchemy. Perhaps better than any of his other graduate students, Nichole Faysonnt thought she understood the underlying emotions that inspired Isaac's quest for factual knowledge of the ancient alchemists. But, until this evening, Nichole had always assumed that the quest of her adviser (and secretly fantasied lover) was more of a diverting hobby than an all-consuming passion.

But like Isaac, Nichole couldn't resist being intrigued by the sense of history reflected in what appeared to be an exceptionally nice reproduction of a page out of an ancient laboratory notebook. Whoever had made the reproduction for Isaac had done an excellent job, she decided. The manipulation of the old world-type paper stock was magnificent. Especially the alteration of the distinctively thick paper fibers—seemingly darkened and worn smooth by the friction of innumerable fingers and uncounted years—that gave the document the full flavor of a priceless original. A beautiful piece of work, she nodded to herself.

"I think so," Isaac replied softly, entranced by the aura that seemed to radiate from the document. For a few moments, he was able to forget his fearful realization that whoever had delivered the envelope—and the terrifying knife—had been in his laboratory just moments ago, less than a dozen feet away from his turned back, entering and departing without making a sound . . .

He handed the authentication letter to Nichole, his eyes still focused on the view-screen.

"My God," she whispered, awestruck as she quickly scanned the typed and signed letter, "It's—an original? How did you—? Where—? And this money?"

Isaac continued to stare at the screen for a few more seconds, unable to break away from the haunting story contained on the thick piece of yellowed paper.

"Look at the page number," he finally said, as much to himself as to Nichole.

"Twelve," Nichole read quickly. "I don't understand . . ."

"It means they have at least eleven more pages. Look at the left-hand edge. You can see where it's been cut with something . . . sharp," he finished, suddenly overwhelmed by the imagery of sharp-edged tools, and the men who could wield them so callously, to cut into something as sacred as a notebook actually written by Maria the Jewess. Almost like cutting into her very body . . . her soul.

"*Who* has eleven more pages? What are you talking about?" Nichole demanded.

Isaac was silent for several moments before he turned to Nichole and stared thoughtfully into her uncomprehending eyes. Then, decisively, he took her white-coated arm in a gentle but firm grasp and directed her toward a nearby lab stool.

"Nichole," he said, taking a deep, steadying breath. "Please sit down and listen to me carefully, without saying anything. There's something I've got to tell you. A very long and complicated story . . ."

High upon the Torrey Pines bluffs overlooking a dark expanse of the Pacific Ocean along the North San Diego County coastline, Kaaren Mueller grasped the thick, scarred, rock-steady hand and took a first cautious step into a water-carved system of deep, twisting gullies that dropped rapidly and precariously down through the sandstone cliffs to the rocky shore far below.

In spite of the hallucinatory flashes of color that continued to disrupt her thought processes, Kaaren understood—Roy, her beautiful friend, lover, and protector, had been insistent—that a slip at the start could easily result in an out-of-control tumble toward one of the numerous outcropping cliff edges . . . and a three-hundred foot fall into empty, black space.

As she worked her way down into the head-high gully, Kaaren felt the first set of swells begin to build deep within her body, disturbing the serene calmness of her surroundings. Swells rising and falling in almost perfect rhythm with the surf she could hear—but couldn't see—as it rose up in the cold darkness far below to crash, embrace and flow against massive, unbending rock.

She stopped her cautiously guided descent long enough to inhale slowly, trying to match her body rhythm to the oscillating sense of calm, knowing that the swells would build in intensity until they released in a series of orgasmic convulsions, thrusting her fermenting body into conflict with a mind that had only just begun to deal with the contradictions of this new dimension of sensuality.

Kaaren felt Roy's hand close firmly around her wrist, pulling gently but insistently. She responded by forcing her mind to concentrate on the placement of each bare foot on the claustrophobically narrow, cold, winding pathway as they continued to descend between the massive rocks. Again and again, she had to force herself to ignore the fascinating patterns of crisply brilliant light relecting off the thick slabs of wet sandstone in her narrowed field of vision.

Fat Man's Misery.

A deeply recessed portion of Kaaren Mueller's drug-hazed mind recorded an awareness: the path was well-named. Misery indeed for any overweight man or woman foolish enough to take this trail down to the beach. Even Roy, her . . . friend? . . . was having difficulty scrunching his heavily muscled shoulders through the tight turns and sudden drop-offs in the rapidly descending chasm, now at least fifteen feet deep and often as narrow as twelve or fourteen inches across.

Kaaren felt Roy hesitate in front of her. Then she stopped again, bracing her free hand against the warmly solid bare back as he pulled himself up, then helped her over a large, rough-surfaced boulder wedged tightly into the gully. As she climbed, Kaaren could feel the periods between the soothing oscillations shorten perceptibly.

"There you go," Roy spoke gruffly as he jammed himself against an outcropping of treacherously fragile sandstone to give her room to slide past. As she did so, Kaaren was intensely aware of the chromatic sensations emanating from every square inch of her upper torso as she brushed against Roy's karate- and surfboard-hardened body—a dependable source of body heat that defied the slowly dropping air temperature.

Kaaren stepped forward, aware now that the reflecting colors had more room to dance, that she and Roy—and someone else?—were now on a flat outcropping of smooth rock that had to be very close to the ocean. She could hear the sound of the roaring waves, taste the salt-laden air, feel the cold . . .

Shivering now that she was fully exposed to the onshore winds, Kaaren moved carefully forward to the edge of the rock mass that interfaced with the ocean. She could sense with her bare feet the chill of the foamy, breaking surf as she listened in color-saturated fascination to the muted roar of the salt water. Sounds that seemed to mimic and then enhance the intensified rush of blood through her arteries . . . and brought on the first of the spasmodic releases.

Shaking from the pleasure and the cold against her bare skin, Kaaren turned to face the pathway, wanting to reach for the comforting body warmth of Roy's muscular arms. In the darkness a few yards away, she saw Roy . . . and then the other one. The strangely distant one with the dark face who didn't seem to care that she loved him too.

She started to move forward, wanting to embrace and absorb

the warmth of the larger, more caring man who had somehow managed to overcome the deep inner protests—both his and hers—that she could not even begin to understand. But then the deeply rising swells began once more.

As Kaaren Mueller stood transfixed on the cold, smooth rock, confused and hurt, the expanding prismatic ribbons of richly hued light seemed to center on the rainbowlike man with the frightening dark face before reflecting brightly off the sharpened edge of shiny wet steel in his hand.

7

AT 11:10 IN THE evening, in a San Diego hotel room, Tom Fogarty was still half-awake, lying in bed and reading through a stack of investigation reports generated by the six members of his Task Force team, when the hotel operator connected Ben Koda's call.

In the span of the next thirty minutes, a number of seemingly unrelated events began to take place simultaneously on both sides of the continental United States.

In Fairfax County, Virginia, the still groggy Director of the Federal Drug Enforcement Administration kissed his wife good-bye and then drove out of his garage at 2:30 in the morning, heading toward his Washington, D.C. office where he would take an emergency call from Special-Agent-in-Charge Thomas Fogarty over a secure phone line.

In a quiet, isolated room deep within the J. Edgar Hoover Building in Washington, D.C., a senior records supervisor took over a terminal and proceeded to enter an Alert Message into the computerized National Crime Information Center network, to the effect that a black male adult named Lafayette Beaumont Raynee, AKA 'Rainbow', was wanted for questioning in the bombing death of Freddy Sanjanovitch, a known narcotics smuggler . . . Raynee known to reside in the San Diego area . . . may be in the company of WMA James Pilgrim . . . WMA Eugene Bylighter, AKA 'Squeek' . . . and WFA Kaaren Mueller . . . all subjects to be considered armed and dangerous . . .

In Needles, California, a small desert town approximately fifty miles north of the Big Bend campsite, Herby Dawson—a crack pilot of widely diverse experience, who now cheerfully supplemented his military retirement by being on call for emergency middle-of-the-night assignments from government people like Thomas Fogarty—sat in the left-hand seat of a very fast combat transport helicopter and went through a hasty but thorough preflight check, while a second man secured a prepackaged array of lethal weaponry and ammunition behind the rear passenger seat.

Each of these events had been initiated by a furiously determined Fogarty, who—after dialing another one of the several hundred phone numbers in his "investigative resources" notebook—immediately got back to Koda with orders for the remaining team members.

Orders that were brief and explicit:

Other than the Alert Message put out over the NCIC law enforcement computer system, there would be no—repeat no—contact made with San Diego law enforcement officials regarding the apparent death of Freddy Sanjanovitch and the disappearance of Kaaren Mueller. Under no circumstances was either Sanjanovitch or Mueller to be identified as a federal agent to any law enforcement officer, regardless of the situation.

Other than a standoff surveillance by Bart Harrington and Sandy Mudd, the team was ordered to stay away from Freddy's and Kaaren's apartments. Harrington and Mudd would rendezvous at a gas station just outside the North Gate of March Air Force Base at 3:00 A.M.—in approximately three and one-half hours—to coordinate that surveillance with Fogarty.

The status and whereabouts of Special Agent Kaaren Mueller was to be determined, ASAP. Highest priority. Operating within the ongoing restraints of the investigation, and until further notice, Ben Koda and Charley Shannon were effectively unleashed.

Find Mueller. Report back immediately.

Go.

* * *

At 11:35 P.M., Pacific time, two leased vehicles—a brand-new Toyota sedan and a well-used pickup truck—roared out of a dirt camp road at Big Bend and sped out in the direction of the small crossroads town of Earp, California, both Koda and Harrington pushing the vehicles well past their recommended operating limits.

They were almost ten miles out of Big Bend, both drivers savagely intent upon reaching the small airport just outside of Earp as quickly as possible, when the cumulative impact of the last two hours finally caught up with Sandy Mudd. She turned to her partner with a stricken look on her ashen face.

"Bart, please, stop the car. Right now!"

The conscious part of Ben Koda's mind was two hundred and five crow-flying miles away, remembering an adolescent playground of dangerously steep cliffs and deep, winding gulleys . . . and trying to construct an approach that was both tactically sound and reasonably safe. It was his subconscious—that portion of his brain reflexively monitoring the continuing emptiness of the black asphalt road ahead, making fine adjustments to the steering wheel and gas pedal as the visible portion of the road rapidly dipped and curved—that remained dependably alert, and responded accordingly when the headlights in the rearview mirror suddenly swerved away. Ben Koda's hands and feet had already begun to downgear the highballing pickup to a controllable brake-speed before the cold, vicious, vengeance-seeking, conscious part of his mind became aware of the situation, and had a chance to demand, "Why?."

Sandy Mudd had the passenger door open and was out of the car before Bart Harrington was able to bring the abused Toyota to a full tire-screeching stop. She dove into the desert night, staggering and falling through several dozen yards of the treacherous ankle-deep sand, before she finally fell to her knees and began to shake and cry and vomit spasmodically.

"Goddamn it . . . Goddamn it . . . God . . ." she shook her head weakly, unable to control the emotionally helpless reaction that had suddenly and unexpectedly overcome the mental walls she'd been building for the past hour. Then she felt her head being lifted gently and supported in two huge, calloused hands.

"Easy, girl. Take it easy now. Ain't nothin' to be ashamed of." Charley Shannon's gruff voice was oddly quiet and soothing as he brushed the vomit and the tears away from her face, absentmindedly wiping his hand on his trouser leg.

"I—I killed him," she whispered between choking sobs.

"Sanjo's dead because I didn't—didn't think—didn't—" Her voice broke in another fit of shaking and sobbing.

"You didn't kill nobody," Shannon spoke softly, steadying the trembling girl in his arms, and using the tail end of his unbuttoned shirt to finish wiping away the partially digested remains of the dinner before taking the canteen from Harrington and helping her to wash out her mouth. "You just got caught up in somethin' you could n' control. Nothin' you could 'a done to change things."

"That's not—what Ben thinks," Mudd whispered softly, still trying to control her ragged breathing and choked voice.

"He's not thinking right now . . . he's just reactin'," Charley Shannon shook his dark-bearded head. "Gonna be a little while before he starts acting civilized again. Probably not till we find out for sure what happened to Kaaren and Sanjo. Meantime, we got a man waitin' for us at Earp. Think you can keep down the rest a' that food till we get to the airport?"

Sandy nodded her head sheepishly as she blinked to clear her eyes, using Shannon's offered arm to pull herself to her feet. She looked down and wrinkled her nose in dismay at her wet and smelly shirt, then shrugged and started back to her car, silently grateful that neither Charley nor Bart offered a hand to keep her upright as they stumbled side by side through the deep, yielding sand back toward the road.

The trio made it to the passenger door of the Toyota before a still badly shaken Sandy was able to speak again.

"Charley?" she whispered.

Shannon had started toward the pickup where Ben Koda was waiting impatiently. He stopped and turned at the sound of her raspy voice.

"They're going to try to draw us in, aren't they?"

"How's that?" The burly agent stood there in the moonlit darkness, thick hands thrust part way down into the too-small front pockets of his jeans, his dark head cocked in a manner that suggested amused curiosity.

"Kaaren. If they weren't going to use her for something—else—then they'd have probably blown her up with Sanjo, wouldn't they?"

Shannon's eyes flicked over toward Bart Harrington for an instant before settling back on Sandy Mudd. Then he nodded his head slowly.

"Yeah, I guess that's probably 'bout right; 'less maybe, like you say, they're plannin' on usin' her for bait. Maybe they're dumb enough to do that. Always hope," the dark-skinned giant shrugged.

Koda was in the process of replacing the CB mike in its dashboard clip when Shannon got into the pickup, closed the door, and looked over at his partner, questioning.

"Chopper'll be down on the pad in five," Koda said, starting up the truck engine and accelerating through the hard-packed sand back onto the road. "Fogarty must have really used his pull on this one. Got us a Sikorsky Black Hawk. Pilot's an ex-military free-lance named Herby Dawson."

"Think Ah heard a' the man," Shannon nodded. "Supposed to be a real crazy motherfucker. Cobra jockey in 'Nam 'fore he turned Spook—or whatever the hell he is now. Heard he flew for Colonel Schroeder back when."

"Sounds like just the man we need," Koda said, his eyes on the road as the speedometer steadied out at seventy-five. "She okay?" he added, after a few moments of silence.

"Just got caught up by the shakes," Shannon shrugged. "Locked in on the idea she got Sanjo killed. Dumped her cookies." Shannon shook his head sadly as he readjusted his oversized bulk into a more comfortable position within the confining truck cab, and then glanced over at his still-too-quiet partner. "Oh yeah, almost forgot. She also thinks you're a real shithead."

Koda snorted, a flicker of amusement passing across his face for a brief moment.

"'Course it'll probably all work out okay anyways," Shannon added contemplatively as he stared out over the probing headlight beams into the desert blackness. "Said she's thinkin' about running off down to the Keys with me after this thing's all over. Do a little fishin' and whatever, seeing's how you don't love her no more."

"Girl's got a real talent for judging character," Koda grunted.

"Yep, that's what Ah figured," Shannon nodded glancing over at his longtime friend and taking note of the body language signs that reassured him that his normally dependable partner was finally start- ing to level out. "Might even turn out to be a half-decent agent some day. Worked out the draw-play all by herself."

"That so?" Koda' eyebrows rose, and he made a slight shrug- ging motion with his shoulders. "Yeah, well that's good. Maybe she'll survive all this shit after all," he said. Then he turned his full con- centration back to the road as the turn sign for the airport rose up in the truck's flickering headlight beams.

* * *

The four long rotor blades of the sleek, massive and powerful Black Hawk had begun to whip slowly through the night air on the illuminated helicopter pad, less than fifty yards away from the main office and hangar of the small airport, when the pickup and the Toyota came to a quick stop next to the sheet metal building.

Driven by a time factor that was rapidly becoming critical, the four agents bailed out of their vehicles and ran into the hangar in search of Herby Dawson. They found a lean, fiftyish man with a white-haired crew cut and a three-day beard filling up a battered metal thermos from a glistening twenty-cup coffee pot.

"Dawson?" Koda asked, walking up to the lean, flight-suited figure, dropping his duffel bag, and extending his hand.

"Herby," the grizzled pilot nodded, returning the firm hand-shake. "Reckon you're Ben, so these three must be Charley, Bart and Sandy. That right?" he asked, quickly noting each affirmative nod. "Okay, good enough. Like to sit and gab with y'all for a spell, but Fogarty tells me you got a little problem with time, so why don't we get ourselves up in the air. Plenty of time to talk while I'm trying to figure out how to fly this thing."

He turned and headed out toward the helicopter pad, whistling cheerfully as he and an equipment-laden Shannon matched longleg-ged strides across the tarmac under the glaring flood lights.

Koda looked quickly at his watch, and then turned to Harrington and Mudd.

"You've got a little less than three hours to make your rendezvous with Fogarty. You'd better get going."

"I'll check us in at the Hotel Circle Ramada. Use that as a connection point," Harrington said.

"Fine," Koda nodded. Then he turned to Sandy Mudd, who had seemingly withdrawn back into her private shell after the departure of the gregarious Herby Dawson. She was staring down at the concrete floor with a distant, unfocused expression.

"You going to be okay?"

She looked up, startled, and then nodded, her eyes focusing into an unblinking look of self-evident determination as she stared back at Koda.

"Yeah, sure," she nodded, her voice distant and raspy.

"You throw up in that Toyota and we're gonna make you turn it back in yourself," Koda chided gently, watching for a telltale break in her expression.

"Next time I'll just upchuck in my purse," she shrugged.

"Okay, I'm convinced," Koda nodded, unable to keep from grinning momentarily, in spite of the impatient rage that was still churning within him. But his eyes were still cold and serious. "You two keep an eye on each other, *and don't get too close*," he added with pointed emphasis. "Understand?"

"Bart thinks he's going anywhere without me the next few hours, he can think again," Sandy said seriously.

"Back-to-back and low profile," Harrington agreed soberly. "We'll watch ourselves. Anybody finds out anything about Freddy, they can drop a dime on Sandy's phone recorder."

"Sounds good," Koda said. "We'll call in when we have something." He was turning to follow Dawson and Shannon out to the loudly whining helicopter when Harrington called out.

"Hey, Benji."

"Yeah?" Koda half-turned.

"You and Charley watch your asses out there too, okay?" Harrington looked more than a little embarrassed, but he didn't bother to conceal the worried expression on his wrinkled and suntanned face. "Been a long time since you two played games like this."

"I hear you, Mother Hen," Koda nodded in agreement, and then ran for the helipad as Dawson began to rev up the night-slashing rotor blades.

Koda had strapped himself into the front passenger seat, and was reaching for the headset as Dawson brought the Sikorsky up a few feet in the air, tail high, and then sent it dipping and gliding smoothly forward out over the tarmac. After making a quick, confirmatory check of the control functions, the pilot looked over at Koda and back at Shannon, received two thumbs-up signals, and then sent the helicopter churning skyward.

As soon as they leveled out at five hundred feet over the desert floor, Dawson used his foot pedal to switch over to his on-board communications system.

"Hear tell you two used to do a little jitterbugging in Slicks with the Air Cavalry few years back," Dawson said casually into his headset mike as he brought the Black Hawk around on an almost due southwest course heading.

"Dinh Tuong Province in the Delta," Koda acknowledged into his mike, watching distractedly as Dawson made quick radio-frequency adjustments on the helicopter's instrument-filled console. "Kinda brings back a lot of bad memories."

"Bet it does. Like maybe Night Raid Teams, Second Battalion,

Thirty-Ninth Infantry?" Dawson asked, his eyes reflexively scanning the night sky for aircraft warning lights as he monitored the sector radio traffic coming in over his ear phones.

"Fogarty feed you all that shit?"

"Said I shouldn't worry about you guys falling out a chopper door," Dawson shrugged. "Just so happens I spent about five years of my life in Dinh Tuong, couple weeks back in July of '69. Flew gunship support for the Slicks on night drops. Figure I mighta helped clear off a drop zone or two for you 'n Charley, one time or another. Crazy-ass world, ain't it?"

Koda grunted and nodded his head in agreement. "Fogarty brief you on our problem?"

"Said I'm supposed to put you over some bluffs at Torrey Pines, ASAP, look around a little bit, maybe drop you off, and then get my ass out of town pronto. Something about one of your people gettin' lost. Anybody I can't outfly asks questions, I'm just out flying charter for an environmental testing company, collecting night air samples." He chuckled and shook his head at the idea.

"It may get a little more complicated than that," Koda said, staring out into the darkness, trying to visualize the geography of the bluff area surrounding the entrance to Fat Man's Misery.

One thing that kept popping back in his mind about the deeply eroded sandstone gullies at Torrey Pines was his father's irritated suggestion that the high, crumbling coastal cliffs were one hell of a place for a couple of dumb thirteen-year-old kids to start learning about common sense. That and the fact that his father had roped them both off of the outcropping just before dusk, when there was still plenty of light, Koda remembered, wincing inwardly at the childhood memory. Moving around out there in the middle of the night was going to be interesting.

"Figured that might be the case," Dawson said. "Otherwise, you'd have probably just gone ahead and used one of the locals. You know, like the police, sheriff, customs, border patrol. Hear tell even the DEA's got a couple whirlybirds hanging around down there on the border." Dawson shrugged again, grinning to himself.

"Sounds like it might get a little crowded," Koda nodded non-committally.

"Might at that," Dawson acknowledged. "'Course we're not exactly gonna announce ourselves, are we? Which reminds me, you boys might want to put on a couple of those down flight jackets. Gonna get a little cold up here in a few minutes."

"Why's that?"

"Time factor," Dawson explained as his eyes continued to flick back and forth from the blackened sky to his green-glowing instrument panel. "Order to get you two out there quick, we're gonna have to go pretty much in a straight line. Trouble is, there's a couple of military installations and one hew-mongous ordnance testing range right smack dab in the way, which we're gonna have to avoid. Happen to know those people out there pretty well. They don't cotton much to unidentified aircraft playin' around in their air space."

"So why don't we just make a quick pass through? Shouldn't be much testing going on out there this time of night," Koda reasoned. "Besides, who's gonna want to drag their ass out of a warm bed just to tell us to go home?"

"Apache, most likely," Dawson suggested in a slow drawl.

"What?"

"Ain't talking 'bout the bows-and-arrows shit. This kinda injun'd take out a whole fuckin' wagon train in one pass, and then go out lookin' for some serious trouble."

Koda stared uncomprehendingly at the grinning pilot.

"Attack chopper, Ben," Dawson explained with cheerfully undisguised enthusiasm. "Huey Apache. One mean mother of a bird, let me tell you. Carries enough ordnance to take on half a battalion single-handed. Flies in the dark like a fuckin' bat. Makes my old Huey Cobra look like a little ol' pussycat," he sighed, shaking his head wistfully.

"And they got those things stationed out here?" Koda asked, realizing immediately it was a foolish question.

"Full squadron at a time," Dawson nodded. "Day and night exercises. Nothing them boys'd like better than to scramble on a juicy little bird like this Black Hawk, neither. Probably give us about half a minute to put down before somebody called dibs, and then opened up on us with his 30-millimeter. Just might be enough left of this here whirlybird to fill a good-sized trash can."

"So we're going to bypass your friends down there, right?"

"Yep. Like I was saying, you boys better get them jackets on. Best line-of-flight's gonna take us over a couple of good-sized mountain ranges. Little over six thousand feet. Just might get a little cold up there."

"Jesus," Koda said, starting to work himself into the jacket that Charley Shannon tossed forward. "Hope the hell Fogarty's making all this worth your while."

"Oh yeah, me and ol' Tom, we got a good thing goin' on these kinda deals," Dawson drawled happily as the powerful helicopter began to climb in the cold night air. "He don't hardly charge me much at all."

At 1:40 A.M., one hour and fourteen minutes after lift-off, the Sikorsky Black Hawk helicopter piloted by ex-Army Warrant Officer Herby Dawson passed directly over the illuminated bridge entrance to the Carlsbad Lagoon just below the coastal town of Oceanside, and then continued westward for about a half mile out over the Pacific Ocean. At the half-mile mark, Dawson turned due south. Then, in absolute violation of all peacetime aviation regulations, he cut off the helicopter's running lights and kept on going.

Five minutes later, less than a hundred yards off shore in almost total darkness, an eleven-thousand-pound, sixty-five-foot-long helicopter hovered gently—much like its fiercely patient namesake—over the black ocean swells, looking down at the high, crumbling wall of the bluffs at Torrey Pines State Reserve.

"Trail drops down to the right, starting just below that split boulder to the left of the trail sign. See where it disappears about twenty feet down?" Koda said, talking into his headset mike, while concentrating on the logistics of conducting a quick visual sweep of the area, when Dawson made his single, fast, and dangerous low-level pass across the face of the cliff.

"Got it," Dawson acknowledged.

There were a lot of things to be looking for when they went over, Koda reminded himself as he checked his seat harness and adjusted his goggles. First of all, Kaaren. Then the kid Bylighter, and maybe even Rainbow if they got lucky. Other traps set around the bait. Vehicles. Possibly even the police.

The only real advantage the men in the hovering helicopter possessed was the almost total darkness—now that thick clouds had drifted over the slivered moon—that temporarily concealed everything except the distinctive thumping sounds of the rotor blades. The darkness and the three pairs of night-vision goggles now being worn by Dawson, Koda and Shannon. Not to mention the infrared searchlight, mounted on the underside of the Sikorsky, that would throw a rapidly moving (and otherwise invisible) twenty-foot-wide-at-the-base cone of greenish light beneath the chopper. Illumination for the IR-sensitive goggles.

"You ready back there, Charley?" Dawson spoke into his mike, his practiced hands holding the huge, rumbling and vibrating war machine in a fixed position over the water, waiting.

Charley Shannon had slid open the side door of the Black Hawk and was sitting out on the edge of the doorway in camouflage battle fatigues, his upper face covered by the binocular night-vision goggles, his large combat-booted feet dangling out into open space, a quick-release safety line snapped onto a loop in his ammo harness, and a loaded pump-action twelve-gauge shotgun held secure and ready across his thighs.

"All set," Shannon growled into his mike.

"Ben?"

Ben Koda was dressed in identical camouflage clothing, except that instead of boots he wore a pair of tread-soled tennis shoes, and instead of the heavy combat harness and shotgun he carried a holstered .45 automatic shoulderstrapped under his left arm and a non-reflective sheath knife on his hip. A large medic's first-aid field pack was nestled tightly against his feet.

"Go to it," Koda said, his mind locked in on the problem. His eyes had already shifted to the first search point.

"Hang on, boys," Dawson grunted as he dove the Sikorsky in toward the distant bluffs.

The gut-wrenching combination of the massive helicopter's growing momentum, and the unpredictable nature of the strong up-drafts along the irregular cliff, seemed certain to smash the dual-turbo-engined assault aircraft against the jutting chunks of sandstone. It was only the power and maneuverability of the carefully designed machine, Dawson's practiced skills, and his unwavering concentration that kept the three men from instant death as they swept down and across the cliff face.

"Two cars at the top, one close to the road." Koda's voice over the radio, distant and distracted.

"Two men, possibly three. Three o'clock. In the rocks." Shannon, expressing pure, predatory anticipation.

"Shit." Dawson . . . his hands reflexively yanking the Black Hawk away from a suddenly visible outcropping before his conscious mind had a chance to consider and comment on the problem in detail.

"Body! Tide level," Koda yelled into his mike. "Herby, bring her around, wide turn, over the water in front of the face . . . low!"

"Copy." Dawson flared the rotor blades and swung the vibrating chopper around in a smooth, pirouetting turn, sending the Sikorsky back down across the rocky cliff face, this time about twenty yards out from the shoreline, and less than six feet above the surging black saltwater.

Koda had already snapped open his seat harness, and was bracing himself at the opened back doorway next to Shannon. He held on tightly to the safety handle at the door, brought the headset mike up to his mouth, and then turned to look at Dawson's back.

"Herby, I'm going out on Charley's 'now.' Soon as I'm out, put him down in the parking lot, fast as you can, and then get the hell out of here. Charley, you copy?"

Koda waited until both Dawson and Shannon gave a thumbs-up signal. Then he threw down the headset, pulled off the night-vision goggles, grabbed hold of the medic's pack, and crouched down at the doorway.

Two seconds later, Shannon yelled "NOW!" into his headset, slapped Koda's leg, and then held on as Dawson swung the rear rotor blade of the helicopter back and away, watching alertly as his partner threw himself out the door in a tuck position, and then plowed almost instantly into the dark water with a huge, billowing splash.

Stunned by the body-shock of the impact and the rapidly numbing cold, Koda allowed himself to remain suspended underwater for a moment while he regained his sense of direction. Then he began to thrash his way to the surface of the black, swirling saltwater one-handed, fighting as he did so to keep the medic's kit from being torn out of his grasp by the powerful underlying crosscurrents. His head cleared the surface, and he quickly exhaled and sucked in a welcome breath. But before he had a chance to clear the stinging water out of his eyes and mouth and catch his breath, he felt his lower body being caught up in a swift shoreward swell.

Accustomed to the unpredictable actions of the coastal waters, and relieved that he hadn't dropped into one of the common—and equally powerful—riptide currents that would have swiftly drawn him away from shore, Koda relaxed, allowing himself to be carried along by the shoreward-driving wave-swell, grateful for the opportunity to recover and prepare for the dangerous trip in through the rocky surf line.

Then, suddenly, the no-longer-distant noise of the crashing waves rapidly grew in volume, and Koda realized that the chilling dark water had started to surge up against something ahead . . . a rock?

Fighting against the impelling force of the swelling wave, Koda twisted to face the shore with both legs forward, ready . . . and then quickly jammed the medic's pack out in front of his face—an instinctively protective move—as his feet jarred against and then slipped off the slick, irregular, seaweed-and-mussel-covered surface of a huge rock mass.

The heavy, water-soaked first-aid kit absorbed most of the impact as the irresistible momentum of the wave thrust Koda into and then over the erosion-smoothed top of the submerged rock. Hurt, stunned and gasping from the glancing blow against his ribcage, he was powerless to keep the pack from being ripped out of his hands. It was all he could do to shield his face with his bruised and torn arms, and to keep air in his lungs as he was propelled by the uncaring ocean into rock after rock, his hands and feet scrambling futilely for a solid hold or footing.

Then the wave crested.

Before Koda could react, he was falling out of the wave. Helpless to do anything other than protect his head, he slammed down through twenty-or-so inches of foaming water into the top of a quasi-solid sandbar built up between two rocks, absorbing the impact on his shoulder as he tucked his head at the last second and rolled. For several long seconds, he tumbled through the churning, deep-water surge created by the endless line of oncoming waves crashing through the rocks, the sand and saltwater penetrating deep into his eyes, ears, nose and mouth. Then one tennis shoe briefly struck bottom, and he realized the frenzied, beach-seeking water was now only neck-deep.

Driven by a determination built on hours of smoldering rage, Koda clawed at the passing rocks with his bleeding hands—fighting for a handhold while trying to protect his battered head—until his rubber-soled shoes could finally dig in against wave-packed sand.

Seconds later, he used the last of his energy to pull himself out of the breakers and up through more slippery rocks onto a wet and cold solid rock ledge.

It took almost a full minute before Ben was able to crawl the twenty-or-so yards across the seaweed-covered flat rocky surface to the spot below a huge wet boulder—wedged firmly into the base of the single upward-leading pathway—where the dark, still, and almost invisible form of Kaaren Mueller lay naked and cold.

Koda could barely make out the features of Kaaren's face in the starlit darkness. And it wasn't until he fumbled for her wrist, to try for a pulse anyway, that he understood the enormity of the death she had suffered.

Both her wrists had been cut, as had both the Achilles tendons above her ankles. Unable to stand, or walk, or climb, Kaaren Mueller had apparently tried to crawl back up Fat Man's Misery on her knees and elbows (Koda could feel with his own bleeding fingers where the toughened skin had torn away) and had come face-to-face with an impossible obstacle as her life slowly drained out across the bleakly cold rock ledge.

The words that Ben whispered might have been human in origin, but the malignant violence lurking beneath the words was something else entirely.

He was still kneeling at Kaaren's side, no longer aware of the nearly paralyzing cold and the agonizing pains that were rapidly sapping away what little strength remained in his battered muscles, when he heard the distant, gritty sound of a boot scraping against a sandy rock above the rhythmic crashing of the surf.

Koda's head came up quickly, and then moved very slowly back and forth as he listened intently, trying to focus in on the most probable location of the sound as he waited for another . . . .

There.

This time it was a clacking noise, like small rocks being knocked against each other. The distracting sounds of the crashing waves, loud and irregular, made it difficult to pinpoint the location. Somewhere above, certainly. To the right?

Another soft, scraping sound, more easily isolated from the ocean sounds now that Koda was alert and waiting. Definitely to the right this time. Maybe twenty or thirty feet up?

Koda's right hand had wrapped around the cold, sand-encrusted grip of the .45 automatic that had amazingly survived the trip to shore. He started to pull the heavy pistol out of the gritty, saltwater-soaked leather holster, even though he knew the handgun would probably jam after the first shot. Then his mind flashed an image of the deep, smooth-edged cuts that had been cruelly inflicted on Kaaren Mueller's wrists and ankles, still sticky-wet beneath his probing fingers in the darkness . . . as though they'd been made with an old-fashioned straight razor.

Something in Ben Koda's mind—a self-protecting inner awareness that had long understood and defended the necessity of civilized behavior—stepped aside. The primeval entity that instantly took its place had no interest in modern, jammable, quick-killing firearms. It demanded something more primitive. Something more sensory. Something on the order of bared teeth . . .

. . . or a sharply clawed hand.

Koda's torn right hand resecured the pistol in his shoulder holster, dropped down to his hip, flicked loose a snap, and then came back up with a groove-handled killing knife, the blackened blade of the familiar weapon held out flat with its deadly cutting edge to the inside.

Ben Koda shook his head and blinked. Then, no longer hindered by the cold or the pain, he levered himself up and over the wedged boulder, landing softly in a semicrouched position on the other side, the knife held out, low and ready, for a sudden upward thrust.

Koda's mouth was half opened, exposing his white teeth in an invisible snarl that allowed him to breathe silently, as he slowly began to move forward and upward along the narrow trail, his eyes and ears probing ahead for another sound. Any sound. Any indication of movement or location.

Step by step, Koda's tennis-shoed feet slid quietly across the steep, rock-strewn pathway, the scraped and cut fingers of his free hand brushing gently against the high, confining dirt walls to guide his movements and anticipate the sudden turns.

Click-click-click.

The sudden noise, unexpectedly loud and sharp in the ocean-saturated darkness, jarred against Koda's highly sensitized ears, setting off a warning alarm in his memory. He jerked away instinctively, jamming his exposed back tightly against the irregular sandstone wall, knife-arm held in tightly against his stomach, muscles poised wire-tight as the civilized portion of his mind wrenched back control.

Click-click-click.

Again. Above and to the left. Louder. Much closer than the scuffling sounds. Electronic?

Then he had it, and the night darkness—once an ally—suddenly became darker, and more threatening.

Radio clicks.

The recon signals the night teams had used in the jungles of the Delta when it was too dangerous to use voice communications over the radios. Just trigger the mike key. One click: stop. Two clicks: go. Three clicks: pull back. Repeat to acknowledge.

Shit.

Koda hesitated, held back by sudden indecision, the numbing vision of a SWAT team set up over Kaaren's body momentarily blanking out the cold, demanding hatred that still flowed through his mind. Charley had been dropped up on top in the parking lot. No shots fired . . .

A rapid scuffling sound—high and to the left, lasting less than four seconds—grated against Koda's ears.

No shouting.

No shots fired.

Three clicks, repeated.

Another rapid movement—this time lateral, across the face of the cliff—galvanized Koda into action.

His fingers guided the way. Touch the rocks and then move—quickly and quietly.

Touch, move. Touch, move. Stop, listen. Repeat. Keep moving.

Whoever they were, they weren't cops.

Touch, move. Touch, move. Stop, listen.

Couldn't be cops.

Touch, move.

Charley'd be screaming his head off by now, loudly demanding his civil rights. . . .

Stop, listen.

Scuffling sounds, moving faster . . . farther away. Bastards!

Touch, move, move.

. . . demanding a lawyer. No way they'd ever take Charley down without making one hell of a racket in the process. And cops wouldn't care about making noise either. Searchlights, helicopters and outside-speakers'd be more like it.

Couldn't be cops.

Touch, move, move.

Koda grunted involuntarily from the exertion and the repressed pain as he forced his agonized muscles to keep climbing the thirty- and forty-degree slopes within the narrow, winding passageway, his ears straining to listen ahead over the muted sounds of the ocean, and the louder sounds of his laboring lungs. A small part of his mind—his awareness—was concentrating on keeping the knife in-tight, ready, in case the hidden figure moving up ahead suddenly turned back. Or in case . . .

Koda's guide-hand brushed against the top of the gulley, warning him that he was coming up on the upper ledge. At the same time, long-forgotten instincts were screaming at him to *stop* and *listen*. Moving too fast. Breathing too hard . . .

Bastard cut her wrists and ankles. Left her to bleed to death down there in the dark. Now he's trying to pull out. Trying to get away before . . .

The soft scrape of a boot against powdered sandstone reached Koda's ears just as a hand slammed hard across his mouth, a second hand closed tightly around the wrist of his knife-hand, and a sudden, heavy impact sent him sprawling face-forward into the now-shallow gulley.

Koda was twisting under the suffocating weight even as his chest struck the solidly packed dirt. He was struggling to use his free hand to lever himself out from under the suffocating weight, to free his knife-hand, trying to ignore the screaming protests of his lungs that there wasn't any more air, when a familiar voice growled sharply in his ear.

"Stay down."

Obediently, Ben stayed face-down in the gulley for a good six or seven seconds, painfully willing his diaphragm to draw oxygen into his still-complaining lungs. Then, when he was finally able to breathe evenly again, he slowly crawled forward to lie prone next the dark figure.

"Take a look," Charley whispered, handing the night vision goggles over to his exhausted partner.

"Jesus Christ," Koda whispered, watching the three dark figures zigzag across the top of the bluff, methodically working their way back to the two cars in the parking lot. All three figures were moving in practiced sequence: two providing cover while one jumped up into a short zigzag run, and then dropped down again to provide cover for the next runner.

Koda had his knife back in its sheath and was reaching for the holstered .45 when Shannon dropped a heavy restraining hand on his shoulder.

"Don't even think about it," Shannon shook his head. "Those boys're carrying them shit-firin' Uzis. Packin' a lotta ammo, too. No way we're gonna put 'em down with the firepower we got. Need a couple .223 and a grenade-chucker, minimum. Ah could'a dropped one of them with the scatter-gun," Shannon went on conversationally, relaxing his grip when he felt his partner's shoulder muscles reluctantly sag in acknowledgment. "Maybe two, if Ah got real lucky. After that, like as not, you'd a' been awful lonely out here. Didn't think much of that idea, knowin' how shit-ass crazy you'd get, wandering around all by yourself in the dark. Probably start thinkin' you could take 'em all on, single-handed." Shannon slapped Koda's shoulder affectionately before removing his hand.

"Yeah, appreciate that," Koda rasped tiredly, watching in exhausted frustration as the zigzagging figures—a Jimmy Pilgrim's professional, three-man dope guarding team—finally piled into one of the two waiting cars, both vehicles then speeding out of the parking lot without bothering to turn on their headlights. "You get a look at Kaaren?"

"Spotted her with Herby's glasses when we came around. Couldn't see much. Looked like she mighta got cut on," Shannon grunted with an apparent lack of emotion.

"Tendons—wrists and heels. Looked like she tried to crawl out. Couldn't get over the rock."

"Yeah?" Charley was quiet for a few seconds. "Well," he finally growled, standing up and helping Koda to his feet, "maybe it's a good thing we didn't try to do the deed on them three boys after all."

"Yeah, why's that?"

"Got a pretty good look at 'em, one at a time," Shannon said, reaching down and picking up the shotgun. "Boots, tight jeans, dark sweaters, watch caps, ammo pouches, Uzis, and stubby-barreled revolvers. No jackets. Didn't see no knives no-where."

"Doesn't mean anything," Koda muttered, starting to shiver from the cold offshore wind against his saltwater-soaked clothes and his physically abused body. "Could've used a folding knife, razor, something like that."

He and Shannon began walking quickly away from the ledge of the bluffs toward the parking lot, uncomfortably aware as they did so that the moon was beginning to drift out of the clouds, streaking the bluffs with faint, eerie shadows.

"Yeah, Ah know," Shannon growled, reaching into one of the large leg-pockets on his combat fatigues, and pulling out a small pack-set radio. "All kinds a' possibilities. But Ah jes' can't help rememberin' what Fogarty told us 'bout that motherfucker Rainbow. Hate like hell to use up mah chances takin' apart the wrong people. Figure Sanjo and Kaaren earned a better deal'n that."

"Yeah, they sure as hell did," Koda nodded, his eyes blinking from exhaustion. "You planning on calling us a taxi with that thing?"

"Finest kind," Shannon nodded. "Ol' Herby said he wasn't leaving till he got a confirmed wave-off from me. Didn't give a shit *what* you and Fogarty said." Shannon motioned toward the edge of the cliffs with the radio. "Probably hanging around out there right now, playin' with himself an' wishin' he had one a' them goddamned Apaches to play with instead."

"I may steal him one before this thing's over," Koda said. "You happen to get license numbers on those cars before you started worrying about my mental health?"

"Sure."

"Then go ahead and call him in," Koda said, the exhaustion now evident in his voice as he squatted down on the asphalt surface of the parking lot. "Don't feel much up to walking any more right now. Besides, we've gotta get a few things settled before it gets light— before people start wandering around down there and find Kaaren."

8

BASKING IN THE dominating influence of Lafayette Beaumont Raynee's singlemindedly erotic imagination in that early morning hour just before sunrise, the light brown feminine body that so closely matched Raynee's idealized concept of sensual perfection grew steadily warmer beneath the firm, steady strokes of the street dealer's rigorously disciplined hands.

The key was patience.

And like any artist who worked at the cutting edge of his physical senses, Lafayette Beaumont Raynee possessed almost infinite patience. Thus, he willingly allocated several minutes to the task of caressing the rounded contours of the extended lower right leg resting seductively on the white silk sheet; his fingers probing with persistent gentleness for any sign of imperfection as the responsive surface absorbed and then radiated the heat generated by his sinewy hands.

It was only when Raynee was finally satisfied—basing his judgment on tactile response alone—that he allowed his sensitized fingers to slide up and over the hard, protruding kneecap, and finally drift out onto the long, firmly smooth expanse of milk-chocolate thigh. . . .

The shrill, jarring ring from the telephone at the edge of the bed broke sharply across the sensual flow of Raynee's meditative awareness, yet the depth of his concentration was such that he willingly tolerated the hammering of the bell five times before reluctantly reaching for the intruding phone.

"Yes?" Raynee's voice was calm, quiet, and dangerously emotionless. He maintained his control because he knew who was calling. Only Jimmy Pilgrim—the one man who had ever managed to intimidate the savagely malevolent Rainbow—possessed the secondary call-numbers needed to access this particular phone.

"I understand our demonstration went well," Pilgrim stated without preamble. "Have you had any response?"

"Nope, nothin' at all. 'Specially nothin' from the General. Maybe the man knows more 'bout tactics 'n we think," Raynee suggested thoughtfully.

"There's nothing in his record to indicate any military talent," Pilgrim responded, his voice cold and impassive. "He was a moderately competent, paper-shuffling bureaucrat. Nothing more."

"Then Ah'd say we'd better keep a real close eye on Locotta," Raynee said. "Little early to be burning our main bridge jes' yet."

"Agreed," the flat, emotionless voice rasped through the earpiece of the phone. "But concentrate on our primary suspect. Probe him. We must be certain of his interests before we move. Absolutely certain," Pilgrim reemphasized pointedly. "We haven't much time left, regardless."

"You got it."

"The first analog," Pilgrim went on, expecting nothing less than complete and dependable obedience from his streetwise assistant. "The thiopene. Have you made any further evaluations?"

"Goin' by how that littl' redheaded Kaaren lady reacted, Ah'd say our professor really knows his shit," Raynee said. "Never seen nothin' this side a' white smack hit that fast an' hard. 'Specially not usin' no needle. Girl had maybe thirty seconds after drinkin' jes' a' littl' bit a' that shit 'fore she legged over t' that john, upchuckin' like she'd done some righteous buttons."

"Peyote?" Pilgrim understood Rainbow's street jargon. He wanted clear confirmation.

"Right on," Rainbow nodded. "Made me think our professor jes' might be tryin' to bo-jive his partners, mixin' a little *mes-ca-leen* in his powder. Know what Ah'm sayin'? Thing is, though, that lady, she didn't hardly stay down long 'nough for righteous button juice. Popped up an' damn near offed that shitassed Squeek 'fore we put her down again."

"How long?" Pilgrim demanded. "Straight talk."

"Maybe an hour," Raynee said, shifting and meshing mental gears with indifferent smoothness. "Hour'n half, outside."

"Perhaps a matter of dosage?"

"First thing Ah'm gonna check out," Raynee nodded agreeably. Bylighter might'a given her a low dose, holding back some for himself."

"Check it out, immediately," Pilgrim ordered. "If he played games with the thiopene, then the test results on the other analog may also be suspect."

"Say what?" Raynee blurted out, genuinely startled by this sudden, incomprehensible bit of new information.

"I said check out *both* analogs . . ." Pilgrim started to repeat, his voice dropping dangerously low, when Raynee interrupted.

"Yeah, that's what Ah'm sayin'. What two analogs? Far as Ah know, the powder Squeek laid on the girl's the only powder the man shipped us."

"Isaac says he sent a second test sample along with the thiopene. Something different. Supposed to have been marked A-seventeen," Pilgrim growled. "He wants test data on both samples as soon as possible so that he can proceed with the series. Are you telling me—?"

"Ah don't know *what* Ah'm telling you, man," Lafayette Beaumont Raynee whispered, his voice suddenly turning as cold and lifeless as that of Pilgrim. "'Ceptin' Ah never heard *nothin'* 'bout no *two* analogs from that boy. But Ah'll tell you what, Ah'm gonna find out 'bout them things, *real quick like.*"

"Do that. I want some answers this evening," Pilgrim rasped. The sound of the distant phone being slammed down into its receiver echoed in Raynee's ear.

Raynee sat on his bed for a few moments in silent contemplation, his face slowly contorting through the progressive stages of cold rage. Then he yelled out through the open doorway of his expansive bedroom.

"ROY, GET YOUR HONKY ASS UP HERE!"

The light-footed sound of tennis shoes coming up the stairway was immediately followed by the sight of the lanky Roy Schultzheimer filling the doorway.

"Squeek," Raynee whispered, his eyes glittering crazily as he stared into the pale blue eyes of his viciously protective assistant. "Ah wanna talk t' that little son of a bitch. *Right now.*"

Eugene Bylighter didn't respond to the early morning pounding on his door. Instead, he remained prone, nude and face up on the ancient foldaway bed. Partially because he was semidrugged and half-asleep. But mostly because he knew what would happen if he moved his skinny, wide-spread legs any closer together. He *knew* that the pain receptors lying horribly vulnerable beneath his massively bruised inner thighs—not to mention the unimaginably sensitive nerve endings trapped within the grotesquely swollen tissues of his triple-sized blue-purple gonads—would never tolerate sudden movement of any sort.

As it was, Bylighter had less than five seconds to consider the possible reasons for the ominous pounding on his door before the cheap drugstore lock gave way under the impact of Roy Schultzheimer's foot with a loud crash.

"Whaa—?"

Eugene Bylighter's slurred question was terminated in mid-breath, and replaced instantly with a short-lived scream as Lafayette Beaumont Raynee's veined, black hand closed tightly around his throat, and then yanked him into an upright but still spread-legged position. The scream was short-lived only because Bylighter fainted at that horrible instant when his baseball-sized gonads were pressed into tight contact with each other against the rough mattress.

"Jesus, that poor son of a bitch," Roy Schultzheimer whispered.

"I want this place taken apart," Raynee said, opening his hand and allowing the now limp and unfeeling Bylighter to flop back onto his mattress. "I'll take the bedroom. You start in the kitchen. *I want that powder,*" he growled as the ever-obedient Schultzheimer began to search the kitchen with practiced and energetic efficiency.

It was simply a matter of logic and experience, rather than any concern about the welfare of Bylighter, that caused Raynee to begin his search by taking apart the bedroom dresser instead of his bed. Thus Bylighter was still, unknowingly, at least thirty seconds away from being dumped off of his soon-to-be shredded mattress when Raynee's ransacking bodyguard opened an empty ice cream container in the rusted kitchen refrigerator, and discovered the two vials.

"Got 'em," Schultzheimer called out. He hurried back into the bedroom, the vials held out victoriously in one hand.

Raynee examined the vials, noting that the "THIOPENE" vial

was empty, and that the one labeled "A-17" was slightly less than half-filled with a tannish-white powder. Then he nodded his head toward the sprawled form of Bylighter and spoke one word.

"Water."

The panful of cold water jarred Bylighter back into a hazy awareness of reality—which consisted of a blurry black image of Rainbow's fearsome eyes glaring down into his own, and the sensation of having his head yanked up by a hand wrapped around his long dirty hair.

"This what you gave that girl?" Raynee spat the words directly into Bylighter's face as he held the empty vial marked "THIOPENE" inches away from the youth's glazed and half-open eyes.

Bylighter tried to nod his head. "Yesss," he whispered faintly.

"You gave her this one? Mixed it in her coke like Ah told you to? That what you're saying?" Raynee demanded, jamming the vial between Bylighter's glassy eyes.

Another weakly attempted nod and whispered assent, as Bylighter tried to focus on what he wanted to tell Rainbow, wanted to tell him so badly . . .

"Then what about this other one? You didn't tell me 'bout the other one—this A-seventeen shit—did you, you little son of a bitch!" Raynee snarled, his fierce, glaring eyes still viciously insistent as he held up the second vial in front of Bylighter's pale, splotchy face.

. . . because he wanted to tell Rainbow everything. *Had* to tell Rainbow everything this time, Bylighter told himself, trying to focus his thoughts at the same time that he was trying to understand what it was that seemed to hurt so much down there, because . . .

"Goddamn it, listen t' me, you little shit-head! Ah wanna *know*, you test this A-seventeen out on anybody?" Raynee demanded, his teeth bared viciously as he flung Bylighter's head back down against the mattress. Then he watched in helpless fury as Bylighter's eyes rolled up and back into his head, completely unaware that Squeek—his fearfully loyal gofer—had been trying to tell him something that was terribly, terribly important.

At ten-fifteen that Sunday morning, San Diego Police criminalist Paul Reinhart received the call that he'd been half-expecting ever since he'd decided to surprise his wife by installing the new bathroom and kitchen sinks while she was out shopping with her sisters.

Reinhart had known that it was a gamble from the start, but he figured the odds were on his side. Most homicide scene call-outs seemed to occur on Friday and Saturday nights between eleven at night and three in the morning. By nine o'clock on a Sunday morning, Reinhart figured, any residual carnage from the previous evening ought to have been discovered and reported. So at nine-fifteen he crossed his fingers, turned off the main water valve to the house, and began dismantling water pipes in the kitchen.

He was just lifting the sink out of the back bathroom cabinet when the phone rang.

The dispatcher explained that the surfers would have probably found her a lot earlier, but the waves had been real low this morning. Not worth going out and getting cold, so everybody had stayed in their cars till it warmed up. Then the kids had to haul their boards back to the top of the cliffs before they called the station. Yeah, soon as possible. Sorry.

Reinhart allowed himself the luxury of closing his eyes, shaking his head and sighing. Then he hurriedly put crude "DO NOT TURN ON WATER!" signs on every faucet and toilet in the house, washed his hands, locked the doors, and ran to his truck . . . telling himself at that moment that it was a good thing his wife was used to surprises.

As Jake Locotta watched from his shaded poolside lounge chair on the spacious brickwork patio of his Palm Springs home, the girl in the thin, tightly stretched, blue-violet swim outfit—the suit that matched her eyes perfectly—stood poised on the diving board for a few enticing moments before she suddenly sprang up, twisted with athletic precision in midair, and then plunged down with barely a splash through the glistening surface of the transparent blue water.

Locotta raised his glass of iced vodka in approval as the girl's blond head popped to the surface, enjoying a moment of anticipatory pleasure as the girl pushed her sun-reflecting, water-soaked hair out of her eyes and then smiled playfully in his direction—displaying sets of closely matched dimples and straight white teeth—before stroking smoothly over to the side of the pool.

As both men watched in silent appreciation, the girl levered herself up out of the pool, and then slowly strolled past their two lounge chairs. Dripping wet, the blue-violet swim suit seemed—if possible—to have become nearly transparent and even more taut against the well-toned muscles and smooth curves of the girl's sensuous body. The resulting exhibition was at once graceful, aesthetic, and unquestionably erotic. As intended.

"So, whaddaya think, Rosey?" Locotta chuckled, sipping sparingly at his cold vodka as his piercing eyes tracked the fluid movements of the stretching fabric until the girl disappeared around the wooden barrier entrance to the showers.

"Feel like I'm at a thousand-dollar peep show," the elderly accountant cracked. "Good thing I forgot what I'm supposed to do with that stuff," he went on in his raspy voice, starting to pick at his Sunday morning fruit-and-cottage cheese brunch. "Damn near need oxygen just to look."

"I'll have Joe set you up a bed, built-in oxygen tent," Locotta promised, winking cheerfully at his longtime associate. "Give you your own controls and everything, so you can boost the flow."

"I'd settle for a little peace of mind about now," Rosenthal commented drily.

"Oh yeah, so what's the problem?" Locotta asked, his husky voice turning noticeably serious. He didn't like hearing about trouble in his territory.

"Jimmy Pilgrim. I'm hearing stories I don't like coming out of the San Diego area."

"Tell me about it," Locotta growled.

"Guy got blown up in an apartment last night, down in Chula Vista. Place was rented by some broad. Tall, pretty, redhead."

"Yeah, so?"

"Girl matching that description was found on the rocks below Torrey Pines this morning. Wrists and ankles cut. Street talk has it the bomb was tied to our dope action."

"The cops put it together?"

"Probably not yet," Rosenthal shook his head. "Police investigators are out at Torrey Pines right now. Sheriff's deputies're working the body in the apartment. Figure it's a little early for the cops to start matching puzzle pieces outside their jurisdiction. Nothing to tie the girl back to the apartment yet, far as any of our people know. She's still listed as a Jane Doe. 'Course, we're not planning on giving them any help."

"Shit," Locotta rasped, his eyes narrowing as he considered the possibilities. "They know better."

"No guarantee Pilgrim or Rainbow are involved," Rosenthal reminded his boss.

"What kind of cuts?" Locotta asked, ignoring his elderly adviser's admonition.

"Thin and deep. Probably razor," Rosenthal acknowledged. "Still . . ."

"We don't need this, Rosey," Locotta muttered unnecessarily as his longtime adviser nodded in understanding.

Al Rosenthal knew full well why a successful narcotics-dealing operation like theirs depended so heavily upon public indifference, if not acceptance. Dope-dealing was something that could be easily overlooked by citizens caught up in their own tangled web of social and economic problems, but the uncontrolled, violent acts of a man like Lafayette Beaumont Raynee—the mind-crazed Rainbow—were something else entirely.

Locotta and Rosenthal both knew that public sentiment wasn't about to overlook a rampaging black, dope-dealing pimp with a taste for straightedged razors—especially not in deep-down conservative San Diego County—regardless of any "laid-back" and "socially-aware," Southern California images to the contrary. There would be a public outcry, letters to editors, pressure put on otherwise complacent politicians and bureaucrats to do something, and do it quickly. They didn't need that.

Jake Locotta's eyes were concealed by his dark sunglasses, but his fingers drummed a slow, menacing beat on the table top.

"Rosey, I want you to to check this thing out personally. Get me the full line."

"I'm already on it, Jake."

"Yeah, figured you would be," Locotta nodded approvingly before continuing. "You contact Pilgrim. Let him know that I'm concerned. *Very* concerned."

"I think he'll know that already," Rosenthal rasped.

"Yeah, but make sure he understands. It's very important that the crazy son of a bitch understands," Locotta snarled, thoroughly irritated that business concerns were preventing him from fully savoring the warm Palm Springs sun. This vacation had been a long time coming, a well-earned reward for all of the effort he'd put into reorganizing his newly consolidated territory. Unless things got out of control, Jake Locotta had no intention of allowing Jimmy Pilgrim or any one else to screw it up.

"Don't worry about it, Jake," Rosenthal whispered as he got up out of the shaded lounge chair. "I'll talk to Pilgrim. You take it easy. Get some sun. A nice dinner. This is supposed to be a vacation, remember?"

"You talk to Pilgrim, Rosey," Locotta nodded agreeably as he blinked his eyes open and then stood up in his bare feet on the cool brick patio. "And I'll get some sun and maybe even a nice dinner. But you know what," he said, turning his head in the direction of the wood barrier at the far end of the pool and smiling pleasantly, "first I think I'm gonna take myself a nice long shower."

Theresa Sanchez, a tragically aged and otherwise burned-out fifteen-year-old runaway, who continued to support her once-valued freedom by turning lethargic twenty-dollar tricks under the watchful supervision of one of Rainbow's seven assistant pimps, was selected pretty much at random to be Jimmy Pilgrim's first guinea pig.

Although in reality it was less a matter of random chance, and more a consequence of her ready availability, that brought the emaciated street girl to Raynee's attention on this particular Sunday morning.

Theresa Sanchez had once been beautiful, childlike and innocent, but that had been almost a lifetime ago. Now, ten months later, the mere thought of trying to book the services of the sadly aged child-whore weeks in advance was enough to bring tears of derisive laughter to the eyes of her callously indifferent pimp.

As it was, her utter lifelessness had already forced Raynee's ever-practical assistant to drop Theresa's basic price by sixty percent over the past month. And even then, it wasn't easy to find customers willing to overlook the depressing aspects of the transaction in order to enjoy a few inexpensive minutes of dubious pleasure.

Theresa was perched on a high bar chair in the center of a mostly darkened back room in the "C" Street Bar, looking slightly dazed, vaguely confused, and mostly indifferent, when her street-weary eyes focused on the all-too-familiar dark face of Lafayette Beaumont Raynee.

Rainbow.

"Hi, 'Bo," she whispered hoarsely, a flicker of something resembling vague interest—mixed with uncertain wariness—crossing her face. Theresa Sanchez had grown increasingly indifferent to occupationally suffered pain during the last ten months of her life, but, like every one else who worked the streets and bars in San Diego, she knew better than to mess with Rainbow.

Raynee ignored the girl's pathetic attempt at a friendly greeting as he walked up to the bar stool, grabbed her stringy black hair in his two muscular hands, and turned her face in the direction of the single, glary light bulb overhead.

"You on somethin', girl?" he growled.

"No . . . no way, man," Theresa Sanchez shook her head quickly, her eyes reflecting an instinctive rejection of anything even vaguely related to the truth. "Honest, 'Bo, I—"

The girl's head recoiled sharply as the violent impact of Raynee's open-handed blow sent her tumbling out of the chair, landing with a heavy thump on the linoleum floor.

"Get your ass back up on that chair, girl," Raynee ordered in a soft, whispery voice.

Wordlessly, she slowly crawled to her feet and then painfully climbed back up onto the chair, her eyes fixed on her tightly clenched hands that had begun to tremble.

"Look at me." The whispered voice was soft and raspy.

Her eyes came up slowly, fearful now, to look helplessly into the cold, black, terrifying eyes.

"What you be on, girl?" Raynee spoke the words slowly, holding the girl's trembling chin gently in one hand.

"Grass," she whispered shakily.

"That all?"

"Yes." Very quietly.

"When?"

"This morning." The words barely were audible now. "Couple hours ago."

"Good stuff?"

The girl shook her head silently, her wide, tearless eyes expressing every bit of the hopelessness of her life as her trembling hands pulled a thin, crumpled number out of her grease-stained jeans and hesitatingly offered it to Raynee. He tore the handrolled cigarette apart in one hand, quickly noting the contents. Mostly stems and seeds. Absolute shit. He tossed the torn cigarette aside contemptuously and turned back to the cowering Sanchez.

"You sure that's all? Nothin' else?"

The girl started to nod, and then shook her head, staring down at her hands again, as much out of embarrassment now as fear.

"You want somethin'?"

The empty brown eyes came quickly up to Raynee's chilling face, expecting to find an expression of sadistically teasing amusement, but searching anyway. Just in case . . .

"Speak up, girl," Raynee growled. "You want something to make you feel good, or not?"

"Yes . . ." she whispered, almost inaudibly, a long-repressed tear starting to form in one street-deadened eye, ". . . please."

Raynee turned to Roy Schultzheimer and the young pimp behind him, who stood waiting in the shadows by the closed door. "Give her one a' them quarter papers."

"What is—?" the youthful pimp started to ask, and then shut

up and quickly busied himself with helping Schultzheimer assemble
the unusually clean "kit" that the pale-eyed bodyguard removed from
his gym bag.

The sharp, hypodermic needle slid smoothly through the
scarred epidermal layer of the girl's inner left arm, and into a thin vein
far more accustomed to shared, blunt-edged and dirty "spikes."
Theresa Sanchez, Raynee, and his assistant, all watched from varying
points of interest as Schultzheimer slowly injected the slightly cloudy
liquid: Schultzheimer concentrating on keeping steady pressure on
the plastic plunger, the youthful assistant enthralled by the band-
wrapped pile of folded paper bindles lying next to Schultzheimer's
sinewy arm, each marked with the notation "A-17," Theresa watching
the cloudy liquid disappear slowly into her distended vein, and
Raynee simply staring into the irises of the girl's deadened eyes.

Schultzheimer released the rubber-tube tourniquet. For almost thirty seconds, the darkened room was filled with eerie silence.

"Feel anythin', girl?" Raynee rasped.

"Little," Theresa whispered. "Nothing much."

Another thirty seconds of silence.

"Now?" Raynee asked, still watching her eyes.

"Yeah, a little bit," she nodded quietly, still staring down at her
arm. Then she looked up at Raynee with eyes that were little more
than deep wells of pain. "Please . . . can I have some more?"

At the northwest corner of Palm and Hawthorne Streets in
downtown El Cajon, a densely populated valley community about ten
miles east of San Diego, Lafayette Beaumont Raynee delivered ten
thick, handrolled cigarettes—each bearing a distinctly inked
number—to a skinny, eighteen-year-old high school dealer named
Alex . . . along with some very specific instructions.

Forty-five minutes later, ten adventuresome high school students who normally purchased a lid of high-grade marijuana from Alex
every Sunday morning were huddled around a coffee table in a run-
down apartment, all impatiently waiting for their chance to try out one
of the new blends of happy weed. Ten varieties. Just in from the Is-
lands. A consumer-testing program, absolutely free, because they
were such good, dependable customers.

He didn't bother to mention that they were also dependably
stupid.

Alex handed out the cigarettes, one at a time, inked a matching
number on the right hand of each test subject, carefully recorded

names and numbers in a small notebook, and then tossed around small boxes of matches.

Alex had been specifically instructed to observe and take notes. He hadn't been informed that the even-numbered joints contained equal amounts of a moderately potent brand of Hawaiian-grown marijuana. He simply recorded the fact that test subjects #2, #4, #6, #8, and #10 all appeared to be mildly stoned, although each youth continued to describe his state of euphoria in greatly varying terms. Like "glassy" . . . and "ripped" . . . and "fucked-up."

Alex also had no idea that the odd-numbered cigarettes contained equivalent amounts of the same marijuana that had been soaked in increasingly concentrated solutions of a new analog drug known only as "A-17." Following his orders precisely, Alex simply recorded the fact that subjects #1 and #3 appeared to be affected very much like all of the even-numbered subjects.

As his eyes continued to flick back and forth among the smokers, Alex happened to notice the oddly glazed expression on test subject #5, an athletic youth with an uncontrollable cowlick. And then, because he was busy scribbling, Alex failed to observe the tremors that caused #7—a normally lively and wide-grinning black youth—to drop his half-consumed cigarette onto the scarred and burned tabletop—

"NO! DON'T LET IT GET ME! NOOOO!"

—in front of #9, who scared the living shit out of everyone in the room—especially Alex—when the Semitic-featured boy suddenly lunged over into the far corner of the small living room, screaming at the top of his lungs as he frantically proceeded to pound and claw his way through the plasterboard wall.

In the girls' bathroom in the basement of a nondenominational church in Escondido—just north of San Diego—three sixteen-year-old high school girls, who were supposed to be taking part in an intolerably boring Youth Activities League meeting, were instead huddled around one of the sinks as a fourth girl unfolded three numbered paper bindles and then dumped the off-white powdery contents into three opened cans of orange drink.

Urged on by their more worldly associate—who assured the three somewhat nervous girls that absolutely *everybody* had tried a little *"Magic Silk Cloud"*—the three girls quickly downed their drinks and then hurried back to the meeting room, reassured and confident that the hour-long lecture wouldn't be quite as boring this Sunday.

It wasn't.

Twenty minutes into the lecture, the girl who had consumed the contents of the bindle marked "A-17-C" politely excused herself, and then lit out for the bathroom as soon as she got out the door. Approximately ten minutes later, "A-17-B" noticed that her stomach and lower intestinal tract were beginning to feel a little strange, and prudently decided to follow her friend. But, having unknowingly consumed a much lesser dose, it wasn't until the lecture was almost over that "A-17-A" fully understood that the physiological effect of taking *Magic Silk Cloud* orally was far more purgative than hallucinogenic.

All of which resulted in a considerable amount of confusion and distress in the girls' bathroom when the panic-stricken "A-17-A" realized—much too late—that the basement bathroom had only two stalls, both of which were very much in use.

As an emergency room team at El Cajon Community Hospital labored to resuscitate a Semitic-featured youth who had long since stopped screaming, Lafayette Beaumont Raynee's team of "scientific" investigators continued to test the effects of Dr. David Isaac's new analog at varying dosage levels.

As the Sunday afternoon wore on, the five testing groups began to report back fairly consistent results to Raynee: namely that the powder in the vial labeled "A-17" produced acceptably hallucinogenic results if smoked or injected in carefully moderated dosages; however, the effects were unpredictably spooky at relatively high dosage levels. As far as everybody was concerned—especially the still-panicked Alex—that made the powder exceedingly dangerous to sell out on the street, legal or otherwise.

All which was not exactly news to Raynee. He'd already figured most of that out for himself, having gone to considerable lengths to determine the actual toxicity of the new analog drug known only as "A-17."

But in contrast to the efforts being reported by some of his badly shaken street dealers, Raynee's experimental methods were both methodical and conclusive. He knew exactly what Isaac's new A-17 analog could and couldn't do, and he was extremely anxious to share those results with Pilgrim and Isaac . . .

. . . just as soon as he and Roy finished helping one of his terrified pimps to get rid of a body hidden in the back room of a downtown bar. A body with rope burns and eight fresh injection marks that had once housed the soul of a beautiful and playful child named Theresa.

EIGHTY KILOGRAM BRICKS. One hundred and seventy-six pounds of tightly compressed white crystalline powder, which calculated out to be around $8,450,000 worth of 86% cocaine.

One hell of a stash to be delivering on a Sunday afternoon, no matter how you counted it, Bobby Lockwood thought as he shut the refrigerator door and quickly moved the now much-lighter appliance into the kitchen of the General's newly purchased home, a structure that the General would never again enter now that the delivery had been confirmed. The pound-dealer cared a great deal about those eighty kilo bricks, Lockwood knew, but not enough to risk getting caught in possession. *That* would be left up to his well paid assistants.

"Last one, General," Lockwood's pony-tailed helper Tim called out, easily flinging the packet up to José, who in turn tossed the kilo-brick gently in through the open doorway of the bedroom.

The General fielded the last of the bricks, then reverently set it into the one remaining space in the otherwise symmetrical stack.

"Eighty . . . check," he acknowledged in a crisp, commanding tone, and then raised his voice slightly to yell down the stairway. "I'd like you to come up when you're finished, if you please, Mr. Lockwood."

Still elated by his recent promotion to one of Jimmy Pilgrim's high-paid distribution teams (in spite of never having knowingly met or seen the much-feared mob boss), Bobby Lockwood shook off his fatigue and hurried up the stairs to join the grey-haired pound-dealer, the man who insisted that every one of his subordinates address him as "General," regardless of their well justified suspicion that he had never actually earned that long-dreamed-of rank.

Lockwood stood by the doorway in properly respectful silence and saw the expression on the General's face: pure, unashamed satisfaction.

Understandable satisfaction, Lockwood decided, because if the rumors he'd heard were correct, the General had only entered the drug distribution business full-time less than eleven months ago, using his first official retirement check and his "supplemental savings" from twenty-eight years of mostly self-serving service in military procurement.

"Looks mighty nice, General," Lockwood said.

"That it does, my boy," the General grunted in agreement as he bent forward to light his cigar.

"Uh, then I guess everything came out okay from our end?" Lockwood asked the question as casually as he could, nervously aware that he was being closely watched and evaluated during his probationary period.

"Couldn't be better," the General shook his head and smiled. "Just wanted to tell you I appreciate the fine job you did for us last week. Goddamned nice work. Credit to the organization. Sure as hell can't build a functional unit with petty criminal minds like that son of a bitch MacKenzie, can we?"

"Ah—no, sir, I guess not. Uh—I'm glad it worked out okay," Lockwood shrugged uncomfortably. He was still unnerved and embittered by the knowledge that Jamie MacKenzie, his one-time friend, was still on the critical list at Scripps Hospital, mostly because nobody had bothered to tell him how severely Jimmy Pilgrim intended to discipline MacKenzie for his unauthorized greed. Lockwood thought momentarily about the horrifying tape he'd been ordered to listen to, and shuddered inwardly.

"Just fine," the General nodded again. "You and the boys have any trouble coming in?"

"Nothing that I'm aware of," Lockwood shook his head. "Seemed to be a routine trip. Pickup at the factory was clean. We made a couple of furniture deliveries before we got here, and we've still got one more bed and four more computer terminals to drop off before we head back. Uh, anything else we can do here, General?" he asked hesitantly. "Gotta get going if we're going to make that last delivery on time."

The General shook his head, dismissed Lockwood with a wave of his hand, and watched out the bedroom window as Lockwood and his two assistants quickly reloaded the dolly onto the truck and drove off.

"So how'd it go?" the General asked, turning to the senior of the three professionally armed and alert men in the upstairs bedroom. "The boy call it right?"

"Looked clean to us, General." The chief security guard shrugged. "No sign of any surveillance. I'd say the kid came up with a real nice scam, setting himself up with that furniture delivery job. Should be able to use it for a couple months at least, long as the store owners don't get suspicious."

"Lockwood's smart, honest, and a hard worker," the General shook his head. "Any businessman with brains'd give his left nut to have a kid like that driving his trucks. They'll keep him on long as they can," he added knowingly, patting his pants pocket for the lighter he invariably left on his desk.

The General took in the sight of his three security guards with a satisfaction that was almost orgasmic, knowing that he *had* to have people like them around to handle the business, because there was no way to anticipate how many of the one hundred and seventy ounce- and gram-dealers might run into problems during the month, in spite of the incredible amount of training, equipment, supplies, personal support and legal services that he and Pilgrim and Locotta were constantly feeding into the operation.

Problems in keeping their mind-softened customers satisfied.

Problems in monitoring and dealing with the ever-shifting maze of probing narcotics investigators and their semicontrolled operators.

Problems in continually trying to identify the latest "turned-over" snitch.

Problems with competing free-lance dealers who muled their own supplies across the Tijuana border, and offered below-market discounts on their ounces.

And equally insidious, the problem of constantly resisting the powerful temptation of easy money. The General shook his head in irritation, reminded that it would be necessary to replace Jamie Mac-Kenzie quickly at U.C.S.D. Too much money walking around that University campus to leave in the hands of just two gram-dealers.

Might as well be back in the military, the General groused to himself, as he considered once again the unending flow of paperwork involved in running his drug dealership. Paperwork that—unlike that in the military system—couldn't be passed down to an office staff of obedient clerks and secretaries. In the all-too-vulnerable world of a pound-dealer, where information was often more valuable than dope, loosely protected records could be just as deadly as a bullet. And better a bullet than a twenty-year term in a federal prison. The ex-military officer shuddered inwardly.

All of which made it goddamned difficult for a leader to function, the General continued to muse. Hell of a thing for the head honcho to have to do his own record-keeping, be his own clerk—even if he *did* have one of those computer terminals to make things easier, and even if it did make sense in the overall scope of protecting the Organization.

But that was just the point, the General reminded himself. You had to protect the Organization, if only to protect yourself, because if you didn't, in a very short time, nothing else would matter. There was always someone standing by, ready to step in your place. Always somebody . . .

The General was very much aware that he was only one of nine pound-dealers in Jimmy Pilgrim's piece of the Organization, responsible for only one of nine territories cut up out of San Diego, Imperial and Riverside Counties. An area which, in turn, comprised only one third of Jake Locotta's Southern California Empire.

In terms of status within Locotta's organization, the General knew that he was just one of at least thirty pound-dealers. Third level, no matter how you looked at it. As in his military career, the General had long ago accepted the fact that the top level was beyond his reach. No three- or four-star clusters on his shoulders in this lifetime. That was the hand he'd been dealt, and he would accept it without complaint, like a soldier.

But one or two stars: That was something else entirely. As far as the General was concerned, a pound-dealer rated a star. No question about it. That made Jimmy Pilgrim a division commander. Two stars. Fucking-A.

In his own mind, the General was convinced that he was a

perfect candidate to step up into Jimmy Pilgrim's job someday. Perhaps someday soon. No question that he was better qualified to run a complex operation than a lowlife pimp like "Rainbow," who couldn't even begin to comprehend the tactical value of camouflage dress and behavior, not to mention the principles of chain-of-command.

A voice interrupted his train of thought.

"Supposed to relay a message to you before we go, General," the security chief tried again. He was accustomed to the General's periodic lapses into daydreaming. "Rainbow wants to meet with you. This evening, if possible. He suggests a reserved private room at your club for seven-thirty."

The General looked around at the room, noting in satisfaction that his three powder jockeys were already hard at work with scales and heat-sealers on the first twenty-pound shipment.

"You tell Mr. Lafayette Beaumont Raynee that I will be pleased to share dinner with him in the private lounge of the Rusty Oar, nineteen-thirty-hours sharp, my treat." The General looked directly into the security chief's eyes. "Not sure I want to risk my reputation at the club, being seen associating with a nigger and all that."

"You want me to tell Rainbow that too?" the chief guard asked, a slow, amused grin spreading across his face.

"Word for word," the General nodded, matching the smile and winking as he placed the fatigue cap with the single chromed star back down over his balding head.

It was just past noon—the hot Southern California sun burning high overhead—when San Diego Police criminalist Paul Reinhart arrived at the top of the Torrey Pines bluffs and first saw the distinctive sign of a major crime scene investigation in process: the seven light-barred patrol units and the ten uniformed officers who were trying to form a barrier between the growing crowd of onlookers, and the small groups of civilian-clothed investigators who were standing at the cliff edge and looking down.

From his position at the entrance to the spacious dirt parking area sloping down and away from the bluffs, the scene was one of just barely controlled chaos. It always took a while for things to get organized at a homicide scene.

"Anyplace safe to park?" Reinhart stuck his head out his car window and asked one of the uniformed officers who was roping off the presumed scene perimeter with lengths of bright yellow plastic surveyor's tape.

The officer looked up at Reinhart and shrugged. "You've got

about ten thousand footprints and tire-tracks to choose from out there already," he said, nodding out across the parking lot. "Guess a few more probably won't hurt much. I wouldn't park too close to the edge though," he added with a tired grin on his dust-and-sweat-streaked face. "Long way down."

"Wonderful," Reinhart nodded, carefully driving his car over what he hoped was a "safe" area. He got out and walked cautiously over to one of the groups of investigators—all of whom were dressed in variations of the very practical scene-search uniform: casual shirt, jeans and tennis shoes. Unlike their coat-and-tie counterparts on TV, this particular CSI team expected to get very wet and dirty before they finished their work.

"Hey, what's our ace bench jockey doing out here?" Reinhart asked, surprised to see criminalist Tina Sun-Wang standing between the two scene technicians and the PD's police photographer.

Sun-Wang was a highly skilled graduate chemist from U.C.S.D. who had been recently hired to upgrade the crime lab's analytical chemistry section. Because of her skill in operating the highly complex lab instruments, the lab director had been extremely reluctant to allow his new chemist to take part in scene investigations, in spite of the protests of Reinhart and the others that she needed a broad range of experience to do her work properly. Besides, if the truth were known, they all liked working with the cheerful and extremely attractive young woman.

"G-c/mass-spec went down yesterday afternoon," Sun-Wang shrugged, her dark eyes squinting in the bright sun. "Can't get the parts until Monday, earliest. Guess the boss man figured this'd be a good time to get my feet wet."

"Yeah, well you're probably gonna get more than just your feet wet on this one," Reinhart smiled grimly, remembering the dispatcher's description of the body. What a way to start, he thought to himself as he surveyed the scene one more time before he finally spotted the senior homicide detective. "Everybody ready to get briefed before we go down?"

The two evidence techs and the photographer—all experienced at this sort of thing—just rolled their eyes and nodded quietly. Tina smiled agreeably.

"Okay," Reinhart shrugged, "let's go to it."

Tina Sun-Wang spent the first part of her crime scene debut that Sunday afternoon getting progressively hot, tired, sweaty, and covered with dirt and plaster powder as she labored on top of the bluffs, intermittently watching Reinhart and the lab photographer work in concert with two homicide detectives, the coroner's investigator, and two white-shirted men from a nearby mortuary to remove Kaaren Mueller's ravaged body from the base of Fat Man's Misery.

She had no idea what to expect in terms of her own emotional reaction as she stood high on the Torrey Pines cliffs and watched the eight men slowly work themselves down into position around a small, sprawled form. But thanks to a few quick instructions offered by the distracted Reinhart (who was about to begin his descent down the outer edge of Fat Man's Misery, in order to avoid destroying the clearly visible footprints that might have been made by the suspects, or any of several hundred other people) Tina did have some idea as to what a trainee crime scene investigator was supposed to do at a scene.

First of all, she was supposed to watch where she stepped, because it was very possible that the killer or killers had walked right along the cliffs where she was now standing. Naturally, Reinhart had explained, it would be helpful if these prints could be preserved from the winds, dogs, beachgoers, cops, and crime scene investigator trainees long enough for their identifiable characteristics to be recorded on film, and maybe even on a plaster cast.

Although, of course, the fact that the uniformed officer had been reasonably accurate in his estimate (there were easily several thousand whole, partial and overlapping foot- and shoeprints of varying sizes and shapes scattered all over the irregular clifftop acreage) made it very difficult, if not impossible, to be appropriately careful.

The obvious solution was for Sun-Wang to stand at the edge of the cliffs, out of the way as much as possible, watch everyone else work, and hope that she hadn't already stepped on a vital piece of evidence. Unfortunately, however, she couldn't do that because there was a great deal of work that needed to be done very quickly, and even a pair of inexperienced hands could be useful.

Secondly, if she didn't know enough to be appropriately careful *all* of the time, she could at least stay alert enough to spot potential items of evidence that, again, *might* be scattered about the crime scene area. Or, then again, might not.

The problem, as Reinhart had hurriedly explained, was that they wouldn't know for sure what was or wasn't relevant evidence until several hours—or even several days—after the scene-search, by which time, of course, it would be much too late to first go back and collect the things they'd either ignored or missed entirely.

Fortunately, Reinhart had had to scramble down the cliffs before he could recite any more instructions. So Sun-Wang spent most of those first four hours moving about the top of Torrey Pines cliffs very carefully, trying to help one of the evidence techs block out sets of what seemed to be relatively fresh shoe- and footprints with small wooden stakes and rolls of brightly colored surveyor's tape, while the second technician worked feverishly to photograph every one of the useful impression marks with a tripod-mounted camera and item-numbered ruler.

At 4:30, the senior detective, the coroner's investigator and the two mortuary attendants brought Kaaren Mueller's body up the cliff in a zippered, opague-white plastic bag, and awkwardly wrestled the body bag into the waiting hearse.

Then, as Sun-Wang continued to watch with uneasy curiosity, the hearse slowly drove away with the coroner's investigator, the two mortuary assistants and the bagged body. The senior detective came over to where she and the two evidence technicians were working, examined a few of the taped-off impression marks, pointed out a few likely candidates for casting, then began working his way back down the cliff.

At 5:15, the police photographer came up for more film, and immediately went back down again, leaving a trail of saltwater in his wake. Somehow, Sun-Wang noticed, the otherwise water-soaked technician had managed to keep his canvas camera bag almost completely dry.

Finally, at 6:45 P.M., they all came back up, exhaustion and frustration etched across every face.

"Didn't find anything around the body," Reinhart muttered tiredly. "How'd you all do up here?"

"Found nine good sets of shoeprints and a couple of huge boot-prints that looked pretty fresh," Tina shrugged. "Most of them had nice, distinct patterns."

"Find any tennis shoes with a couple of deep gouges in the right heel?" Rinehart asked.

"Yeah, sure did," one of the technicians nodded. "Anything worth casting down there?"

"Possible series of four, about halfway down," Reinhart said. "Marked 'em out with green tape. You might try to get at them before it gets dark. Don't worry if you can't, though. We got plenty of pictures."

"I'll hit those first and finish up here later," the scene technician said. "Always set up lights back here tonight if we have to . . . or work on them tomorrow," he added with just a trace of prophetic resignation in his voice. "So, you guys going to the post?"

"On our way now, soon as we can get into some dry clothes," Reinhart nodded tiredly. "Gonna give ol' Tina a real show for her quarter."

The private lounge on the upper deck of the Rusty Oar offered a splendid environment for the rich and influential to dine in seclusion without risking the possibility of having their digestion spoiled by reporters, competing lobbyists, and other inquisitive investigators. The six private dining areas were arranged on the semicircular deck in such a manner that each table had an unobstructed view of the ocean, and more important, no view whatsoever of the occupants of the other five tables.

Exactly the setting that Jimmy Pilgrim wanted for the opening moves of his new game.

Knowing of Raynee's preference for lowlife haunts and habits, the early arriving General had expected to easily take and hold the psychological high-ground in this elegant setting. But he had been jarred by the sight of an exquisitely dressed Raynee being deferentially escorted to the table.

The familiar street-hustling demeanor of Lafayette Beaumont Raynee had vanished. In its place was a quietly reserved man with a neatly trimmed Afro and manicured fingernails, who looked and acted exactly like a goddamned university professor, the General thought. From the soles of his spit-shined Gucci loafers to the collars of his beautifully coordinated silk shirt and dinner jacket, Raynee presented an incredible image of elevated class, taste and sophistication.

But even more disturbing to the General than the startling appearance of his nominal superior was the fact that he had no idea if Jimmy Pilgrim's security chief had actually delivered his bravely spoken, but later regretted, message. If the cold-minded delivery guard had done so, there was no indication at all in Raynee's amused eyes or friendly smile as he nodded his head in silent greeting and allowed himself to be seated at the small private table.

Decidedly uncomfortable now, the General allowed his eyes to shift away from Raynee's disarming expression, searching for something appropriate to say. It was only then that he was aware that one of the waiters had quietly added a third place setting to the table.

The General started to turn in his chair to call the man back for an explanation—and then suddenly found himself staring up into the cold, dispassionate eyes of the one man he feared above all others.

A bearded man wearing horn-rimmed glasses and a three-piece suit.

A game-playing madman named Jimmy Pilgrim.

In the few moments it took the attentive waiters to provide the three elegantly dressed diners with menus and pre-dinner cocktails, the General struggled to bring his shattered mental processes back under control.

"An excellent choice," Pilgrim nodded approvingly as he raised a fine crystal glass in salute and gestured out at the panoramic view of the light-speckled coastline.

"Glad you like it," the General nodded cautiously.

"I trust that you're satisfied with the recent shipment?" Pilgrim inquired.

"Certainly," the General nodded, trying to decide whether or not to accept Rainbow's unbelievable transformation and Jimmy Pilgrim's deliberately theatrical arrival at face value.

The whole thing was probably just another one of Pilgrim's mind games, the General told himself, but he had to remain extremely cautious and alert nonetheless. Having served with marginal success as a high-level federal executive, the General knew full well of the dangers of underestimating an opponent, especially one of higher rank. He had no illusions that Jimmy Pilgrim and Lafayette Beaumont Raynee were anything other than a pair of exceptionally vicious and dangerous individuals, regardless of the exterior they happened to be displaying at the moment.

"The quality appears to be consistent, and the weights are accurate. What more can I ask?" the General shrugged, offering a congenial smile.

"Perhaps a product that is, shall we say, more marketable?" Pilgrim suggested, motioning to the waiter that he was ready to order.

"What?" The General's alcohol-reddened face registered amusement, disbelief and confusion all at the same time. "If there's anything out on the street more marketable than . . ." he began and then hesitated, noting the waiter's approach.

"Are you gentlemen ready to order?"

"Yes, certainly," Jimmy Pilgrim nodded. He left the menu closed on the table. "I found the poached salmon to be exceptional last Saturday."

"We received a fresh shipment this morning from Anchorage," the waiter nodded, disdaining the use of a check form as he picked up the unneeded menu. "The chef advises that the quality is again superb."

Pilgrim and Raynee silently nodded their acceptance.

"And for you, sir," the waiter turned to the General.

"My friends have dependably excellent tastes," the General gestured slightly with this head.

"Perhaps you could select an appropriate salad and vegetable?" Pilgrim suggested to the properly agreeable waiter. "And also, if you would, a very nice bottle of wine to compliment the salmon. *My* treat," Jimmy Pilgrim glanced across the table, bringing up a relaxed hand to brush aside the General's automatic protest before smiling back up at the waiter. "We have a great deal to celebrate this evening."

"My pleasure, sir." The waiter nodded and then quickly departed.

"Now, then, where were we," Jimmy Pilgrim said, smiling.

"I haven't the slightest idea," the General shook his head slowly, unable to maintain his expression of curious amusement. "I find myself distracted by an overwhelming urge to apologize for a few, ah, incautious remarks I made earlier this morning. If for no other reason than a suspicion that 'Bo would make a very interesting addition to a foursome at my club. But the odd thing is," the General added pointedly, meeting Raynee's amused gaze squarely, "I don't understand why I should feel this way at all."

Raynee laughed delightedly, and then raised his wineglass in salute, the stem appearing dangerously fragile in his black, muscular hand.

"Perhaps you two are more alike than you'd both care to admit, in spite of your obvious differences," Pilgrim suggested cryptically. "At any rate, I'm sure that 'Bo would be happy to accept your invitation— but I believe we have more important things to discuss than golf. Money, for example."

The General raised his eyebrows, but said nothing.

"As you are aware," Pilgrim continued, "the Chairman of our— Corporation—has, for some months now, been personally involved in upgrading our management system."

"To the benefit of all concerned," the General nodded, shifting instinctively into a bureaucratic kiss-ass demeanor.

"Yes, I agree," Pilgrim growled, inwardly amused at the predictable pound-dealer. "But apparently this was only the first step. It seems that the next phase in the reorganization involves a complete reevaluation of our product line. A check, if you will, to be sure we're pushing the most marketable items."

The General blinked, and then looked around quickly to confirm their isolation.

"Is Locotta out of his mind?" he whispered. "If you've got anything out there more marketable than cocaine, I'll caddy Rainbow around the entire eighteen holes at my club, piggyback."

"A grievous temptation for 'Bo, I'm sure," Pilgrim smiled coldly as Raynee's eyes gleamed with wicked amusement, "but I doubt that either of you could afford the resulting attention. Consider this, instead: How would you like to handle a line of merchandise *just* as marketable as The Lady, at the same retail price, but at one-half of the wholesale cost?"

"Somebody's hallucinating," the General stated flatly, forgetting in his confusion that he would have never dreamed of talking to Jimmy Pilgrim like this under ordinary circumstances.

"The cost factor is, of course, intriguing," Pilgrim continued, apparently unaffected by his subordinate's outburst. "But I believe there are other considerations which offer a more telling argument."

"What the hell are you talking about?" the General whispered.

"You'll agree that it is often necessary to cope with a wide range of—ah—environmental hazards in marketing our products? Many of which can entail serious legal complications?"

"All right," the General nodded slowly, waiting.

"Then why not switch to a product line that is *just* as potent, *just* as appealing to the general public, but with virtually zero environmental hazard problems?" Pilgrim said reasonably.

"You're shitting me," the General responded, barely remembering to keep his voice low.

"Ah, you see, you *are* interested," Jimmy Pilgrim nodded. "So am I. Now then, let's carry it one step further. Let's assume for the moment that you've been selected to distribute this new product line under an exclusive trial franchise for one year. Essentially a corner on the market."

"You're talking about a product that looks the same . . .?"

"Yes."

"And reacts . . .?"

"Better."

"And there are no . . . legal problems?" the General added, still incredulous.

"None whatsoever," Pilgrim said matter-of-factly.

"Then what the hell—" the General started in, and then hesitated as Raynee brought up a warning hand.

The waiter cleared his throat and waited for Jimmy Pilgrim's signal before approaching the table.

"I have selected a splendid Riesling to accompany the salmon," the waiter began, "but I thought you gentlemen might appreciate the opportunity to view a truly exceptional Mondavi Chardonnay. Perhaps something to consider for an anniversary celebration." He gently and reverently placed the two-hundred-dollar bottle in Jimmy Pilgrim's steady hands.

Pilgrim held the dusty bottle for a few moments, reading the label with apparent interest. Then he looked up at the waiter through his black-framed glasses—his eyes resembling cold, black stones—and nodded.

"Yes," he said, "this is exactly what I had in mind for my friend this evening."

10

IN HIS SAN DIEGO hotel room, Special-Agent-in-Charge Tom Fogarty sat with an after-dinner bottle of beer and listened as Bart Harrington completed his summary.

". . . the initial scene report, Sanjo's body was too badly burned and mutilated for visual identification. Nothing usable in the remains of his wallet. For the moment, he's listed as John Doe Twenty-seven. Far as we know, they haven't found anything yet that would tie him back to his apartment."

Fogarty's eyebrows came up suddenly. "The car . . ."

"We got lucky on that," Harrington said. "Sanjo apparently parked it around the block from Kaaren's apartment before he went in. Turned out to be about fifty feet outside the scene perimeter. Sandy and I spotted it on our second pass-through. She managed to hot-wire the ignition in the middle of a bunch of neighborhood gawkers while I stood up on the hood and acted like a goddamned crime scene groupie."

"Detectives'll find Sanjo's keys eventually," Fogarty said. "We'd better make sure the lease papers are clean, just to be safe."

Harrington nodded. "We went through his apartment last night. Pulled his personal gear, emptied the trashcans, wiped everything down for prints, and then left a note for the manager saying he was checking out. Far as I can tell, we've got Sanjo pretty well covered. Kaaren's the big problem."

"Police ID her yet?"

"Don't think so," Harrington shook his head, "but it's just a matter of time until they tie her back to what's left of her apartment. That's always been the problem with using a girl like Mueller in a covert operation. Too easy for people to remember her face, especially considering all the time she and Sanjo spent hitting the bars. Gotta figure it won't take the sheriff's deputies long to match the apartment manager's description of Kaaren with the Unidentified Body poster the PD's going to be putting out any time now," the veteran agent added. "Especially when one of those deputies takes a few minutes out to read a newspaper, and then starts thinking about the time factor."

"Not much we can do about that. What about her family?" Fogarty asked. "Friends? Neighbors?"

"Not an immediate problem," Harrington shrugged, looking up from his notes. "Her parents are traveling in Europe. They're not due back for three weeks. As for her friends," Harrington said thoughtfully, "she grew up in Sacramento. Hadn't been back in California for almost eight years, until we sent her into San Diego with Sandy. Of course, the police will eventually distribute her photo to outside jurisdictions, unless we—"

"No contact," Fogarty shook his head. "Not unless everything goes to shit. We can't risk it yet. We've got to take the chance."

"There's a further complication," Harrington said, closing one of the file folders. "Our friend at J. Edgar is a little concerned—"

"Oh, shit, the teletype," Fogarty muttered, closing his eyes in frustration.

"Right," Harrington nodded. "Kaaren used her real name on the rental agreement. As soon as someone in the sheriff's office runs her name on a record check, our teletype's going to kick out clear as day. No way we can pull the 'want' now without causing one hell of a trail. Which means you've got to get ready to explain why the DEA happens to be interested in Lafayette Beaumont Raynee, Eugene Bylighter, and a woman named Kaaren Mueller who turns up dead at the base of Torrey Pines."

"And no matter what we say, they're still going to pull in Rainbow and Bylighter for questioning, which means Pilgrim'll know he's being probed," Fogarty finished. "GODDAMN IT!" He slammed his fist on the arm of his chair, spilling some of the rapidly warming beer.

"Sending Ben and Charley in was just a long shot," Harrington shrugged. "The teletype was the only real chance you could give her. You had to do it."

"I know, I know. But Jesus . . ." Fogarty couldn't finish.

"We may have an acceptable option," Harrington suggested.

Fogarty's head came up quickly. "What's that?"

"Ben's got a buddy working at the sheriff's office down here. Guy he grew up with. Narcotics detective named Martin DeLaura. Ben says the guy'd probably be willing to help. Better yet, he knows how to keep his mouth shut. Wouldn't be all that hard to sidetrack the investigation if we've got an inside man. Figure you'd have to bring DeLaura in on the operation, though. Give him something to cover his ass."

"Just him?"

"Be nice, but you gotta figure DeLaura'll want the sheriff hooked in on the deal," Harrington shrugged. "Serious business, playing games with a homicide investigation on your own time."

"You know what kind of risk Ben and Charley are going to be taking if word of this operation spreads? Just one slip by anyone—"

"They know. They still want to do it."

"Then maybe the relevant question is why," Fogarty said softly.

Harrington was quiet for a few moments, staring at the file folders in quiet contemplation.

"I think you know why," he finally said.

"Yeah. And that's exactly what keeps me awake nights. I can't let it go down like that," Fogarty said flatly.

Harrington remained silent.

"Listen, Bart, I want those bastards as bad as anyone else on the team," Fogarty went on. "We're going to take them down, no question about it, but we're going to do it clean. Gradual infiltration— that's the only way we can get at Locotta. We can't just go out and hit Pilgrim and Rainbow like we're a goddamned Phoenix operation."

"But—"

Fogarty looked up and caught the set expression on Harrington's face.

"*For Christ's sake, Bart, we don't know for sure they're the ones who killed them!*" Fogarty slammed his fist on the arm of his chair and glared at the quietly defiant agent.

"That's true," Harrington admitted. "We don't know. We may

never know, for that matter. But the pattern's about as clear as it could be. The phone games, a delayed trigger-bomb wired in to Ben's call, those knife-cuts on Kaaren. Pilgrim and Rainbow might just as well have signed their fucking names on the bodies," the normally quiet and steady veteran special agent snarled.

Fogarty suddenly threw back his head and laughed.

"Jesus Christ, Harrington," he said, shaking his head, a saddened expression passing across his fatigued eyes. "I wanted you on this team because I needed somebody who could work an operation by the book—help me keep *my* ass out of trouble. Now you're the one who wants to call in an air strike."

"Yeah, I guess you're right," Harrington shrugged in embarrassment. "Guess I got a little carried away. Look, Tom, I'm not suggesting you should send Ben and Charley in with authorization to waste those assholes the first chance they get. Our target's Locotta, I know that and they know that. We're gonna work our way up to Locotta, and then go back and kick doors on Pilgrim and Rainbow. They put up any kind of fight, tough shit; they come out in bags. I understand how the game is supposed to be played," Harrington emphasized fiercely with his wide-open hands. "I just . . ." Then he closed his eyes and shook his head. "Ah shit, Tom, I don't know . . . I guess this is just one of those times I don't see much point in playing the game by the rules."

"Seems to me that's what got Ben in trouble in 'Nam," Fogarty reminded pointedly.

"Yeah, I guess that's right," Harrington said. "But did you ever hear *why* he crossed over into Cambodia?"

"No. It wasn't mentioned in his file. Never figured it was any of my business."

"Charley laid it out for me a couple nights ago over a few beers," Harrington said. "Whole thing started with a Viet Cong raid team that kept coming across the border at night, hitting at dug-in units, and then hauling-ass back to their Cambodian sanctuary before anyone could cut 'em off."

"Just like Korea," Fogarty snorted.

"Yeah, except it seems that our intelligence units got word that this particular team was out to make a live-body snatch. Only thing is, they had orders to be selective. Hanoi wanted a black prisoner."

"What for?"

"Propaganda," Harrington shrugged. "Makes sense. Drag a grown-up ghetto kid across the border where we can't get at him, crank up the washing machine and do a little brain-scrubbing until the kid understands what a shit-ass deal he got from his good old honky Uncle Sam. Then put him out front for the TV cameras."

"Jesus."

"Yeah, hell of an idea. So good that our brass decided they'd better send in one of their hot-shot night raid teams to put a rapid halt to that kind of crap—which just happened to include a couple of buck sergeants named Koda and Shannon. The lieutenant in charge of the operation apparently figured he'd split his two fire-teams up for a little hammer-and-anvil action. Charley's team was the anvil. They dug in just inside the border while Ben's team stood by their Slick . . . uh . . . transport helicopter," Harrington explained, noting Fogarty's confused look, ". . . in full combat gear, waiting for the word to swing the hammer. They almost pulled it off, too."

"Almost?"

"The VC team crossed over late that evening," Harrington went on. "Bypassed Charley's anvil position and surprised a fortified Marine outpost two clicks—uh, kilometers—southwest. Chopped the radio hut with a tank rocket right off, killed five Marines, and wounded seven others before the VC finally figured out that everyone left in one piece was a paleface, and then took off. Time one of the Marines got to the backup radio and called for the hammer, the VC were already crossing the border."

"That's when Ben went over?" Fogarty asked.

"Not exactly," Harrington shook his head. "His chopper went up soon as the call came out. Came over the border just as one of the Cobra pilots spotted movement and lit up the area with a parachute flare, pinning maybe twenty-five VC flat to the deck. At this point, they're maybe a hundred yards on the Cambodian side—no big deal, 'long as everybody stayed cool. So while one of the Cobras keeps the VC facedown in the mud, the second gunship clears out a drop zone for Ben's Slick."

"Sounds like one hell of a confused mess," Forgarty commented.

"I don't know," Harrington shrugged. "According to Charley, it was pretty typical for the night teams. In this case, it was just a reversal of the original plan. Only now Ben's team was supposed to drop in and set up a new anvil while Charley's people load up and play hammer. Except the Slick pilot taking in Ben's fire team makes the mistake of radioing in his position just as he's coming in for the drop. Lieutenant hears the broadcast, figures the whole world knows what he's about to do, chickens out, and calls off the assault."

Harrington shook his head.

"Can you believe it?" he asked sadly. "Nine hotshot air assault troops in a chopper, armed to the teeth and itching to land, with two Cobra gunships for air support, and the lieutenant calls them back. They had those kidnapping bastards caught out in the open, and the shavetail son of a bitch didn't have the balls to cross a goddamned line in the dirt."

"I tend to sympathize with the lieutenant," Fogarty commented drily, "but I don't follow . . ."

"So while Ben's throwing a shit-fit up in the chopper because his pilot's already turning around, Charley's fire team's following orders too. They're pulling out of their position—getting ready to load up in their chopper—and then *they* get hit just as their Slick touches down for the pickup, because the slimy bastards cut back across again. Chopper takes an RPG rocket in the fuel tank, blowing chopper pieces, flaming gasoline and troopers all over the pickup zone. Next thing Charley knows, he's tied up and being dragged across the border by three grunting, sweating and cussing VCs—two older guys and one kid—while their buddies keep dropping out to mount a rearguard action."

"Jesus," Fogarty whispered.

"You think you've got supervisory problems," Harrington snorted as he paused to take a sip of his beer. "Get a load of this part. Here's this poor goddamned second lieutenant, right? He's put in command of a raid team that's supposed to put a stop to this kidnapping-black-GIs shit. So he lays out a battle plan that'd do his old war college proud—hammers, anvils, the works. Standard West Point stuff. Ten minutes later, the VC hit an outpost, outrun his hammer, slip past his anvil, cut back, take out one of his Slicks, chop up half his raid team, and are now in the process of dragging the only black noncom in the entire fucking outfit back across the border into Cambodia. Right? So just about then, his other Slick pilot starts screaming over the radio that Sergeant Koda has a loaded .45 stuck in his ear and that they're now going across after Sergeant Charley Shannon in violation of umpteen fucking international agreements."

"Jesus, no wonder those two are so tight," Fogarty shook his head in disbelief.

"You haven't even heard the best part," Harrington grinned. "The lieutenant tries to ground his gunships, hoping Ben'll pull back on his own without air support, but the two Cobra pilots aren't having any of it. Both of them suddenly develop radio trouble, mostly because they're already across the border and tearing up the countryside with gatling guns, rockets, grenades, flares, and anything else they can throw out the windows, trying to keep Charley in sight and clear a path for Ben's team—who are now on the ground and going fucking apeshit, cutting their way through the rear guards."

"Nine guys taking on a twenty-five man VC raid team in a jungle at night?"

"Nine guys and the two Cobras," Harrington reminded. "Except by the time Ben catches up with the three assholes who are still trying to drag two hundred pounds of thrashing and kicking ghetto kid through the jungle, one of the Cobras is down and Ben's the only one left from his team still on his feet . . . and he's so goddamned mad, scared and shot-up that he can't see straight.

"Accordin' to Charley, Ben overran them like a fuckin' momma grizzly going after her only cub, screaming like he was crazy and laying into the bastards with his rifle, swinging it like a club 'cause I guess he couldn't shoot with Charley in the way. Broke his rifle apart on the second guy's head, and went after the young one with a knife when the stupid little son of a bitch tried to cut Charley's throat before taking off. By the time Charley managed to roll over and knock Ben away, he'd already gutted the kid out and was busy pounding his face flat with a rock."

"He lost it."

"Yeah, guess so. Either on the run in, or during the next five days and nights while he and Charley got lost trying to work their way back out. According to Charley, they had to hide and sleep by day, travel at night, fighting off leeches, snakes, bugs, immersion foot, wound infections, VC patrols, diarrhea, the works. By the time a chopper found them, Ben was completely gone. Charley's the one who got them back in, and then *he* spent the next three days in the brig for breaking the lieutenant's jaw when he found out the s.o.b. was filing court-martial charges against Ben."

"Court-martial? You gotta be shitting me," Fogarty blurted out.

"Not counting the six casualties on Charley's fire team, it cost the unit eight men, two Slicks and one of the Cobras to rescue one man," Harrington said. "Not to mention the little detail about violating the sovereign rights of Cambodia. Guess the lieutenant didn't figure the whole thing should have to come down on his head. Man might'a been right, but he made a bad mistake in not getting transferred out of the area before he filed his charges. Fortunately, somebody at the General Staff level took a look at the overall situation and decided the whole thing amounted to a draw. Besides, the lieutenant wasn't going to be up to testifying for a few weeks anyway."

"A convenient solution," Fogarty nodded, and then turned to stare directly at his longtime agent friend. "But that doesn't help us much with *our* little problem, does it?"

"Vietnam was a long time ago, Tom."

"And you still think Ben's capable of making a clean buy off of Rainbow and Pilgrim, and then working his way in to Locotta without flipping out and committing murder?"

"If he and Charley can get in, they'll pull it off," Harrington nodded. "It's a different situation. Besides, like you said, they don't know for sure who dumped Freddy and Kaaren either."

"And when they find out?"

Harrington hesitated for a few moments before answering. "I guess I don't know," he admitted. "But I *do* know the only way in to Locotta is through one of his major dealers. We're already partway in on Pilgrim. We pull back now, we've got to deal with Freddy and Kaaren on an official level, and then start over with a new team— assuming that you'd *get* a new team."

"You know the answer to that one," Fogarty growled.

"So where are we at now?" Harrington asked, acknowledging the accuracy of Fogarty's response by changing the subject.

"A test run," Fogarty said. "A small buy's been set up for Thursday evening. Five ounces of coke. Dealer working for a man they call the General—one of Pilgrim and Rainbow's pound-dealers. Remote possibility Rainbow may show up. Needless to say, Director's going to be real interested in this one," Fogarty added. "I don't think he cares much for all this secret-operation business within the agency. Probably makes him real nervous."

"He's not the only one," Harrington commented.

"So the day after tomorrow we find out something, don't we?" Fogarty said, taking another sip at his drink and staring at the wall again.

"One way or the other," Harrington nodded, standing up. "Oh yeah, one thing I forgot to mention."

"Yeah, what's that?" Fogarty said, the fatigue clearly visible on his face as he stretched out in his chair.

"Remember that young VC kid I told you about? The one Ben tried to smash flat with a rock?"

"Yeah, what about him?"

"According to Charley, Ben didn't realize it 'till after they went at each other with the knives. Turned out the kid was a lot younger than either of 'em thought, and kinda cute too . . . for a little VC girl."

* * *

Charley Shannon quickly placed the partially cleaned slide assembly back on the grease-streaked hotel towel, along with the rest of
the dismantled .45 automatic pistol, and then reached for the phone
before it could ring a second time.

"Shannon."

"Charley, this is Sandy. Just checking in to make sure you guys
are okay."

"Yeah, Sandy," Shannon rumbled quietly. "We're doin' just
fine. Can't say the same for a couple of our buddies, though."

"Yeah, I know. We got the word from Harrington," Sandy
Mudd whispered softly, and then hesitated. "Uh . . . Charley, Bart
said something about Ben getting hurt . . . ?"

"Nah, he's just scraped up a little. Bounced off a couple rocks.
He'll be fine. Don't you worry none."

"I'm not—" Mudd started to protest, and then gave up in the
face of Charley's quiet laughter. "Listen," she said, talking quickly to
cover her embarrassment, "we're going out to get something to eat.
You guys want to join us?"

"Better give us a rain check," Shannon replied. "Ben's still
sacked out. Figure I oughta let him sleep while he can. Might be a
while 'fore he gets another chance."

"Okay, we'll check in with you guys tomorrow. You both take
care."

"Oh yeah, we're gonna take care all right," Charley Shannon
chuckled. "Gonna take care of everything."

Humming contentedly, Shannon gently placed the phone back
on its receiver, and then returned to the familiar time-passing task of
meticulously swabbing the encrusted salt and sand particles out of his
partner's sidearm.

At the arched entryway to the main dining room of Chez
Pierre, one of the most expensive French restaurants in Palm Springs,
a quietly self-assured elderly man stepped up to the maître d'hôtel and
whispered a name.

The immediate response of the immaculately tuxedoed major-
domo was both properly respectful and inconspicuous. A discreet flash
of the maître d's fingers and the directed gaze of his eyes identified the
table and the message. The waiter nodded his head slightly in acknowledgment, strode quickly over to the isolated table for two,
glanced momentarily into the blue-violet eyes of Jake Locotta's stun-

ning blond companion, and then bent down and whispered quietly into his ear.

Moments later, the delicious blond with the deep-water eyes walked gracefully in the direction of the ladies' room as Al Rosenthal slid into the still warm and fragrant chair.

"So what's up?" Locotta inquired, directing his adviser to sample the steaming plate of stir-fried shrimp and scallops.

"Not much," Rosenthal mumbled as he chewed the tender seafood. "Haven't been able to get in contact with Pilgrim. Raynee neither, for that matter," he added.

"They trying to avoid you?" Locotta growled.

"Looks that way," Rosenthal nodded.

"Any reason you know about?" Locotta demanded, his suspicious mind becoming alert.

"No," Rosenthal shook his head. "I left word that we want some answers back from the southern region. Twenty-four hours, max."

Locotta considered that statement for a few moments, then nodded approvingly. "Yeah, that's fine, but don't wait any longer," he said. "I want a tight rein kept on that goddamned Pilgrim."

"Man makes us money," Rosenthal reminded gently.

"Yeah, but I don't trust that devious son of a bitch. Never have. You keep an eye on him," Locotta ordered.

"Meantime," Rosenthal continued, "I did a little checking with some of our inside sources. Far as they know, there's no tie-in on the killings to any of our franchises. But . . ." Rosenthal hesitated, ". . . there's a couple of very interesting rumors floating around on the street."

"Such as?" Locotta asked.

"First of all, the guy and the broad were definitely involved with dope. No question about it. The real question is who, and where, and how."

"Probably free-lancers," Locotta mumbled through a mouthful of steamed cauliflower. "Three-to-one, Pilgrim blew 'em outta the picture."

Rosenthal nodded his head in agreement. "But the other information's a little more disturbing," he said. "The word is that Jimmy Pilgrim's coming out with some new kind of dope. Something the cops can't touch."

Jake Locotta's eyes came up sharply. "You know anything about that?" he demanded.

Rosenthal shook his head. "I figure it's probably some of that caffeine shit," he rasped. "But still . . ."

"Stupid bastard's probably trying to slide into the bubble-gum trade," Locotta growled, twisting his heavy jaw muscles into a scowl. "We don't want any part of that crap. He knows better."

"Want me to look into it?"

"Yeah," Locotta nodded, resting his fork on top of the remaining vegetable on his plate as he stared at his longtime friend, "you do that, Rosey. Put out the word to Pilgrim and that nigger pimp Rainbow. You tell them I want a phone call. I want to know what's going on down here, *right now!*"

Locotta shook his head in irritation as his trusted adviser started to get up from the table. "Let 'em know I'm serious, Rosey," he said, glaring. "We've got a lot a' money invested in this area. I'm not about to let a little game-playing son of a bitch like Jimmy Pilgrim screw things up for us now!"

By the time that Paul Reinhart and Tina Sun-Wang arrived at the mortuary at 7:35 that Sunday evening, the senior detective and the coroner's investigator were already standing around one of the three heavy, aluminum-tray autopsy tables, helping the pathologist—a balding, red-mustached doctor—carefully remove the sand-and-dirt-encrusted zipper bag from under Kaaren Mueller's pale body.

The smell hit Sun-Wang as soon as she stepped into the small, brightly-lit basement room. It was a very distinct and unsettling odor that was difficult for the novice forensic scientist to pin down—an odor that she would soon learn to recognize as the distinctly pervasive after-smell of death.

The pathologist looked up from his labors long enough to glare at Tina's unfamiliar pale face.

"You belong here, Miss?" he asked, actually directing his question at Reinhart.

"One of our new criminalists, doc," Reinhart explained as he knelt down on the wall-to-wall sheet-linoleum floor and opened up his collection kit. "Name's Tina Sun-Wang. Say hi to Dr. Jack-the-Ripper Carney," Reinhart said to Sun-Wang, grinning up at Carney. "Tina here just finished working her first crime scene, so we figured it was about time she got checked out on the blood and gore."

"Sign her in," the pathologist nodded, apparently satisfied. "Afraid she's not going to see much blood with this one. Talk about a waste . . ." Carney shook his head, examining the features of the cold, glassy-eyed corpse as he readied his equipment. "We'll see what we can do about the gore, though, soon as your mangy excuse for a photographer figures out how to load his camera."

As the pathologist went back to his work, the seemingly insult-proof police photographer took thirty-or-so large-format shots of Kaaren Mueller from various sides and angles under Dr. Carney's directed guidance. Then, as the photographer stepped over to a nearby counter to mark his film rolls and reload for the next series, Tina Sun-Wang moved in closer to watch uneasily as Reinhart and Carney first collected fingernail scrappings, then oral, anal and vaginal swabs, and finally combed and plucked head and pubic hair samples.

Neither Reinhart or Carney seemed to be the least bit embarrassed or inhibited by the presence of a female in the room, a fact that vaguely registered somewhere in Tina's numbed mind.

"Probably raped," Carney muttered to no one in particular. "Don't expect you'll find much, though."

Reinhart grunted an acknowledgment as he quickly marked the label on a glass tube with his name, date, time, and the case and item numbers.

Sun-Wang tried to follow Carney's and Reinhart's activities as the pathologist and criminalist worked methodically to transfer the samples into labeled vials and envelopes, but her eyes kept shifting back to the awful wounds on Kaaren Mueller's wrists and ankles, a fact that didn't escape Carney's notice.

"Somebody did a hell of a job on her, didn't they," Carney commented drily as he reached down with his plastic-gloved hands to examine the horribly clean-sliced wounds.

Sun-Wang nodded mutely. The once-beautiful body wasn't really human—just some sort of laboratory specimen—Sun-Wang realized, wondering how many autopsies you had to attend to develop such a detached attitude. More than one, she decided.

"Tell you what, Tina," Carney added absentmindedly, "you help that old, broken-down detective over there find the fellow who did this. Strap him down nice and tight on this table here. And I'll be happy to perform the vasectomy, free of charge. Might even let you help if you're interested." Dr. Jack-the-Ripper Carney's coldly detached gaze bored into Tina Sun-Wang.

The room was suddenly quiet as Sun-Wang grew aware that everyone in the room—Reinhart, the photographer, the "broken-down" senior detective, the coroner's investigator, and Carney—was watching her . . . and waiting?

Tina stared down at the spine-chilling wounds once again, not at all sure that she should say what she felt like saying.

"Long as I get to use a dull knife," she finally whispered, "you've got a deal."

The quiet tension in the room immediately broke up into an explosion of brief, tired laughter. The senior detective grinned at Carney and Reinhart, winked approvingly at Sun-Wang, and then went back to scribbling in his notebook with a slow, nodding smile on his face.

"You'll make it okay, Tina," Carney said gruffly. "So why don't you get in close here so you can see what happens when somebody decides to turn the lights off on a human body."

If Sun-Wang thought that the sight of the dead girl on the table was the most unnerving thing she'd ever seen in her life, she quickly changed her mind as Carney's steady hand drew the sharp scalpel blade down the girl's chest as he made the standard "Y-cut" incision. As Tina watched, the nervously sick feeling growing in her stomach, the layers of skin and fat peeled back smoothly under the steady advance of the slicing blade. The death odor, even stronger now, began to fill the room.

"Now, let's see if the son of a bitch really did manage to drain her dry," Carney mumbled as he cut away the front of the ribcage with a short, curve-bladed tile cutter, and then slipped the tip of a small plastic suction bulb—that, as far as the now thoroughly nauseated Sun-Wang was concerned, looked an awful lot like the apparatus her mother used to baste turkeys—into a small incision in the heart.

"There," Carney said, his gruff voice taking on a note of satisfaction as he transferred about four teaspoons of blood into a tube being held by Reinhart, "we'll see what kind of tox work-up you people can do with that."

"Tox?" Sun-Wang whispered weakly, grateful for any distraction that she could focus her numbed mind on for a few moments. "You mean like in poisons?"

"That's the idea," Carney grunted.

"But . . . isn't it . . . I mean, isn't it obvious what killed her?" Sun-Wang asked, unable to comprehend what was going on.

"I'll tell you what, young lady," Carney said calmly, looking up from the shiny lobe of liver he held in both hands, "the first thing you're going to have to learn in this business is that you never, ever, want to start making hasty assumptions."

11

THANKS TO THE distracting hum of the malfunctioning TV set, the sprawled occupants of Room 205 were completely unaware of the three unexpected visitors who had been knocking discreetly at their door for the past thirty seconds.

"Room service."

Ben and Charley looked over at each other across the four feet of space separating the two queen-sized beds in their deluxe suite. Unlike the still half-dressed Koda, who had slept peacefully right up to their wake-up call, Charley Shannon had been showered, shaved and dressed in jeans and a bright orange-and-brown Hawaiian shirt since six-thirty that Monday morning. If anyone in the room had ordered room service, it would have been Charley.

Shannon shrugged his broad shoulders, shook his head at the unvoiced question, and then smoothly reached under his pillow and palmed a loaded .45 automatic as Koda began to move cautiously toward the chain-locked door, ignoring the painful tightness of the nu-

merous purpled bruises and scrapes that stood out darkly against the
tanned skin of his bare arms, shoulders, chest and back.

Coming up to the right side of the door, opposite the doorknob,
Koda gripped the door frame just above the top set of hinges and then
leaned his upper body out to the side—keeping his torso away from
the high-probability target area surrounding the doorknob and se-
curity-chain—and took a quick look through the peephole.

Then after shaking his head in amused disgust, Koda quickly
unchained and opened the door, reached out, and snatched one of the
large, still-warm paper bags out of Bart Harrington's hands before
stepping aside to let in Harrington, Sandy Mudd and Thomas Fogarty.

"Morning, boys," Fogarty said cheerfully as he walked into the
room ahead of the other two agents and immediately turned off the TV
set. "Nice to see you two up and about . . . more or less," he added
pointedly, his eyes flickering from the bare-chested Koda to the gener-
ally messy condition of the room.

"Somebody must'a finally given you that Academy lecture on
how to go about motivating people, Fogarty," Koda muttered, his
hand already digging into the opened bag as he savored the aroma of
freshly cooked eggs and meaty bacon. "Put 'em up in a first-class dive,
starve 'em for a little while, and then bring in junk food. Works every
time."

As Fogarty opted for the comfort and dignity of the room's single stuffed chair, Charley replaced the pistol under his pillow while
Bart and Sandy began handing out fried-egg-and-bacon sandwiches,
orange juice and coffee, Shannon winking appreciatively—and getting
no response—as the still solemn-faced Mudd absentmindedly stacked
four of the styrofoam-packaged breakfast meals next to his pillow.

She'd been that way ever since he and Ben had brought back
the confirmation of Kaaren's death, Shannon realized—concerned because in spite of his reservations, and unlike his partner, Charley truly
believed there was a place and a need for competent women in covert
law enforcement work. Especially women like Sandy Mudd.

But in spite of her deep-seated depression over the death of her
ex-roommate and partner, it was immediately obvious to Shannon that
Sandy Mudd could still be distracted. For one thing, he had noticed
that she seemed to be making a continuous effort not to wince every
time her eyes flickered across Ben Koda's purpled, scabbed and meth-
iolated wounds.

Charley Shannon was still trying to figure out how to make use
of this interesting bit of information when the problem was taken out

of his hands. Predictably, perhaps, Shannon wasn't the only agent in the small room who had noticed Mudd's expressions.

"Ah, you might consider putting on a shirt, Benji," Bart Harrington commented from his feet-up-on-the-table position in one of the upright chairs surrounding the round breakfast table. "Not that any of us boys are all that squeamish about pain—long as it's yours—but you're just liable to get my partner here turned on, you keep walking around like that. And Lord knows what might happen then," Harrington rolled his eyes suggestively.

There was a split-second delay in Sandy's reaction; then she smiled. "Probably not much, way he looks," Mudd shook her head with a disappointed sigh, and accepted a grinning hand-slap from Charley.

As both Harrington and Shannon expected, Sandy quickly discovered that it was relatively easy to keep up her end of the banter. If nothing else, it helped her to ignore a pervasive feeling of numbness that she couldn't seem to drive out of her mind. Besides, she knew they were going to have to start talking about Kaaren before too long, anyway.

"Mighty nice of you to do this, Fogarty," Koda mumbled through another large bite of egg and bacon as he agreeably struggled into a T-shirt, and then settled down cautiously on his unmade bed. "Downright suspiciously decent in fact. What gives?"

"Didn't want to tempt you boys into committing a little malfeasance of office, come voucher time. At least not any more than necessary," Fogarty commented drily, taking note—as the others had—of the ragged edge to Ben's voice. "Figuring in the cost of this room, you boys could just about order up a piece of dry toast with what's going to be left out of your per diem."

Fogarty looked around the room and then shook his head in feigned disgust at the quasi-elegant surroundings. Like the special agents he supervised, Tom Fogarty was more accustomed to staying in under-thirty-bucks-a-night motel rooms, and saving the remainder of his allotted daily funds for food and beer. Besides, the TVs usually worked better.

"Don't worry about it none, boss," Shannon rumbled as he reached for one of the bags. "Ah already ate up his per diem yesterday, while he was dreamin' 'bout bein' a gen-u-wine samurai hero. 'Sides, he don't do nuthin' much anyway. No reason he should be eatin' like honest workin' folks."

Koda smiled, offering his partner a thumbs-up gesture as he

silently polished off the remains of the first sandwich and dug into the bag for another one.

"I don't suppose you got around to checking into a hospital, like I told you to do?" Fogarty asked as he eyed the bandaged cuts on Koda's hands and feet, and then immediately recognized his error as he saw the smoldering rage flicker in Koda's eyes before he brought himself back under control. Too close to the raw spot, Fogarty realized. Much too close.

"Lard-ass emergency clinic," Koda said in a tight, semijoking voice, gesturing with his shaggy black head over at the sprawled Shannon. "Figured we were better off not attracting too much attention around this neighborhood," he shrugged, "seeing's how Charley's still half-decent at first aid, and nothing feels like it's broken. Besides, I made out a hell of a lot better than Sanjo or Kaaren," Koda added with uncontainable bitterness, his dark eyes flickering dangerously again.

"There was nothing that you—or any one of us here—could have done for either one of them," Fogarty said forcefully. "You know that."

Koda opened his mouth, ready to vent his pent-up anger and frustration, and then nodded his head in a half-apology. "Yeah, I suppose. So what's the picture?"

"The situation regarding Sanjo and Kaaren is stable for the moment," Fogarty said, "but it's not likely to stay that way. We're going to have to divert the investigations fairly quickly if we're going to stay clear. This may be an appropriate time for you to contact your friend DeLaura. We're going to need some inside help with the locals. Think he'll go for it?"

"Yeah, sure, no problem," Koda said.

"So the Director's not pulling us out?" Charley Shannon sounded genuinely surprised.

"No," Fogarty shook his head. "Not yet, anyway. He's got some ideas on containment, but we'll get to that in a moment. Right now, we've got to agree on a course of action regarding Locotta."

"Back door," Bart Harrington commented over his cardboard cup of steaming coffee. "Still the only way to go, far as I'm concerned."

"You mean Pilgrim and Rainbow, right?" Koda asked, the chill in his voice betraying his sudden, intense interest.

"Sure," Harrington shrugged, as if to say "who else?"

"We're already partway in on Pilgrim," Fogarty nodded. "If we try to go in through the other two—LaQue or Nogales—we're going to lose time, and that's a significant factor right now. We don't have a lot of time left to pull this thing off. We've got to move fast. Still cautiously," he added, almost as an afterthought, "but very fast, nonetheless."

"Agreed," Koda nodded. "So let's do it. What's the problem?"

"The relevant question is *how*, Benjamin," Fogarty reminded.

"We buy our way in low, like we talked about before," Sandy Mudd offered quietly. "The original idea was to go in through a low-level weak link. We've already got a good entry point marked out. So why not use him?"

"You mean Bylighter?" Fogarty asked, one eyebrow rising curiously.

"Sure," she nodded. "If we're going to go in as free-lance dealers, why not? It would fit the pattern, so far. And like Ben said," she went on determinedly when no one else spoke up, "if they thought that Kaaren and Sanjo were federal agents, they wouldn't have . . ." she hesitated on the word.

"That's right," Koda interrupted, "they wouldn't have, period. People like Locotta, Pilgrim or Rainbow aren't going to open up on a federal agent over a penetration attempt. A major buy, maybe, but not a penetration. Especially when they don't know what's coming down, right?"

"Sounds reasonable," Fogarty said. Koda looked around the room, waiting for someone else to object. No one did.

"Okay," Koda continued, "if we assume Sanjo and Kaaren got hit because they looked too much like small-time competition, then it isn't likely that they'll be expecting another approach from the same angle. Especially from free-lancers, which gives us just enough of an edge to make it work. We'll just come in a little heavier. And like Sandy said," he added, "we *know* the Bylighter kid's vulnerable. I say let's do it."

"Ahh, maybe we're not . . ." Shannon started to add something, but Fogarty broke in before Charley got a chance to voice a sudden suspicion that he knew precisely where their ever-manipulative supervisor was heading.

"I think you're both right," Tom Fogarty said. "Bylighter still seems to be the most accessible entry point we've found so far. We know they're going to be watching him closely, but that just makes our follow-up that much easier if we can pull off the entry. Means we have to be *extremely* cautious in our approach," he added. "But even so, it shouldn't be all that difficult to gain his confidence."

"Especially since he and I have already talked a couple of

times, apart from Kaaren," Sandy added quickly. "Squeek only saw us talking together once and that looked like a chance meeting, so he's not all that likely to be suspicious—"

"BULLSHIT!" Koda exploded, coming up off the bed, his eyes blazing. "Who the hell said anything—"

"—or scared of *me*," she continued, lunging up out of her chair with her fists clenched, glaring defiantly at Koda, "*because I'm a woman*, and nobody's going to be expecting a *woman* to come back at them. Not after Kaaren. *Isn't that right?*" She practically spat the last words through her bared teeth.

"I don't give a shit *what* they expect . . ." Ben started in—but he was interrupted by the deep, rumbling voice of Shannon.

"Ben!"

Koda whirled around and glared at his partner, who remained sprawled on the bed with his head propped up on a couple of pillows, a sad smile spread across his face.

"You tell her," Koda demanded, gesturing back at the defiant Mudd. "Maybe she'll listen to *you*. Go ahead, tell her—"

"—that she's right?" Shannon asked. "Ah don't need to do that. She knows it. So does everybody else in this room, 'ceptin' you, an' that's probably 'cause you're a dumbass male chauvinist. Can't help it, Ah guess, jes' the way you are," Shannon shrugged sympathetically.

"For Christ's sake, Charley . . ." Koda started to shake his head, an almost pleading look in his eyes.

"That's the way it is, partner," Shannon spoke softly. "Might's well go with the flow. Besides," he added, deliberately shifting dialects, "it's about the only way you and I are *ever* gonna get a shot at my asshole blood brother. And I just wouldn't want to miss out on that . . . you know what I mean?" The gentle smile remained fixed on Charley's face, but the expression in his eyes had changed perceptibly. It didn't match the smile at all.

Koda stood quietly for a few moments, his eyes focused on some distant point. Then he nodded his head.

"Okay," he said, immediately shifting over to Fogarty, deliberately avoiding the accusing eyes of the still-standing and now stone-faced Sandy Mudd, "but Charley and I are going to watch her every minute she's out there on the street with those bastards. And I mean every fucking minute," he said emphatically. Then he turned suddenly to stare directly into the widened eyes of the startled Mudd. "Any argument with that?" he demanded.

"Not from me." Sandy Mudd carefully maintained a neutral

expression, determined to keep her underlying fears to herself. She wasn't about to confess to anything, but the idea of having Ben Koda and Charley Shannon as personal bodyguards for the next few days appealed to her far more than she was willing to admit to anyone . . . especially herself.

"Won't hurt my feelings none either, in case anyone's interested," Bart Harrington added innocently from the sidelines, causing a sudden, tension-releasing burst of laughter in the room that neither a relieved Sandy Mudd nor a still-shaken Ben Koda could resist joining.

"We wouldn't have it any other way, Ben," Fogarty nodded, thoroughly satisfied with the way the mood in the room had shifted. "But before we all start getting overly worried about Harrington's fragile hide, I think it's about time you made that phone call . . . ."

For the first time since Isaac could remember, Nichole Faysonnt was not at her lab desk when he walked into his university laboratory office at precisely 8:30 that Monday morning.

Uneasy and concerned, for reasons he couldn't quite explain, Professor David Isaac sat down at his desk and forced himself through the irritating routine of dealing with the never-ending flow of university memos, evaluations, studies, purchase orders and other assorted papers that were continuously dumped into his in-box, hoping that the much-despised paperwork would take his mind off Nichole's unusual absence.

It didn't.

Shrugging uneasily, he tossed the five-inch-thick pile of stapled, clipped and rubber-band-wrapped papers back into his in-box, and walked out into the familiar serenity of his laboratory to find a more productive way to occupy himself for the next twenty minutes.

At 8:56, Isaac looked around the otherwise empty research lab one last time, and then closed the back panel of a troublesome analytical instrument that was still in need of some repair work, preferably by someone capable of focusing his or her attention on complex wiring diagrams. Isaac's normally well-disciplined mind simply wasn't up to the task.

Sighing in frustration, the distracted professor reluctantly stepped away from the lab bench, picked up his lecture folder, and walked down the hallway to his waiting nine o'clock chemistry class.

At 9:45, Dr. David Isaac finally realized that the bored expression on the face of a normally alert and inquisitive sophomore in the first row was shared by virtually everyone in the lecture room. Nodding his head in shared sympathy, Isaac quickly concluded his dispirited lecture on molecular bonding, then disappeared through the door adjoining the podium before anyone had a chance to question his curious lack of inspiration.

Mildly and irrationally despondent, he turned away from the lingering sense of loneliness that permeated the quiet lab room—intent on escaping into the cool, quiet sanctuary of his isolated office—and suddenly found himself staring directly into the wide, expectant eyes of Nichole Faysonnt.

"I thought—" Isaac started to say, his voice oddly tight, and then his words were cut off by a gentle hand placed firmly against his lips, then quickly replaced by a softly warm mouth that seemed to melt sensuously against his own for a few long, time-stopping moments.

Nichole was the one to finally pull back, her hands clasping his fingers tightly, preventing his hands from moving reflexively up the sides of her lab coat but, at the same time, keeping him in close. Having forced herself to go this far, she had no intention of backing away, though inwardly she was trembling.

"I had to think . . . about what you told me Saturday night," she whispered in a husky voice as she stared up into Isaac's face. For the first time he realized that her brownish-green eyes were filled with gold-colored flecks.

If anything, Nichole seemed just as confused and unnerved as Isaac by her sudden, impulsive action.

"I wasn't ready to . . . talk with you this morning," she continued in a soft, tightly restrained voice. "So I stayed in the library until you went to class, and then came down here . . . to wait for you."

Isaac could still feel the lingering warmth of her lips, the same kind of enticing warmth that radiated from her small, smooth and soft, and yet amazingly strong hands. Even Nichole's familiar lab coat seemed to draw in his attention, forming a soft white backdrop for her long, silky-dark hair.

Isaac knew what it meant to want—more than anything else—something that was forbidden, something that he couldn't (or was it shouldn't?) have. But this time, even the missing pages of the Maria notebook—Pilgrim's brilliantly enticing lure—seemed to pale in comparison to Nichole's gold-flecked eyes.

"I wanted you to know . . ." he began hesitantly, and then stopped because he hadn't the slightest idea of what he was going to say. She's a *student* for Christ's sake, he raged hopelessly at himself, even though he *knew* that she was much more than that. He shook his head, trying to erase the forbidden, erotic images that were filling his mind, and tried to start over again.

"It was important to me that you understood what . . . why . . ."

"I know," she nodded, squeezing his hands tighter, her eyes refusing to shift away under his impassioned gaze. "That's why I . . . want to help you," she whispered softly. "I really do."

They had been sitting in Isaac's private research laboratory for almost three hours, side-by-side, talking quietly, and occasionally touching each other briefly with knees, arms and hands in gentle movements that were deliberately slow, cautious and almost non-suggestive, because they were both still strangely, almost adolescently uncertain of themselves and each other. Then the phone rang loudly, causing them to jerk away from each other guiltily.

Isaac picked up the phone, and then spent almost five minutes talking guardedly, answering mostly in monosyllables as he shifted his eyes back and forth between the securely closed door of the lab and the curious expression in Nichole's eyes.

Twice, as Nichole watched and listened, Isaac was clearly surprised by something being said on the other end of the line. Both times, he blinked and hesitated for a few moments to think carefully before answering. Something about building a lab, and testing the analogs, Nichole deciphered from Isaac's end of the conversation. Finally, Isaac hung up the phone and looked up at Nichole.

"It was Pilgrim, wasn't it?" she asked.

Isaac nodded. "They've already tested the first analogs I gave them—the thiopene and A-Seventeen."

"You gave them A-Seventeen? But that was going to be the last of the A-series. Why . . . ?"

"I wanted a quick check on the first group, to see if we were headed in the right direction. Apparently we weren't," Isaac shrugged, a residue of uneasiness still evident in his eyes. "Pilgrim says that the hallucinogenic effects were frequently unpleasant, and varied considerably among the first test subjects, even at similar dosage levels."

Nichole blinked in confusion, much as Isaac had done when he received the news from Pilgrim.

"Also," Isaac went on, "it seems that dosage levels are more critical than we might have anticipated. According to their tests, the optimum-dose range was extremely narrow, something on the order of plus-or-minus five milligrams."

"That's odd," Nichole shook her head, a perplexed expression crossing her face. "I would have expected results like that from the thiopene, if only because it's so similar to PCP. But I am very . . . surprised . . . that A-Seventeen generated an unpleasant reaction. I mean, the entire series is based on two well-documented visual receptor sites. If anything, the results should have been . . . I don't know . . . visually pleasant at least. Intense coloration, things of that sort. Nothing spectacular, perhaps, but at least somewhat enjoyable. You don't suppose . . . ?"

"An accidental switch?"

Nichole nodded.

"It's certainly possible," Isaac shrugged, "but not at all consistent with the levels of sophistication and professionalism they've demonstrated so far. Logically, you'd assume that they would closely monitor their testing. If we can't assume that . . ."

"It's frustrating, isn't it?"

Isaac looked up and blinked uncertainly. "What do you mean, frustrating?"

"I don't know," she shook her head sadly. "It's just that . . . the whole idea of our getting involved with Pilgrim was the tremendous opportunity to test whole *series* of psychotropic analogs on human subjects, something the Government would never allow us to do. And now we discover we can't even trust them to record the data properly."

"Nichole, you must understand that these people are not at all concerned about our research data," Isaac smiled grimly. "Pilgrim is a very practical man. He wants results. As long as we come up with useful analogs, he'll continue to test for us, but he certainly doesn't understand, much less *care* about the scientific value of what we're doing. It's just something we're going to have to deal with as we go along."

"So what do we do about the rest of the A-series?" she asked. "Should we scrap Eight through Sixteen, or send them out as the next test batch?"

"I'm not sure it'd be wise to continue the series," he said after a few moments of quiet contemplation. "It's conceivable that Pilgrim understands enough of what we're doing to realize that all of the analogs in the A-series would be closely related. If one failed . . ."

"But it would be extremely helpful to be *sure* about those receptor sites before going on to the next series," Nichole persisted, not at all willing to give up on the analogs she had personally designed on her computer screen. "The calculations were so promising. And besides, they wouldn't have to know . . ."

"No, they wouldn't," Isaac nodded. "Not if we change the prefix from 'A' to 'B'. They'd never know, would they?" The concerned expression on his face slowly shifted to a relaxed and satisfied smile.

"I'll do that this evening," Nichole offered hesitantly, "if there's nothing else . . ."

"There is something else," Isaac said. "As it turns out, Pilgrim was very satisfied with the thiopene. In fact, they want to start making large batches—fifty or even a hundred pounds at a time—right away, and they want me to design . . ." he smiled, and then shook his head at the imagery as he stared down at his tightly clenched hands, ". . . an 'underground laboratory.' Can you believe that?"

"Are we going to?"

Isaac looked up, startled by the girl's deliberate emphasis on the sharing pronoun. He realized that this moment was the point of departure. From now on there could be no more hesitations . . . no more uncertainties, because they could no longer afford to be hesitant and uncertain about each other in dealing with an unpredictable man like Pilgrim . . . and his silent messengers, Isaac remembered. Still, he delayed for a few moments before he finally answered.

"Yes."

"Will it be . . . difficult?"

She probably meant dangerous, Isaac realized, but answered, "No, not really," carefully diverting the conversation away from his real concern. "The chemistry is straightforward enough. A simple bromothiopene Grignard reaction with the piperidine carbonitrile—which we will have to prepare ourselves through a series of intermediates. It seems that the Drug Enforcement Administration is monitoring the sale of piperidine very carefully, in order to locate labs making PCP."

"Is that a problem?"

"No," he shook his head. "Or at least not for us," he smiled. "If there is a problem, it will be in modifying the synthesis routine—particularly the steps involving the cyanide solution and ether—so that it can be safely run by . . ." Isaac shook his head wearily, ". . . an undergraduate chemistry student."

"That's something else I don't understand," she said. "Why use inexperienced undergraduates to do something like this? I mean, surely, with all the money that must be involved in this business, you'd think they would have some first class *chemists* to run their labs."

"I'm curious about that also," Isaac admitted. "I suppose the idealistic answer would be that they have trouble getting good professional chemists to do this sort of thing; however . . ." he let his words drop off, leaving the ironies unspoken.

"So you think they don't have anybody else?" Nichole pressed.

"I think they must have other chemists," Isaac shook his head. "For some reason Pilgrim just doesn't want to use them . . ."

"So he goes and lures kids out of college?" she finished.

"Apparently," he nodded.

Nichole's eyes suddenly opened wide. "Do you think it could be one of ours?"

"No," Isaac laughed, "At least I certainly hope not. In fact, I have Pilgrim's assurances that their, uh, lab people will be from other parts of the state. Nonetheless, we will still have to take precautions to make certain that neither of us is ever recognized while we are actively working on this project. I don't think we can depend upon Pilgrim and his friends . . ." Isaac shuddered inwardly at the memory of the covert delivery of the sharpened scalpel, ". . . to be overly concerned about our welfare . . . or our future."

12

FROM DR. DAVID ISAAC's admittedly naive and limited understanding of organized crime in Southern California, it seemed logical that Jimmy Pilgrim would have little reason to be interested—one way or the other—in the long-term welfare of two university chemists . . .

. . . which was probably just as well, because the professor would have been reduced to a state of bowel-loosening terror had he really *understood* what it meant for Jimmy Pilgrim to be absolutely indifferent about the welfare of another human being.

The simple fact that Isaac didn't understand the enormity of the dangers involved in associating with a psychopath like Pilgrim was evident from his actions—or lack thereof—immediately following the delivery of the Maria relic and the warning scalpel.

Which was to say: Isaac had not panicked . . . nor had he tried to run, observations which thoroughly intrigued the two surveillance specialists assigned to keep the professor under loose, rotating observation. Mostly because they happened to know, with a degree of confidence bordering on certainty, that any street dealer in San Diego

169

County who had received a bladed warning at night from Rainbow would have been long gone by morning. And if not, the thought of hustling a little tail from a friendly college coed would have been the *last* thing on his fearfully impotent mind.

Thus, as far as these two professionals were concerned, Dr. David Isaac either had balls that "hung to the ground" or, more likely, was a typical university professor who didn't have enough "street sense" to be scared shitless.

But then, too, even if Rainbow—who certainly *did* understand—had tried to educate a brilliant and learned man like David Isaac into the fearsome realities of associating with a madman like Pilgrim, the effort would have been wasted. Simply because a civilized man like Isaac couldn't begin to comprehend the graduated markings on Jimmy Pilgrim's mental yardstick—markings that depicted with horrifying clarity his absolute indifference toward the welfare of other human beings.

At the low end of that yardstick, there was the benign indifference with which Pilgrim viewed almost everyone, and necessarily included the vast majority of his associates. In effect, if any of these people possessed something that Jimmy Pilgrim wanted—money, influence or power—he was perfectly willing to show some interest. Otherwise, their existence didn't matter, one way or another. Didn't matter at all.

The second upscale mark was reserved for those unfortunate souls who lived in a constant state of uneasy fear that they might inadvertently displease Jimmy Pilgrim for any number of minor reasons. These were basically illogical fears, because Pilgrim rarely even acknowledged the existence of his low-level underlings, who usually went to a great deal of trouble to remain as inconspicuous as possible. Simply because, as one low-level employee put it nervously, it was one thing for Jimmy Pilgrim not to care about a person one way or another, but it was something else again *entirely* if he decided not to care about that person on an active basis.

Perhaps appropriately then, the third gradation up Pilgrim's curious yardstick marked the transition between passive and active lack of interest on the part of the shadow-dwelling crime boss, a transition that was possibly still within the range of Dr. David Isaac's logic-based understanding.

Simply stated, to reach third-level status on Pilgrim's scale, the offending individual had to cross him in such a manner that he actually took notice, and yet remained pretty much indifferent as to how that individual was reprimanded, which could involve anything from a split lip to a bullet in the knee cap. The point was that, as far as Pilgrim was concerned, it simply didn't matter.

And in fact, it wasn't until a person attained fourth-level status that Pilgrim seriously began to take interest, finally caring enough to orchestrate the means of punishment—usually for the benefit of others who might profit by the warning. But even at this elevated stage of "interest," it rarely mattered to Pilgrim how—or how long—the individual suffered in the process, only that everyone else got the message.

Professor Isaac might not have understood this distinction, but Freddy Sanjanovitch and Kaaren Mueller certainly had. They had both received that level of attention from Jimmy Pilgrim before they died.

Understandably then, the fourth mark on Jimmy Pilgrim's yardstick represented a degree of savagery well beyond the comprehension of most civilized men and women who had not experienced the vulgarities of life, first-hand, in a military combat zone. But, in truth, it was really the fifth and final level—the point at which he began to seriously *care* about inflicting agonizing, unbearable pain upon an individual—that would have been utterly incomprehensible to a civilized man like Dr. David Isaac.

There were, of course, those who *did* understand the twisted personality of Pilgrim. Victims like Ralph Barreno, the crippled state narcotics agent, and Jamie MacKenzie, the now mute and paralyzed gram-dealer. Associates like Bobby Lockwood and the General. And even the deadly, street-stalking Rainbow. They all understood. As did many of the pursuers, like Ben Koda and Charley Shannon, who had long since accustomed themselves to crossing over into a netherworld of deceit and lawlessness where fear and violence were simply weapons to be faced and utilized in turn. They too understood Jimmy Pilgrim's mania, all too well.

But the one individual within Pilgrim's domain who was vividly, absolutely *aware* of what it meant to live in total fear—the one person who would do *anything whatsoever* to avoid the terrifying scrutiny of Jimmy Pilgrim and his dreaded assistant, Rainbow—was a much lesser individual than any of those aforementioned: a much maligned and now severly injured street youth named Squeek, who had already made one unforgivable (and so far undiscovered) blunder in the service of his ruthless employers . . . and on this particular Tuesday morning was about to make yet another.

*   *   *

To suggest that Eugene Bylighter now existed in a state of almost unbearable mental and physical agony was a classic example of understatement.

Less than seventy-two hours after he had received the series of sledgehammer knee blows to the groin, Bylighter painfully crawled out of his ransacked apartment before dawn to return to his job at the Hole-in-One donut shop.

Not because there weren't others who could take over the relatively simple cut-out tasks of arranging for the home delivery of moderately priced teenaged call girls and moderately cut gram-bindles of cocaine to less discriminating customers, while at the same time washing trays, making coffee, icing donuts, hauling trash, and wiping the painted-metal tables outside the Mob-owned donut shop. But, rather, because Bylighter was absolutely terrified that Rainbow or Pilgrim might decide that a cheap throwaway kid named Squeek had finally become completely unreliable . . . or, much worse, a liability.

It would have done Bylighter's already terror-haunted mind little good to learn that Rainbow had come to that very conclusion long ago.

In point of fact, Bylighter was still being allowed to function as a thoroughly expendable go-between only because Jimmy Pilgrim had decided that it might be rewarding to put the occasionally useful gofer—who had unaccountably been the focal point of the still unexplained penetration attempt by Kaaren Mueller and her boyfriend— back out on the street . . . and then wait to see exactly who or what started sniffing around the bait.

Bylighter was blissfully ignorant of the event's significance when—as he was cautiously and painfully moving between a pair of solidly mounted enameled-steel tables to collect a gooey wad of discarded waxy papers and half-empty coffee cups—a warmly firm hand dropped down over his thin, shaky wrist.

"Squeek?"

"Uhhh—!" Bylighter reacted to the sudden, unexpected contact by jerking back, immediately causing his face to turn pale and his forehead to break out in a heavy sweat when his legs rubbed much-too-closely together. All but fainting from the stabbing pain, Bylighter was unable to prevent an agonized moan from escaping between his tightly clenched teeth as he grabbed at the table to steady himself.

"Jesus, Squeek, are you okay?" The expression in Sandy Mudd's eyes reflected only a sense of immediate self-concern, which, in truth, was all that she felt. Bylighter looked like he was going to vomit or faint at any moment—most likely on her table.

"Uh, yeah—sure," he whispered weakly, blinking away at the hazy film in front of his eyes before he was able to focus on the girl's face—

"God, you look awful. Here, why don't you sit down a minute, take a rest." Mudd helped to steady the trembling youth as he cautiously settled into the opposite metal seat.

"I guess—I just don't feel too good right now," Bylighter admitted, still blinking and shaking from the effects of the residual pain as he tried to remember the woman's name. Susan? Or Sue? Or . . .? "Sandy?" he finally asked.

"Yeah, that's right," Sandy nodded, offering a friendly smile as she reminded herself to ignore Bylighter's characteristic abused-puppy demeanor, an appearance she had reason to believe might be dangerously deceptive.

Tom Fogarty had managed to obtain a bootlegged copy of the preliminary autopsy report on Kaaren Mueller, and had made certain that Sandy and the rest of the team read each stomach-twisting page before they went out to make the arranged contact with Bylighter.

As far as Sandy was concerned, the report had been excessively graphic. In addition to documenting the extensive rope burns around both wrists, the deep apparent razor cuts, and the extent of the confirmed sexual assault, the pathologist had also noted the presence of humanlike skin fragments lodged between four of Mueller's front teeth, suggesting that at least one of her assailants had likely suffered some visible injuries in the process of committing the vicious assault.

From her vantage point across from the partially slumped youth, Sandy imagined that she could just about make out teeth marks within the bruised area on Bylighter's neck that was almost completely covered by his high-collared shirt. In fact, the sight of the presumably recent injury was almost enough to send the relatively nonviolent special agent lunging across the table to even the score for her ex-roommate and partner. The only thing that held her back was the fact that she couldn't believe that a malnourished adolescent like Squeek was physically capable of assaulting, raping and murdering a highly trained and motivated special agent like Kaaren.

Which didn't necessarily mean anything, Mudd told herself, because the purpled bruise mark on the scrawny youth's neck appeared to be very fresh . . .

"You're the one I talked to a few days ago," Bylighter broke into her thoughts. "The one who wanted to score some hash for . . . a boat party, wasn't it?" Bylighter tried to reconstruct his fragmented memory of their previous conversation. Something about a yacht out in Newport Harbor and an older boyfriend, he vaguely remembered.

"Yeah, I did," Sandy nodded, "but when I came back for the directions, I couldn't find you."

"Yeah, well—I—ah—got involved in some heavy stuff, you know," Bylighter shrugged uneasily, nervously aware that he was treading on extremely dangerous ground. "You still interested?" he asked, uneasy and hopeful at the same time, thinking that a couple of good contacts might be just what he needed to get back in good graces with Rainbow. "I might be able to—"

"No, not really," Sandy shook her head. "At least, not hash."

"Oh, hey, grass isn't any sweat—"

"No, that's not it either, Squeek," Sandy shook her head again. "To tell you the truth, I'm not even sure myself what I'm looking for. I thought maybe—since you're supposed to know a lot about the action around here—I mean, at least everybody around here says you do—"

"Oh yeah?" Bylighter gulped and grinned sheepishly, trying unsuccessfully to conceal the sense of manful pride that was almost enough to make him forget about the waves of pain still emanating from his swollen crotch. "Well, I mean—yeah, if you can tell me what you're after," he half-stuttered. "I mean—I guess I got some good connections. Good as anybody else around here. Oughta be able to get whatever it is you want," he finished lamely.

"That's just it, Squeek, I don't really *know* what I want. See, the thing is . . ." Mudd lowered her head slightly to whisper conspiratorially, even though there was no one else sitting at any of the adjoining tables, ". . . these three guys I'm staying with . . ."

"Three guys?" Bylighter's eyes widened in disbelief.

"Yeah, well, you know," Sandy shrugged, pretending embarrassment, "it works out okay. Anyway, I was kinda kidding them about—some things." She hesitated, no longer certain where this ad-libbing was taking her, but still determined to take advantage of Bylighter's well-known weakness. She and Kaaren had discussed several possible variations of this basic approach during the past few weeks. "Anyway, I ended up promising them that I'd get something—better—than hash to keep us—you know, going—"

"Oh, you mean . . . ?" In spite of his slow uptake, Bylighter was hooked.

"Yeah, sure," Sandy nodded, her cheeks taking on an un-

feigned reddish blush, "that's what I mean. I thought maybe that some
coke . . . ?"

"Oh, yeah, coke'll do it," Bylighter nodded knowingly. "I mean
it'll really—keep things going, and I *know* I can turn you on to some
decent stuff, but—" And he couldn't help himself. "—you know, I just
might be able to get you something that'd work even better."

"Better than coke?" Sandy whispered, perplexed by the sudden, unexpected turn in the conversation.

"Oh yeah. God, let me tell you, this stuff *really does it*," he
winked with unashamed implication.

"You've tried it?"

"Oh, yeah, a couple of times," Bylighter lied. "But you know
what's the best part? It's not even illegal."

"So what is it? I mean, it's not Spanish Fly or anything like that,
is it?" Sandy asked quickly, now thoroughly frustrated by the realization that she had probably just talked herself right out of an illicit sale.
Shit, she muttered to herself, knowing that she *had* to work her way
back in, somehow.

"Oh no, nothing like that . . . I guess. It's more like . . . anyway, I thought maybe we could work out some kind of . . . uh . . .
deal, you know," Bylighter added quickly, scurrying back to more solid
ground. He'd already heard a couple of street-hyped stories about a
young redheaded fox who'd been found dumped off the Torrey Pines
cliffs. In fact, he'd heard enough to be justifiably suspicious that it
might be the same girl he'd helped Rainbow and Roy kidnap last Saturday . . . and to *know* that he'd sure as hell better keep his mouth
shut. Somebody was bound to come around asking questions, and
even though he was pretty sure he'd met this girl Sandy long before he
had anything to do with Kaaren, it was always possible . . .

"Listen," Bylighter went on hurriedly, "I've got a couple of
grams of this new stuff I might be willing to share, if maybe—you
know—you and I—could sorta—" For some reason that Bylighter
couldn't quite fathom, Sandy Mudd had a motherly look about her: a
look suggesting that she just might be willing to add Bylighter to her
fun-loving foursome if he played his cards right.

But the card that Bylighter played inadvertently gave Sandy
Mudd the angle she'd been looking for.

"Hey, that stuff sounds good, Squeek," she said. "And I really
appreciate your offer, but, you know, it's going to be a long boat trip. At
least a week. I figure we'll need at least a couple of ounces . . ."

"Ounces?" Bylighter looked crestfallen.

"Oh yeah, at least," Mudd nodded her head. "But listen, you know, if you could turn my boyfriends on to a couple of o-z's of good rock coke, maybe you and I could work out a separate deal later—you know—for some of that new stuff?"

Getting awful close to entrapment, even if I'm not in Kaaren's league, Sandy reminded herself nervously. But the trouble was, damn near anything she said that even remotely suggested an intimate relationship could be considered entrapment for a horny little bastard like Bylighter. Gotta say *something*, she rationalized, deliberately keeping her eyes on the youth's pale, mottled face—and, more important, away from a certain van with dark-tinted windows that was effectively concealed among several similar vans in a dealer's show lot across the street.

"Couple-ounce deal's too big for me to handle," Bylighter admitted with a sheepish shrug. "But listen, I can turn you over to my connection. You meet with him and he'll—"

"Whoa, not me, Squeek," Mudd laughed, holding up her hands. "I'm too chicken to carry bread like that around this neighborhood. I'll let two of my boyfriends bring the money. They can do the deal, then maybe later . . ." Mudd reminded gently.

"Oh, yeah." Bylighter visibly brightened. "Hey, well listen, this is the way it's gotta go. You gotta tell me what these guys look like, how they'll be dressed, so I can let my, uh, connection know that they're cool, you know."

"Sure, no problem," Mudd shrugged indifferently. "I'd say Ben's about six foot or so. Kinda long black hair. Blue eyes. Mustache. Real dark tanned. He'll probably be wearing a pair of tight blue jeans and—" Sandy Mudd felt her face color as she remembered, too late, the small microchip transmitter she had personally mounted in her belt-buckle.

Her sudden embarrassment was obvious, even to Bylighter.

"Ah, I guess he must be, uh, kinda like your favorite?" Bylighter asked cautiously.

"What? Oh, uh—yeah, I guess, something like that," Sandy Mudd forced the words out, fiercely determined to keep the story line going, and hoping desperately that Charley would be the one who was monitoring the recorder. Please, God, not Ben, she whispered to herself.

"So, what about the other guy?"

"Who—Charley?" Sandy Mudd asked, suddenly finding it very difficult to concentrate. She was beginning to regret having successfully talked Fogarty into temporarily lifting his restriction on the use of concealed body transmitters. Goddamn transmitter, she raged inwardly, barely able to repress the urge to rip the revealing belt-buckle off right there at the table, but knowing full well that the ever-horny teenager would be sure to misinterpret *that* action. Damned things *were* dangerous, although admittedly not in the way that the reluctant special-agent-in-charge had argued, Mudd realized with a certain degree of chagrined embarrassment.

"Yeah," Bylighter nodded, suddenly more self-confident, and even a little intrigued as a result of the older girl's apparent confusion. "So what's this Charley guy look like," he demanded. "I mean, how're we gonna recognize the dude?"

"Oh, I don't think you guys'll have much trouble recognizing Charley," Sandy Mudd suddenly smiled, her eyes twinkling in ready anticipation as she prepared herself to savor the predictable expression on Bylighter's face. "He's just a little bit different from Ben . . . ."

"Looks like they're going to stop in this time," Charley Shannon muttered darkly from his back-window position in the rear of the surveillance van.

From the two high-backed seats in the front section of a van with dark-tinted windows that was parked—among seventeen similar vans—across the street from Bylighter's donut shop habitat, Ben Koda and Martin DeLaura watched the driver of the white pickup truck signal and then slowly turn into the parking lot. The same shabby white pickup had already made four slow runs past the donut shop during the last forty-five minutes.

As the three officers watched in silence, two clean-shaven men, both dressed in white coveralls, worked their way out of the passenger side door of the now-familiar pickup. The two men walked casually past Bylighter and Mudd—who were still sitting at their outside table, heads bent in conversation—and stopped in front of the order window.

The driver remained in the bucket-and-ladder festooned vehicle, seemingly uninterested in the five couples and two foursomes eating and talking at the outdoor tables. He was hopefully unaware of the three men who had been waiting in the van with stoic patience since four-thirty in the morning.

"Whaddaya think?" Koda asked.

"Those guys are either exactly what they appear to be, or they're awful damned good," DeLaura commented as he shifted the viewfield of his binoculars to each of the three men in succession.

"They sure as hell *look* like a team of solvent jockeys loading up on coffee and donuts before work."

"Ever run across any of 'em before?" Koda asked.

DeLaura set the binoculars down on the van's center console, and then took a small sip from a warm can of lemon-flavored tea while he carefully considered the question. A veteran of innumerable stakeouts during his fifteen-year law enforcement career—the last six in the San Diego Sheriff's Vice/Narcotics Unit—DeLaura knew better than to overload his vulnerable bladder too early in the course of an extended surveillance operation. The only bathroom facilities readily available to the three men for at least another hour consisted of four wide-mouthed plastic jars stored away in the back of the rented van for such emergencies, along with a two-day stock of easy-to-consume food and drink, and a roll of toilet paper.

The problem was simple: It was rarely possible for a surveillance team to predict how long they'd have to remain in place on any particular stakeout. It could be a matter of one or two stuffy, leg-cramping hours, or just as easily an equal number of days, with the only alternative to one of the wide-mouthed jars being a wait for total darkness and then a quick sneak out to the nearest facilities—often a nearby tree—praying all the while that the assholes didn't decide to make their move at that very inopportune moment. As a result, it didn't take long for a professional surveillance team to lose all inhibitions regarding their bodily functions.

"Don't recognize the faces," the balding detective finally admitted, "but I'm not sure I'd want to hire one of them to paint my house."

"Yeah, why's that?" Koda asked, gently tapping his fingers against the ring of keys hanging out of the ignition as he watched the two athletic-looking "painters" walk away from the order window and then sit down two tables away from Mudd and Bylighter, apparently waiting for fresh coffee to go with their take-out order. Koda's hand moved down to the padded pouch hanging from the right side of the driver's seat, confirming the orientation of the loaded-and-locked .45 automatic pistol, and then moved back to the key ring in the ignition.

"Take a close look at their coveralls, and then their boots," DeLaura suggested.

Koda made a minute adjustment to the focus ring of the spotting scope that was quick-release mounted on the van console, just barely peeking up and over the dashboard padding, as he peered through the single eyepiece.

"Don't get very messy, do they?" Koda said quietly, nodding his head in sudden understanding.

"Never saw a painter yet who didn't have paint spots all over himself. Shit, I can't even pop the top off a paint can without getting covered with the friggin' stuff," DeLaura muttered as he scribbled the date, time and the license number of the pickup in a half-filled notebook marked "PHOTOS." Then he reached down between his legs for a battered, long-lensed 35-millimeter camera.

"Hear tell your buddy Pilgrim's got a hotshot trio of baby-sitters on his payroll," DeLaura added reflectively as he steadied the lens tube on the dash, pushed the filter-protected end of the lens up tight against the tinted window, and then focused on the back portion of the waiting driver's head. "Might match up with those playmates of yours out on the cliffs the other night."

"Yeah, just might," Ben Koda nodded, slowly going from face to face with the spotting scope. "Charley, you want to check these guys out from up here?"

"Comin' up, jes' a second," Shannon grunted, waiting until De-Laura's camera stopped making rapid click-whirring sounds, and then moving cautiously forward so as not to cause any outwardly visible movement of the van.

Kneeling between the two front seats, Shannon carefully transferred the earphones for the tape recorder connected to the radio-receiver over to his partner, and then picked up DeLaura's binoculars. He spent a few seconds examining each of the figures through the darkened field-of-vision created by the black-tinted window glass of the van, and then set the field glasses back down next to DeLaura with a noncommittal shrug.

"Could be," Shannon muttered as he took the padded earphones back from Koda. "Didn't see much in the way of faces the other night. Small dude facing this way could be one of 'em, real easy. Looks like both of them could fit, far as body size and shape. Can't tell about the driver."

"Not enough to confirm?" DeLaura asked.

"Nah, but don't count them mothers out," the darkly bearded agent growled tightly, shaking his head as he replaced the earphones and then returned to monitoring the conversation between Mudd and Bylighter. The pump shotgun and DeLaura's scoped autoloading rifle lay loaded and ready behind the front seats, both within easy reach of Koda and DeLaura—who were alert and ready to provide short- or long-range protection for their partner the instant that Charley Shannon called the shot.

"Here they go," DeLaura whispered quickly as the taller of the two men stood up and walked over to pick up the take-out order while the shorter, more scraggly member of the trio walked casually around the building, seemingly in search of a bathroom.

"He took the long way around to the johns," Koda noted. "Could be checking out the scenery, looking for tags."

"Yeah, and here he comes, back around the other way," De-Laura added, shifting the camera quickly and squeezing off another frame as the man's full face came into view. "Good thing we didn't try to set up in the parking lot. These bastards would'a made us in a hot tick. Look at the way the son of a bitch's checking out the cars, kinda casual-like."

As the two impassively-faced men met at the corner of the do-nut shop, and then turned back toward their truck, they passed right by Mudd and Bylighter's table. This caused Charley Shannon to brush his fingers casually across the grip-end of his hip-holstered automatic. At the same time, he was trying to detect any signs of unusual ner-vousness in Eugene Bylighter's voice, a difficult task at best because Bylighter *always* talked like he was about ready to shit in his pants when he was in the presence of a sexually mature female. DeLaura had quietly exchanged his camera for a more useful long-barreled .357 Magnum revolver as the fingers of Ben Koda's right hand tightened around the head of the van's ignition key.

"They're going," Koda whispered as he and DeLaura watched the pickup slowly back out of its parking space.

"We gonna tail 'em?" DeLaura asked, slipping the hollowpoint-loaded handgun back into its concealed shoulder holster with a quiet sigh of relief as the bucket-rattling pickup truck turned slowly out of the parking lot.

"No way," Koda shook his head firmly. "Far as I'm concerned, those guys can run straight back to Locotta, or wherever the hell they came from. We're staying on Sandy till she hooks back up with Bart, period. Plenty of time to play games with those bastards later." He turned around in his seat to look at his partner. "How's it sounding for a buy?"

"Ah think she's jes' 'bout got it nailed," Shannon mumbled, and nodded his head slowly as he continued to monitor the silently run-ning recorder. Then Shannon's eyes flicked up to those of his partner as an amused grin slowly spread across his now visibly relaxed face. "Jes' so long's you remember t' wear them ass-tight jeans a' yours when we go in," he added, his dark eyes twinkling with unexplained amuse-ment.

* * *

Jimmy Pilgrim received a call from Rainbow at approximately 8:30 that morning.

"You're certain she was clean?" Pilgrim asked after Raynee had spent almost five minutes detailing Bylighter's recent activities as live bait.

"No, not certain," Raynee said. "Boys didn't have time t' set up a sweep for a transmitter. Made a pretty good visual check of the area, though, an' got a few pictures of the girl. Didn't spot no activity. Followed her back to Newport, an' confirmed she's shacking with a dude living out on a boat in the harbor. Big money, looks a' the boat. 'Cording t' the harbormaster, the dude goes by the name a' Bart Harrington. Showed up a few weeks ago. Dock space's got a long lease to a third party co-op. Runnin' the registration now. We'll get you more on the whole group, couple a' days."

"Fine, you keep on top of this one yourself," Pilgrim ordered. "If the contact through Bylighter is coincidental, and the girl and her friends are legitimate, we'll turn the action over to the General. But I want to be *certain* that she isn't tied in with the Mueller girl in *any* manner. Absolutely certain."

"Gotcha. You still gonna stay down for a while?" Raynee asked.

"Until we're certain who we're dealing with," Pilgrim replied coldly.

"Ah hear tell ol' man Locotta ain't too happy. Wants t' get hold a' you or me real bad. 'Specially you."

"What does he want?" Pilgrim grunted indifferently.

"Think he's heard some stories we might be comin' out with some new shit. Kinda hard t' advertise without the man hearin' things, ain't it?"

"We expected that," Pilgrim reminded. "We have decoys available. It's time we made use of them."

"Ah hear ya," Raynee chuckled. "Meanwhile, you got any problems with the sale t' this Mudd broad?"

"For how much?"

"Couple ounces."

"No, let it go through, but monitor it closely. Use one of the General's dealers if necessary, but make certain that Bylighter's the only one in position to take the fall."

"Gotcha," Raynee acknowledged.

"In the meantime, we will continue to move forward with the prototype lab. I assume you've given our alchemist proper notification."

"The man's been notified. Don't know that he *knows* 'bout i
.yet though," Raynee chuckled contentedly, remembering his recent
diversion.

"I'm sure he'll get the message," Pilgrim responded coldly.
"Let me know if he doesn't respond properly. In the meantime, I'll
contact Mike Theiss to let him know we're going to need a firm funding commitment very shortly. The time to solidify our financial backing is drawing very near. Theiss may want to talk to you also. If so, try
to be reassuring."

"He's gonna be skittish," Raynee predicted. "Them banker
friends a' his didn't like what they heard last week."

"We will remind him that the time factor is becoming critical. If
they want to keep on making profitable investments, then they're
going to have to choose. Right now."

"What if they decide they don't wanna come over t' our action?" Raynee inquired cautiously.

"Then we'll apply pressure," Pilgrim replied icily. "Theiss
should understand by now that there's only one choice. He and his
friends have no other options."

At 8:45 Tuesday morning, the phone in Jake Locotta's Palm
Springs suite rang four times before the Mob boss was able to pull
himself up out of the bed and reach the switch on the rectangular box
beneath the phone. He thumbed a second switch to activate the
scrambler, and then waited for the door to the spacious adjoining bath
to close behind the lithe form of the departing blond-headed woman.
Then he waited a few more seconds until he heard the muted sounds
of bath water running.

"Locotta."

"Jake . . . Al. Sorry to disturb you this early."

"No big deal," Locotta growled, irritated as ever by the fuzzy
tones generated by the computer-chip-controlled, voice-scrambling
device. He despised the "son of a bitch box," as he called it, but, at the
same time thoroughly appreciated its usefulness. With approximately
three hundred and seventy billion possible codes to break, Jake Locotta's worries about federal wire taps were a thing of the past. At least
he hoped to hell they were. "Whaddaya got, Rosey?"

"Word is, all the action on this 'new dope' shit's comin' outta
the General's area."

"Yeah? So what's Pilgrim got to say?"

"Haven't been able to contact him yet. Picked up an interest
rumor, though. Possibility the General mighta moved out on his ov

"You trying to tell me a fuckin' tin-starred boot-licker like the General'd have the balls to go independent on Jimmy Pilgrim?" Locotta's voice broke into a guttural laugh. "Don't gimme that shit, Rosey. Fuckin' Pilgrim'd tear that lard-assed bureaucrat apart with his bare hands, he pulled something like that. Either that or he'd set that crazy-ass nigger loose on him."

"Yeah, I know, but just the same, everybody I talked to says Pilgrim's just flat-ass disappeared. Nobody's seen him lately."

"You tell his people I want a call from Jimmy Pilgrim by ten o'clock tomorrow morning," Locotta spoke quietly. "I don't get a call by then, I send Tassio down there to get some answers, any way he wants. You tell them that, Rosey. And you keep checking this thing out, understand? I want some answers." The scrambler device gave off a nervous buzzing sound under the sharp impact of the disconnecting phone.

Dr. David Isaac awoke to a curious perception of nearby, radiating warmth, a sensation that he wasn't quite able to identify, but yet one that—for some inexplicable reason—seemed deliciously familiar and sensuous. And possibly even forbidden, although he couldn't begin to imagine why.

As Isaac continued to drift lazily in a state of semiconscious awareness, the alert portions of his brain tried to fit the nerve sensation data into a recognizable pattern . . . until suddenly, the heat-generating body twitched in a preawakening movement of its own, causing bare legs, haunches and back to shift slightly against the fleshy spoon formed by the professor's legs, groin and stomach . . . and the nerve data suddenly crystallized into a series of flickering, erotic images of . . .

Nichole?

Isaac increased the pressure of his left hand very slightly for a moment, released immediately, and then brought his hand up, barely brushing against the soft, radiating skin as it moved slowly down and forward, sliding across the gently curved abdomen, the protruding lower ribcage, the solidly concave sternum, then up along an incredibly soft, rounding slope that . . .

As Isaac willed his hand to settle ever so slowly, in gentle increments, against the wonderfully smooth, small globe of the girl's left breast, feeling the soft, varying texture of the areola against his palm, Nichole Faysonnt groaned quietly. Whereupon, even as he felt the dominating nipple slowly begin to harden and distend against the steady, gentle pressure of his hand, Dr. David Isaac became fully aware—as did an awakening Nichole—that certain portions of his circulatory tissues apparently had a will of their own.

In the span of the seven or eight minutes that followed, the two scientists—mentor and student—remained vocally silent and virtually immobile on the thick, yielding mattress, neither of them willing to risk interrupting the slow, steady momentum of their intensifying desire for each other.

As the morning heat in the room gradually intensified, causing the contacting surfaces of the two bodies to be separated by a thin, lubricating film of sweat, Isaac's firmly placed hand began to slip unintentionally down and across Nichole's engorged nipple . . . and the young graduate student finally lost control with a sudden, loud groan of surrender around . . .

"No . . ." she pleaded, tossing her long, dark hair wildly against her flushed cheeks and her desire-widened eyes, barely able to get the words out as Isaac reached for her: ". . . let me."

. . . and impaled herself over Isaac's sprawled hips with a sudden hissing intake of breath, a barely contained scream of pure sensual pleasure as she quickly thrust her hands down against Isaac's shoulders and pushed her upper body away from his heaving chest, her eyes locked on his . . .

"No, don't move!" the young woman whispered, imploring Isaac with her eyes as she fought to keep her own body under tight control, to prevent it from lunging toward the inevitable ledge as she hovered above him—her arms and their upper bodies forming a right angle that joined tightly at their unmoving loins—because she wanted it to last. "Don't move," she whispered again. "Please, just let me . . ."

. . . and then closing her eyes and whimpering uncontrollably, her inexperienced body trembling and straining forward as Isaac's searching hands found and caressed and stroked her tightly swollen breasts that seemed to be igniting . . .

"Yes . . ."

. . . a flame that threatened to . . .

"Yes, yes, that's it! Just like that! Don't stop, don't . . .!"

. . . engulf Nichole Faysonnt's entire body in a rapidly surging wave of pleasure that she couldn't stop as her body surrendered to the spasmodic sensations that caused her to throw her head back and open her eyes and mouth wider and wider . . . until she screamed in consummated pleasure.

Then her eyes focused on the envelope pinned tightly to the wall—just over her head—by the wickedly sharpened bowie knife, and she screamed again, this time loud and long and fearfully.

13

THE BATTERED AND rusted pickup truck looked abandoned, parked deep within a grove of trees near a tract of old World War II vintage cinder block houses. There were no lights in the truck, no visible movement outside, and there was no sign of a driver.

Although, in fact, the driver had been sitting several yards away, in the dark, for over an hour now, leaning back against a reasonably comfortable tree trunk and patiently nursing a cup of coffee while watching the front of a specific house across the culvert.

The faint crunching sound of a boot stepping into a patch of partially dried pine needles warned of the approach of a shadowy figure through the tall swamp pines. The figure moved forward silently in the direction of the seemingly unconcerned driver.

"Good thing your feet aren't any bigger," Ben Koda shook his head, acknowledging his partner's arrival. "People in that house'd start thinking they got some kinda elephant stompin' around their backyard."

"Have to wander through the living room and kick over the TV 'fore them boys'd pay any mind," Shannon chuckled. "Security's a mite lax."

"Spot anybody?"

"At least three inside the house. One of them's the watchdog. Couldn't make any other faces. Video monitors on the front and back doors. Low-light, not enhanced, best Ah could tell. Nobody staked out on the perimeter that Ah could see, 'less they're set up in one a' the other houses." Charley Shannon shrugged.

"So who do you figure?" Koda asked.

"Probably 'bout like we expected. Ounce-dealer and at least the one guard. Might even see the General hisself, we get lucky."

"You don't figure Rainbow?"

"Nah," Shannon shook his head, "not logical. Deal's set too low. Man like Rainbow ain't gonna show his face over a few ounces. Take at least a pound before he'd get curious."

"Or a lid of grass."

"Yeah, there's always that too," Shannon acknowledged, "but like Fogarty says, we gotta block out that kind a' thinkin'. Jes' forget about it. All we gotta do is walk into that house and shoot the shit, do a little deal on a couple ounces of powder, set up for the next one, say 'thank you kindly, sirs' real nice and polite-like, and then get our butts out the door. All there is to it, except'n for one little thing. We blow this one, my man, and we are *out* of it, period."

"Yeah, I know," Koda sighed in exasperation. "Just play it cool and walk the dog like we're told. I'm trying, Charley. I really am trying."

"Hey, man, it's jes' a game, remember?" Shannon chuckled. "Ain't nothin' but a silly-ass game. We done it hundreds a' times. Easiest thing in the world. Only thing different 'bout this one is these people are gonna try t' play with our minds a little 'fore they deal. No big thing. All we gotta do is shuck and jive with them suckers, an' then slide out the back door with a handful of o-z's. Just one step at a time. Deal in low, work our way up t' the General, then go flat out for Rainbow and Pilgrim. Time we're finished kickin' ass an' takin' names, ol' Locotta ain't gonna have shit for an organization."

Koda nodded. "Okay, *compadre*, you got me convinced we're the good guys in this friggin' popcorn movie," he said, standing up stiffly in the darkness. "Let's go get it over with before I forget my lines."

Koda backed the truck onto the main road, went on forward turning right onto the dimly lit side road, then left in front of the house they'd been watching. There was no one in the window or at the door, as far as either of them could see. Koda drove past the house, continued down to the end of the street, made a U-turn, and then came back up the street at the same unhurried speed.

"Anybody out front?"

"No, but it looked like somebody picked us up on the front monitor," Shannon said.

"Figured as much," Koda nodded as he parked the truck across the street from the house. "So let's go see if we can catch them off-balance anyway." He stepped down out of the truck, as Shannon switched over to the driver's seat. "Anything special you'd like for a 'go/no-go' signal?"

"Let's stick with one of the standards," Koda said. "Everything checks out, I'll send the muscle-boy out with my watch. Dial set to six o'clock."

"Ninety-degree switch-over?"

"Yeah. Nine o'clock, come in cautious. Midnight, I'm in deep shit," Koda said in confirmation. "How about a quick gun check? Might as well play it all by the book."

Charley Shannon drew the .45 automatic out and checked it over. "Six o'clock, loaded and locked," he said calmly. "Do it."

Koda's knock was answered by a man who seemed to possess all of the characteristics of a grudgingly retired Marine drill instructor. Koda scanned the squared-off face, optimistically searching for some indication—however slight—of compassion, or maybe even a sense of humor. No way. Koda figured Square Jaw had to be the baby-sitter.

"Yeah?"

"Name's Ben. I got an appointment."

Then somber-faced, crew-cut guardian stared into Ben Koda's unblinking eyes. "Come on in," he growled. As he closed the door sharply, he grabbed Koda by the arm and spun him back face-forward into the plasterboard wall.

"What the—"

"Take it easy, ace," the guard grunted, jamming Koda tight against the wall. "Gotta make sure you're clean before I let you go in there. The man don't like visitors coming in here carrying guns." Square Jaw spoke conversationally as he conducted a professional pat-down with his free right hand. "But it doesn't look like you're carrying much anyway, sport," the guard chuckled as he brought his probing hand up into Koda's crotch, grinning knowingly at his victim's tightly controlled nonreaction before switching arms and patting down Koda's left side.

"Too bad," Square Jaw sighed. "Kinda hoped I'd find something. Give me an excuse to rip that fucking mustache off your little baby face," the guard grinned maliciously, catching one end of Koda's mustache between two of his thick fingers and giving it a solid tug.

"That's okay, fella. Tell you the truth, I kinda enjoyed it," Koda said, winking affably as he patted the guard about six inches below the globe-and-anchor belt buckle with the back of his hand, observing with satisfied amusement the expressions of surprise, disbelief and then anger that flashed across the man's eyes.

"Listen to me, asshole," the ex-Marine snarled, thrusting a clenched fist up into Koda's face, "maybe you think all this is just fun and games—"

"Uh-uh, careful, friend," Koda cautioned as he shook his head and then glanced up meaningfully at the video camera lens partially concealed within a massive hanging planter box, "you don't want to say anything you might regret later on. Boss man might not understand all that enthusiasm. Know what I mean?"

"You're clean, pal," the security guard snarled, still working to control his ragged breathing. "Get your ass on in there. Down the hall, first door to the left," he motioned with a jerk of his angular head as he stepped back away from the hallway.

"Appreciate that," Koda nodded pleasantly. He started down the hall, stopped at the doorway and turned back to the closely trailing guard. "Hey, man, no hard feelings, okay? Maybe we can get together over a few beers sometime, after this deal's over. Talk about all the cute jar-heads we used to know." He glanced down suggestively at the guard's crotch, and then winked again.

"Count on it, asshole," Square Jaw whispered savagely as he reached past Koda and opened the door, grudgingly allowing the agent to enter the room.

Koda's eyes went first to the two men standing in front of the fireplace, about ten feet away from a huge couch that partially surrounded a redwood-slab table. Five small, sealed plastic packets were lying on top of the table, each presumably containing a measured ounce of white crystalline powder, a clear indication that the deal was on.

The man standing closest to the cocaine packets was the ounce dealer that he and Charley had already met through intermediaries, Koda noted.

The second man had a protruding paunch for a stomach, and a brand-new fatigue hat with a single bronze star that almost completely covered his side-walled, grey-white crew cut.

Well I'll be damned, Koda thought, the General himself. Looks like we made it to the big time after all.

"Hey, man, we expected you a lot earlier," the General's ounce dealer said smoothly, motioning for Koda to sit at one end of the couch. The paunchy man remained standing in front of the fireplace with his hands deep in his pants pockets. "You and your buddy, what's his name? The spade?"

"You mean Charley?" Koda asked calmly. "He's outside."

"Tell him to come in," the grey-white-haired man ordered.

"No, I don't think so," Koda shook his head slowly. "Leastwise, not until I'm a little more comfortable with the situation in here," he added pointedly.

"You're worried about being *comfortable*?" the elderly man asked, seemingly caught off guard by Ben Koda's comment. "What makes you think . . . ?"

"See, the thing is," Koda interrupted, "I talked to your partner here the other day, told him we were interested in doing a deal this evening. But, you know, he never said anything about having a fucking brigadier general for a partner. So, what I'm trying to tell you is, I'd like to know who the hell *you* are—and what you're doing here—*before* we go any further," Koda emphasized. "I figure I'm being reasonable, seein's how it's my money."

"Well, I'd say that makes us even, Mr. Koda, because I don't know much about you either. Certainly, I don't know enough about you *or* your friend to seriously consider offering you a franchise . . ."

"Uh, I don't mean to be rude, General," Koda interrupted again, the sarcasm evident in his voice, "but I don't remember saying anything about wanting to work for you people.

"See, it's like this, General," he went on after that failed to get a reaction. "Charley and I contacted you because we're interested in going into business on our own, and we heard you handled the wholesale action in this area. But, General, Charley and I don't cotton much to working with a bunch of fruitcakes. Too fucking dangerous, if you know what I mean."

The expression in the red-streaked eyes—watching warily beneath the fatigue cap—flickered back and forth between anger and confusion, and then seemed to settle on some sort of bewildered amusement.

"Perhaps we've been a little too presumptuous, Mr. Koda," the potbellied man shrugged off-handedly. "We thought you and your partner might be interested in a long-term agreement. Something in the neighborhood of five ounces a week, with a generous credit structure. However, in view of your concerns, perhaps a less, uh, serious arrangement might be in order."

"Actually, we were thinking of something a little more serious," Koda responded. "Like something on the order of twenty pounds a month, starting this evening. Cash terms, ten percent in advance, the remainder upon delivery. Something like that would be just fine with us."

The grey-white-haired man blinked again.

"You guys brought a hundred and twenty thousand dollars *here, with you?*" the General's ounce dealer whispered in disbelief.

"Hundred and thirty," Koda corrected calmly. "We're offering sixty-five a pound, five thousand cash bonus for guaranteed delivery. Thing is, we're not real interested in being on the tail end of the delivery line, if you people happen to come up short some month."

The General's ounce dealer was clearly out of his depth. He just looked up at his boss, incredulously wide-eyed. The potbellied ex-bureaucrat continued to stare silently at Koda for a few more moments, when a deep, loud voice from inside the adjoining dining room interrupted.

"Well, don't just stand there, General," the voice demanded, "answer the man. Tell Mr. Koda we'll be happy t' separate him from his money." The side door connecting to the dining room opened slowly, and a man with a deep ebony complexion stepped dramatically into the living room.

Under normal circumstances, it would have taken a lot to distract Ben Koda from the new arrival's unsettling grin and his gleaming, seemingly drug-crazed eyes. But in this instance, the outrageous display of clothing did the trick nicely.

The man was a living spectrum of color . . . from the brilliant red tam-o'-shanter resting at a careless angle on top of his Afro, down through the gradually shifting hues of orange, yellow, green, and blue of his neck-tied 'kerchief, patterned shirt, Bermuda shorts and high socks, to the deep, gloss-shined, burgundy of his high-heeled alligator shoes.

"Don't tell me," Koda said, shaking his head slowly, his eyes locked in on the black, dimpled face. "You gotta be Rainbow."

"Thass right," the ominously smiling figure nodded mockingly. "'Course Ah don't rightly know who you be jes' yet, do Ah, Mr. Ben-ja-min Koda?"

"No, you don't," said Koda.

"An' since you been tryin' to get mah attention all this time, Ah figure it's 'bout time you'n me got ourselves acquainted. Whadda you think 'bout that?"

"Fine with me," Koda shrugged warily, feeling the growing tension in the room.

"Thass good," the black dealer drawled. "'Cause we're gonna start our littl' intro-duction by havin' the General here put a little attention-getter upside your head. Yeah, thass right, jes' like that," he nodded.

Koda was peripherally aware of the snub-nosed revolver in the General's hand, now pointed directly at his left temple, but he chose to concentrate his attention on the eyes that gleamed dangerously beneath the jaunty tam-o'-shanter.

"Now then, Mr. Ben-ja-min Koda," the still-grinning Rainbow rasped, "did Ah hear you mention somethin' 'bout a hundred thirty thousand dollars?"

"'That's right," Koda acknowledged, feeling his chest and arm muscles begin to tighten involuntarily.

"Ah think Ah'd like t' see that money, you don' mind."

"But I *do* mind," Koda replied in a reasonable tone of voice. "You want to talk business, you can start by tellin' your little toy soldier here to shove that gun up his ass."

The wickedly gleaming eyes widened noticeably, and then the wide, taunting, white-enameled grin broke into sudden laughter.

"Man, you sure 'nuff don' back down much, do you?" Rainbow shook his head. "Thing is, though, Ah jes' don' think Ah trust you all that much. Leastways, not jes' yet," he added significantly. "Guess you probably got your man out there holdin' the money. That so?"

"That's right."

"Thass good. Ah like dealin' with a man who works real careful-like." The dealer looked over at his security guard. "Jack, mah man, why don' you jes' go on outside an' in-vite—" The black dealer hesitated, and looked back over at Koda questioningly.

"Charley."

"Yeah, thass right. You go outside'n tell Mr. *Charley* t' get his black ass in here 'fore we start talkin' serious shit with Mr. Ben-ja-min Koda here. An' you make *sure* he 'cepts mah invite." The black dealer grinned.

"My pleasure," Square Jaw said with a malicious smile. He started to turn toward the door, and then came up short at the sound of Ben Koda's voice.

"You gonna need that stupid son of a bitch for something else later on?"

"What you jivin' 'bout, man?" Rainbow demanded.

"Your Iwo-Jima-reject over there," Koda replied, motioning with his head toward the guard.

"Guess Ah might," the black dealer nodded slowly. "You sayin' mah man's gonna have himself a problem?"

"He might find this helpful," Koda answered, removing his wristwatch, resetting the hands to nine o'clock. "Then again," Koda shrugged indifferently. "He's welcome to try persuading Charley his own way. Tell you the truth, I don't really much give a shit, myself."

Rainbow blinked thoughtfully. "Take the man his watch," he finally said.

The guard walked sullenly over to the couch, yanked the watch out of Koda's hand, and disappeared out the door.

Less than four minutes later, Square Jaw reentered the room. He positioned himself between the door and the couch, standing shoulder to shoulder with Shannon, who seemed blissfully unaware of the bodyguard's threatening glare. Charley Shannon took in the entire room with one rapid glance, and then turned to stare openly at the most eye-catching object in the room.

"Shee-it, don't you beat all," he said with a grin, shaking his head slowly at the rainbow-clothed dealer. Then his eyes shifted to the disconcerted General and the short-barreled revolver before settling on his partner. "See you're still havin' trouble relatin' with folks," he drawled.

"Kinda looks that way, doesn't it?" Koda nodded, slowly reaching down and picking up two of the plastic-wrapped packets, and holding one up for Shannon to see. "Offered these people good money for this stuff. Doesn't sound like they're all that interested though," he added, turning the packet in his right hand to peer closely at the chunky powder inside. "Far as I can tell . . ."

The snap of the spring-loaded steel blade jarred across Koda's sensory nerves, causing him to freeze in place even as the razor edge sliced through the tightly stretched side of the plastic pouch in his hand.

The compressed acrid-smelling powder burst out of its container and spilled out over Koda's unmoving hand and legs, and down onto the table and floor.

Before Koda could react, Rainbow's hand closed around the front of Koda's shirt and yanked him to his feet, bringing their sweating faces inches apart, the cold, flat knife blade pressed tight against the side of Koda's neck.

"Thing is, my man," Rainbow whispered to Koda, "there's somethin' 'bout you jes' don' set right. Know what I mean?"

"You're out of your fuckin' mind," Koda replied quietly, staring deep into the crazed eyes.

"Ah don' know what it is," the black dealer continued, "but somethin' 'bout you jes' ain't right, 'cause you act like you don' even *care* 'bout how Ah cut mah powder."

"Hey, man, you're making a mistake. Back off," Charley Shannon warned, starting toward Rainbow, and suddenly finding his way blocked by Square Jaw.

Rainbow seemed to ignore the outburst by Shannon.

"Only dude Ah ever met, didn't care how his powder's cut, be the Man," he went on, oblivious to the chilling expression in Ben Koda's eyes. "'Cause all he wants t' do is make his buy and split. You hear what Ah'm saying, *sucker?*" the black dealer hissed, as the knife blade slid down tight against the front of Ben Koda's chest, easily slicing through the threads of the top button on his shirt.

"I'm telling you, man, you're pushing it too hard," Charley Shannon insisted, ignoring the movement of Square Jaw—who had suddenly stepped in close, slamming a beefy hand over Shannon's right wrist.

Nobody else in the room had moved, and the star-capped General looked just as confused and uncertain as his ounce dealer.

"An' you *know* what we do to the Man, don' you?" the black dealer whispered fiercely, staring directly into Ben Koda's eyes. "Even them little foxy ladies, ones that think they can play the game too. We jes' take 'em down to the water—" The blade sliced down through the second button.

"Ben, he's testin' you—back off!" Charley yelled, starting to move forward again.

"Shut your face, nigger-boy," Square Jaw snarled, thrusting the palm of one hand into Shannon's chest and shoving him backwards.

"—and then we jes' start cuttin'," Rainbow's voice broke into a maddened giggle just as the blade cut into the third button, and the entity crouched deep in Koda's mind lunged.

"BEN, DON'T—!"

Ben Koda released his pent-up rage in a long, guttural scream as he twisted counterclockwise, blocking the knife past his chest with his open-palmed right hand and forearm. Then, before the startled, off-balance dealer could recover, Koda slashed his right arm back, driving a powerful backhanded tight fist into the man's unprotected face—

breaking nose cartilage and splitting both lips in a spray of bright-red blood. The black dealer spun to the floor, the knife jarring loose out of his hand.

"HOLD IT UP IN THERE!"

"BEN, STOP—Agghhh!" Charley Shannon grunted as Square Jaw's fist slammed hard into his stomach.

Shannon stumbled forward, bent at the waist, and then came back up—snarling viciously—in a lunging head-on, rib-crunching tackle that sent both men crashing into the couch, taking the panicked ounce dealer and the disbelieving General down with them in a tangle of arms, legs and breaking furniture.

"You fuckin' honky . . ." Rainbow snarled through bloodied lips, the crazed madness in his eyes now replaced with a different kind of rage as he lunged up at Koda, missing with a vicious forward kick aimed at Koda's groin, and screaming in pain as the edge of Koda's tennis shoe slammed sharply into his left knee—just before a punishing, full-body-twisting, *ki-yi'd* karate punch to his lower chest dropped him to the floor.

Groaning in agony, and bleeding profusely from the mouth and nose, the black dealer felt the knuckles of his right hand brush against the open-bladed knife . . .

. . . just as the silence in the room was shattered by a roar of anger and an explosion of breaking glass and wood as Charley Shannon surged up out of the tangled pile of bodies, power-lifted Square Jaw over his head, and heaved the still-struggling guard through the front window of the house.

Shannon heard the sound of a hammer being cocked, spun around in time to see Rainbow try to come up on one knee with the knife in his hand . . . going for Koda, who was in a crouched position less than ten feet away, with the General's cocked revolver extended out in two tightly clenched hands.

Before Shannon could move or yell, the concussive, eardrum-piercing sound of a .38 Police Special roared twice in the closed room . . . and then a third time as Ben Koda brought the weapon up from the black dealer's chest, centered the sights right between the dealer's panic-and-pain-shocked eyes, and triggered the third round.

"CEASE FIRE, GODDAMN IT!" The loud voice roared again over the loudspeaker. "KODA, THIS IS FOGARTY. DO YOU HEAR ME? CEASE FIRE!"

"Oh, Christ," the man with the bloody split lips and the smashed nose and the mangled red tam-o'-shanter that hung limply from one side of the twisted Afro wig whispered as he stared in disbelief at the smoking barrel of the blank-loaded pistol in Koda's hands.

Charley Shannon was the first one to get to his partner, grabbing the smoking handgun out of Koda's hands just as the first of the men from the adjacent buildings in the Federal Law Enforcement Training Center burst into the room.

As the five DEA special agents sat in the secured and sound-proofed conference room, staring silently at the flickering television monitor, the video tape reenacted the sequence of events that had taken place less than an hour earlier in one of the Practical Exercise Houses on the far eastern edge of the Glynco, Georgia Federal law enforcement training facility.

Shannon shook his head and mumbled something unintelligible as the shimmering video image of the mock guard (in reality, a recently retired Marine instructor with a now-well-documented racial bias who lived in nearby Brunswick) disappeared through the all-too-real window frame in a spray of shattering glass and wood.

Then it was Koda's turn to wince in sympathetic pain and dismay as the FLETC weaponless control instructor who had volunteerd to play-act the part of Rainbow absorbed the successive impacts of Koda's open-handed knife-parry, the stunning backhand punch to his face, the crippling side-kick to his exposed knee, and the final, devastating fist-punch to his unprotected diaphragm.

Ben Koda averted his eyes during the final moments of the tape, not wanting to look at the visibly terrified and shocked face as the bloodied officer crumbled under the imagined impact of each projectile from the blank-loaded .38.

The only sound in the room was the DEA training director's whispered curse.

"IT'S YOUR OWN GODDAMNED FAULT, THORNTON!" Shannon roared, coming up out of his chair and slamming his clenched fist onto the heavy conference table.

"I admit we let it go further than necessary," DEA training director Jim Thornton snapped as he glared back at Shannon. "That doesn't mean it wasn't a valid test. In fact . . ."

"In fact, you *know* the actors can flip out in one of these scenarios just as easily as the players can," Sandy finished for Shannon. "It's happened at Glynco at least a dozen times that I know of," she added pointedly. "Maybe you'd care to review one of your old training tapes. Like maybe the one where you tried to choke the hooker who tried to kick you in the balls because . . ."

"All right," the training director nodded, raising his hands in reluctant surrender as a still-muttering Shannon sat back down. "So maybe Jackson got a little carried away with his role-playing. You're right, it's happened before. But it's not necessarily his fault. We *told* him to push it. He just . . ."

"It was the knife that set the whole thing off, Jim," Bart Harrington interrupted calmly. "Not Jackson's play-acting. You could see it coming, as soon as he cut that bag of coke in Ben's hand. From where I'm sitting, it was just a case of bad judgment, letting Jackson use a real knife."

"Yeah, maybe so," Thornton acknowledged, "but don't forget, you know this Rainbow's a knife-freak. And he doesn't play with fucking rubber knives, either. Besides, that was the whole point of the exercise. If one of you people can't handle the idea of buying dope off of someone like Rainbow,"—Thornton glared at Koda—"*we have to know about it now!*"

Thornton's raised voice finally jarred Ben out of his trancelike state. He shook his head slightly and looked up at the training director. "Jackson gonna be okay?" he asked quietly.

"He's not going to be playing much racquetball for a while," Thornton replied sarcastically, and then shook his head in self-disgust. "Sorry, that was a cheap shot. They're taking him in for X-rays now. Probably tore the cartilage and ligaments in the knee."

"Shit," Koda whispered.

"Man brought it down on himself," Charley broke in. "Broken knee's a long sight better'n a .38 slug between the eyes, which is what he'd a' taken in the field. Maybe he learned something out of it. Make him a better instructor. But Jackson's knee's not the problem, right now," he emphasized with his deep voice. "*We are.* So what're we gonna do now?"

"That's up to Fogarty," Thornton shrugged. "If he thinks you guys can't make a clean buy off of Rainbow and Pilgrim . . ."

"Goddamn it, Jim!" Koda came up out of his chair, his eyes flaming, "you didn't prove shit with this half-assed fire drill, and you know it! Charley and I've made buys off people so fucking paranoid they wouldn't trust their own mother not to rip them off. We're not going to screw up when it's for real. We're going to go in on the General for a few ounces, just like we planned. When we're set up to do pounds, the General's going to have to take us up to Rainbow and Pilgrim. That's the way their system works. We buy into their operation . . ."

"And then you guys blow them away before we get a chance at Locotta?" Thornton suggested.

"Bullshit!" Charley slammed his fist on the table and glared at Thornton, as one of the FLETC electronic technicians walked into the room with a tape recorder in his hands, immediately followed by Tom Fogarty.

"All right, that's enough," Fogarty said sarcastically. "Before anybody says, or does . . ." he glared pointedly at Koda, Shannon and then Mudd, ". . . anything else that *he* or *she* might later regret, I would like everyone here to kindly shut up and listen to this tape. Anybody going to have trouble keeping a lid on it for a few minutes?" Everybody in the room remained silent.

"Good. Now listen up. This particular tape was received from what we're going to call a confidential government source approximately three hours ago," Fogarty continued as if nothing unusual had occurred between the members of his Task Force team during the last few hours. "For clarification, neither the subjects involved nor the location of the intercept has been disclosed to us, probably because there isn't any monitoring authority on file for the tap."

"You telling us that tape doesn't exist, officially?" Koda asked.

"Yeah, that's about it," Fogarty nodded. "Although, for our purposes, I don't think the question of legality is of any real significance. Listen for yourself," he said as he pressed the "PLAY" button on the recorder and a scratchy, muffled conversation began to fill the room.

"Hey Rainbow, this is Mike Theiss."

"Yeah, man, how's it going?"

"Real good. Listen, I got your message to call in. Can I give you a number?"

"Do it."

"Two-two-seven . . . five-five-nine-two."

"Gotcha. Gimme fifteen."

Click.

The tape continued to turn for a few seconds, silent. A phone rang once, then another click, and the conversation filled the room again.

"'Bo?"

"Yeah, man, go ahead. We're clean."

"A double phone-booth tap?" Koda's eyebrows came up. "How the hell did they . . . ?" Fogarty waved for him to be quiet.

"Listen, Rainbow. It's about that deal Jimmy and I were talking about the other night . . ."

"Yeah, what about it? Sounds too fuckin' good t' believe, don't it?"

"You guys are talking about one hell of a lot of cash up front, my friend."

Laughter.

"Hey, listen, 'Bo. I'm not shitting you. I mean, it's like I told Jimmy, I can cover a few million on my own, no sweat. But what the hell am I going to tell the rest of our backers on a deal like this?"

"Lay it out for 'em, man. Give it to 'em straight, cold turkey. They got enough sense t' keep their mouths shut. What we're talkin' 'bout is turning the dope market right over on its fuckin' head, man. Right on its fuckin' head!"

"Yeah, I understand what you're saying, 'Bo. That's just it. I mean, have you guys really sat down and thought about what's gonna happen if you and Pilgrim actually try out this theory . . . ?"

"The analogs ain't no theory, man. They's facts. We're talkin' stone cold legal dope. You can deal it, smoke it . . . pour it in your ear, that's what you like. You can even sell it to a narc, 'long as you're real careful 'bout what you say. Thing is, it just don't matter. Don't you people understand? The Man, he can't do a fuckin' thing. Long's we deal it right, the powder ain't nothin' but legal."

"Yeah, but 'Bo, listen. Are you sure this isn't just another way of dealing those prescription fakes? You know, the stuff that looks legit, but the capsules are filled with fake speed, like caffeine or something?"

"Naw, no way, man. Listen to me now. That shit you're talkin' 'bout, that's just nickle-dime stuff. Kiddie-dope. People on the street, they're hep to that action. What we're talkin' 'bout here is the righteous stuff. Real he-man shit. Genuine, mind-rippin', hal-lucinatin' d-o-p-e, man. Only thing different is it's stone-cold legal. Ain't you people *never* gonna understand what we're tryin' t' tell you?"

"We understand, 'Bo. And listen, don't get me wrong, it sounds good. The money especially . . . it sounds god-awful good. But Jesus, 'Bo, what you and Jimmy are talking about is so goddamned spooky. I mean, you're not just talking about taking on the cops and rubbing their noses in it, 'Bo."

"No, we ain't. That's exactly right, brother."

More laughter.

"Yeah, but Jesus, 'Bo, you're talking real bad trouble on the street. I mean first-class serious trouble. You're talking about fucking over organized crime, for God's sake! I mean, Jesus, the Family alone's gotta have billions invested into cocaine and heroin. Fucking billions!

No way in the world they're gonna roll over on that kind of investment. And when they find out it's us . . . Jesus, I don't even want to think about it," the voice trembled. "Listen to me, 'Bo. We gotta talk this thing out with Jimmy a little more . . ."

"No way, man. Listen to me now. The Pilgrim, he's got this thing wired. We got ourselves an ace-number-one chemist dude doin' the dope, and he ain't a fuckin' freak like Drobeck neither. Man's got a mind light-years 'head a' his time, you dig what Ah'm sayin'? An' what he's doin', see, he's makin' the Pilgrim a whole shit-pile a' these analogs. Remember what we told you? They're all jes' like the real dope, except'n each one's jes' a little bit different than the real shit, chemically, an' that means they gotta be legal. So all we gotta do is test 'em out, find out which ones *really* do the deed. An' let me tell you, man, some of them really *do it*. Even better than The Lady."

"Come on, 'Bo . . ."

"I'm tellin' you, man, I seen it happen, personal. An' let me tell you somethin' else. Our first lady guinea pig, she turned out t be one turned-on, whacked-out little fox. So like I'm sayin', the ones what do the deed, we're gonna put out in kilo lots . . . one analog at a time. The cops wanna stop it, they gotta change the law real specific-like, make each analog illegal. So you figure we got maybe a year t' deal each one. An' who you think the people on the street gonna be buyin' from, all this time? People sellin' shit they can go to jail for, or people sellin' *legal*, mind-blowin' dope . . . like us? Jes' think 'bout all that bread, man. Jes' think about it!"

"Jesus." Almost a whispered prayer.

"Ain't it the truth," the voice agreed. "An' 'member now, come law-changin' time, all we gotta do's jes' burn the lab t' the ground an' move on t' the next one—don't leave no trace a' nothin' illegal. No big deal 'cause we're gonna have lots a' them anyways. Ain't that right?"

"Franchises, just like McDonald's," the voice agreed wondrously.

"Thass it. We play it right an' I'm telling you, man, there ain't nothin' the Feds or the cops or anybody else can do t' stop us, jes' so long as Locotta's people don't get to us 'fore we set things up . . . and they ain't goin' to, 'cause we gonna stay *low* t' the ground. Ain't that right?"

"But what about Lester . . .?"

"Hey, man, didn't Jimmy take care a' ol' Lester like Ah said he would?"

"Uh, yeah, I guess . . . but what about this chemist guy, 'Bo? I mean, who is he? How come we haven't heard about him before?"

"Beats the shit outta me, man. He's jes' some university dude. All Ah know is Pilgrim calls the man his alchemist."

"An alchemist? A modern-day alchemist who makes legal dope? Jesus, that's all right 'Bo. That is really all right. An alchemist, for Christ sake . . . !"

Tom Fogarty shut off the recorder. The conference room was silent. "So tell me, Ben," he asked quietly, finally breaking the silence, "you still think you and Charley can go back out on the street and buy a pound of cocaine off Jimmy Pilgrim?"

14

As a result of the three-hour time difference between the high desert region of southern California and the low-lying swamplands of Glynco, Georgia, the southwest Mojave Desert sky was still marvelously alight with brilliant, sunset-reflecting wisps of red-orange cirrus clouds as David Isaac and Nichole Faysonnt finally came to the mountaintop end of their long and exhausting desert journey.

Although, in fact, it hadn't been all that long a drive. Only one hundred and twenty-one miles, the last twelve winding up a high rock-mountain road that provided a beautifully scenic view of the Joshua-treed desert floor, the distinctive high-altitude smell of the evergreen pines, the crisply chilled taste of smogless air, and the quiet solitude of the mountain itself.

The two-and-a-half-hour drive should have been a relaxing and pleasant experience for two people in love. And it would have been, had these lovers not been distracted by a multitude of conflicting emotions . . . such as lust, greed, ambition, curiosity, not to mention a growing awareness of their own amateurish uncertainty that had begun to shift into pure, unadulterated fear.

Instead of two hot-blooded lovers eagerly anticipating their arrival at an isolated mountain cabin, it was two tired, cramped, hot, distracted, and emotionally exhausted scientist-conspirators who finally stumbled out of the small Volkswagen bug at the top of Eagle Mountain and stretched gratefully as they took in deep, invigorating breaths of the cold mountain air.

Hand-in-hand, they walked down to the edge of the high cliff overhang where they stood silently, watching as the flame-hued cloud-streaks gradually darkened—finally fading into shades of grey surrounded by a darkening blue.

"I think we missed out on the best part," Nichole whispered, holding Isaac's arm tightly with both hands as she stared out into the growing darkness, not wanting to look at his face. Afraid that she would see a frozen mask of apprehension that would mirror her own.

"No," Isaac shook his head. "It was out there all the time. We just weren't paying enough attention." He turned his head to kiss Nichole and then smiled reassuringly. "There'll be other sunsets. Ones just as beautiful."

"God, I hope so," she whispered fervently.

"You've got to remember, they're not as smart as they want us to believe," Isaac said, trying to reassure himself as much as Nichole. "They're dangerous, and vicious and arrogant, certainly. No question about that. And they're obviously very good at sneaking around in the middle of the night and playing games with . . . people like us."

He shook his head, remembering how his stomach had twisted in horror when he first realized that Nichole's screams were rising in pitch, from passion to something very much resembling . . . terror? How he had looked up in the direction of Nichole's wide-eyed stare to see the long blade-edge of the horrifying knife glistening sharply out from the impaled wall less than three feet above his head. How he had been unable, later, to become effectively aroused, and somehow, still couldn't . . .

"But that's all right," Isaac went on quickly. "We can deal with their games, because we know they make mistakes, just like everyone else—their testing of the A-Seventeen analog being a prime example."

Isaac paused, considering carefully what he was about to say, and then went on. "So what we have to do is to stay alert, and be ready to take immediate advantage of any mistake that affects us. If we can do that, we'll be all right. Agreed?"

Nichole took a deep breath and nodded her head shakily.

"Good," he said, the growing nervousness evident in his voice. "So now let's get to work, and get it done, so we can get out of here."

In another basement—actually a bunkerlike series of offices and workrooms nestled beneath his expensive hillside Del Mar home that overlooked the Pacific Ocean—Lafayette Beaumont Raynee sat alone and very still in a twenty-by-forty-foot room that was almost completely black, thinking about the interwoven elements that influenced his highly enriched life—past, present and future—as he waited for Simon Drobeck's gift to appear.

It was a gift that Rainbow treasured even more than the dozens of ancient weapons that lined the walls of his cavelike underground office. He was fascinated by the histories of violent death that had been documented for every one of the honed blades—the stories of sweaty, straining effort suddenly terminated by a dreadfully swift slash or thrust, yet he relished Simon Drobeck's gift even more . . . because Drobeck's gift was something special.

It was death itself. A living, breathing, slithering, silent death that recognized no equal in its fabled ability to instill terror within a man, no matter how fearsome or fearless he might appear to others.

With the weapons themselves, Raynee could only brush his fingers across the carefully honed edges and imagine the terror that each weapon had evoked. But with Drobeck's gift, he could actually experience the gut-level fear of approaching death . . . and he craved that sensation more than anything else he could imagine.

The only source of illumination in the coal-black room was a single purple bulb mounted high overhead, radiating a nearly invisible deep purple glow, and producing brightly visible light where it struck a fluorescent material. The bulb was the only protection that Lafayette Beaumont Raynee's dreaded "Rainbow personality" would allow himself in satisfying his compulsion to experience over and over again the sensation of approaching death.

And even then, he reminded himself, the light could burn out at any time . . .

. . . because aside from a few threads on his clothing, there were only two objects in this room capable of absorbing the deep purple radiation and giving off that eerie brilliant, yellow-orange glow when . . .

There!

A single yellow-orange spot suddenly appeared at the far left-hand corner of the room. It rose up slowly, turning from side to side so that Raynee could occasionally see that there were, in fact, two glow-

ing spots. Two yellow-orange spots that would sharply resolve themselves into the two fiercely glowing, fluorescent eyes . . .

. . . of Naja, king of the serpents . . .

. . . as the creature slithered forward in the darkness, searching
out the creature who dared to sit in the darkness and watch its approach, never really able to judge the distance accurately as the cobra's
invisible length stretched forward . . .

The telephone in the office next door rang loudly, jarring
Raynee's intensely focused attention. Reluctantly he reached up and
switched on a light, suddenly bathing the room in a soft blue glow that
made the cobra's eyes seem to fluoresce even more brilliantly as it rose
up to a third of its sixteen-foot length and expanded its hood, watching
with motionless intensity as Raynee picked up the unused snake hook
and then stepped out of the room through the single narrow door.

Reaching for the telephone on his desk, his hand brushed
across the package containing the ten screw-capped glass vials, the ten
new analogs, neatly labeled B-8 thru B-16, that he had just received
from Isaac. Each of them contained about ten grams of a white crystalline powder representing the possible future—and power—of
Jimmy Pilgrim and Rainbow. Ten new analogs, at least one of which
just might be the future replacement for heroin and cocaine, or if
nothing else, the immediate replacement for the thiopene analog . . .
which hadn't turned out to be quite what he and Pilgrim were after,
but was certainly going to be satisfactory for their trial run.

"Rainbow," he whispered.

"Pilgrim," the gravelly voice rasped. "Talk to me."

Obediently, Raynee described in detail the ongoing status of
his assignments.

Michael Theiss, their West Coast banker and financial con-
sultant, was now firmly committed to acquiring all of the necessary
funding for the franchised labs. He was still very nervous, to be sure,
but committed nonetheless.

The new analogs were in.

The prototype lab for the thiopene analog production was being
set up by Isaac and his girlfriend right now. It would be ready in time.

There were some problems with the analog-testing program
that Jimmy Pilgrim needed to understand.

"Tell me," Pilgrim demanded.

Raynee explained how he had begun his testing of Isaac's A-17
analog with some readily available, upper-middle-class high school
kids—whose influential parents hadn't been the least bit amused
about being summoned to emergency rooms . . . only to find out from

the police officers that their treasured offspring had damn near over-dosed on some as yet undetermined drug.

The result had been some very intense political pressure put on a couple of small-city police chiefs—who didn't need any prodding in the first place to come down hard on people dealing to high school kids. Two of Raynee's top assistants had been forced to make rapid transfers out of the southern California area. The selection of test subjects would have to be more carefully considered.

"Work it out, and keep testing," Pilgrim ordered. "We need that data."

"You got it."

"So what about Locotta?" Pilgrim demanded.

"Few more a' Jake's people been nosing 'round down here lately," Raynee said. "Ol' Rosey himself's been spreadin' the word that Locotta's real serious 'bout wantin' t' hear from you 'fore ten o'clock tomorrow morning."

"We knew that already," Pilgrim growled.

"Yeah, but it seems like Locotta's gettin' a little impatient," Raynee chuckled. "Hear tell Joe Tassio's in town."

"Oh?" Pilgrim's voice took on a mildly amused tone.

"Think maybe it's 'bout time we did a little talkin'?" Raynee suggested.

There was a pause while Pilgrim seemed to consider this latest bit of intelligence. "Yes," he said finally, "this is an excellent time to provide our friends with a distracting decoy. Give them something to think about while we complete our arrangements."

"Gonna give them boys lotta things t' think 'bout," Raynee chuckled happily to himself, discovering as usual that he was laughing into an empty phone.

After hanging up, Lafayette Beaumont Raynee sat quietly in his chair for a few moments, contemplating the crystalline beauty of the glistening white powder in each of the vials, wondering which—if any of them—it would be. His sensitive hands gently felt for, held and then fondled one of the precision-matched, flat-gripped throwing knives on his desk. His knowing fingers tested the thin edges, searching for the balance point. Then, in a too-quick-to-be-seen motion, his hand blurred forward . . . sending the knife spinning into the chest of the black, wall-mounted, silhouette target with a solid *thump!*

Satisfied with the balance of the knife and the visual purity of the crystals, Raynee reached for the phone again.

"Skylight and Squeek," he whispered. "In my office. One hour."

* * *

By the time that Bylighter was rudely awakened, forcibly dressed in a stained T-shirt and grimy jeans, and then delivered to the underground entrance to Rainbow's office by Roy Schultzheimer, the trembling donut-shop hustler was on the verge of helpless tears.

Schultzheimer finally had to help Bylighter out of the back seat of the car, walking him through the underground garage over to the steel door. The silent bodyguard thumbed a button, nodded toward an overhanging video camera, and shoved Bylighter forward with an impatient grunt as the electronically-controlled door snapped open with a loud *click*!

As Bylighter stumbled forward he heard the heavy door slam shut behind him, and looked up to discover he was standing alone at one end of a curious, boxlike, wooden framework that extended forward about eight feet before funneling out into a darkened open room where he could see Rainbow and someone else with curly blond hair sitting at a desk. A large wrestling mat filled the rest of the room. It was immediately obvious to Bylighter that he couldn't enter the room without passing through the curiously threatening framework.

"Walk up here, boy," Raynee ordered.

"What . . . ?" Bylighter blurted.

"And hold it, *right there*," Raynee commanded as Bylighter saw the throwing knife held balanced and poised in Rainbow's raised hand.

Bylighter came to an immediate stop, his eyes bulging with fear. At that instant, an overhead light switched on over his head, bathing his face with a greenish glow.

"Get your ass in here and sit down, boy," Raynee growled.

Bylighter moved forward hesitantly, and then sat down as directed. Then he jerked away with a terrified squeak as Raynee's hand suddenly lashed forward, sending the knife whirling past Bylighter's head to bury itself in the forehead of the black silhouette target mounted on the cork-lined door.

Triggered by the spinning blade, the ultrasensitive metal detectors in the framework responded, causing a light over the door to glow bright red.

Bylighter was vaguely aware of having urinated in his pants, but he didn't care. His face was ashen, he was shaking uncontrollably with fear, and he couldn't even begin to take his eyes off the other two identical knives resting on the desk top within an inch of Rainbow's right hand.

"Don't look like you're wired, boy," Raynee whispered menacingly.

"Wh—why—? No, God no, I'm—not," Bylighter stuttered, shaking his head wildly, his hands frozen in place on the chair arms. "Why would I—? I mean, Jesus, Rainbow, I *wouldn't*—ever."

"Ah know, boy. Didn't figure you *would*," Raynee went on, indifferent to Bylighter's frantic denials. "But now that Ah *know* you *didn't* . . ." Raynee paused significantly, ". . . you might's well meet your new partner." Raynee motioned with his black-Afroed head. "Skylight, honey, this here boy is Squeek. One Ah told you 'bout."

For the first time since Bylighter had stepped into Raynee's dark, intimidating office, he was able to shift his gaze away from the terrifying collection of wall-mounted knives, swords, and battle axes, and onto the small, blond-haired figure sitting quietly in a chair about six feet from his own.

The first thing that occurred to the still-shaken Bylighter was that the girl wasn't real. She couldn't be. She was too smooth. Too . . . perfect. Somehow, Rainbow had managed to capture an angel, poured her into some sort of thin, silky, spiderweb of a dress, and directed her to just sit there in his terrifying underground office and glow.

The girl—and she *was* real—was absolutely the most beautiful creature he had ever seen in his entire life. Far more erotic than any of the fantasy figures in his well-worn supply of *Playboy* and *Penthouse* magazines. Bylighter saw the light-blond curls that flowed gently down to the girl's soft, smooth, bare shoulders, took in the curvaceous body that was not at all concealed by the thin fabric of her long dress. Then he saw the full, sensuous lips readily forming a wide, loving, curiously amused smile, the dimpled cheeks, and the small pug nose.

But when his eyes came up to those two deep, knowing pools of glowing azure—eyes that seemd to promise a never-ending night of aggressively erotic pleasure—the youth finally understood that the diminutive, angelic Skylight was the furthest thing from an angel that he could possibly imagine.

Once Dr. David Isaac and Nichole Faysonnt had begun to assemble the component parts of their "underground" laboratory, the terrifying memories of the previous morning seemed to gradually fade away—much in the manner of the shifting, reddish-orange hues in the sunset-reflecting cirrus clouds.

Although the analogy of sunset wasn't all that consoling, Isaac reminded himself as he got down on his hands and knees to examine the rust-crusted water-cut-off valves under the basement sink. He knew that, like the vanished sun, the source of their early-morning terror would not leave them alone for long. Given sufficient time both were certain to return, one as inevitable as the other.

David Isaac was finally beginning to understand how Jimmy Pilgrim's malicious mind worked, and what he understood he didn't like at all.

Fortunately for Isaac, however, the limitations of the block-wall basement as a site for a safe and functional illicit drug laboratory provided plenty of distracting problems.

Most of the problems were mechanical: blocked ventilation ducts, clogged drain pipes, shorting circuit breakers and broken light bulbs. However, the ever-encroaching desert still managed to add a few natural hazards of its own, including a seemingly unlimited supply of dirt, sand, bugs and spiders . . . and a lively and inquisitive little kangaroo rat that refused to be cornered, caught or dislodged from its basement home.

Working nonstop, it took the pair almost two full hours to bring the basement up to a minimum standard of acceptability, which didn't necessarily include the still-elusive kangaroo rat. After making a third unsuccessful attempt to corner the tiny creature, Nichole decided to name it after her distant father's racy British sports car.

Finally realizing that further efforts to evict "Mini-Cooper" from his habitat were doomed to failure, Isaac and Nichole gave up, taking a thirty-minute break instead to wash up and eat before taking on the far more demanding task of assembling the complex chemistry apparatus.

Like Isaac, Nichole Faysonnt was at heart a highly competent and enthusiastic lab-bench chemist who thoroughly enjoyed the challenge of a difficult problem. In spite of the recent fear and confusion that had been added to her new relationship with Isaac, she seemed to find comfort in functioning as part of a team: unpacking heavy-walled glassware as each piece was needed, using metal clamps, ring supports, and thick dabs of stopcock grease to mount, connect and seal each ground-glass tapered joint.

As each piece of glassware was moved into position, they stopped to rinse critical reaction surfaces with distilled water, readjusted the clamps and support rods, and then neatly set the packing materials aside before going on to the next step.

Once mounted in place, each of the huge, spherical glass reaction vessels was connected with more joint grease to the intricate blown-glass reflux condensers—which in turn were connected to the basement waterlines and drains by lengths of clear plastic tubing.

Thick-walled rubber vacuum lines were connected between

the pump and the equally thick-walled glass flasks to filter the crystalized compounds out of the mother liquids.

A small tab-A-to-slot-B fume hood was assembled, hooked to the vents, and then stocked with the trays and dessicators that would ultimately dry the pure, filtered crystals into piles of fluffy white powder.

Step by step, the dirty, cobwebby basement of the isolated desert-mountain home began—much to Isaac's and Nichole's amusement—to take on the appearance of an alchemist's dungeon laboratory.

In something less than three hours, the two professional chemists had the basic "cooking" apparatus for preparing five- and ten-kilogram batches of the thiopene analog in place. They took a couple of minutes out to savor the interwoven beauty of the glistening pyrex structure, and to recheck their work. Then, as Isaac went over the electrical connections, Nichole went outside to the car and quickly returned with some far-less-sophisticated chemical apparatus.

Five minutes later, as Isaac knelt in front of a complex vacuum pump, reviewing in his mind how he was going to run a ground wire to one of the nearby water pipes, the invigorating aroma of freshly brewing coffee began to fill the basement.

Once Isaac was satisfied that the vacuum pump was securely grounded, he and Nichole took a welcomed twenty-minute coffee break, and Isaac—easily lapsing into his accustomed role as mentor—explained to Nichole why the expensive set of vapor condensers was absolutely critical to the success of the entire project.

"From a safety standpoint, we certainly can't allow any buildup of cyanide or ether to occur—" Isaac began his explanation as he sipped gratefully at the hot coffee. \

"Sure, basic lab safety," Nichole nodded her head impatiently. "I understand all that, but what I'm saying is why not just vent the vapors outside, instead of containing them at the reaction and drying sites?" she asked reasonably. "Those condensers must have cost a bundle."

"Don't tell me you're suddenly concerned about spending Pilgrim's money," Isaac teased, grinning in amusement.

"No, not at all," Nichole shook her head wearily. "It's just that it doesn't make sense. Why go to the expense of running all the vents through condensers, when all we're really doing is increasing the danger of an explosion? With the ventilation we've added, cyanide exposure will be minimal. And you've grounded all of the electrical equipment, so there shouldn't be any serious concern about an ether fire—unless their chemist is foolish enough to use a flame down here;

in which case . . ." she shrugged, looking around the earth-contained basement.

"But you're still thinking like a chemist." Isaac shook his head. "You're forgetting the one critical factor: In an underground laboratory, concealment can be just as important as safety . . . and if our assumptions are correct, perhaps even more so. At any rate, Pilgrim certainly can't afford to have anyone discover the location of this lab. And you know how easily even trace amounts of ethyl ether or cyanide can be detected in the air outside a chemistry lab."

"So we set up a contained system that increases the risk of some student chemist searing his lungs with a flash fire, or shutting off his metabolism with cyanide, just so . . . ?"

"But we aren't the ones who are putting that individual at risk," Isaac reminded gently. "We've agreed to provide Pilgrim with a system that functions as requested. Beyond that, we can only assume that the "chemist" they use will know enough to make frequent checks for leaks . . ."

"And know enough about ether not to smoke while he works," Nichole added.

"That too," he nodded. "But regardless of all that, we simply can't hold ourselves responsible for the foolish actions of others."

"But—" she started to protest.

"It's the same with the analogs themselves," he went on insistently. "People are going to continue to take drugs, regardless of who makes them, and somebody is going to reap the benefits of that production. As it happens, you and I now have the unique opportunity to develop and test a fascinating group of analog compounds that may drastically alter our present concepts of neurological chemistry."

"But at the expense—" Nichole tried again, determined to play devil's advocate until she had resolved her own uneasiness with their illicit project.

"—of a few individuals who would almost certainly destroy themselves with heroin or PCP anyway," Isaac finished. "A foolish waste of their lives."

"I suppose that's true."

"You *know* it's true," Isaac went on firmly. "The ethical concept of using guinea pigs of *any* species—including *Homo sapiens*—is certainly open to debate, but let's be honest with ourselves. Where would we—as scientists—be, in terms of scientific advancement, if we didn't encourage the use of guinea pigs?"

"I know, but—"

"Nichole," Isaac said, "you and I can make hundreds of computer projections. We can evaluate, estimate and theorize. But until we actually test those analogs out on a wide spectrum of human beings, we simply won't *know* how they work. And under the current government rules and regulations, it would be years—perhaps even decades—before we could even *begin* to properly test a single analog. And with so many possibilities, so many viable structures," Isaac shook his head and sighed, "neither you or I could even scratch the surface in our lifetimes. At least not . . . legally."

Nichole was quiet now, pensive but no longer arguing. More than anything else, she wanted desperately for everything to be back the way it was before Isaac had been changed by the Maria documents—and that terrifying knife, she shuddered. But it was too late to turn back now. Much too late. To survive now as researchers and as lovers—to survive at all—they could only go forward.

"So, inevitably, we return to the same point," Isaac shrugged. "This man Pilgrim has provided us with an enormous opportunity. I contend that we would be foolish—professionally, historically, and perhaps even ethically—if we turn away from this once-in-a-lifetime chance to probe the chemical depths of the human mind."

"And fail to follow in the footsteps of Maria?" Nichole whispered, staring directly into Isaac's pained eyes.

"Yes, that too," Isaac nodded. "It's clear in her notes that she was trying to tell all of us something critically important. I think we owe it to her legacy—and to ourselves—to listen very carefully."

"GODDAMNIT, YOU LITTLE SHIT-HEAD! Are you *listenin'* t' what Ah'm tellin' you?" Rainbow demanded, slamming his hand down on the desk top and glaring at Bylighter after his attention once again shifted over to the blond-haired girl.

"Uhhh!—" Bylighter jerked his head around, his mouth suddenly dry with fear. "Uh, uh—y-y-yeah, s-sure, Rainbow—I've been listening, honest!"

"Then Ah wanna hear it back," Raynee snarled, pointing at the terrified youth with one of the throwing knives. "Talk t' me!"

"Uh, me and Skylight," Bylighter began, stuttering helplessly, "we're—we're supposed to t-t-test out those n-new analogs. G-give them to the hookers, s-s-some t' the j-johns. See which ones g-give—"

"An' you're gonna help her, right out a' that fuckin' donut shop, jes' like Ah told you. And you're gonna do *anything* she tells you t' do. And you're *not* gonna fuck up this time. You understand what Ah'm sayin', boy?"

Bylighter nodded frantically, unable to speak, his eyes bulging with fear as he watched the point of the thick, double-edged knife-blade center on his bony chest.

"WELL?!"

"I—I—understand," Bylighter managed to squeak out through his fear-constricted larynx. "Jesus, Rainbow—I m-mean—I won't—"

"Ah *know* you won't," Raynee glared. "Now you tell me again 'bout that girl an' her friends. The one you said's been hittin' you up for them ounces."

"Uh—uh—I think they're s-still interested—I guess. I told them—told 'em I'd meet with them tomorrow, 'round noon. See if I can g-get something arranged. Then I guess . . ."

"Get the fuck outta here," Raynee growled, "an' change them pants 'fore you shit in 'em too."

"B-but what about the—"

"GET OUTTA HERE!"

As Raynee and Skylight watched with unconcealed amusement, Bylighter shot up out of his chair and ran, disappearing through the barely opened door as Raynee released the lock-mechanism at his desk.

"I don't believe it, he really did piss in his pants," Skylight shook her head slowly in wonder.

"Ain't much to that boy," Raynee acknowledged, tossing the throwing knife down on the desk top with a snort of disgust. "Here, Ah want you t' take these here analogs," he said, shoving the package of screw-capped vials over to Skylight. "Put 'em up in tenth-gram bindles. Mark 'em with the numbers so we can keep track." Raynee shook his Afroed head in irritation. "Gettin' so Ah can't trust that little shithead t' do nuttin' right any more."

"I've never seen anyone so absolutely pathetic," Skylight replied, transferring the vials to her purse. "I still don't understand why you keep him around. It's not like you," she added suggestively.

"Times when a huntin' man wants t' draw somethin' in real close," Raynee whispered, "like as not, he's gonna go find hisself a decoy; somethin' that's gonna make a whole lotta noise an' attract a shitload a' attention. But the man, he don' wanna use somethin' good . . . jes' some throwaway shit. Know what Ah mean? Lotta people 'round here gonna be out huntin' 'fore long," Raynee smiled. "Might get kinda hard t' tell who's huntin' who. You gonna be able t' handle it all?"

"You mean Squeek?" Skylight's cheeks dimpled into a disbelieving grin as she laughed.

"Squeek, the girls, the johns . . . the whole fuckin' gig. Gonna get kinda crazy 'round this neighborhood. Might even have t' act like you *like* that boy, comes down t' it." Raynee continued to smile, but not with his eyes.

Skylight returned his gaze with a look that was equally cold and indifferent, and then whispered as she brought the fingers of her right hand slowly up the front of her skin-tight dress. "You know that I can."

Crouched low under one of the new, oily-smelling additions to his basement habitat, the tiny kangaroo rat who had unknowingly taken on the name "Mini-Cooper" uneasily sensed that the vibrations on the cement floor—and the noises in the echoing room—had changed. Instead of the two huge creatures who had made wonderful additions to his subterranean home, there were now two different creatures moving around in the basement—both still huge and noisy, but nonetheless different.

True to the inherent nature of his species, the small rodent was curious. So much so that he was willing to stop his incessant nibbling and brave the blinding overhead lights in order to see what treasures these new creatures might provide.

Cautiously, he hopped out from beneath the protective vacuum pump, and then froze in place as he sensed the danger . . .

. . . and leaped high in the air, emitting a tiny, panicked squeal as the triangular head of the huge snake slashed forward just beneath his tiny, springlike legs.

Mini-Cooper had less than a second to spare before the snake recovered with a hiss of rage and then struck once again, the small desert rodent almost wasting that second by futilely scratching at the concrete floor—instinctively trying to kick non-existent grains of blinding sand into the eyes of the horrible creature—before leaping into a pile of disassembled cardboard boxes that, at best, would provide only a temporary sanctuary.

Frantically burrowing deep within the cardboard and shredded paper, the little kangaroo rat finally stopped and crouched down as his tiny lungs worked feverishly to renew his energy reserves. There he discovered that his primary defense mechanism—his ability to hear whispery-faint noises with his huge ears—was being drowned out by waves of meaningless giggling sounds.

Out in the middle of the basement room, Simon Drobeck continued to giggle to himself, thoroughly enjoying the antics of his excited pet as he began to photograph Isaac's laboratory in detail with a

Polaroid camera, savoring the knowledge that the tiny kangaroo rat would now be listening in terror for the first slithering approach-sounds of the huge, hungry snake that now shared his once-secure home.

15

THE COPS ALL called it the graveyard shift, suggesting, and probably even savoring, the illusion of a lone patrol car moving slowly and quietly through fog-shrouded rows of marble headstones between the hours of midnight and dawn.

It was an illusion that became all the more intriguing with the discovery that the implied nervousness, the discomforts and sensations of ever-approaching danger were, in fact, based on a reality that had very little to do with the spiritual underworld.

Its reality, instead, was comprised of bone-chilling night air in even the warmest of climates, of glary streetlights that made the darkened alleys and fields appear even more desolate and dangerous, of lonely, isolated patrol beats with only the intermittent chatter of dispatched radio traffic for company, and of the murderers and rapists and burglars who preferred to caper during those dark, quiet hours.

All of this said a great deal about the police officers and sheriff's deputies who aggressively sought out assignments on the graveyard shift. Especially the ones who truly enjoyed prowling the almost-empty streets as they searched patiently for furtive movement in the shadowy darkness—searching for burglars, arsonists, dope-dealers and all of the other scumbags who worked their own graveyard shifts—while waiting to receive one of the cherished hot calls that were guaranteed to send the adrenaline levels of even the most street-hardened veteran skyrocketing once again. Like Rainbow's street people, the graveyard cops too had a habit to feed.

The type of call itself didn't matter to the graveyard cops. Robbery, rape, assault or burglary . . . it all amounted to the same thing. Because all they really wanted was for one of the criminal-type assholes to pop up in the open long enough to commit a single illicit act. Just one would do fine. Then the fun would begin . . .

. . . which probably explained why Rainbow chose to wait deep in the shadows of an almost-empty parking lot in downtown San Diego until the probing beam of the slowly moving patrol car's searchlight went on by.

Then too, Raynee's choice might have been influenced by the knowledge that the name Lafayette Beaumont Raynee, AKA Rainbow, was prominently recorded in the police computer files, with a coded "flag" advising any querying patrol officer that he had just hit the jackpot. Dope and prostitutes. Aggravated assault. Possible murder. Most likely armed with at least two knives. Certainly dangerous. Definitely worth rousting. And by the way, don't worry too much about hurting his feelings. He ain't got none.

Raynee wasn't the least bit afraid of confronting any police officer in San Diego County, but at the same time he wasn't eager to tangle with a radio patrol car in a downtown San Diego alley at 3:25 in the morning . . . for the very simple and logical reason that it wouldn't be one-on-one very long.

Not on a stop of AKA Rainbow.

That was one of the first lessons that Raynee had learned in the ghetto streets of Harlem: that it never stayed one-on-one with a cop if they even *thought* you might be a badass.

Go after a lawman with ready access to a radio, and the odds very quickly shifted to three-, five-, or even ten-on-one. Which was to say: two, five or ten aggressive-type graveyard cops—not one of whom had the slightest interest in getting into a man-to-man, eyeball-to-eyeball street fight with a crazy, knife-wielding black dude like Rainbow. Certainly not when they could just as easily deal with him from a distance. Like at about seven yards with a couple of .357 hollow-points, or a low-aimed round of number-four buckshot.

Raynee knew the razor-edged combat knife he held tight

against his thigh could easily drop a single police officer, given the proper circumstances, but a pair of officers was a different situation entirely. And besides, the bladed weapon that Raynee held lovingly in his right hand was meant for someone else.

For a fearsome man in his own right who went by the name of Joe Tassio.

Locotta's man.

Content to be patient, Lafayette Beaumont Raynee waited in the shadows until he was rewarded with the sharp clicking sound of the back door to the bar.

The first man out the door was one of Tassio's hired guns—a gangly, large-framed professional killer, who looked up and found himself moving slowly and carefully back into the darkened office, the terrifyingly sharp K-Bar knife pressed tight against one of the pulsating jugular veins in his neck.

In a matter of a few moments, the shaken gunman was sitting at a desk in the reilluminated office with his hands flat and immobile on the desk top, watching nervously as Raynee first unloaded and then tossed the licensed pistol over to the red-faced bodyguard's employer.

Joe Tassio caught the pistol one-handed, glared disgustedly at his high-paid associate, then tossed the weapon to the floor near the desk with a grunt of apparent indifference.

"Nice to see ya again, Rainbow," Tassio growled, eyeing the knife in Raynee's hand as he carefully sat back down in the chair, prudently keeping his knuckle-scarred hands out in open view, even though it was clearly understood by all three men in the room that Joe Tassio never carried a gun. He much preferred to use his powerful bare hands.

One other point of mutual understanding was that Joe Tassio had little reason to be concerned about his welfare . . . at least for the moment. It was obvious—especially to Tassio's bodyguard—that had Rainbow been so inclined, Joe Tassio would have long since been one of two bodies lying sprawled and bleeding on the floor.

The fact that Tassio was still alive—Raynee having stepped back from his surprise advantage into a standoff position where he held minimal, although still effective, control—suggested to the professional enforcer that it might be foolish to test the crushing strength of his hands against the reputed speed and viciousness of Raynee's knife, at least in this particular setting. There would be other opportunities . . . at some later date and time.

Joe Tassio was curious. He'd been sent down to San Diego to find Jimmy Pilgrim and to get certain information. All things considered, which included Tassio's wary respect of Raynee's street reputation, it seemed prudent to listen to what the grinning pimp had to say. Matters of ego and proper respect could always be resolved at that later date and time.

"Understand you been askin' 'round 'bout me," Raynee offered, his wide smile filled with gleaming white teeth.

"You and Jimmy," Tassio growled. "Locotta's been hearing a lotta loose talk about your operation down here. Wants to have a serious talk with you two, real quick-like. Especially Pilgrim."

Tassio hesitated, uncertain as to how far to push Raynee. "The thing is, you guys've been kinda hard to track down lately," he added accusingly.

"Ain't been much interested in talkin' t' people lately," Raynee chuckled. "Got me a lotta things cookin' down here. Serious shit. Gotta make sure Ah got things straight in mah head 'fore Ah go 'round talkin' business with the boss man. Hear what Ah'm sayin'?"

Tassio blinked. The first piece of information had been offered.

"Since when does Jimmy Pilgrim let you do his talking for him?" Tassio demanded.

"Mah main man's been kinda outta touch lately," Raynee shrugged, still smiling pleasantly. "So Ah been takin' care a' business, best way Ah know how."

"How far out of touch, Rainbow?" Tassio whispered with just a touch of menace.

"Way far out of it, man," Raynee grinned savagely. "Far fuckin' out. Know what Ah mean?"

Tassio considered that bit of information for a moment.

"You want me to relay that message to Jake?"

"Ah'd appreciate it," Raynee nodded slowly, turning his head momentarily to smile pleasantly at the fidgety bodyguard. "Figure the boss man don' want no trouble down here. Leastwise, not so long's Ah can keep the bread movin' up his way. Can't see no sense in you an' me gettin' all heated up ovah little action in mah territory, seein's how you probably got plenty t' keep yerself busy up north. Pissin' contest might git downright ugly. Know what Ah mean?"

"Yeah, it might at that," Tassio nodded thoughtfully, smiling calmly at Rainbow before favoring his uncomfortable bodyguard with a meaningful glare.

"Figured you an' Ah could talk business, man-t'-man like," Raynee chuckled. "You always was willin' t' listen polite-like t' us jive-ass niggers."

"I'll pass the word on to Jake," Tassio muttered, ignoring

Raynee's pointed sarcasm. "Anything else you wanna talk about?" Tassio stood up, slowly and carefully, very much in tune with the underlying threat of violent death in Raynee's voice. His bodyguard stayed put.

"Naw. Don't wanna take up any mo' your time," Raynee shook his head, slowly and easily backing out of the doorway. "Nice talkin' with you."

"Hey, Rainbow," Tassio called out, watching the black pimp's eyes carefully as Raynee stepped back into the darkened hallway. "Listen, tell Jimmy I hope things work out okay. Hate to see him get hurt over all this." Tassio's one last attempt at the confirmation.

"Now don' you go worryin' 'bout Jimmy Pilgrim none," Raynee admonished from the hallway. "He be doin' jes' fine where he be. Matter a' fact, he ain't hurt'n none at all," Raynee laughed, then disappeared into the darkness.

By 4:30 in the morning, much to Simon Drobeck's amusement, his persistent python had managed to corner the terrified kangaroo rat within a small pile of shredded newspaper in a dusty corner of the basement. The frantic scurrying sounds of the trapped rodent so appealed to Drobeck's perverse nature that he had to stop his survey of Dr. David Isaac's recently constructed underground laboratory just to watch the rodent's final moments of paralyzed fear. His moment of sensual anticipation was interrupted by the arrival of Bobby Lockwood.

"Drobeck?" Lockwood called out as he came in through the basement stairs door, his blindfold having been removed by Schultzheimer upstairs. "We're ready—OH SHIT!" he blurted out as he spotted the dark, shifting coils of the huge python at the opposite side of the underground room. "Goddamn it, Drobeck, I warned you—"

"Be quiet," Drobeck hissed.

Bobby Lockwood stared in revulsion for a moment as the weaving head of the huge snake followed the jerking bits of paper. Then he exploded.

"ALL RIGHT, FUCK IT!" Lockwood yelled, causing Drobeck to spin around on his stool in horror as the sharp metallic snap of a round being chambered into a .380 automatic pistol echoed through the basement.

"WHAT—? NO, WAIT!" Drobeck screamed as he saw the small weapon come up in Lockwood's hand. Drobeck threw himself off the stool and scrambled into the heaving mass of rubbery coils, finally coming up with a savagely hissing head in one fat hand and loops of twisting, muscular snake in the other, turning his fat body to protect the snake. He glared accusingly at the curly-haired youth—who had just been driven up the mountain to help Drobeck photograph, sketch and chart out the highly secret lab.

"How dare you!" Drobeck shrieked.

"I warned you before, Drobeck," Bobby Lockwood shook his head, his voice shaky as he moved the aim-point of the small pistol away from Drobeck's protruding stomach, realizing as his brief moment of insanity faded that he didn't dare shoot Drobeck because he knew Jimmy Pilgrim and Rainbow needed the son of a bitch. "Goddamn it, I *warned* you."

"I'm in charge here," Drobeck hissed. "You were brought up here to do exactly what I—"

"Bullshit!" Lockwood snarled. "You know I can't stand being around that fucking snake. You want me and Tim to help you work this place, then you get that fucking thing outta here. Right now! I mean it, man," he added with a meaningful motion of the lowered pistol.

"I'll put her away . . . for now," Drobeck muttered sullenly, glaring at Lockwood as he stomped up the stairs with his still-thrashing pet to complain to Schultzheimer, ignoring Lockwood's ponytailed helper, Tim, as he edged his way down the stairs.

"Jesus, that guy's a number one fruitcake," Tim commented.

"Yeah, and that's about all he is, far as I'm concerned," Lockwood nodded as he replaced the illegally concealed pistol in his leg holster. "Trouble is, I hear Rainbow likes the ugly son of a bitch."

"So what are we supposed to do, move all this stuff?"

"Nope," Lockwood said as he handed his assistant an SX-70 Polaroid camera and a bag of film packs and flash bars. "Supposed to help Drobeck take pictures and sketch out how all those pieces of glassware are hooked together. According to Roy, we're supposed to make another lab just like this one somewhere else. Six more, in fact."

Tim shook his head in disgust. "Didn't you say they just got through building this place, and they haven't even used it yet?"

"Yeah, far as I know."

"So what's the deal? Everybody in this outfit crazy like Drobeck?"

"Beats the shit outta me," Lockwood shrugged, watching the little kangaroo rat he had inadvertently rescued as it suddenly broke into a frenzied series of small hops across the cement floor of the basement. "I just work for the dudes. Learned a long time ago it don't pay to screw up or ask a lotta questions," he added, as he thought once again about the fate of his ex-gram-dealer buddy, Jamie MacKenzie.

Raynee was stretched lazily out on the wide expanse of his bed, when the red phone on the nightstand rang loudly. Six A.M. exactly. Right on time.

"This mah Thursday morning wake-up call?" Raynee yawned.

"Understand you had a little talk with Tassio," Jimmy Pilgrim rasped into the telephone.

"Yeah, Ah heard the dude might be checkin' out the bars, askin' 'round 'bout us bad boys. An' sure enuf, he was," Raynee laughed. "So what happened, me and him, we had a little *conversation,* couple hours ago. Nice an' friendly like, more or less."

"And?"

"Ah figure somebody oughta be wakin' up ol' man Locotta any time 'bout now, tellin' him that Jimmy Pilgrim's crazy-ass nigger might a' done did the deed on his boss man."

Pilgrim responded in a way that actually startled Raynee. He laughed. Or at least the explosive, guttural noises that caused a chill to run down Lafayette Beaumont Raynee's spine *sounded* like laughter. It wasn't always easy to tell with Pilgrim.

"They're getting impatient," Pilgrim chuckled. "Locotta'll be putting taps on our phones if he hasn't already. We should start using our message-switching system as soon as we can."

"It's almost ready to go," Raynee said. "Got a couple more a' them new computer terminals t' deliver, then we're ready."

"Fine—but in the meantime, I've got a rather difficult task for you," Pilgrim whispered, as the almost human laughter died in his throat; an effect that always made Raynee uneasy. Raynee much preferred to deal with Pilgrim when he was predictably cold and indifferent, not when he was in his game-playing mood. The thing was, *nobody* liked to deal with a game-playing madman like Jimmy Pilgrim, not even Rainbow.

"Yeah?"

"We have to confirm the sales aspect of the analog theory," Pilgrim said. "Make a test run."

"Job don't sound all that difficult," Raynee drawled. "Ah miss somethin'?"

"In this case, it will be useful to have a buyer available to take the fall. An expendable buyer," Pilgrim added helpfully.

"You want it wired from both ends," Raynee said. "Lots a' possibilities inna deal like that. What kinda volume you got in mind?"

"Ounces. Pound at the outside. Drobeck's going to prepare a one-pound test batch of the thiopene analog in the new lab. The powder should be available by Saturday."

"Kinda hate to see a pound a' that shit go out on our rep," Raynee said quietly. "The buzz ain't all that predictable."

"The effects won't matter," Pilgrim growled, his voice reverting to its normally cold indifference. "If the deal is worked properly, the powder won't reach the streets." Pilgrim paused. "What about that girl and her friends from Newport? The ones who tried to hit up Bylighter for the coke last week. That deal still running?"

"Still on," Raynee replied. "Squeek's supposed t' connect with 'em today, 'round noontime, after he an' Skylight get their shit t'gether with our lay-lady guinea pigs. Not sure I like it, though."

"You think they're heat?"

"Don't know," Raynee admitted. "Background's comin' back clean so far. No hooks back t' that other fox. But Ah ain't 'xactly what you'd call *convinced* jes' yet. Figurin' on passin' them over to the General anyways. You wanna do the switch on them?"

"Yes," Pilgrim said. "One way or the other, I think they'll work out just fine."

By nine o'clock that Thursday morning, Eugene Bylighter was back at the donut shop, groggy from lack of sleep, and up to his elbows in sudsy, lukewarm water.

He was going through the motions of cleaning a stack of thirty-inch-square metal donut pans, when he suddenly became aware that another body was standing there. A body topped with curly golden hair and a pair of brilliant blue eyes. An irresistible body that offered the promise of unimagined sexual pleasures. The very same body, in fact, that he had been daydreaming about almost constantly since he awoke that morning.

The graceful, athletic, seductive body of Skylight.

"You ready to go to work?" the diminutive young woman said in a quiet, firm voice.

Bylighter nodded mutely.

"Then get it in gear. We've got a lot of people to see this morning."

As far as Bylighter was concerned, the next three hours of his life came about as close to pure heaven as he figured he'd ever get. Heaven, in his case, consisted of the passenger bucket seat of a twenty-thousand-dollar metallic-flake blue Porsche, high-quality music on a five-speaker stereo system possessing thirty-odd buttons, levers and knobs, and a state of mental ecstasy that bordered on the orgasmic, simply from the physical pleasure of sitting next to Skylight in the cockpit-like sports car interior.

Bylighter obediently made a dozen five-bindle deliveries of the new "B"-series of analogs to the first twelve girls in Skylight's mental address book.

It never occurred to Bylighter to question the obvious: why Rainbow would want him to do an important task that Skylight could have just as easily done herself, or why she would go to considerable lengths at each of the drop points to keep herself and her readily identifiable Porsche well out of sight. Bylighter was content with his lot, blissfully unaware that he might soon become the focal point of a very serious and deadly game.

Oddly enough, his childlike naiveté also provided a certain amount of amusement for Skylight—who, in addition to stimulating his long-frustrated libido, decided to give him an education in the mechanics of organized prostitution.

Among other things, Bylighter quickly learned that there were considerable differences between the lifestyles of the overworked runaways who plied the street corners and bars for short-time customers in his own neighborhood and those of the very well paid, part-time call girls on Skylight's payroll.

In the matter of clothing, for example, Bylighter's streetwalking acquaintances tended to favor the basic style: a bright-colored, skin-tight leotard worn with a contrasting, extremely short skirt and a pair of very high-heeled shoes. While the overall effect was unquestionably crude and tasteless, the advertised product was easily recognizable from a distance, critical element in luring one of the anxious johns driving around in search of a quick pickup.

Rainbow's high-priced call girls had little use for such high-visibility advertising. They depended on Skylight to make their initial contacts. Repeat business was entirely dependent on their subsequent efforts and enthusiasm. As such, Skylight also arranged for her girls to be provided with a wide selection of expensive outfits ranging from exquisite dinner gowns to filmy baby-doll nighties. Skylight and her girls understood that it was the proffered illusion of personal interest, and the quality of their services—rather than the illicit thrill of quickly purchased sex—that brought their customers back for more.

And as to the clients themselves, here again it was a matter of quality versus quantity. Under Skylight's management, her girls rarely had to "service" more than one john—that is, one healthy, bathed, vigorous, and often even affectionate customer—a night. In an expensive hotel room, of course. All of which was in direct contrast to the working conditions of Bylighter's runaway friends, who tried to work in as many tricks as possible during a single evening, ideally without having to remove their leotards or move too far away from their favorite street corner in the process.

And then there was the matter of price.

Vaguely aware that his street associates were usually willing to accept a twenty—and occasionally even a ten—for extremely "basic" services, Bylighter was dumbfounded to learn that a call-out order for one of Skylight's girls started at one hundred dollars for the first hour, in advance, MasterCard and Visa being perfectly acceptable.

The question might just as well have been written in block letters across Bylighter's acne-scarred face.

"You really want to know what I'd charge, don't you, Squeek?" Skylight said matter-of-factly as she power-turned the low-slung Porsche onto the freeway on-ramp.

"Uh—uh, well," Bylighter stammered. "I—I guess I didn't think—"

"Didn't think what? That I don't trick?" Skylight turned to look at Bylighter, an expression of mildly incredulous disbelief on her dimpled, smiling face. "Is that what you really think?"

"Uh—yeah, I guess. I—uh, I mean, I guess I thought you were more—uh—I mean—"

"More selective?" Skylight suggested, her eyes twinkling playfully.

Bylighter could only nod his head, but he felt his stomach twist in what could only be described as an overpowering surge of adolescent jealousy. Somehow, for some illogical reason, it didn't seem right that, having found her, he should have to share her.

"You really don't understand, do you?" Skylight shook her head in amazement.

Bylighter looked up, his eyes questioning.

"Squeek, you happen to be looking at somebody who's about as selective as she can get and still trick. And I *do* trick, Squeek, believe me—with just about anybody who can meet my price."

"A—a—anybody?" Bylighter couldn't believe his ears.

"Long as he's got the bucks and the balls," Skylight nodded matter-of-factly.

"Even—me?" He almost choked on the words.

Skylight turned her head briefly to stare at Bylighter, her eyes widening in surprise. She started to laugh and then remembered

Rainbow's admonition. She might have to like the little bastard. She allowed her face to dimple into a smile that damn near set Bylighter's groin on fire. "Yeah, maybe even you, Squeek," she said. "You come up with my price—straight five or fifteen—and I'm yours."

"Five—dollars?" Bylighter's mouth dropped. "You mean you'd—?"

"Jesus, Squeek, you really are something, aren't you? Where the hell'd Rainbow find you anyway?"

"Well—I—"

"Listen, babe, my price happens to be five *hundred* dollars, for one hour. You want an overnighter, it's fifteen. Hundred, that is," she added with a dimpled wink.

"Five—hundred—dollars?" Bylighter whispered weakly, his spirits sinking. "A—a—an hour—it just d-doesn't seem like much t-time—"

"Sometimes an hour can be a *very* long time, Squeek," Skylight laughed. "Anyway, it's always been plenty long enough for most of the guys I know," she added with a knowing grin. "Why, you figure you could handle more?"

"I—I don't have five hundred dollars," Bylighter choked out, trying very hard to keep the desperate, pleading tone out of his voice. "But I got . . . I got something that's worth five hundred—easy."

"Oh yeah, what's that?"

"About f-five spoons worth of the h-hottest p-powder on the street," he tried.

"You're trying to buy me with some of Jimmy Pilgrim's new dope?" Skylight glanced over at Bylighter with a look of pure shock on her face. "Jesus Christ, Squeek, what the hell're you using for brains? You know what Rainbow'd do to you if I told him?"

"No, no," Bylighter shook his head frantically. "I don't mean the new stuff. It's something else . . . something special I—uh—kinda saved back from the first tests. It's really d-dynamite, I'm tellin' you, only see—" Bylighter hesitated, unable to figure out how to explain the screwup with the A-17 and the thiopene analogs to Skylight without telling her the whole story. A story that would certainly get back to Rainbow.

"No way, Squeek. Cash money. That's the only way it works. You come up with five bills and we'll talk about it some more. In the meantime," she added, "we've still got a lot more deliveries to make, but it's almost twelve. Weren't you supposed to be back at the shop by noon?"

"I—I'm gonna get that money," Bylighter said with a strange

sense of determination that he had never experienced before in his life.

"Squeek, quit thinking about your fucking joint for a minute and *listen* to me. Do you want to go back to the shop?" Skylight repeated patiently.

"No," he whispered, shaking his head despondently. He wasn't going to get to have her after all. It wasn't fair. It just wasn't fair. "No," he whispered again, "I don't wanna go back. Let's go finish the deliveries to your—uh—uh—" he stammered helplessly, then hurried on. "Then maybe we can go do the street girls. It'll go faster," he promised, "'cause I—uh—I guess I kinda know them better. You know." Bylighter couldn't stand the idea of leaving Skylight. Not yet.

The golden-haired girl shrugged. "Your funeral, kid," she said, and then turned off the freeway en route to the next high-rise apartment building on her list.

"Yeah, well, that's okay," Bylighter whispered, mostly to himself. "'cause I'm gonna figure out how to get me that money. You'll see."

16

THE YOUNG DAY manager who was supposed to be manning the sales counter was busily reading a tattered comic book while alternately wiping his runny nose on the back of his hand and then using that same hand to dip a stack of greasy plain donuts, one by one, into a vat of thinly-colored glaze icing. He looked up apprehensively as the two tired, irritable men entered the back room of the donut shop.

"Uh—help you guys?"

"We're looking for a kid named Bylighter," Koda said, forcibly blanking out the sudden, unappetizing realization that he and Charley had each consumed two identically glazed, grease-soaked donuts about an hour earlier.

"You mean Squeek? He ain't here," the youth sniffled helpfully.

"Yeah, we can see that," Koda nodded. "We were supposed to meet him here at noon."

"Don't think he'll be here," the youth shrugged. "Uh, either you guys want a fresh donut?"

"Another time, maybe." Koda shook his head and then, hurrying on before his equally dismayed partner found his voice, "Think maybe you could tell us *why* you don't think he'll be here?"

"Mostly 'cause he left here, oh 'long about nine this morning with the most beautiful piece of grade-A-prime ass I ever did see." The sniffling youth started to describe Skylight as best he could, only to be interrupted by an immediately suspicious and disbelieving Koda.

"You sure we're talking about the same Bylighter?"

"Dumb-shit guy, about eighteen, wall-to-wall zits?" The youth took a big bite out of the donut. "Ain't got enough brains to blow his—"

"That . . . sounds like Bylighter," Koda broke in quickly. "I don't suppose you'd happen to know where they might be heading?"

"If I was him, I'd be . . ."

"Uh, yeah. In other words, you're not real sure, that about it?" Koda interrupted again.

"Naw, guess not," the kid admitted. "Might be makin' some rounds, though. Droppin' off some shit to some of the girls. Guess you two must be the guys he's setting up the deal on to score some crystal lady, huh?"

Koda blinked. "Say what?"

"You know, man, the crystal. Cocaine." The runny-nosed face looked up at Koda and Shannon quizzically. "Aw c'mon, you guys know what I'm talkin' about. Squeek told me this morning he was settin' up a deal with some big-ass nig—"

The young manager suddenly realized what he was saying, glanced up quickly at Charley's maliciously smiling face, then made a very hasty search of his limited vocabulary. "—uh, b-black dude, and another guy with black hair and a mustache," he hurried on, nervously giving Charley another quick, flickering look. "I mean, that's gotta be you guys, don't it?"

"Squeek *told you* we were coming by to score some coke?" Koda couldn't believe his ears. Or, more to the point, he couldn't believe that this was the quality of the people Jimmy Pilgrim and Rainbow were depending on to take over the dope trade from Jake Locotta and his highly organized criminals. The guys with the meat-hooks, the fifty-five-gallon oil drums and the concrete. Jesus, he thought, the whole thing didn't even begin to make sense.

"Oh, yeah, sure. No big thing. See, what it is, Squeek ain't exactly good at keeping his mouth shut, you know? Only I guess you guys didn't know that, huh?" The youth looked back and forth at the two dumbfounded agents for a few more seconds before it all finally seemed to sink in. "Oh—yeah. Jeeze, I guess I shouldn't be saying

anything about the coke, huh? I mean, like, you guys could be narcs—
or something, huh?"

Charley Shannon rolled his eyes skyward and then turned for
the door, muttering to himself.

"Hey, man—like, you know, I'm sorry," the kid said, a hurt look
appearing on his grimy face. "I mean, I didn't think—"

"Hey, don't worry about it, kid," Koda said. "No harm done. I
mean, at least this way, you know we're not cops. Right?"

The kid started to grin in heartfelt relief, but then his smiling
expression suddenly crinkled into blinking confusion. "Uh—how do I
know that?"

"Simple," Koda shrugged, turning to follow his still muttering
partner out the door so he wouldn't have to watch when the kid started
nodding to himself in sudden, happy and complacent understanding.
"How many cops do you know who'd turn down a free donut?"

According to the intricately wood-framed digital clock on Rainbow's bedstand, it was precisely 3:16 in the afternoon on a Thursday,
which meant that Roy Schultzheimer would be waiting by his phone
for instructions.

"You ready to do some hard work?" Raynee asked without preamble.

"Sure, boss. Watcha got?" Roy Schultzheimer was always ready
to go to work for Rainbow. He didn't necessarily understand all of the
whys and wherefores, but then he really didn't care, either. Mostly
because Rainbow and Jimmy Pilgrim continued to provide him with
everything he wanted out of life: money for his basic living and entertainment needs, a ready supply of amiable women, a daily workout
with Raynee at the contact martial arts he loved, and perhaps most
important, the constant opportunity to inflict physical pain upon some
deserving individual. In effect, every possible work-incentive that a
brutal and violent man like Roy Schultzheimer could ask for. Certainly
enough to ensure that he would make himself available for Raynee's
instructions at any time of the day or night.

"Ah want you t' find Bylighter for me."

"That doesn't sound too difficult," Schultzheimer chuckled.

"Wouldn't be, normally," Raynee agreed, "but Ah don't want
you t' be makin' contact with that boy yourself. Use a pay phone t'
check 'round. Pick one at random. You know how t' work it. Thing is,
Ah wanna know what's goin' down on that little deal a' his with the
little fox from Newport. One what's got the sugar daddy with the
boat."

"That the one who's supposed to be shacking with the three dudes?"

"That's the lady," Raynee said. "I wanna know if'n they're still interested in a' couple o-z's, crystal. Get back t' me real quick-like, now, hear?"

"Be a hell of a lot quicker if I could just go out and kick the little asshole's door," Schultzheimer suggested.

Raynee chuckled quietly. "No, no, my man. Can't let you do that. Thing is, we got our little Squeek all staked out now, nice'n pretty-like. Don't want nobody backtrackin' in on our action thru that boy no more. Dig?"

"I'll get back to you," Schultzheimer said affirmatively.

"You do that."

It took Schultzheimer almost two hours to track Bylighter to the shared apartment of two hard-living young hookers named Raggedy Ann and Raggedy Annie. They were in the process of enthusiastically receiving their alloted share of the new analog powders (very enthusiastically, in fact, because neither of the girls could remember the last time that Rainbow—or anyone else for that matter—had offered them free dope) when they received Schultzheimer's call. Bylighter was ordered to remain at the girls' apartment until he received a call from Rainbow. It came about two minutes later.

"Roy tell you what Ah wanna know?" Raynee demanded when the terrified youth finally answered the phone.

"Uh—uh—yeah. Yeah, he—he told me," Bylighter stuttered frantically, "but I don't—I mean, I got busy helping Skylight, so I didn't—I mean, I kinda forgot—"

"You tryin' t' tell me you didn't meet with them folks like you was supposed to?" Raynee demanded in an ominously vicious tone.

"I can still get hold of them, anytime you want," Bylighter promised hurriedly, having no idea at all whether or not he really could. "Have the deal set up right away. Anytime you—"

"Sunday."

"W-what—?" Bylighter stuttered.

"I want the deal set for Sunday," Raynee growled. "Thiopene analog. Half a pound."

"But they don't—" Bylighter protested desperately.

"Thiopene analog—half a pound—on Sunday," Raynee whispered menacingly. "You got trouble with your friggin' ears, boy?"

"No—no," Bylighter shook his head, oblivious of the wide-eyed looks he was getting from Raggedy Ann and Annie. "It's just—I mean—I need some money to set the deal," he whined. "I need five hundred dollars—"

"What-for you need that kinda money?" Raynee demanded.

"For Skylight," Bylighter blurted out before he could stop himself. "I-I mean—"

Raynee closed his eyes, asking himself once again how Bylighter's value as a sacrificial goat could possibly be worth all the hassle and frustration. But then, if Jimmy Pilgrim said the kid had value, he did, Raynee shrugged. No two ways 'bout it. Besides, the more he thought about it, the funnier it got.

"You really think a little dirt-bag like you can jes' go out an' buy a piece a' ass off a' stone fox like that Skylight?" It was all that Raynee could do to keep himself from breaking out into convulsive laughter.

"She said she would—" Bylighter whispered miserably.

"Shit-all-mighty," Raynee sighed. "Ah oughta jes' cut them balls off a' you right now, put you outta your fuckin' misery once'n fer all."

"But—but—!" Bylighter's squeaky voice almost went off the scale.

"Listen to me, you little honky asshole," Raynee snarled into the phone. "You ever wanna get yourself a piece a' ass, then you get that deal set up fer Sunday, like Ah'm tellin' you to. You hear what Ah'm sayin', boy?"

Bylighter choked out something desperately affirmative.

"That's what Ah wanted t' hear," Raynee nodded, his voice dropping down in a soothing, almost sympathetic tone. "An' you listen t' me now . . . listen what Ah'm tellin' you. You want that bread for Skylight, you gotta start listenin' with your head, 'stead a' your good-fer-nuthin' balls."

"But—"

"Use your head, boy," Raynee repeated insistently. "Listen t' me now. You the one who's settin' up the deal—ain't that right? Well then, shit, man doin' all that work, he oughta be gettin' hisself a gawd-damned finder's fee fer his trouble. You understand what Ah'm sayin'?"

"Uh—yeah, Rainbow, I—I understand. Jesus, that's right. Maybe I can get myself some kind of finder's fee," Bylighter whispered as a laughing Rainbow hung up the phone, leaving Bylighter to shake his head at the wonder of it all. After all this time, he was beginning to believe—to really *believe*—that they just might be able to pull it off.

* * *

According to the coded schedule in Raynee's notebook, he had
another twenty minutes to wait until the General would be standing
by his scrambled telephone—one of the phones purchased by Jimmy
Pilgrim as a temporary communications system until he had his much-
safer, computer-coded message-switching system in place.

"Hello?"

"How're you doing, General?"

"Kind of impatient," he chided cautiously. "I've been waiting
for your call. I believe we have some business to take care of."

"You mean the analogs?"

"Yes, exactly," the General acknowledged. "I was wondering
when I can expect delivery of the first shipment."

"In a few days," Raynee said. "Matter of fact, Pilgrim's setting
up the production line right now. Meantime, though, we figure we
oughta be doin' a little market testing. See what kind a' response we
get on the street 'fore we get too heavy in this stuff. No sense alienat-
ing our regular customers if'n it ain't gonna go over."

"That sounds reasonable," the General said. "What'd you folks
have in mind?"

"One of our street gofers tripped over some people looking t'
buy a couple ounces coke in your area." Raynee went on to describe
Bylighter's contact with Sandy Mudd and her three "boyfriends."

"You figure they'll go for the switch?"

Raynee smiled to himself, thankful that he could handle this
part of the operation over a telephone. He wasn't sure he'd have been
able to keep a straight face, dealing person-to-person. And then too,
Raynee reminded himself, it wasn't a good idea to get too careless
around the General. Man might'a been a shit-ass bureaucrat, but it
didn't figure a dude could last around Washington, D.C.-type politics
for twenty years without learning something about backstabbing.

"Might," Raynee said. "Thing is, we're figurin' on offering
these people a half-pound at the two-ounce price. They like it, like we
know they're gonna, then they're probably gonna deal off what they
can't use right away. Shouldn't be too hard to keep track a' their action
for a few days. Let them take any heat that comes down."

"In other words," the General said, "if it goes to shit, they take
the fall. And if the stuff sells, like you say it's going to, then we're still
the only source." The General paused momentarily and then nodded
his head. "I like it. Fact is, I like it a lot."

"Thought you'd see it that way," Raynee chuckled. "Thing is,
though, we figure you'll wanna use the best salesman you got, make

sure these people go 'long with the program. Hell of a lot ridin' on this buy. Bad time t' be makin' dumb-ass mistakes."

"I'll see to it personally," the General snapped. "What's the background look like on these people?"

"No guarantees, but they're coming back clean so far. We're runnin' a trace back on the boat now. Shouldn't be any problem, anyway, though—long as you talk it right—seein's how the stuff's legal in the first place. But Ah'd play it real cautious-like anyways," Raynee added. "Ain't no need t' get too 'lax with this shit jes' yet."

"I agree. So what's the action?" the General asked.

"Told the kid t' set the deal up for this Sunday. We'll get the powder to you, night 'fore. You set the site, handle all the local details. Oh yeah," Raynee added, "supposed to tell you . . . Pilgrim figured you'd wanna do the deed yerself. Said Ah should tell you, man like you oughta be able t' handle a' half-pound deal like this blindfolded."

"Tell Jimmy I appreciate his confidence, but I'll keep my eyes open on this one, just the same," the General grinned, matching Raynee's responsive laughter, as the phone clicked.

By 6:30 Thursday evening, Joe Tassio and Al Rosenthal had each finished updating Jake Locotta on the uncertain situation in Jimmy Pilgrim's San Diego area. Having had their say, both trusted lieutenants sat back in the huge living room of Locotta's Palm Springs retreat and waited for the silent, contemplative mob chieftain to finish lighting his fifth cigar of the day. An ominous sign.

Locotta finally looked up from the smoldering length of Cuban tobacco and fixed his cold, introspective eyes on Tassio.

"You think he's dead?"

"No." Tassio's growled response was immediate and firm.

Locotta turned his gaze to his longtime accountant, adviser, and personal friend. "Rosey?"

"I don't think so, Jake," the aged counselor rasped. "Doesn't make sense. Not with all this other business about new dope on the street. Doesn't add up right."

"You don't think Raynee's capable of icing Jimmy Pilgrim?" Locotta directed the question at both of his advisers, but Tassio offered up the obvious answer.

"I don't know more'n one or two people out there who could go up against Jimmy, face-to-face, and walk away from it," the deadly enforcer growled. "Thing is though, Rainbow's one of 'em. I just don't think he knows it. Or, if he does, maybe he just doesn't believe it. Either way, Jimmy's got one hell of a mind-lock on that nigger."

"Raynee may be capable of dumping Pilgrim," Rosenthal added, "but the relevant question is: Would he want to? I don't think so. I just don't see a street player like Raynee going after the number-one spot. Not his thing."

"Which means . . ." Locotta glared at the two men.

". . . that Pilgrim's gotta be setting up a game on us," Tassio finished. "Don't see it any other way."

"Rosey?"

The elderly accountant shrugged. "I think we gotta go with the assumption that Jimmy Pilgrim is *capable* of communicating with us, *and* responding to our warning. He just doesn't want to."

"Then what you're gonna do," Locotta growled, turning his angry gaze back on Tassio, "you're gonna give Jimmy Pilgrim a warning! Something he's *not* gonna ignore!"

As it happened, Thursday evening was a slow night for large-scale dope deliveries in the General's metropolitan San Diego area.

In fact, the last-minute order that Bobby Lockwood was scheduled to deliver to an ounce-dealer in Mission Beach—at eight o'clock that evening—was specifically listed on the General's schedule as a low priority drop. Only a half-pound brick of 86% cocaine, invoiced at $30,000. No big deal.

Under the General's meticulously organized control system, no big deal meant that only three people would be involved in the delivery: the curly-haired Lockwood, armed with his Browning .380 automatic; his ponytailed assistant, Tim, with his lead-filled baseball bat; and the Mexican immigrant named José, who carried a sharp-edged switchblade knife in each of his carefully polished boots and a third strapped to his right wrist, and had a sawed-off pump shotgun in the delivery van.

Bobby, Tim and José. Three well-armed and trustworthy employees, each of whom had demonstrated an ability and a willingness to defend their boss's dope on at least one prior occasion. The General felt that was plenty of protection for an eight-ounce shipment of coke.

And of course he was right. The three armed young men should have been plenty, because in the past three years—ever since Jimmy Pilgrim and Rainbow had been transferred down to San Diego to put a rapid halt to the intramural skirmishes conducted among the highly competitive pound-dealers—there hadn't been one rip-off of a major dope transfer in the San Diego area. Not one.

Which explained why, at 8:25 that evening, Bobby Lockwood remained completely unconcerned after he had walked up the long driveway to discover that the address provided by the ounce-dealer was for an abandoned house at the end of a narrow, hidden access road.

Reasonably assuming that he had made a mistake in copying down the address, Lockwood turned back toward the delivery truck and saw José standing next to the rear door, where he was supposed to be. Except he was standing between two other darkened figures with his hands held high over his head.

"Hey, what the hell—!" Lockwood started to yell out, when he suddenly found himself face-to-face with a stocky, grey-haired man he had never seen before.

"Don't play it stupid, kid. Just shut up and listen," Joe Tassio growled, holding his thick arms loose at his sides.

"Who the hell are—UUHHHH!"

A tightly-clenched fist slammed across the youth's vulnerable jaw as Lockwood made precisely the stupid decision that Tassio had anticipated, and went for his gun.

Unfortunately for Lockwood, his right hand had already closed around the grip of the small automatic pistol when Tassio's blow sent him spinning to the ground in a mouth-and-nose-bleeding daze. And even though he was badly hurt, he foolishly tried to come back up to his feet, not really even aware that he still had hold of the gun. The result was that Lockwood screamed loudly, then mercifully fainted when Tassio coolly stepped forward, slapped one of his brick-and-mortar-toughtened hands over the slide-action of the automatic, and twisted the weapon out of Lockwood's hand with a crunch of breaking wrist bones.

Lockwood's ponytailed assistant, Tim, proved to be equally self-assured, and even less fortunate.

At first, Tim wasn't even aware that anything out of the ordinary was happening, until he saw the shadowy figure step in front of Lockwood on the driveway. He saw Lockwood spin away from the vicious roundhouse punch. As Tim got out of the delivery van cab with the lead-filled bat clenched tightly in his hand, Lockwood's scream split the night air.

Joe Tassio saw the ponytailed youth coming, and waited, smiling, until the bat was sweeping down in an overhead arc toward his forehead.

Then, timing the move perfectly in the glary darkness, Tassio reached up to absorb the heavy impact of the bat's thick end with the palms of his scarred hands—and then ripped it out of the youth's grasp. Tim barely had time to grunt in surprise before Tassio drove the grip-end of the bat deep into the pit of his stomach, causing the youth to vomit explosively as he dropped face-forward and helpless to the ground. Tassio then grabbed one of Tim's limp wrists, lifted it up, and brought the thick end of the bat down sharply against the muscular upper arm. The crack-sound of breaking bone was clearly audible.

The normal procedure would have been for Tassio to start with the elbows—one or both, depending upon the severity of the offense—and then move on down to the knees.

In this situation, however, Bobby Lockwood, Tim and José were not the offenders; they were simply the unfortunates who had been elected to bear the brunt of Jake Locotta's message. And because Joe Tassio happened to appreciate aggressive bravery on the part of his employees, he had already decided against permanently crippling the three members of Jimmy Pilgrim's delivery team. Compound fractures would serve the same purpose.

But Joe Tassio never got around to explaining his decision to José, who understood the normal method of operation all too well, saw Tassio reach for Tim's other arm—the lethal bat poised for another bone-breaking swing—and decided he liked his elbows and knees just fine the way they were.

The closest of Tassio's watchdogs to José heard and recognized the snap of the wrist-concealed switchblade just in time to absorb the thrust of the double-edged blade with the palm of his outstretched hand instead of his belly button.

Hissing from the pain, the street-experienced enforcer deliberately clamped his uninjured hand over José's knife hand, controlling the deadly weapon long enough for his partner to smash the frame of a .357 revolver into the side of José's head.

After a few moments of silent deliberation, during which time he expertly bound his assistant's wounded hand with a clean handkerchief, Joe Tassio reached down for José's right wrist, and then shattered the elbow joint with a single sharp blow of the heavy, leaded bat.

When the police came upon the delivery van in the course of their routine graveyard patrol sweeps, they discovered three severely beaten young men lying unconscious in the driveway of the dark, empty house.

They searched the van and found a few pieces of furniture and a blood-smeared baseball bat. But they didn't find a pump shotgun, or a .380 Browning automatic, or any of the three switch-bladed knives, and they *certainly* didn't find an eight-ounce "half-brick" of 86% cocaine . . . for the simple reason that they were no longer there.

The furniture store owner came down to the station, identified his van, confirmed that Bobby Lockwood had no scheduled deliveries that night, and suggested that the whole thing was probably union-related. He admitted he'd been expecting something like this ever since he'd hired the aggressively independent youth. He also advised the police officers that he would probably fire Lockwood for un-authorized use of the van.

With that bit of vaguely useful information, the night-duty detective attempted to question the single conscious victim—Bobby Lockwood—after the emergency room physician finished applying strips of water-soaked plaster bandage to his broken wrist. As the detective made several probes at what seemed to be the obvious areas of concern, Lockwood found it less and less difficult to act appropriately dazed, dumbfounded and ignorant—especially ignorant.

As a result, Lockwood learned a great deal about what had happened to his delivery team, and the detective learned absolutely nothing at all, which was exactly what Jake Locotta and Joe Tassio had in mind all along.

17

AT EXACTLY 8 o'clock the next morning, a woman who identified herself as Elizabeth Lockwood came into Bobby Lockwood's hospital room and proceeded to make an appropriately concerned fuss over the entire situation, as she helped her son get dressed and settled comfortably into the mandated wheelchair while listening carefully to the doctor's cautionary prescriptions.

After Elizabeth Lockwood paid her son's hospital bill in cash, accepted the receipt and signed the Recommended Follow-up Treatment sheet supplied by the emergency room physician, mother and son walked slowly out to a late model Lincoln Continental, got in, and drove out of the parking lot at a sedate speed.

For the next fifteen minutes, Mrs. Lockwood drove the Lincoln through the streets of Linda Vista—a small bedroom community just north of San Diego—at that same slow, cautious pace. As she did so, she cautiously examined her rear- and side-view mirrors every thirty seconds or so. During the entire time, neither she or Bobby Lockwood spoke a word to each other.

Then Mrs. Lockwood took one last look in her mirrors, made a quick turn at the next street corner, immediately made another right, and then pulled into an underground parking lot. She waited there for a few moments, making sure that none of the "suspicious" vehicles she had noted during the past fifteen minutes had followed them in. Then she turned to face her "son."

"Aisle seven, white-over-blue Dodge van," she said, no longer bothering to smile. "Ask for Sam."

"Thanks a lot, Mom," Bobby Lockwood mumbled through his tender, swollen jaw as he cautiously levered himself out of the vehicle.

"Anytime, son," she replied indifferently, wadding up the Recommended Follow-up Treatment sheet and the receipt and tossing them into a nearby trashcan before heading for the lot's rear exit.

Forty-five minutes and two car-switches later, Bobby Lockwood was sitting on a comfortable sofa, sipping cautiously at a welcome glass of cold Moosehead beer, and trying to explain to the General exactly what had happened during the past twelve hours. Or, more to the point, exactly what he thought had happened.

"And you're sure the cops didn't find the coke?" the General asked when Lockwood finished going through his story the second time.

"Hey, it's like I told you . . . for all I know, they took it home with them," Lockwood shrugged, wincing at the pain caused by the excessive movement of his jaw. "Maybe Tim or José saw what went down, I don't know, but I sure as hell didn't."

At this particular moment, all Bobby Lockwood really wanted to do was to go home and lie down for about a week until his wrist and jaw stopped throbbing. But he knew it wasn't going to work out that way. Not when one of the General's highly regarded delivery teams had been ripped off. And especially not when the action involved a half-pound of high-grade coke, which was to say, thirty thousand dollars of the General's hard-earned money.

"Listen," Lockwood said, finally judging that he had satisfied the basic points of the General's determined interrogation, "does anybody know how Tim or José's doing? I mean, they wouldn't tell me anything at the hospital," he added quietly.

"Tim's okay. José was still unconscious as of a half-hour ago," the General mumbled distractedly, drumming his fingers on the lamp table as he worked his way through all of the varied possibilities once again, trying to get several of the seemingly conflicting details straight in his head. Finally, he reached for the scrambled phone next to his single-starred hat.

Raynee answered the phone sleepily, but he quickly came wide awake as the General's words began to make sense.

"Anybody get a description?" Raynee demanded after the general finished trying to summarize the situation.

The General repeated the description of the man who had confronted Lockwood, looking over at the nodding youth a couple of times to confirm a particular detail.

"You know, now that I think of it, that description kinda sounds like—" the General started to suggest when Raynee interrupted him.

"He ever seen Tassio?" Raynee growled.

"No, I don't think so," the General shook his head, feeling his stomach start to tighten up as Rainbow vocalized his unspoken fears. The General looked over at the severely beaten Lockwood and repeated Raynee's question, and then felt even more uneasy when he read the look of stunned horror in Bobby Lockwood's eyes. Clearly, as far as Lockwood knew, he had never seen Joe Tassio face-to-face, but the youth had certainly heard of the man.

"Jesus, you think it was Tassio?" the General asked Raynee nervously, trying to ignore the stricken expression on Bobby Lockwood's face. "Why the hell would they—"

"Naw, ain't likely Tassio'd come stompin' 'round down here, 'out tellin' us. Probably jes' some shit-head happens t' look like that ugly wop bastard," Raynee chuckled. "Don't you worry 'bout it none, General. We're cool with the main man. It's probably jes' some freelancer shit. You let Jimmy an' me do a little checkin' 'round, take care 'a business with them fuckers. Ain't gonna let nobody mess 'round in Jimmy Pilgrim's territory, you dig?"

"Yeah, sure," the General nodded distractedly. "Say, listen, speaking of the competition—ah, I guess we're going to be a little slow on deliveries till I can get another drop-team set up."

"Don't worry 'bout it," Raynee said soothingly. "You jes' get the stuff packaged. Ah'll send some a' the boys down to help out. 'Sides, don't forget, ain't gonna be long 'fore you're gonna be the main powder dude 'round here with all that new analog shit. Ain't gonna haf'ta worry none 'bout competition no mo', 'cause we're gonna *be* the business in Diego County, you dig? An' if *that* don't make Jake Locotta stand up an' kiss that fuckin' silver star a' yours, Ah jes' don't know what."

"Yeah, I guess it oughta really make his day when we finally deal out the competition around here," the General nodded, feeling a little less uneasy now that he remembered his starring role in Pilgrim's analog test project. Raynee was right. It didn't make sense that Joe Tassio would be muscling in on one of his top managers just as this new project was getting off the ground. Had to be one of the outside competitors feeling his oats a little. Serve those bastards right when Jimmy Pilgrim and Rainbow came down hard on their asses, the General told himself consolingly.

"Gonna make the man's day, no shit," Raynee laughed in agreement. "Listen now, you get yourself ready t' deal out the last a' them eighty keys, you hear? Like we said, anything you can't get rid of, we'll take back two-for-one on the new stuff. Meanwhile, me an' Jimmy, we'll take care a' the other bullshit."

"Fine with me," the General nodded.

"Oh yeah, one more thing," Raynee added, still smiling to himself, "why don't you jes' send that Lockwood out mah way. Special delivery. Think Ah'd like t' have me a' little talk with that boy."

"Jesus Christ, you *sure* they didn't say when they'd be coming back?" Eugene Bylighter pleaded, looking up from the uncooperative telephone after making yet another connection with Sandy Mudd's answering machine. He'd been dialing the same number every half hour since seven o'clock that morning. Four hours ago.

"Hey, man, it's like I've been trying to tell you all fucking morning," the still-sniffling donut shop manager repeated, "the dudes didn't say *when*, or *where*, or even *if* they was comin' back. And you ask me, they *ain't* coming back, neither. Not after the way you left them hanging out to dry yesterday."

"Naw, no way," Bylighter shook his head. "They'll be back. I mean, Jesus, it's not like I . . ." Bylighter's voice trailed off weakly. He wasn't to the point of crying . . . yet . . . but he was getting close.

"And besides, what the hell good's it gonna do ya to keep calling the broad's apartment?" the manager went on. "I mean, like it's Friday, right? You know she works at some kind of office. So whaddaya figure she's gonna be doing at eleven o'clock on a Friday morning? Waiting around her place to see if you're gonna call her ten fucking times, 'stead a' nine? Shee-it," the manager snorted, shaking his head in disgust.

"I'm tellin' you, man, I *gotta* find her, get that deal set up," Bylighter whispered, biting nervously at an almost nonexistent fingernail. "If I don't—"

The phone rang.

"Yeah, hello, Sandy?" Bylighter blurted out hopefully, and

then cringed inwardly as he recognized the decidedly nonfeminine voice.

"Ah been waiting t' hear from you," the voice growled. "What's happenin'?"

"Uh—uh—she's, I mean, she's supposed to b-be calling me b-back any second now," Bylighter stuttered.

"She better be," Raynee snarled. "Remember what Ah told you? Thiopene analog. Half a pound. Sunday night. Ten-thirty. Hotel Clairmont. Right?"

"Uh—ye-yeah, r-r-right, honest, y-you can depend—"

"You still got that number Ah gave you?"

"Uh—uh—" Bylighter searched frantically through the scraps of paper on the disheveled desk top. "Yeah, yeah—here it is." He brought the sweat-stained piece of paper up in his trembling hand. "Uh—two-seven-five—"

"You get the deal set, you call that number," Raynee said. "Man's waitin' t' hear from you." Then he slammed the receiver down before he had to listen to any more of Bylighter's terrified chatter.

"Some days that goddamned son of a bitch ain't worth pissin' on," Raynee shook his head in irritation as he reached down in his lap to redirect the pocket-probing course of Simon Drobeck's python. As far as the sixteen-foot, arm-thick snake was concerned, Lafayette Beaumont Raynee was too big to eat and too gentle with his strong, stroking hands to be a threat, and was merely a convenient source of welcome body heat and intriguingly deep pockets.

Using the thumb-edge of his steady right hand, Raynee brought the smooth, sliding neck of the lightly mottled python up slowly until he could feel the gentle, flickering touch of the reddish forked tongue brush against the tip of his dark-brown nose. Then he moved his hand out away from his face until the elongated, triangular head with the cold, unblinking eyes came into focus—eyes so very much like his own.

"All right now," Raynee rasped, allowing his gaze to slide past the still curiously probing snake's head, and past the bald, wrinkly head of the python's criminally demented owner, to focus on the nervously pale face of Bobby Lockwood, "Ah want you t' tell me an' Drobeck here all 'bout that chemistry stuff you been studyin' out at that university."

By 1:45 Friday afternoon, an increasingly frantic Eugene Bylighter had made exactly eighteen attempts to call Sandy Mudd from the Donut Shop. He had long since given up trying to leave recorded messages on the maddeningly repetitious machine. Mostly because he couldn't think of anything else to say.

"I mean, Jesus, how many ways can you ask a girl to call you back on a thirty-second recording?" Bylighter mumbled to the unresponsive phone. But this time, to Bylighter's amazement, the phone responded by ringing loudly.

"UH—UH—HELLO!" Bylighter blurted into the receiver breathlessly, trying to keep his voice calm and his hands steady, and not really succeeding at either. "Uh—I m-mean—hello, S-Sandy?"

"WHAT THE HELL YOU DOING?" Raggedy Annie screamed into the phone, blasting Bylighter's ear away from the receiver.

"Oh shit, Jesus I'm uh—uh—I'm, I'm s-sorry," Bylighter stuttered shakily, "I thought—"

"And I ain't Sandy neither, whoever the hell she is," the tough-minded street girl snarled. "This is Annie. Remember?"

"Oh yeah, hey—sure, Annie, I—uh—uh. Listen, jeeze—I'm sorry but, you know, it's like—I mean, I gotta hang up. I gotta call—"

"You better *not* hang up on me, you little pecker-head," Raggedy Annie warned. " 'Less you want me t' tell Rainbow you're screwing up this new-dope test of his."

"Whadda ya mean?" Bylighter felt his stomach twist. "I—I'm—"

"Skylight said we was supposed to call in the results, soon as we got 'em. So I'm callin' in."

"Yeah, but—but aren't you supposed to call Skylight? I mean, nobody told me—"

"I can't get hold of Skylight," Raggedy Annie explained. "So, since you're her number-one gofer this week, I'm callin' *you* and givin' *you* the results so you can tell Rainbow yourself. Understand?"

"Oh—uh, yeah, sure," Bylighter nodded nervously. "Okay, listen, I'll write it down—only you gotta hurry, 'cause—"

"You tell Rainbow that Ann and me, we tried all them B-vitamins he gave us. The whole goddamned bunch. B-thirteen, fourteen, fifteen and sixteen."

"Jesus, you took all of them? I mean, weren't you supposed to, uh, I mean, you know, try 'em out on your, uh, friends?"

"Shit-howdy, honey," Raggedy Annie laughed, seeming to have forgotten her previous burst of anger, "Ann and me, we ain't about to give anything to our friends we ain't tried out on ourselves first. 'Sides, that's the reason I'm callin'. Y' see, we want you and Skylight to get us some more a' that B-Sixteen." Raggedy Annie suddenly burst into a fit of giggles. "Jesus, stuff sounds like a fuckin' bomber, don't it?"

"You want—more?"

"Hell yes we want more, honey-butt! Listen, you write this down now. That thirteen, it didn't do much, ya know. Good for a little pepper-upper, that's all. Fourteen, you got maybe a little flash of color. Nothin' all that much, but you know you had something. And fifteen, it wasn't all that bad neither. Kinda like a triple dose of fourteen with a little coke on the side, ya know? Streaky stuff.

"But let me tell you, baby," Raggedy Annie went on, sounding more animated over the phone than Bylighter could ever remember her being in person, "that B-Sixteen, that was somethin'. Goddamn, them colors was somethin'! Like livin' inna fuckin' rainbow, ya know. And I ain't shittin' ya, honey," she giggled again, "that stuff, it made me and Ann so horny, we'd a' even given *you* a free ride, just for the pure hell of it. And let me tell you what, honey, they *ever* come up with the next one in line—B-Seventeen or whatever—you better make goddamn fuckin' sure me and Ann get some a' that Power-Rainbow first."

"Uh . . . yeah, sure, Annie," Bylighter nodded, only vaguely aware of what Raggedy Annie was saying because he was increasingly conscious of the time passing. He had to get Raggedy Annie off the phone. Sandy could be trying to call him at any minute. Possibly even right now.

"Hey, shit, Annie," he started in without really thinking, "I can probably get you some of that seventeen, no sweat. Thing is, though, right now I'm kinda—"

"YOU GOT SOME SEVENTEEN!" Raggedy Annie practically erupted through the phone.

"Uh—well, yeah, sorta—I guess. I mean, uh—I only got a little, but, uh—" Annie's words had done something to Eugene Bylighter's mind that he had never experienced before. He was actually trying to put two and two together. Trying to *think*—and scaring the living shit out of himself in the process. The colors. Rainbow colors. That girl, Kaaren, she'd been laughing and whispering and crying about . . . colors. Lots of colors. Rainbows of colors, he remembered. Those were her exact words.

Jesus.

Bylighter was rapidly putting two and two together and coming up with the number seventeen. The number on the vial that Rainbow and Roy had taken from his refrigerator that night. The one they'd tested out later and said didn't do much. It was the thiopene one they liked better. The one he was supposed to have given to the girl—Kaaren. Only the thing was, *they didn't know* . . .

Didn't know he'd dropped the vials in the cat's water.

Didn't know he couldn't figure out which one was which anyway after he'd put the new labels on, so he'd mixed half-and-half in the coke, just to be sure. Half from the one vial and half from the other, so he'd be absolutely sure he was giving her some of the thiopene.

Didn't know he'd squirreled away most of the other half of the powder from the "thiopene"-labeled vial, so they *wouldn't* ever know, and then cut out a little bit—not very much, just a little—of the A-17 for himself too, because they wouldn't ever know about that either . . .

Except that if B-14, 15 and 16 produced brighter and brighter colors, like Raggedy Annie had said, then didn't that mean the A-17—the one that gave *really* bright rainbow colors—had to be the next one in line after the B-16? Maybe he'd made another mistake? Written an "A" instead of a "B" when he'd relabeled the vials? Bylighter shook his head, horribly confused by the mass of swirling numbers and thoughts in his head. Thoughts that, for some reason, he *knew* he had to understand, because . . .

"GODDAMNIT, ANSWER ME! YOU REALLY GOT SEVENTEEN? HONEST TO GOD—THEY REALLY MADE SOME POWER RAINBOW?" Raggedy Annie screamed again.

. . . of Rainbow. He knew about the colors. He'd heard the girl Kaaren whispering and laughing and crying about the rainbow colors too. Thought it was funny. If he found out—

"GODDAMNIT, YOU SON OF A BITCH!" Raggedy Annie really screamed this time.

—about Raggedy Annie's colors—

"YOU GIVE ME SOME OF THAT SEVENTEEN OR I'M GONNA GO STRAIGHT TO RAINBOW—"

—and realized what he—Bylighter—must have done, realized that he must have switched the vials or done something to screw up the test because Kaaren must have been given the A-17 too, along with the thiopene—

". . . AND TELL HIM YOU'RE HOLDING OUT ON US . . ."

—and found out that he—Bylighter—had stashed away some of the powder. Except that instead of having only a little bit of the A-17, like he thought . . .

". . . WON'T GIVE US ANY OF THE GOOD STUFF!"

. . . he had almost half a vial of the stuff . . . that might even be

better than the B-16 stuff that—what had she said?—made Raggedy
Annie and Raggedy Ann so horny that they'd . . . ?

"Jesus," he whispered out loud.

"ALL RIGHT, YOU LITTLE FUCKER—"

"NO—NO, WAIT," Bylighter yelled frantically. "Listen—
please," he begged, "just listen to me." He was whispering now, almost crying again from the desperate, swirling combination of mind-
crazed fear and hope. "You don't have to go to Rainbow. I—I'll get you
some of that Seventeen."

For the fifth time that Friday afternoon, San Diego Police criminalist Tina Sun-Wang made a series of calculated adjustments to the
control panel of the computer-monitored gas chromatograph, and then
injected five microliters of the solvent extract from Kaaren Mueller's
blood into the inlet port of the analytical instrument.

Next to the gas chromatograph on the laboratory bench-top, a
wire-connected recorder began to whirr noisily as a small ink pen responded to electronic signals from the sensitive detectors in the instrument by moving up and down a slowly unrolling length of chart
paper, indicating as it did so the presence of minute amounts of chemical compounds in the blood extract.

As Tina watched expectantly, the fine red pen-line graphically
recorded the presence of the new set of known compounds she'd
mixed and injected with the blood extract. As she continued to watch,
hoping against the odds, the pen moved up and down rapidly to form
the familiar PCP peak, and then surged up and down twice more,
again producing the two distinct peaks on the finely gridded chart
paper that—as she'd half expected—didn't match any of the known
drug compounds.

Tina glared silently at the slowly moving chart paper for a few
moments, and then muttered a clearly audible and very uncharacteristic curse.

"Still got trouble?" Paul Reinhart asked, looking up from the
wire-strewn innards of another instrument—this one partially disassembled—that took up a good third of the floor space in the primary
instrument room of the San Diego Police crime laboratory. He came
over and looked at the recorder chart.

"Same two peaks," Reinhart noted. "What'd you run this
time?"

"Mescaline, psilocybin, serotonin, PCP, couple of the catechol-
amines," Tina Sun-Wang muttered.

"You know, every time you run that extract, one of those peaks comes out awfully close to PCP," Reinhart commented. "You sure you haven't got a metabolite?"

"Ran the whole PCP series twice," Sun-Wang shook her head. "No match."

"You ever manage to get them separated for the UV?" Reinhart asked, knowing how difficult and frustrating the analytical problems— especially the toxicology ones—could get. The trouble was, there were *so* many possibilities, literally thousands and thousands. And nowhere near enough time to work them out, he reminded himself, looking at the row of fifty-odd blood extracts on Tina Sun-Wang's bench-top, all waiting their turn to flow past the GC's electronic detectors.

"Yeah, I think so," Sun-Wang nodded, pointing at two torn-off sections of chart paper tacked on the wall over her nearby desk, each bearing a unique, multicurved ultraviolet frequency scan. "Pulled those out of the urine this morning. GC peaks match on blood and urine, so there couldn't have been much in the way of metabolic action. Same problem though," she shrugged tiredly. "No match with any of the UV or GC reference charts."

"Anything on thin-layer?" he asked, after staring at the red-lined charts.

"That's next," she nodded, "but I can't spend much more time on this one. Gotta get all those negative-alcohols run before Monday court, or the D.A.'ll be screaming," she added morosely, motioning with her head at the rows of blood-filled vials waiting for analysis. "Saving the liver and brain for last. Sure would help if we could get that mass-spec working. Give me a lot better idea what I'm dealing with."

"I called again this morning. Repairman's backed up till next Wednesday," Reinhart said. "Meanwhile, we're gonna have to work things the slow way . . . like we always used to do before we hired ourselves a fancy instrument chemist," the senior criminalist chuckled.

"I think I need to go back and get another degree," Tina Sun-Wang muttered to herself as she reached down for the vial again in preparation for making one more injection. "A few courses in alchemy might be useful about now."

"Don't let it get you down," Reinhart replied as he went back to setting the probes of a voltmeter against a pair of terminals on one of the suspect circuit boards. "No matter how much you study, there's always something new coming up. You start letting it bother you, you'll just go nuts."

"I guess you're used to running into things like this," Sun-Wang said, motioning with her head at Kaaren Mueller's autopsy blood sample. "Stuff you can't identify?"

"All the time," Reinhart grunted as he rechecked the voltage reading against the listing in the repair manual. "Always somebody out there trying something different, looking for a better way to get away with murder. That's okay, though," Reinhart added, looking up at Tina with a tired grin on his face. "When you get right down to it, that's what makes this job so interesting."

By 7:30 that Friday evening, Bobby Lockwood was beginning to wonder if his life wasn't getting to be just a little *too* interesting—if not downright dangerous.

Less than twenty-four hours after receiving the worst beating of his life, he had taken another major step in his illicit career.

But this time it was a little different. Instead of selling gram bindles of cocaine on the streets of La Jolla, or working as a covert quality-control buy-man for the General, or delivering unimaginably large amounts of high-grade dope for Jimmy Pilgrim and Rainbow, Lockwood now found himself locked in the basement of an old mountain cabin with Simon Drobeck, a caged thirteen-foot python, a bewildering array of chemistry lab glassware, a brand-new computer terminal that wasn't working yet, and a cookbook for making something called "the thiopene analog"—whatever the hell *that* was.

From dope dealer to headhunter to mule . . . and finally to underground chemist. Or, more accurately, to underground chemist's helper, Lockwood reminded himself as he watched Drobeck transfer the first simmering batch of cloudy liquid precursors into one of the shiny, clean glass beakers. Both he and Drobeck knew how little he'd actually learned during that disastrous Chemistry 1 lab course at U.C.S.D. All Lockwood could figure was that Pilgrim and Rainbow had to be awfully short on chemists to draft somebody like him into the job. Either that, or there was something else going on that he didn't know about, which was always a possibility.

In spite of his minimal qualifications as a dope chemist, Bobby had definitely taken some major steps in his illicit career during the past few days. But the question was, had he gone forward, backward, or sideways?

Lockwood turned his attention to his assigned task of mixing carefully measured amounts of the bottled chemicals with an old-fashioned mortar and pestle, awkwardly trying to hold the quart-sized ceramic grinding bowl steady with his cast-covered hand. He blinked his eyes, still not used to the distracting presence of the ethyl-ether vapors that filled the room—in spite of Dr. David Isaac's elaborate precautions—because with his plaster-encased hand, Bobby couldn't help spilling small amounts of the rapidly vaporizing solvent as he poured can after can into the reaction vessels.

Forward, backward, or sideways. As his aggressively adventuresome father had always told him, you had to be going in one of those directions if you were going anywhere at all, which made a certain amount of sense, Lockwood told himself. He just wished to hell he knew which one of those pathways he'd staggered onto this time.

18

AT 6:45 SATURDAY morning, a little over fourteen hours after having locked themselves into the cold, dank basement of the Eagle Mountain cabin, Bobby Lockwood watched with red, swollen eyes as a groggy Simon Drobeck weighed the three hundred and forty grams of wet, glistening, milk-chocolate-colored crystals they had scraped out of darkly encrusted glass reaction flasks.

They were almost finished now.

According to Drobeck's calculations, they could expect to recover something in the neighborhood of two hundred and fifty grams—just over a half pound—of the finished product, once the crystals were dried. A half-pound of one-one-two-thienyl-cyclohexyl-piperidine, the simple thiopene analog of PCP. Exactly what Jimmy Pilgrim had ordered.

"That it?" Bobby Lockwood asked, standing in front of the quietly rumbling fume hood next to Drobeck as the elderly chemist transferred the crystals to a large cookie sheet, then used a large metal-bladed spatula to spread the pile of brownish crystals evenly under the warm-air currents from two stand-mounted hair dryers.

"The last step," Drobeck nodded, yawning sleepily as he continued to gently fluff and turn the drying crystals with the spatula, working to speed up the evaporation of the solvent from the salt-crystallized compound.

"So how come it still looks dirty?" Lockwood asked. "I thought the stuff was supposed to turn out white."

"Most pure organic compounds *are* white," Drobeck nodded, continuing to make the slow, methodical chopping and turning motions with the spatula, "as I'm sure this one would be too, if it were absolutely pure, which, of course, it isn't."

"You mean we didn't do it right?" Lockwood asked, a worried expression suddenly appearing on his fatigue-lined face.

During the last fourteen hours, Lockwood's impression of Simon Drobeck had undergone a gradual and significant change, mostly for the better. Although Bobby still thought Drobeck was mentally deranged in his passion for snakes, he had come to almost admire the elderly chemist's dedication to his craft.

Drobeck might not have been brilliant enough to figure out the analog business on his own, Lockwood thought, but the old fart worked hard, in spite of the hundred-or-so extra pounds of lard he carried around under his straining belt. And too, Drobeck always double-checked their work to be certain that everything was being done correctly. Thus, it had never occurred to Lockwood that the chemist might make a mistake in producing the analog.

"It went fine," Drobeck shook his head. "The procedure suggests we can expect somewhere between eight and fifteen percent contamination—mostly unreacted materials. I think we're well within that range. We could always clean it up further, of course," the old man yawned, "but that would take far more time than we have available. Besides, I think this batch will do nicely for what they have in mind."

"You're *sure*," Lockwood asked nervously, not at all anxious to get on Jimmy Pilgrim's shit-list.

"Yes, of course I'm sure," Drobeck nodded impatiently. "Here, you keep turning the crystals," he said, handing the spatula over to Lockwood. "I have to make a phone call."

The effects of his all-night labor showing clearly on the fleshy folds of his deeply lines face, Drobeck shuffled over to the far corner of the underground laboratory.

There, to Bobby's immediate dismay, Drobeck bent forward, unlatched the cage, and removed the cold, quiet, and—from Lockwood's hopeful perspective—seemingly dead python. After wrapping the heavy, rubbery and unmoving coils across his chest like a bandolier, Drobeck spent a few moments whispering to his pet while stroking one of his pale, puffy hands across the reptile's glossy-scaled skin, causing Lockwood to shudder when the thick coils began to move in response to the sudden warmth from Drobeck's obese body.

Smiling happily as the heavy-bodied snake sluggishly began to flatten itself tightly against his white-coated bulk, Drobeck reached up and began to dial a series of numbers on the wall phone.

"Drobeck," he said after waiting patiently for a few moments. "Message relay. Tell Rainbow that everything went fine. The powder will be ready within an hour," he added, his voice echoing throughout the basement as he continued to caress the snake.

Over on the opposite side of the underground laboratory, Bobby turned his back to Drobeck and tried to concentrate on working the solvent out of the slowly drying crystals, unable to watch the progressively animated nature of the cruelly indifferent beast and its master, as Lockwood remembered the reptilian horror he had unknowingly helped to unleash on his friend, Jamie MacKenzie.

Back in San Diego, where Simon Drobeck's message was being relayed to Rainbow, a metamorphosis of a different sort was taking place.

As unlikely as it might have seemed, it was becoming more and more evident that Eugene Bylighter might be growing up. Although perhaps the term "growing up" was overstating the situation a bit. Perhaps it was more accurate just to say that he was changing. Whether that change was for the better or for the worse had yet to be determined.

If there was any one indicator that confirmed the emotional upheaval taking place within Eugene Bylighter, it was without a doubt his resistance to what had to be a grievous temptation: to dump the rest of the A-17 powder he'd given Kaaren down his throat, and then wait to experience what he knew would be the most mind-blowing "trip" of his entire life.

It was a temptation that the "old" Bylighter would have surrendered to long ago, had he not been convinced that the powder Rainbow had ordered him to mix in Mueller's drink was some sort of poison. In fact, it was only Kaaren's "spaced-out" reaction to just a few sips of the heavily diluted drug mixture (and especially her whispered ravings about colors) that convinced Bylighter he must have given her a massive dose of the hallucinogen; and that kept him from tossing the remaining "thiopene" powder down his sink.

But now . . . now that he was *sure* the powder he'd skimmed from the relabeled 'THIOPENE' vial was the A-17 analog—the drug that had blown Kaaren Mueller's mind, just as the B-16 had set Raggedy Ann and Annie off on their "rainbow" trip—it was all that Bylighter could do to keep himself from ripping into the hidden bindle and experiencing the whole rush himself.

But Bylighter could control himself now, because he really *had* changed. For the first time in his entire life, he was beginning to think ahead. He'd even come up with a plan—albeit a slobbering vision of improbable ecstasy—that had become the very cornerstone of his existence.

But there was a catch: To make his plan work, Bylighter needed every bit of his secreted supply of "Power-Rainbow." He'd already been forced to give up half of his treasured stash to Raggedy Ann and Raggedy Annie, barely managing to save the rest for himself, and only then by threatening to tell Rainbow. Which meant that he didn't dare try even a little bit of the wondrous powder, because he had no idea how much he'd need . . .

. . . and because he knew if he tried even a little, he'd want more. He'd *always* wanted more.

Concentrate on the plan, he kept telling himself again and again. *Had* to concentrate on his plan—and Skylight!—if he was going to have enough of the A-17 powder to make it work. The plan . . .

. . . and five hundred dollars, he suddenly remembered, feeling sick to his stomach again as Rainbow's terrifying voice echoed in his mind. It was already Saturday morning, and he was supposed to have the thiopene deal set up for Sunday. But he knew he'd never get the deal set up, never have a chance to get his five hundred dollars, unless he could find . . .

"About time you showed up around here, Squeek," the voice said from the doorway.

Bylighter spun around. He couldn't believe his ears or eyes.

"SANDY! Jesus, it's—I mean, goddamn, I been trying to get hold of you—tryin' to find you *so bad*—I—I—" It was all that Bylighter could do to keep from grabbing the girl and hugging her and crying all at the same time.

It was fortunate that he held himself back, however, because the smoldering look that had suddenly appeared in Sandy Mudd's eyes—a look that matched the clenched fist at the end of her solidly muscled forearm—was one of pure hatred.

All because of a single bit of circumstantial evidence.

Bylighter had the two top buttons of his shirt undone. From her position across the room, Sandy could easily see the fading—but still distinct—set of teeth marks on his pale, skinny neck. Teeth marks almost certainly made by Kaaren. Her partner who had been raped, cut, and left out in the cold, salty-wet darkness to die with a tiny bit of skin in her teeth.

At that moment, Sandy Mudd wanted to kill Bylighter, rip his throat out with her bare hands, and then walk out the door without ever looking back. She knew she could do it. Probably could even justify it if she worked her story right, damaged the transmitter first and then rearranged the scene to make it look like self-defense . . .

Except that she couldn't, because she understood now that they were right. Bylighter wasn't enough. Like Ben Koda, Charley Shannon and the others, Sandy Mudd wanted every one of them.

"You weren't trying all that hard to find us last Thursday, were you, *buddy?*" Mudd said accusingly, glaring at Bylighter.

"Oh—yeah, uh, Jesus, I m-mean I'm really s-s-sorry," he stuttered. "Listen, I really tried—"

"Yeah? Well, you must not have tried very hard," Mudd went on. "My friends said they waited around here for a couple *hours* and you never showed."

"I—I know," Bylighter swallowed nervously, frantically trying to figure out how he could talk his way back into the girl's good graces. He *needed* her so badly. "Listen, honest, I—I tried to call you, God, I don't know, I bet at least twenty times yesterday. Left messages and everything. I guess you must a' been out, uh, on that boat or some-thin', huh?"

"No, as a matter of fact, my boyfriends were so pissed-off 'cause they didn't get the coke, they decided they didn't even want to take the boat out. Ask me how happy I am about *that*," Mudd demanded, maliciously waiting a good five or six seconds, while Bylighter stared helplessly, before going on.

"Anyway," she said, dropping the tone of her voice ever-so-slightly, and staring directly into Bylighter's eyes, "they said we might go out next week, *if* . . ." She left the rest of the sentence unspoken.

It took Bylighter a few seconds.

"Oh—you mean, if I—"

Sandy nodded her head slowly. "Yeah, that's right. I talked them into giving you another try."

"Uh—yeah," Bylighter nodded, taking a deep breath, trying to remember how he'd planned it all out. How he was going to sweet-talk her into taking a half-pound of the thiopene instead of the cocaine. "Listen, the thing is, high-grade coke's kinda at a premium right now . . ."

"You mean that after all that talk, you still can't come up with a couple goddamn ounces?" Sandy Mudd asked incredulously. "Jesus, what kind of connection are you, anyway, Squeek?"

"Uh, yeah—well, I guess things haven't been working out too well so far, huh?" Bylighter looked up at Mudd and realized he was right on the verge of losing her. "But—but the thing is," he hurried on, "I've been really working hard for you, tryin' to score you some of that new stuff on the street everybody's lookin' for."

"You mean that stuff you were talking about last Thursday? Look, Squeek, it's like I already told you, my friends aren't interested . . ."

"Yeah, I know, but—listen, remember the price I offered you for the coke?"

"Sure. Twenty-five hundred an ounce. Five grand for the pair, with maybe a ten-percent discount if we come back. Hell of a deal," she added sarcastically. "What about it?"

"Well—uh, see, I kinda talked my boss into making you and your friends a real special deal, seein's how I, uh, you know, kinda screwed up last week. Anyway, what he's gonna do, he's gonna let me sell you guys a half-pound of this new thiopene analog stuff he's comin' out with this month for—uh—almost the same price. You know, kinda like a—a trial offer," Bylighter smiled hopefully.

"You're trying to sell us a half-pound of something we've never heard of before for five grand?" Sandy Mudd stared at Bylighter in disbelief.

"Well—uh, actually, it's gonna come out to f-fifty-five hundred, on account of—uh—I gotta get five hundred out front, you know, to like set the deal 'cause this stuff's so special . . ."

"Oh, and now you want five hundred out front. What's that, your commission?" Mudd asked suspiciously.

"Huh? Oh, uh—uh, n-no, n-n-not exactly—uh, I mean, sorta, you know. Like I gotta make things right with my boss. You know how it is . . .?" Bylighter tried hopefully.

Sandy Mudd shook her head. "I don't know, Squeek. I don't

think my friends are gonna be too interested. Like I told you, we really like to do crystal. Besides, what're we gonna do with a half-pound of this thiopene stuff, even if it is any good? There's only four of us, for Christ's sake."

"Oh hey, listen, soon as the thiopene starts coming out, they're gonna be gettin' at least double what they get for coke . . . 'cause, like, they say it's gonna be legal for a long time. I mean, can you believe that? Mind-blowin' dope you can't get busted for? Jesus, I mean, you guys'll make a fortune offa what you don't use."

"And the bottom line is you can't get the coke anyway, right?" Mudd asked, shaking her head in exasperation.

"Well—yeah, I mean, at least not for, you know, maybe a—uh, week or two at the outside. But Jesus, honest to God, Sandy," Bylighter pleaded, "I'm tellin' you, this stuff's twice as good as coke."

"All right, I'll tell you what," Mudd nodded. "Let me call my friends, see what they want to do."

"Oh yeah, sure—hey, just go ahead and use the phone here—"

"That's okay, Squeek," Mudd shook her head. "There's a pay phone outside. Be a little more private, if you know what I mean."

"Oh—uh, sure—yeah, I understand," Bylighter nodded nervously, "I just thought . . ."

"You stay here and I'll go make my phone call," Sandy Mudd said firmly. "I'll lay it out for them, just the way you told me. They think it's okay, we'll go for it. Okay? If not," Mudd shrugged, "that's the way it is."

"Yeah—sure." Bylighter nodded, looking like a small puppy that had just been abandoned for the first time as Sandy turned and walked out of the back room of the donut shop. She quickly walked across the street, stepped into the glass-walled booth, closed the door, fed a quarter into the slot, took a quick look around to be sure, and then began to punch a memorized sequence of numbers very quickly.

Tom Fogarty stood at the open window of his third-floor hotel room and stared silently out at the distant ocean, the nonscrambled, five-watt, high-band radio held ready in his hand, while Bart Harrington continued to talk on the telephone.,

"Okay, listen," Harrington said after he finished scribbling on the legal pad, "you stay where you are. We'll be back to you within five. Okay? Yeah, I know. Hang in there, kid."

Harrington hung up the phone and looked up at Fogarty. "Now what?"

Fogarty held up a silencing hand, then keyed the radio. "Homestead to Outrider, do you copy?"

"Outrider, go," Ben Koda's voice cracked over the small radio speaker.

"Can you copy, Roadrunner?"

"Negative."

Walls of the building probably blocking the transmitter, Fogarty nodded to himself. "Any sign of your playmates?"

"That's a negative, Homestead. Playin' all by ourselves out here. What's going down?"

"Got a minor problem. Roadrunner's going to maintain position for about five. Do you have a clear visual?"

"Affirmative, Homestead. Line-of-sight. Advise problem."

"Indian Giver's back to his old song-and-dance. Temporary time-out. Roadrunner's going back into the game, soon as we figure out the rules. Want you people to keep the playground clear."

The radio speaker clicked twice in acknowledgment.

"Any suggestions?" Fogarty asked, setting the radio down carefully on the breakfast table.

"Why buy if it isn't illegal?" Harrington shrugged.

"One, Bylighter's still the only decent contact we've got with these assholes, two, we won't know if that shit's legal or not till we get a sample, and three, the son of a bitch can't come up with any coke anyway."

"Least that's what he says now." Harrington nodded. "Thing is, though, if the stuff's legal, we lose our twist at the first gate. Then what?"

"I don't know," Fogarty admitted. "Not much we can do . . . unless things change when Locotta decides to deal himself in," he added ominously.

"Only one other choice, the way I see it, if we want to get ourselves into the game first," Harrington said, puffing contemplatively on his pipe.

"Yeah, what's that?" Fogarty demanded.

"Increase the pressure."

Sandy walked back into the shop, closed the door firmly, and turned to stare directly into the nervous Bylighter's eyes.

"No deal," Mudd said, shaking her head firmly.

"But—but—" Bylighter started in, his voice rising in pitch.

"Listen to me. Squeek, that's the way it is. The guys aren't gonna lay out five grand for something they've never heard of. You want to deal with us, you gotta come up with the coke."

Bylighter looked as though he was going to cry. "But I'm tellin' you, this new stuff—" he tried again, pleading.

"You're not listening, Squeek," Mudd interrupted, "it's five grand for two ounces of coke, or nothing—period."

Bylighter's head and hands seemed to be caught in some sort of random, erratic motion. He kept frantically trying to figure out something . . . anything that might change her mind.

"Okay,"—Mudd shrugged—"see you around sometime." She turned to open the door, and Bylighter's newly changed, goal-oriented mind surged into action.

"NO, WAIT!" he yelled, "Listen—" he tried to catch his breath, feeling his heart pounding and his hands shaking, "—listen, I—I'll—*get* you the coke. Somehow, I don't—but I'll get it for you," he nodded hurriedly. "But I gotta have that five hundred—"

"And that's another thing," Mudd said, realizing that she was enjoying the sight of Bylighter practically begging on his knees, "no front money. You wanna kick in, say, a quarter-ounce or so of that new stuff, we'll get you five bills under the table. *But not up front,*" Mudd emphasized. "Now where do we do the deal?"

"Uh—they s-said, p-park outside H-Hotel C-C-Clairmont," Bylighter stuttered, teary-eyed. "T-ten-thirty. . . ."

"Okay, park outside the Clairmont. Ten-thirty P.M., day after tomorrow." Mudd nodded, watching Bylighter cautiously.

"Well . . .?" Mudd demanded.

"Yeah—okay, ten-thirty, day after tomorrow." Bylighter nodded, snuffling as he wiped at his eyes and nose. "Just don't forget my five hundred," he whispered pleadingly as Mudd closed the door behind her, telling himself that somehow, everything just might work out all right for Sunday after all, if he could just get his hands on that coke. . . .

He wouldn't realize until later on that morning, as he was trying to get up the nerve to call Rainbow, that the day after tomorrow was a Monday.

Isolated in the otherwise empty chemistry laboratory, Dr. David Isaac and Nichole Faysonnt were deeply involved in working out the next analog series for Jimmy Pilgrim when they received a very brief phone call.

This time it was Isaac who walked out into the darkened parking lot to retrieve the manila envelope out of his battered Volkswagen while Nichole watched nervously from the upstairs window. But, aside from Isaac's weather-beaten bug, and the night-janitor's motorcycle, the parking lot was empty.

Isaac slowly removed first the folded sheets of paper, and then—much more slowly—the sealed, clear-plastic pouch containing the second of the single yellowed sheets of parchment bearing Maria's scribbled notations.

As Isaac stood at the laboratory bench and stared wordlessly at the ancient, history-soaked document, Nichole was reading quickly through the sheath of hand-printed notes.

"We were right," she whispered, "look, right here . . ." she held one of the sheets of lined paper under Isaac's eyes, pointing with her finger. "Look, starting at B-Eleven . . . all the way through Sixteen. Look at those results. 'Mild high'; 'nice trip, but too short'; 'flashy colors'; 'space warp'; 'pure sex'; 'dynamite!'" One by one, Nichole read off the list of descriptions provided by Skylight's test subjects.

"What about B-Ten," Isaac said. "Four test subjects: 'died', 'convulsions and coma', 'severe vaginal bleeding', and . . . 'died.'"

"Yes, I know, I . . . saw that too," Nichole whispered quietly, but then, unable to help herself, she became animated again. "But look, especially the Twelve-through-Sixteen series . . . there, look right there, see how it's progressive?"

"And the colors." Isaac nodded, starting to feel a little of Nichole's regained enthusiasm in spite of himself. "Exactly as we predicted, given the availability of that receptor site. It should have had a nice effect."

"It must have." Nichole nodded. "Look at what else they wrote here," she said, handing Isaac another one of the hand-printed pages.

"Computer message system now in operation. Destroy all written records regarding analogs immediately," Isaac read. "Sounds reasonable," he nodded. "They're getting ready to start production."

"Does that mean my lab notebook too?" Nichole asked, looking shocked at the thought of burning her carefully maintained records.

"No, I think we can keep a lab notebook without causing too much harm." Isaac shrugged. "In fact, I think it's essential that we keep back something of our own . . . just in case."

"But if they—?"

"Don't worry." Isaac smiled reassuringly. "They'll never know we have it."

"They also want a cookbook method for B-sixteen, as soon as possible." Nichole read as Isaac started to turn back to the plastic-protected Maria document.

"Yes, I suppose they would want to start with that one." Isaac nodded distractedly. "That shouldn't be too difficult for us."

"All of the procedures are in the memory files." Nichole shrugged. "They gave us an access code to their computer system, so I can transfer it across to them right now if you want. But there's something else too. They want to know if B-Sixteen can be produced in the same lab—with the same equipment and glassware—as the thio-pene."

Isaac thought for a moment, walking through the synthesis pro-cedures for the A/B-16 analog in his head. "Tell them yes." He finally nodded. "We'll make a minor modification in the reflux step. Much easier than setting up another lab for our . . . friends," he snorted, shaking his head as he continued to stare at the torn and stained piece of the Maria parchment, trying to absorb the almost-sensory historical details in the tightly scribbled notations of the long-dead alchemist.

"Yes, but . . ." Nichole hesitated, bringing her small hand up to rub gently against Isaac's stomach, feeling his muscles tighten— involuntarily?—". . . aren't you forgetting something?"

Isaac shifted his mind and eyes away from the ancient parch-ment to stare at Nichole. "Forgetting something?"

Nichole nodded, staring up into Isaac's eyes as she continued to stroke his stomach, willing his muscles—and his mind—to relax. "A-Seventeen," she whispered. "If Sixteen was as good as they say, as colorful and . . . erotic," she hesitated at the word, "then can you imagine what A-Seventeen must be like?"

"It almost makes you wonder, doesn't it?" He nodded solemnly.

"What?" She blinked, not completely sure she understood what Isaac was saying.

"Analog Seventeen," he said quietly. "It makes you wonder if they really know what we gave them."

The three people in Jimmy Pilgrim's organization who *did* know something about the effects of the A-17 analog had no interest whatsoever in sharing their knowledge with their fearsome employer.

Two of these people—Raggedy Ann and Raggedy Annie—had been locked in a mutually sweaty, blissful embrace for almost six hours, with no apparent end in sight to the waves of ever-shifting and intensely stimulating colors that swirled, flowed and flashed across every pleasure-sensitive neuron in their bodies as they lay moaning and exhausted, but still trembling amid uncharted depths of passion in each other's arms.

The third individual also had other things on his mind which, at the moment, were far more pressing than any sense of loyalty to his fearsome employers. Problems such as trying to move as quietly as he possibly could through the downstairs floor of a darkened house in a decidedly upscale neighborhood, trying desperately to see where he was going, and trying not to trip over anything and wake up the guy upstairs, and most important, trying in what had to be the darkest house he had ever been in in his life to find something—*anything*—that might be worth five hundred dollars to a fence.

Actually, Eugene Bylighter had never really made the conscious decision to burglarize a house in order to obtain the money for Skylight. Somehow, at some point after realizing that he had once again irretrievably screwed up something for Rainbow, Bylighter simply decided that he had to do *something* . . . and that it didn't really matter what.

Bylighter didn't know anything about guns, knives, ignition systems or locks, so he simply wandered around the dark residential back alleys of south San Diego for about three hours until he found a house in the adjoining town of National City with an open upstairs window and a backyard that didn't have a dog.

After using an old wooden stepladder from a neighboring yard, he spent another ten minutes creeping breathlessly across the carpeted floor of the upstairs bedroom and hallway, and then slowly down the long stairway and into the dark living room . . . and family room . . . and den, where he finally found what he was looking for.

In the darkness, it took Bylighter a good twenty minutes to disconnect and then carefully coil all of the wires and cords interconnecting the portable television set, stereo, graphic equalizer, video recorder, antennas, and speakers.

Then, as carefully as he could, Bylighter gently stacked the video recorder on top of the TV, and the stereo on top of the recorder, lifted the seventy-odd pounds of expensive electronics gear up in his scrawny, trembling arms . . . and was staggering toward the doorway when the ever-watchful and mischievous Fates finally decided it was time to give him the finger once again.

As he moved along the wall, one of the dangling coils of wire managed to catch on a light switch, immediately filling the room with blinding light. This in turn caused a terrified Bylighter to scream and throw his hands high in the air . . . sending the television, tube-first, into the corner of a huge oak desk, the stereo and equalizer into two of the suddenly blinding lamps on the same desk, and the video recorder into a shiny chrome cart filled with a carefully selected assortment of fine liquors.

The virtually simultaneous implosion, explosion, shattering crashes, and small fires—ignited when sparks from two of the broken lamps came into contact with a spray of 151-proof alcohol—resulted in the complete destruction of the den and most of its contents.

The carnage was later described by a clearly impressed sheriff's investigator as "mind-blowing," which was probably as good a description as any, considering the state of Eugene Bylighter's ravaged mind when he found himself staring wide-eyed and openmouthed at the flames as they licked upward toward the long black robes of a Superior Court Judge.

Ben Koda, Charley Shannon, Bart Harrington and Sandy Mudd were sitting in Ben and Charley's motel room, discussing the implications of the latest twist in their hunt for Jimmy Pilgrim and Rainbow when the phone rang.

"Yeah?" Shannon answered, and then handed the phone over to Koda. "It's DeLaura."

"Yeah, Marty, what's up?" Koda asked.

"You know that kid we were staked out on the other day at the donut shop?"

"Bylighter? Yeah, sure. What about him?"

"Well, you'd better be sittin' down, buddy, 'cause you're not gonna believe this . . ."

19

GIVEN THE NATURE and magnitude of the incident, and the delicious irony of the individuals involved, it took about fifteen minutes for the word to spread throughout the entire night watch of the San Diego Sheriff's Department—thanks to the efforts of the first two deputies at the scene, who quickly discovered that it wasn't necessary to exaggerate a single detail of their story. It was simply *too good*, just the way it was . . .

"Aw, c'mon, you're shittin' me."

"Honest to God, I'm tellin' ya . . ."

"You mean *Eugene* Bylighter? *Squeek*? Nawww."

And on and on.

Until by the time that Bylighter had been booked, strip-searched, showered, deloused, dressed in a pair of baggy coveralls, photographed and fingerprinted, the woebegone youth had become a virtual cellblock celebrity.

As a consequence, every night-watch deputy on duty who happened to be anywhere near the station found some excuse to stop by the jail and wander past Bylighter's cell to stop and stare in un-abashed, head-shaking amazement at the miserable-looking kid who'd had the fucking balls to ransack the residence of Judge Harold "Hangin' Roy" Beene.

Just had to reassure themselves that the guy everybody was talking about was really *the* Eugene Bylighter . . .

. . . whose epic tale of derring-do had perhaps been best summed up by one of the first officers at the scene, who was overheard to tell his police pals, "Honest to God, there we were, just rollin' up on the call, when we see the kid and then the old white-haired bastard himself come bustin' out the front window, bare-ass naked with his flamin' robes in one hand and some kind'a walkin' stick in the other, screaming his fuckin' head off and tryin' to beat the kid to death with the goddamned stick and tryin' to stomp his robes out—*barefoot*, I swear to God!—all at the same time! I'm tellin' you guys straight-out, I *never* seen such a fuckin' sight in all my life!"

This caused one of the head-shaking officers to suggest that Squeek Bylighter was a cinch to become the first *res*-burgler in the history of the San Diego County Court System to receive the death penalty during his arraignment, a comment which, in turn, inspired a narc and two homicide detectives to set up the first office pool betting on Bylighter's gaveled-down sentence.

The predictable result being that some of this information fi-nally filtered down through the various grapevines, rumor mills and telephone lines to reach Lafayette Beaumont Raynee at his home at a little after eight that Sunday morning.

The first thought that occurred to Rainbow after hanging up the phone was that somehow, he was going to beat Judge "Hangin' Roy" Beene to Eugene Bylighter's scrawny neck if he had to do the job himself.

Then he thought about it all a little longer, and was actually chuckling to himself, visualizing the flaming-robes-and-cane scene on Judge Beene's front lawn, by the time he got Jimmy Pilgrim on the phone.

"Whatcha' think?" Raynee asked after he had finished briefing Pilgrim on the situation offering his suggestion.

"I think that our Mr. Bylighter is so incredibly, brilliantly inept and stupid that it would be a shame . . . and also a waste . . . to dispose of him just yet," Pilgrim whispered coldly. "He's doing the job we want much better than we could have ever hoped. What about the thiopene? Will it be available?"

"Picked it up this morning. Also got the cookbook for the B-16 analog. Figure we oughta be in production in a couple days."

"Fine. The sooner the better. You handle the details with the General. I'll make the necessary arrangements with the lawyers."

"Hey, man," Raynee whispered euphorically, caught up in the flow of his own enthusiasm as he anticipated the game-playing violence to come, "tell me true, now, it's gonna work, ain't it? I mean, we're gonna pull it off slick, ain't that right?"

"Yes, my friend," Pilgrim rasped, "it's all going to work out . . . *just fine.*"

The General was sitting out on the spacious rear deck of his hillside La Jolla home, consuming his strawberry-daiquiri-and-scrambled-egg breakfast, reading the morning paper, when the deck phone rang.

"Good morning." The General smiled cheerfully as he recognized Raynee's voice. "I trust you have good news."

"Jes' about got the deal lined up," Raynee said with disarming cheerfulness. "Got a few details t' iron out, but it's lookin' like Sunday evening 'round ten-thirty. Park outside the Clairmont Hotel in Lemon Grove do you okay?"

"That'll be just fine." The General nodded. "Did you pick up any more intelligence on the boat owner?"

"Dude seems a mite kinky 'bout sharin' his lady friend." Raynee chuckled, "but Ah guess that don' mean much 'round Newport. Man's finances trackin' back real nice-like though. People what know him figure he's jes' out spendin' his daddy's money. Other hand, two dudes he and his lady hang out with beginnin' t' look down-right heavy. Roy's bringin' you over couple pictures Loot took a' them boys. Give ya a little look-see what we're dealin' with, 'fore you go runnin' 'round that park."

"Fair enough." The General nodded. "What about the dope?"

"Roy gets there, you gonna have yourself a little thio-pene," Raynee said. "'Bout a half-pound, be exact."

"And the main line?"

"Plannin' on goin' into production in a couple days, soon as this test works out," Raynee said. "Gonna be nice bein' rich. 'Course Ah ain't 'xactly figured out yet how Ah'm gonna spend all that money," he sighed with a giggling laugh.

"I'm sure we'll all manage somehow." The General chuckled in return.

"No doubt 'bout it." Raynee nodded. "Listen, now, you watch yourself out there, come Monday. Can't 'ford t' be losin' man like you, this point a' the game."

"Rest assured I'll have my best interests in mind *at all times*," the General emphasized, sharing Rainbow's laughter as he hung up the phone.

The General continued to sit out on his warm deck, staring out over his beautiful ocean view and thinking to himself how interesting it was that during their entire conversation Raynee hadn't once mentioned the recent, awkward fate of Eugene Bylighter.

Very interesting indeed, because based on his own grapevine, the General figured that an eighteen-year-old, dumb-shit kid like Bylighter would probably find it difficult to carry out his end of a half-pound narcotics transaction from the vantage point of an eight-by-ten jail cell.

Bylighter had just finished his microwaved frozen breakfast, and was hopelessly lost in his jumbled thoughts, when the ceiling-mounted speaker high overhead blared out his name.

"Bylighter, up. Got a visitor."

The message didn't do much for the dejected youth, because he couldn't think of anybody who cared enough about him to go through the hassle of making a jail visit. He figured it was probably a mistake, or at best maybe a priest.

When the jailer came to unlock his cell and escort him over to one of the visitors' rooms. Eugene Bylighter didn't even bother to ask the obvious question.

"Looks like you got yourself a hotshot lawyer, kid." The jailer grinned as he opened the door to the visitors' room with an oversized brass key. "Good luck."

"Huh?" Bylighter said, suddenly very interested in asking questions, but much too late as the door shut behind him with a loud clang. Then he turned to look around and saw an extremely distinguished-looking grey-haired man in a three-piece, pinstriped suit sitting on the opposite side of the small conference table.

The man looked up at Bylighter with a calm, pleasant, and seemingly even friendly expression on his face, and then motioned for Bylighter to sit down.

"You *sure* you wanna talk with me?" Bylighter asked, absolutely certain now that someone had made a mistake. Even to a poorly-developed sense of discrimination like Bylighter's, this man did

not look at all like a typically overworked and dispirited public de-
fender.

"You are Eugene Bylighter, aren't you?"

"Uh—yeah."

"Then yes, I *do* want to talk with you." The grey-haired man
nodded. "I'm Alberton Cahoon, attorney-at-law," he said, reaching
out and taking Bylighter's limp hand in a firm grip for a moment before
motioning to one of the empty chairs. "Please sit down."

Bylighter sat, looking around nervously as if expecting to be
yelled at by someone at any second. The man watched Bylighter's
nervous antics for a few moments and then said gently, "If you're concerned that someone may be monitoring our conversation, please
don't be. Contrary to what you may have heard, the sheriff's department does respect the sanctity of the lawyer-client relationship."

"N-no, that's not—uh, I—uh, guess what I mean is, I can't
afford a lawyer," Bylighter shrugged sheepishly, his eyes downcast.

"On the contrary, Mr. Bylighter," Alberton Cahoon smiled,
"your ability to pay my fee is not in question here. As a matter of fact,
all of your legal expenses are being taken care of by your employer."

"Huh?" Bylighter looked up in disbelief.

"Apparently, they think very highly of you," the grey-haired
lawyer suggested. "After all, they did deliver a retainer check for five
thousand dollars to our office this morning, as promised."

Bylighter's jaw dropped open.

"However," Alberton Cahoon went on calmly, "let's not waste
our time with things that don't concern us. As for your case, there are
certainly a number of promising avenues for a successful defense. Perhaps I can discuss these with you in more detail sometime later, after
you've been released."

"Released?" Bylighter almost choked on the word, absolutely
convinced now that he had to be hallucinating.

"On bail, of course," Cahoon said as if that explained everything. "I reviewed the initial case reports this morning. As things
stand right now, there's no reason we can't arrange for you to be released at your arraignment tomorrow morning."

"B-b-but—the judge." Bylighter shook his head. "He—he
said—"

"Yes, I'm sure that Judge Beene said many things." Cahoon
smiled calmly, as though the prospect of having a client who had very
nearly been beaten to death by a superior court judge running naked
and amok in his front yard with his court robes on fire was an everyday

occurrence, simply a matter of sorting out the minor details, each of which would be dealt with accordingly.

"As I'm sure you realize by now," Cahoon went on sympathetically, "Judge Beene is a rather colorful and easily excited individual. Nonetheless, I'm confident that we can come to—what shall we call it?—a mutually agreeable understanding?"

"I—I don't believe any of this." Bylighter shook his head. "I-I'm sorry, b-but I just don't understand—what's going on," he whispered shakily.

"Oh yes, of course." Cahoon nodded in sudden comprehension. "You really don't understand the process, do you?"

"No—I guess I don't—" Bylighter whispered, shaking his head pathetically.

"You see, in an arrangement such as this," Alberton Cahoon explained gently, sounding as though he were lecturing a freshman law class, "it's customary that your employers may expect you to do something for them in return. Quid pro quo. A favor, as it were."

"Quid . . . a favor? They want *me* to do *them* a favor?"

"I believe that's *exactly* what they have in mind," Cahoon said as he reached into his briefcase for a lined yellow legal pad. "Perhaps if I explain the situation to you in more detail."

While Bylighter was in the process of being enlightened by Mr. Cahoon as to his newly elevated status and responsibilities within Jimmy Pilgrim's tightly controlled organization, two members of that very same organization were engaged in a vaguely similar exchange of services and favors.

Although within the trade Raggedy Annie and Raggedy Ann were really more of a "specialty item" than a "service"—in fact, they were little more than a rough-edged team of bull-and-bear dykes who didn't really mind tripping out with their mildly perverted johns and janes—and as such they were *very* expensive.

Which was why when asked as a favor to supply a little mind-lubricant to get things "warmed up" a bit, Raggedy Annie didn't think twice about offering to share a small portion of their dwindling supply of "Power-Rainbow" (as she and Ann now called the A-17 analog) with Wee-Willie, who, in addition to being an upwardly mobile and otherwise highly ambitious member of the local school board, happened to be one of their more frequent customers.

As a consequence of their generosity, Raggedy Annie, Raggedy Ann and Wee-Willie spent a little over three hours together in a session that William Benson Sandcastle III later described to the other three members of his club foursome on the sixth tee as an experience better than sex, booze and golf all rolled into one.

At that very moment, a similar confession was being made by Raggedy Annie, who whispered to her completely understanding and equally confused playmate, "You know, for a couple of hours there, I really think I loved that guy."

In another apartment, this one near the San Diego campus of the University of California, a young woman who was experiencing a very similar state of mental confusion finished mixing a carefully measured portion of the A-17 analog into two cups of freshly brewed coffee and then walked out onto her second-story balcony that overlooked a wide expanse of landscaped grass and small trees.

David Isaac looked up from the plastic-encased document that was purported to be a part of Maria-the-Jewess's lab notes as Nichole Faysonnt set one of the steaming cups down in front of her mentor and lover.

"Are you feeling all right, Nichole?" Isaac asked, his eyebrows furrowing in concern. "You seem be very . . . distracted lately."

She smiled knowingly. As a matter of fact, she *had* been very distracted, ever since she had deliberately consumed a very conservative dose of the A-17 analog, and subsequently experienced a mild form of the chromatic hallucinations while gazing calmly at the suddenly very clear and understandable scribbled notes of Maria.

For reasons that she couldn't even begin to explain, Nichole now felt that she truly understood the pains, the anxieties, and the frustrations that the determined Maria must have experienced in stepping upon the forbidden territory of the male alchemists. But now that she knew . . .

"It's nothing." Nichole smiled warmly at her lover, who she knew would also understand . . . very, very soon. "Drink your coffee," she said encouragingly. "It's all going to work out fine. I'm sure of it now."

While William Benson Sandcastle III, Raggedy Annie and Raggedy Ann were each busily engaged in trying to explain their shared experiences, a San Diego sheriff's deputy suddenly began paying serious attention to what the distinguished, grey-haired man sitting in front of him was saying.

Very close attention, indeed, because although he wasn't absolutely sure, Sergeant Wilbur Hallstead of the Sheriff's Vice/Narcotics Unit thought he had just heard the magic words that meant promotion.

Then, after listening very carefully to the lawyer for a few more minutes, Sergeant Hallstead excused himself, walked hurriedly through a series of controlled doors to the jail office, and then quickly dialed the office number of Detective Martin DeLaura.

"Narcotics."

"Marty, this is Hallstead. I'm down in the jail. Visitors' room. Get your ass down here, pronto!"

"What—?"

"I think we got the General," Hallstead said cryptically, and then hung up before DeLaura had a chance to question his supervisor as to what the hell he was talking about.

Two minutes later, an irritated but still curious Martin DeLaura walked into the secured visitors' room, and then came up short as he observed the very distinguished-looking man sitting patiently across the table from Sergeant Wilbur Hallstead. A man who looked very much out of place, but not a bit disconcerted by his surroundings.

"Come in, Marty." Hallstead smiled cheerfully, waving DeLaura over to a third chair. "This is Mr. Alberton Cahoon, from the law firm of Jason, Saul, and Cahoon," Hallstead said.

"Martin DeLaura, one of my top narcotics investigators," Hallstead went on expansively, causing DeLaura's eyebrows to rise, a reaction that Cahoon noted with well-concealed amusement.

"Ah yes, Detective DeLaura, I'm afraid that we—that is to say, the various members of my firm—are well acquainted with your reputation," Alberton Cahoon said. "At the risk of seeming overly patronizing, Martin, let me also add—in all seriousness, I assure you—that you have forced us to earn our money on several occasions. Although I believe we're actually even at the moment, eight and eight, if I have my numbers correct."

"Something like that," DeLaura shrugged indifferently. He had experienced too many dealings with lawyers like Cahoon during his thirteen-year law enforcement career. None of them pleasant.

"I guess you must be the General's lawyer, Mr. Cahoon," DeLaura suggested with neutral politeness.

"Not exactly, Martin," Cahoon chuckled, his blue-grey eyes twinkling. "Actually, my firm has been retained to represent the interests of a Mr. Eugene Bylighter."

DeLaura blinked, and then stared at the poker-faced lawyer for a few moments. "You're shitting me," he said finally.

"Marty—" Hallstead growled a warning.

"No, no, that's perfectly all right," Mr. Alberton Cahoon raised his hand and shook his head slightly. "Martin is quite justified in being—shall we say—startled."

"Try suspicious," DeLaura suggested. "I don't suppose you're gonna tell us who's paying the freight?"

"No, I'm afraid not. Client privileges, et cetera, et cetera. I'm sure you understand how the game is played, Martin," Cahoon announced, continuing to display a serene smile. "However, I *am* authorized to tell you what I've just told Sergeant Hallstead. Namely that my client is willing to make a deal."

"A DEAL? You came all the way down here to tell me that Bylighter wants to make a *deal*? Jesus, Cahoon, begging your fucking pardon and all that, but you gotta be crazy." DeLaura shook his head. "I mean, aside from the minor problem that Bylighter's case doesn't even involve narcotics, you got any *idea* what Hangin' Roy's got lined up for that poor son of a bitch?"

"I understand the charges are, shall we say, substantial." Cahoon nodded, still smiling serenely. "Actually, to be perfectly frank with you both, I'm sorely tempted to talk Mr. Bylighter into pleading not guilty and demanding a trial, simply for the opportunity to cross-examine Judge Beene on his amazingly violent response to a rather . . . minor violation.

"However," the lawyer continued with a sigh, "we really can't indulge ourselves like that at the expense of our client—I suppose. Anyway, speaking on behalf of my clients, we feel that we may be in an excellent position to offer a deal. Although perhaps the word 'exchange' would be more appropriate."

"Who the hell—?" DeLaura started to say, and then his mouth fell open when it all clicked into place. "Jesus—" he whispered.

"Yes, exactly." Cahoon nodded. "Mr. Bylighter, my client," he reminded unnecessarily, "in exchange for a man you call the General."

DeLaura sat stunned for a few moments, then turned to his grinning supervisor.

"For Christ's sake, Hallstead, what's the matter with you?" DeLaura protested, "you know we can't make a deal like this. I mean, the D.A.'s—"

"I believe that Sergeant Hallstead has already been in contact with the district attorney, Martin," Cahoon interrupted. "As I'm sure you are aware, there are any number of, uh, influential people who would like nothing better than to see this nefarious General put out of business. Especially now—" Cahoon added with a seemingly sad, head-shaking smile, "—that we are rapidly approaching an election year."

"Jesus," DeLaura whispered again, staring down at the table and shaking his head again as he considered several of the most likely underlying manipulations. He looked up at Alberton Cahoon. "You ever have trouble sleeping at night, counselor?"

"Actually, yes." The elderly man nodded seriously. "Although I console myself with the belief that, on occasion, my efforts as a lawyer may eliminate the need for—shall we say—a more violent means of resolution? A self-serving rationalization, to be sure, but it does help, Martin. For whatever it matters, I can assure you of that."

Martin DeLaura closed his eyes for a moment and nodded his head slowly. "So—how's it supposed to work?"

"Mr. Bylighter, upon his release, will follow his instructions to contact a certain young lady and her friends, who have apparently already agreed to purchase some merchandise—cocaine, as I am told—directly or indirectly from the General himself. The transaction will take place tomorrow evening at approximately ten-thirty, in the park across from the old Clairmont Hotel in Lemon Grove," Cahoon said, reaching into his briefcase, removing a number of black-and-white photographs.

"These are surveillance photos taken of the woman I mentioned and her two gentlemen friends," Cahoon added, handing them over to the suddenly silent detective.

"Assuming that everyone involved really *does* want the General," Alberton Cahoon went on gently, "we—that is to say, of course, my clients—will make the necessary arrangements for Mr. Bylighter to carry on with his intended plans."

"And Judge Beene?" DeLaura asked quietly, continuing to stare blankly at the photographs.

"I am prepared to assist the district attorney in convincing the judge that my client represents a much lesser threat to society as a whole than does a man like the General," Cahoon said. "I have every reason to believe that my argument will be convincing. Presumably it will then be up to you and Sergeant Hallstead to handle all of the . . . subsequent details."

Back in his office, a badly shaken Martin DeLaura reached quickly for his desk phone.

By the time that the motel room phone had rung three times, DeLaura's mind was working feverishly, trying to assemble all of the cross-linking problems into some sort of logical order.

By the fourth ring, he'd decided the only thing that was even halfway clear about this whole mess was that it was much too late to be thinking about briefing the sheriff on his own little deal with Ben Koda. No way in the world, now, that he'd be able—

"Hello?"

"Ben, this is Marty."

"Yeah, buddy, how's it—"

"Listen, man," DeLaura interrupted, "can you get hold of Sandy, real quick-like, get her set up to take a call at her apartment?"

"No problem." Koda shrugged. "So what the hell's going down now?"

"You know that deal the Bylighter kid was gonna set up for you guys? The two ounces of coke?" DeLaura went on hurriedly.

"Shit," Koda growled disgustedly, "what about it?"

"You better be sittin' down again, partner. You guys really aren't gonna believe this one—"

20

THE FOLLOWING MONDAY morning, at nine o'clock, Eugene Bylighter stood quietly in his "SDSO JAIL"-emblazoned overalls and listened in wonder as his sixteen-hundred-dollar-a-day attorney presented a brief yet concise argument to an equally incredulous but certainly impressed municipal court judge.

In truth, it *was* an eye-opening performance by the prestigious law firm of Jason, Saul and Cahoon. So much so that even the long-suffering court bailiff came fully awake when Alberton Cahoon advised the Court in a firm and dignified voice that Eugene Bylighter, his wrongly accused client, was pleading not guilty of all charges, in need of extra time to adequately prepare his defense, and making a perfectly reasonable request to be released on his own recognizance pending trial.

"Mr. Bylighter," the judge said, turning his attention to the accused, "you have heard the charges being brought against you by the deputy district attorney, and you have heard the statements made by your own counsel. Is it, in fact, your wish to plead not guilty to the charges with which you are accused?"

"Y-you m-mean, d-d-did I do it?" Bylighter's voice quivered.

"Ah, Mr. Cahoon . . ." the judge said with a sigh and then waited patiently while the distinguished attorney-at-law whispered a few words of advice to his clearly confused client.

"Oh—uh, yes, sir, your honor. I'm, uh, not guilty." Bylighter nodded unconvincingly.

"Thank you, Mr. Bylighter," the judge said with barely restrained sarcasm, gazing down at his hands for a moment in what might have been silent prayer, and then shaking his head and sighing before continuing on. "Your pretrial hearing will be set for September twelfth in Division Eight of this Court. Your request for O.R. release is denied. Bail is set at fifty thousand dollars." The judge brought his head up from the arraignment documents and looked across at Bylighter's attorney. "Do I assume correctly, Mr. Cahoon, that you are prepared to arrange for your client's bail?"

"Yes, your honor," Cahoon said politely.

"Mr. Bylighter," the judge asked, "may I assume that you are aware of the serious consequences involved should you fail to show up for your scheduled pretrial hearing?"

"Uh—uh, y-yes, sir." Bylighter nodded.

"I can assure the Court that my client will be fully advised of the very serious nature of his responsibilities in this matter," Cahoon offered quietly.

"Yes, I'm quite sure he will be, Mr. Cahoon." The judge nodded with weary sarcasm as he handed the arraignment documents to the court clerk. "Next case."

After obediently signing a bewildering stack of legal papers that he didn't even pretend to understand, and then signing for his clothes, keys and pocket money, Eugene Bylighter walked outside of the courthouse with his attorney.

"You *do* understand what you are required to do this evening, I trust?" Alberton Cahoon asked with a patient and perhaps even kindly expression in his gentle, steady eyes. "Specifically, you are to meet Detective DeLaura at the McDonald's restaurant across the street from the Clairmont Hotel at precisely five o'clock this afternoon . . . correct?"

"Uh, yes, sir." Bylighter nodded, swallowing nervously as he looked around the street.

"Then if I may offer one more bit of advice before saying good-bye, Eugene," Cahoon spoke in a gentle tone.

"Yes, sir?" Bylighter whispered, looking around nervously.

"Do what they tell you, son. Do exactly what they tell you, and don't even think about running away. They are quite serious about all of this, I can assure you. Quite serious, indeed." With that, Alberton Cahoon turned and walked back inside the courthouse.

It took Bylighter almost ten minutes to find an unoccupied phone booth. As directed, his first call was to Rainbow. He stuttered quickly, listened carefully, nodded his head nervously several times, and then hung up when the phone buzzed loudly in his ear. Then he made a second call to a number he had committed to memory.

"H-hello, Skylight?"

The seductive voice at the other end of the line hesitated, and then broke into cheerfully surprised laughter. "Squeek, is that you?"

"Uh—y-yeah, it's me," Bylighter stuttered happily, his heart pounding loudly.

"Where are you calling from?"

"Uh, in a phone booth out on 'C' street. They kinda let me out. See, I—"

"Yeah, I know, Rainbow told me about it. Jesus, Squeek, you really got yourself in some deep shit."

"God, I know—"

"Wait a minute," Skylight interrupted, "you gotta tell it to me straight. Did you really hit Hangin' Roy's place just to get that five hundred?" •

"Uh—well, yeah—sorta."

"Jesus, you really *are* a horny bastard, aren't you?"

"Yeah—I guess," Bylighter admitted sheepishly. "B-but the thing is, I got the money."

"What?" Skylight laughed incredulously. "But I thought you got caught before—"

"Yeah, but see—uh, I kinda made a deal with some people. I guess maybe Rainbow told you . . . ?"

Skylight hesitated for a few moments.

"Yeah, I know what's going down at the Clairmont tonight. So?"

"Well, see, the thing is, since I'm kinda the middleman in this deal, I'm gonna get a finder's fee. Five hundred dollars," Bylighter said proudly. "And, uh, my—uh, friends, they're kinda, you know, gonna rent me a room at the hotel, overlookin' the park. So I thought maybe . . ." Bylighter went on hurriedly before his heart burst through his ribcage, ". . . maybe you could come up there and watch me make the deal, and then afterwards, uh, you know, maybe we could stay up there and watch the whole thing go down, and then, uh, you know, kinda . . . celebrate, like you said?"

For a few long moments, the phone in Bylighter's sweaty hand was silent as Skylight considered her instructions.

"Okay, Squeek!" Skylight laughed. "If you want me bad enough to burg a judge's house . . . then I guess you've got yourself a deal."

Jake Locotta looked up from his poolside Palm Springs lounge chair as Al Rosenthal sat down in the adjoining seat.

"Well?"

"Word is," Rosenthal rasped, "our friend the General's got a deal goin' down this evening. Half-pound of that new shit. Interesting thing is, he might be gonna do it himself."

"So they didn't take our warning seriously, huh, Rosey?"

"Apparently not." Rosenthal shrugged.

"I want you to put a camera out on that deal, Rosey," Locotta ordered. "I wanna see for myself what the hell's happening down here before I shut Pilgrim down!"

"You think they're running a game?"

"I don't know, Rosey." Locotta shrugged his oily, sunburned shoulders. "Maybe Pilgrim, or Raynee, or the General. Maybe all three of 'em. Maybe they're all just playin' with each other. I don't know. But I'll tell you this, it isn't gonna matter!" he growled, "'cause whatever kinda game's going down in my territory—"

"—you wanna know the players," Rosenthal finished for his fearsome boss.

"Every one of them, Rosey," Locotta whispered menacingly. "Every fucking name!"

Minutes after hanging up on Bylighter, Lafayette Beaumont Raynee was on the scrambled phone with Jimmy Pilgrim.

"Squeek jes' called," Raynee said.

"And?"

"D.A. went for the deal. Sounded like them folks been wantin' a shot at the General for a long time. Knew them jive-ass turkeys couldn't resist a little fat-cat bait," Raynee chuckled.

"What about Bylighter?" Pilgrim demanded.

"Boy's got himself *all kind* a' babysitters." Raynee laughed. "Them an' us. Don't worry, though, Ah ain't gonna let *nuthin'* happen t' that boy 'fore our deal goes down," Raynee added reassuringly. "Gonna take care of all that, personal-like."

"Fine," Pilgrim said. "Any indication the General knows about Bylighter's problem?"

"Always possible." Raynee shrugged. "But it ain't likely. No reason for him t' be tuned-in onna little shit-head gofer like Squeek. Not his problem."

"What about the newspapers?"

"Couple columns 'bout Hangin' Roy's house being hit. Said the suspect's a juvenile. No name. 'Sides, the General don't even know who's settin' the deal up anyways. An' even if he did, he's still gonna be too busy worryin' his ass off 'bout that hit by Tassio."

"And he also knows the powder's not illegal," Pilgrim added. "This ought to be *very* interesting. The deal still set with the Mudd girl and her boyfriends?"

"Sure is."

"What about their background?"

"Ain't found nuthin' yet. 'Course like you said, guess it don't really matter much if'n they turn out t' be narcs anyways, do it?"

"Actually, it would be much more informative if they *were* narcs," Pilgrim said. "Our test would be more conclusive, and it might very well explain the other girl and her friend."

"Gets kinda complicated, don't it?" Raynee chuckled.

"Yes," Pilgrim whispered coldly. "That's why we're going to monitor this deal very carefully. We have to demonstrate the analog theory to Michael Theiss and our other backers, but we must be extremely cautious in doing so," Pilgrim reminded. "Locotta won't be satisfied to issue warnings much longer. We can expect him to unleash Tassio at any time now."

"Ah hear ya." Raynee nodded. "Got everythin' ready and waitin'."

"I'm glad to hear that," Pilgrim rasped approvingly. "But for the moment, avoid Tassio if at all possible. It's bad enough that we're using Bylighter. We don't want the bait to be too obvious. By tomorrow morning, we should have a much better understanding . . . of many things."

Out on the deck of his ocean-view home, the man who had suddenly become the focal point of a number of critical career decisions during the past few days was deeply involved in a discussion with one of his more trustworthy ounce-dealers.

"Now you're sure you understand what I'm saying?" the General asked patiently.

"I wait in the car with the engine running till you give the signal." Lennie Orrson nodded, smiling patiently beneath a pair of black wraparound sunglasses. "I get the high sign, I cut the engine, come out, and do my thing. Easiest five grand I ever made."

"Maybe," the General reminded.

"You really thinking setup?" Orrson cocked his head curiously as he tapped the band-wrapped package of fifty hundred-dollar bills against the General's deck table.

"No, not really." The General shook his head. "Or let's say I don't see anybody in the organization turning on Pilgrim or Rainbow. But just the same—"

"—you like to cover your ass," Orrson added, grinning.

"A longtime habit." The General nodded. "Even made arrangements to have the powder tested before the sale, just in case—"

"—these guys turn out to be narcs?" Orrson suggested.

"Whether or not they're narcs shouldn't affect us seriously." The General shrugged. "For the simple reason that we aren't going to be selling anything illegal. That's the whole idea behind the analog sales theory, remember?"

"So we're cool, no matter who or what—just so long as we're real careful about the sales-in-lieu-of bit, right?"

"Careful and alert." The General nodded. "And then, too, our 'outposts' should also provide us with some useful intelligence during the exchange."

"So what it all comes down to, you're paying me a five-grand bonus just to cover your ass. That about it, General?" Orrson grinned.

"One of the first things I learned in working for the federal government, Lennie." The General smiled. "And I don't see this business as being all that much different."

"Yeah, how so?"

"Simple." The General shrugged. "Any time you see a deal being worked out between two or three agencies—people, whatever—you can figure there's at least two or three strategies being set up at cross purposes to make sure *somebody* gets the short and dirty end of the stick.

"In this case," the ex-bureaucrat explained, "I just want to make sure that somebody isn't *me*."

* * *

Had Detective Martin DeLaura been privy to the conversation taking place between Lennie Orrson and his overly suspicious employer, DeLaura would have been startled to learn that he and the General were very much alike . . . at least in the sense that they shared very similar feelings of professional paranoia.

Like the General, Martin DeLaura had suddenly found himself caught in the crosscurrents of several conflicting under-the-table manipulations, a situation that he didn't care for at all. Especially when he considered his vulnerability in two uncomfortably related areas: his deepening involvement with Koda and Shannon, and an ongoing murder investigation.

Glaring at his promotion-hungry supervisor, and the equally self-serving deputy district attorney, DeLaura warned them, "I'm tellin' you guys, you can't trust this little asshole. He's gonna go sideways on us."

"But you *are* still keeping an eye on him, aren't you," the deputy prosecutor inquired.

"Hell, that kid can't take a shit in a public john what we don't go in and count the toilet paper," DeLaura growled. "We lose him and Hangin' Roy'll be building a gallows right outside our fuckin' office. That's not what I'm talkin' about."

"Marty, we've heard all this—" Sergeant Wilbur Hallstead started in.

"Yeah, but you aren't *listening*. I'm tellin' ya, there's no way in the world that a kid like Bylighter's gonna play games with the southern California mob, I don't care *what* that crazy-ass judge threatened to do to him."

"Marty, what the hell's the matter with you?" Hallstead demanded. "Here we got ourselves an easy shot at the General, and now you—"

"And I'm tellin' you the fuckin' General's not gonna do a little two-ounce coke deal himself!" DeLaura slammed his fist on his desk. "Especially with someone like Bylighter setting up the deal," DeLaura added. "It's crazy. That's what the son of a bitch hires his ounce dealers for."

"Mr. Bylighter is simply going to see to it that a prearranged sale takes place in our presence, Martin," the deputy D.A. reminded. "He's not taking a man in. And he didn't say that the General was definitely going to be there. Only that he *might* be there."

"And you don't think that this whole fuckin' deal's a setup?" DeLaura demanded incredulously.

"Why should we think that?" the deputy D.A. asked curiously, completely unaffected by DeLaura's ranting.

"WHO THE FUCK D'YOU THINK HIRED THAT SON OF A BITCH CAHOON . . . BYLIGHTER'S FAIRY GODMOTHER?" DeLaura exploded.

"Marty!" Hallstead warned.

"And how 'bout the bail?" DeLaura went on, his face twisted with anger. "Who the hell d'you think put up fifty thousand dollars for that little asshole's bail?!"

"I don't know who hired Mr. Cahoon *or* who paid Bylighter's bail," the deputy D.A. explained patiently, "and to be perfectly frank, I really don't care."

"WHAT?" DeLaura came up out of his chair, his face livid.

"It's all perfectly logical, Martin," the deputy D.A. said calmly. "Look at it this way. Even if this *is* an intramural setup, as you suggest, what do we have to lose by letting the deal go through?"

"I'll tell you what—"

"Because what we're going to do, Martin," the deputy D.A. interrupted, "is we're going to video-record the entire transaction between these three as-yet-unidentified individuals, and the General . . . *or* his designated dealer," the prosecutor added. "If the General shows up himself and makes the deal, then you and your men will take him down, right there at the scene. And if he doesn't show, then we'll simply allow the deal to go through, follow the three buyers away from the area, and then, as you people say, 'twist' them into agreeing to work with us instead of going to jail. Eventually, through these, uh, cooperative citizens, we will continue to up the ante until we finally arrange a purchase that will entice the General to participate."

Martin DeLaura just sat, slowly shaking his head.

"So you see, Martin," the prosecutor went on, "even if someone *is* setting up the General, what does it matter? We're still going to get him, one way or another. And after all," he added pointedly, "it's not like we care if the mob is actively trying to do him in. They'd just replace him with someone else anyway. Can't you see what we're saying, Martin," the deputy D.A. implored. "It really *doesn't* matter."

"Except of course this way, you just might get your pictures put in the newspaper," DeLaura muttered darkly.

The deputy D.A. smiled cheerfully.

"Oh yes, and one other thing," the prosecutor added. "As you know, we initially agreed that Bylighter could walk away from the deal as soon as the primaries were brought together. However, I've changed my mind about that, and arranged for consent monitoring authority. We want to have him wired and standing nearby to record as much of the exchange as possible."

"Oh we do, do we?" DeLaura growled.

"Yes, Martin." The deputy D.A. nodded. "Sergeant Hallstead and I think that a tape may be, shall we say, most useful in convincing our three, uh, cooperative citizens to remain cooperative."

"What the D.A. is saying, Marty," Hallstead explained, "is we'd like you to explain the situation to the kid. Talk him into being cooperative. Tell him it's for his own safety . . . something like that."

"You see, Martin," the prosecutor added confidently, "based on our previous conversations with Mr. Bylighter, I really don't think he's going to be too happy about wearing a transmitter. Perhaps you can help him see things differently, help him understand that it really *is* for his own good."

At 12:30 that Monday afternoon, DeLaura leaned his aching head against the headrest of Ben Koda's motel bed, and waited patiently until Koda, Shannon and Mudd quieted down before taking another sip of his coke and then finishing his hurried briefing.

"I'm tellin' you people," DeLaura said, punctuating with his almost-empty coke can, "I don't have any control over this deal. The D.A.'s running Bylighter like his own private snitch. Bad enough the kid's gonna be wired, but the real kicker is now Bylighter's claiming the General himself might show up to make the deal."

"So—" Sandy Mudd started to say.

"I'm tellin' you," DeLaura insisted, "if the General hands over that dope in person, it's gonna be buy-bust time, no matter what, so make goddamned sure you people don't do anything to get yourselves shot."

DeLaura took a last swig and tossed the empty can in a nearby trashcan.

"Any suggestions?" Ben Koda asked as he and Charley and Sandy looked at each other.

"If the bust does go down, I'll try to be in position to arrest you three. Best I can do." DeLaura shrugged. "Unless you're willing to let me cut the deal wide open right now."

"Appreciate that," Charley Shannon rumbled quietly, "but we got other plans."

"We want the General a whole lot more than they do," Sandy Mudd added. "We've gotta go higher."

"Yeah, well the thing is," DeLaura went on, "you all better hope like hell the General doesn't show up on this one. 'Cause if he does," the veteran detective muttered grimly, "ain't no fuckin' way around it, you people are gonna lose."

21

By 5:30 MONDAY afternoon, the nosy registration clerk at the aging Clairmont Hotel had convinced himself that some sort of newsworthy event was about to take place somewhere in the vicinity of his hotel.

The problem, of course, was that he had no idea at all as to what was going to occur, or when, or where, or even if, for that matter.

But whatever *was* going on, it had to be big, the curious clerk told himself as he waited impatiently for the fourth group of men checking in that afternoon with heavy equipment cases and tripods to finish filling out their registration cards. After all, it wasn't every day that camera crews from *four* television networks got together in a second-class, run-down hotel like the Clairmont.

It was all very exciting—and, at the same time, very frustrating—because so far none of the arriving guests had been willing to say anything at all about their business at the Clairmont, which, as far as the clerk was concerned, all but confirmed his suspicion that something important had to be going on.

But so far, all he'd been able to determine was that whatever it was, it had to have something to do with the wretchedly maintained park next door, because every one of the four equipment-laden groups he'd checked in this Monday afternoon had demanded a room with a view of the park. And that certainly didn't make any sense to him. He suspected that the vast majority of the Clairmont Hotel's regular clientele wouldn't have noticed if the windows in their rooms had been boarded shut. It was that kind of hotel.

Of course, there was one other thing that he did know. The first two groups were from ABC and CBS, because they had stickers bearing the familiar logos all over their equipment cases.

In fact, he'd even tried to be helpful when the CBS crew checked in by advising the crew leader—in all confidence, or course—that the ABC team had checked in about an hour earlier. It was a judiciously risked indiscretion that resulted in little more than an indifferent shrug and a grunt from the head of Jimmy Pilgrim's three-man delivery protection team, not the sort of grateful response that the desk clerk had hoped for at all.

And then, when the most professional-looking crew showed up a half-hour later, wheeling in a dizzying array of seemingly brand-new equipment cases bearing no logo labels at all, the clerk's sly comment that "you guys must be NBC, because ABC and CBS have already checked in," was rewarded with a flickering glance of momentary confusion from Al Rosenthal, who quickly paid for two adjoining eighth-floor "penthouse" suites overlooking the park with a handful of brand-new fifty-dollar bills, leaving the thrice frustrated clerk even more irritable.

By the time the fourth group (clearly an underfinanced, local subsidiary station, the clerk decided, judging by their ragged equipment boxes and the unbelievably wretched demeanor of their runny-nosed assistant) stormed into the lobby and demanded three rooms with a park-side view, the clerk was in no mood at all to be helpful.

Explaining haughtily that most people reserved their rooms well in advance during the tourist season, the clerk offered the clearly impatient and certainly overbearing man—whom he had no reason to recognize as one of San Diego's up-and-coming deputy district attorneys—three rooms on the fifth floor with the worst possible view of the park he could find, adding snippishly that the only other rooms available were on the opposite side of the hotel with a much better view of the far-distant ocean.

Check-in of the fourth group was then further delayed when it was discovered that one of the MasterCards offered for payment had expired three weeks earlier, enabling the clerk to stand at the counter with a self-satisfied smirk on his face as the men tried to argue about who was going to get paid on whose voucher without making it too obvious that the whole thing was starting out like a typical government operation.

By the time the last group came up with enough cash to cover their room charges in full, the clerk saw no reason at all to direct them toward the one functioning set of elevators at the far end of the hotel. Nor did he bother to advise the clearly second-rate journalists that their competition was already in place and probably long since ready for whatever was going to happen.

This last bit of petty vengeance kept the clerk satisfied for a good fifteen minutes, until the most erotic, blond-haired young woman the clerk had ever seen in his life came in through the front door, walked across the lobby to the front desk, and asked for the room number of a Mr. Eugene Bylighter—a name that the stunned clerk immediately recognized as belonging to the last group's unbelievably wretched assistant. The one with the brightly acned face and the gruesomely runny nose.

By 9:30 that evening—after a weary Martin DeLaura finally finished helping the deputy district attorney's disorganized surveillance team set up their mostly outdated equipment, and was heading back down the hall toward Eugene Bylighter's room—the horny youth had long since become acquainted with a few basic facts of life.

Bylighter had learned that in spite of his celebrated efforts to earn five hundred dollars the hard way, and in spite of the fact that—as promised—he'd brought with him his folded bindle of the "Power-Rainbow" that Raggedy Annie had been raving about to Skylight, first things always came first in certain lines of work.

First things in Skylight's case being five hundred dollars, to be placed in her securely locking purse before Bylighter even thought about getting his hands anywhere near her. Although, in truth, Skylight wasn't concerned about having to follow through with her enticing promise to Bylighter. Rainbow had already reassured her on that score. Such dedication wasn't going to be necessary at all.

Tired, irritated, and worried about more things than he cared to think about, DeLaura unlocked the door to Bylighter's room, walked in, shut the door, turned, and was halfway across the room when his eyes suddenly locked on the image of Skylight sprawled across the double bed.

For a long moment, DeLaura stood there with his mouth hanging open and his eyes switching back and forth from Bylighter to—

"Who in the *hell* are you?" DeLaura finally managed to rasp.

"Uh—uh, t-that's—uh, Skylight," Bylighter stuttered as the angelic-faced girl gave DeLaura a slow, professional evaluation with her soft, promising eyes.

"You must be Detective DeLaura," Skylight finally said in a whispery voice, licking her full, soft, smiling lips almost imperceptibly as she slid her silky-hosed legs slowly across the wide bed so that she was leaning back against the headboard.

Detective Martin DeLaura suddenly found himself fighting the irrational desire to toss Bylighter out of the fifth-floor window and then jump on the girl's absolutely mouth-watering bones.

"That's right." DeLaura nodded, finally remembering the demeanor required of his profession. "Uh, you don't mind my asking . . ."

"Uh—Skylight's kinda like my, uh, girlfriend," Bylighter said.

"She's your WHAT?" DeLaura blinked.

"Squèek and I have what you might call a relationship with a great deal of *potential*," Skylight offered in explanation.

"Potential . . . ?" DeLaura stared at the seductively smiling violet eyes before his long experience in Vice/Narcotics finally took hold. "You mean . . . ?"

Skylight nodded brightly.

"I don't fucking believe this," DeLaura whispered, turning to Bylighter. "You brought a—"

"Actually it's not really—or at least, not *officially*—what you think, officer," Skylight interrupted with a playful grin. "After all, he didn't bring the money, like he said he would."

"Oh yes I did!" Bylighter broke in frantically. "I—uh, I mean, I'll have it, 'soon as he gives it to me," Bylighter nodded toward DeLaura, desperately trying to reassure the clearly disbelieving Skylight.

"As soon as *who* gives it to you?" Martin DeLaura demanded incredulously, not at all sure he had heard the words correctly. "You think *I'm* gonna pay—"

"You promised me!" Bylighter squealed. "You said you'd give me five hundred dollars if I—"

"FIVE HUNDRED DOLLARS? You're gonna give this broad five hundred dollars just to . . . ?" DeLaura couldn't go on.

". . . to experience the most enjoyable hour he's ever had in his life?" Skylight suggested helpfully, actually managing to sound modest. "Although I suppose if you *both* want . . ."

"I don't want to hear about it." DeLaura shook his head firmly.

"I don't even want to *think* about it. You," he growled, glaring over at Bylighter, "get your goddamned ass over here!" He held up a small metal box with a long attached antenna, and a roll of stretch bandage.

"W-w-what's that?" Bylighter squeaked as he came forward obediently.

"It's the wire you're gonna wear, 'cause the fuckin' D.A. wants ya to," DeLaura explained as he grabbed Bylighter, pulled up his shirt and began wrapping the transmitter against the small of Bylighter's back with the stretch bandage and tape.

"B-but—you, you never said," Bylighter whimpered.

"Listen to me, you little shit-head," DeLaura growled menacingly as he spun Bylighter around, grabbed him with both hands by the collar, and glared directly into his weepy eyes. "You want these five bills . . ." DeLaura reached into his shirt pocket and held up a wad of folded currency, ". . . then you're gonna stand out there and act like you're a fuckin' microphone while the deal's going down."

"BUT—BUT—!"

"SHADDUP!" DeLaura screamed.

"B-but—" Bylighter whimpered.

"You want the money, shit-head?" DeLaura demanded in a raspy whisper.

"Y-yes." Bylighter nodded several times.

"Then at *exactly* ten-twenty P.M., you're gonna get your butt out there in that park like I told you to. Otherwise, I'm gonna take you back to that house you ransacked and *personally* hand you over to Hangin' Roy. You understand what I'm saying?"

"Bu—but—"

"BUT WHAT!" DeLaura demanded.

"I—I d-don't have a watch!"

"Jesus, Mother of Mary . . ." DeLaura muttered, starting to unstrap his own watch when Skylight spoke up.

"That's all right, officer," she said, holding up her watch-adorned wrist. "I'll make sure he gets out there in plenty of time. After all, I have a stake in this too. And besides," she added coyly, "I wouldn't want you to have to come back for your watch . . . later . . . and interrupt us."

Skylight then laughed in pure, unrestrained delight as Detective Martin DeLaura slammed the door behind his rapidly departing back.

22

AT 10:25 MONDAY evening, a terrified Eugene Bylighter stepped out-side the front door of the Clairmont Hotel and began walking across the street toward the thickly foliaged and dimly lit neighborhood park, on legs that threatened to crumple underneath him at any moment out of pure, honest-to-God fear.

Given his mental condition—derived, for the most part, from his nervous awareness of the betraying transmitter strapped to his skinny back—it was probably just as well that Bylighter didn't know that his exit from the hotel had been duly noted by at least twenty-eight interested observers. And that wasn't even counting the still-curious hotel clerk, who had been sitting by himself on a cold, wet bench in the middle of the darkened park for over an hour, waiting to see if something important *was* going to happen, and Skylight, who would have been watching except that she was much too busy search-ing Bylighter's room for the promised bindle of "Power-Rainbow."

In fact, it was definitely better that he didn't know, because the amount of effort (in terms of expensive equipment as well as man-power) being devoted to the active surveillance of a throwaway kid like Bylighter was mind-boggling in its scope, and truly beyond his comprehension.

In the floor-separated rooms occupied by Jimmy Pilgrim's and Jake Locotta's surveillance teams, pairs of highly paid, professional technicians immediately activated their expensive night-vision-enhanced video cameras, each team independently recording Bylighter's shaky steps with a telephoto lens. As they began recording, both teams confirmed their radio contact with a total of five armed men placed in static positions in and around the park.

In a room two floors down and one window to the right from Jimmy Pilgrim's surveillance team, the two men selected by the slightly less extravagant General to monitor his thiopene sale were following Bylighter's movements with a pair of second-generation night-vision scopes, one of which was attached to a .223 semi-automatic rifle with a twenty-round magazine. They, too, were in radio contact with a ground spotter in the park, who was responsible for calling the shots in the event that anything other than a law enforcement-type raid was directed against their boss.

In all, the surveillance efforts put on by the various players operating under the loose designation of "organized crime" were, in fact, exceptionally well organized and professional in almost every way imaginable—the only possible qualifier being that, as yet, not one of the three multipositioned teams had detected the presence of the other two.

At the less-sophisticated end of the surveillance scale, however, it was a different story entirely. There, DeLaura and the already swearing deputy D.A. had been reduced to watching their terrified snitch with almost useless pairs of binoculars, while the faithful Sergeant Hallstead monitored Bylighter's ragged breathing over a crackling receiver. As they did so, a pair of "volunteer" D.A. investigators, with no technical training whatsoever, worked frantically to try to figure out why two Vietnam War-vintage night-scopes and an eight-year-old black-and-white video camera had all managed to stop working within the span of a half-hour.

It went without saying that the deputy D.A.'s surveillance crew had no idea that there were three other camera and spotter teams working in and around the Clairmont Hotel. And based upon the steady stream of cussing from DeLaura and the increasingly apprehensive deputy prosecutor, if it hadn't been for the miraculously still-functioning transmitter, they wouldn't have been all *that* sure about Bylighter.

The only person who had a reasonably accurate idea as to the number of people involved in the surveillance of the General's planned drug deal was Tom Fogarty, who had stationed himself in a top-floor hotel room perched diagonally across from the Clairmont Hotel—and directly across from the adjacent neighborhood park—at ten o'clock that morning.

Thanks to a constant stream of reports from a deeply concealed perimeter outpost manned by Bart Harrington, and the spotting efforts of Sandy Mudd, Charley Shannon and Ben Koda, Fogarty had accurate descriptions of the eight "bad-guys" who were still somewhere in the hotel, the five who were scattered about on the ground, the D.A.'s team inside, at least three more unknowns on the ground who hadn't made any contacts, and thus could be on anybody's side, and the hotel desk clerk shivering out there in the middle of the park.

"Looks like a friggin' free-fire zone jes' waitin' t' happen," Shannon commented as he continued to monitor the occasionally shifting movements of one of the motorbike-mounted ground troops—designated team unknown—with a night-vision scope.

"I'm not sure I like the idea of you two going out there," Fogarty said quietly.

"You mean 'we three' don't you?" Sandy inquired casually, keeping her opened eye pressed against the viewfinder of her night-vision-enhanced 35mm camera as she tried to get a shot of a blond-haired face she'd spotted earlier in one of the far windows of the hotel, knowing as she did so that Kaaren Mueller would have had it on the first try.

Fogarty started to say that it went double for her, and then thought better of it. "Then it's about time you *three* got going," he said, checking his watch. "Ten-thirty on the dot. We've got a visual confirmation from Bart that Bylighter's out there. Looks like he's waiting for you people out in the middle of the park."

"Then let's go do it," Ben Koda said as he pulled the loaded .45 automatic out of the waistband of his jeans and dropped it on one of the beds. "You two ready?"

"Guess so," Mudd whispered, setting her camera down on the table and taking a deep, quiet breath.

"'Bout time we started earning all this high-class livin'," Shannon grunted.

Charley's shoulder-holstered .45 and Sandy's 9mm Walther

joined Ben's pistol on the mattress. The three unarmed agents were almost at the door when . . .

"Hey, you people . . ." Fogarty started to say something and then hesitated.

"Yeah, boss? Gonna tell us not to stay out too late?" Koda chuckled mischievously in the darkness, feeling himself settling into his relaxed, role-playing mode now that it was all—finally—starting to happen.

"Like her back in by midnight," Fogarty growled. "Just watch yourselves out—hold on," the pensive supervising agent said, bringing a hand up quickly as he stood silently in the quasi-darkness with the small pack-set radio held tight against his ear.

Then he put the radio down.

"That was Bart," he said, his voice echoing strangely in the darkened room as he turned to face his three agents. "He thinks he just spotted Rainbow."

Eugene Bylighter had been standing nervously under a dimly flickering park light for almost five minutes when he finally spotted the familiar silhouettes of Sandy Mudd and her two friends.

"Hey, S-Sandy!" the shaking youth called out, stuttering through his chattering teeth. "I-I'm over h-here!"

"What's the matter, Squeek, you cold?" Sandy asked as she came up to the nervously shuffling Bylighter, forcing herself to concentrate on her role even as Ben and Charley continued to search the surrounding black tree-trunks and shadows carefully, watching for the approach of the vicious killer they all wanted very badly.

"Nah, just—you know, kinda anxious to get this thing goin'," Bylighter shrugged, his eyes shying away from the brief, penetrating glare of Charley Shannon.

"Squeek, these are my friends I told you about," Sandy Mudd said. "Ben and Charley."

"Oh yeah—uh, hi!" Bylighter nodded nervously, keeping his trembling hands deep in his jacket pockets.

"Where's your man?" Ben Koda demanded, ignoring Bylighter's teeth-chattering smile.

"Uh—uh, I guess he's—"

At that moment, two vehicles going past the park in opposite directions, on opposite sides of the park, suddenly pulled over to the curb in unison. As Koda, Shannon, Mudd, Bylighter and about thirty other interested onlookers watched from various concealed positions around the darkened park, the near door of the car parked on the far side of the park from the Clairmont Hotel opened and a man with a very distinctive black-starred hat and potbelly stepped out onto the curb.

"Well I'll be a son of a bitch," Ben Koda whispered as he, Bylighter, Charley Shannon and Sandy Mudd watched the potbellied man work his way forward in their direction.

The words "It's him!" echoed off five sets of hotel-room walls— four in the Clairmont and one on the top floor of the hotel diagonally across the street.

With the exception of the rifle-mounted night-scope that continued to scan the area around Koda, Shannon, Mudd and Bylighter, and the malfunctioning gear being feverishly torn apart by the D.A.'s team, every piece of optical equipment in the Clairmont Hotel immediately focused on the General as he approached the four dark, shadowy figures with his hands—like Bylighter's—deep in his pockets.

"Good evening." The drug dealer nodded calmly as he walked up to the quiet foursome. "I'm afraid we picked a rather unfortunate place to meet, but, as I'm sure you understand, there *are* advantages," he commented, surveying the surrounding darkness and taking note of the briefcase in Charley Shannon's left hand.

"I know Squeek, of course," the grey-haired man went on, nodding pleasantly at Bylighter, "and I assume you must be Sandy," he said, smiling and nodding his starred fatigue hat at Mudd, "but I don't believe—" he said, turning to Koda and Shannon.

"Ben," Ben Koda said, keeping his hands on his hips—loose and ready—as the General made no effort to remove his hands from the trench coat. "That's Charley," Koda gestured with his head over at his partner.

"Ben and Charley." The General nodded as though placing their names in a prelabeled file. "All right."

"What do you say we get outta the light, find us a place to talk," Koda suggested.

"Uh, I think there's already somebody—" Bylighter started to say, but he was interrupted by Shannon, who growled, "He'll move."

With Shannon and Koda in the lead, the five shadowy figures walked over to the semicircle of metal park benches and stood there, staring down at the shivering hotel clerk.

"We'd like to sit here," Koda said simply.

"I'm sorry." The hotel clerk glared haughtily in spite of his mixed feelings of anticipation and apprehension, "but I've been here—" Which was as far as he got before he found himself being picked up by the suddenly constricting collar of his windbreaker and staring directly into the glaring white eyes of an otherwise very black man.

"Get the fuck outta here," Shannon hissed as he released the now absolutely scared shitless clerk, who seemed to disappear into the darkness even before his shoes hit the ground.

Charley Shannon winked at the General, growled "all yours," and then turned and walked the thirty feet or so back to the dimly glowing lamppost. There, he put the briefcase down so that it was clearly illuminated under the flickering lamp light. Then he too disappeared into the shadowy blackness of the surrounding trees.

"I take it you're not too worried about someone stealing your briefcase?" the General commented.

"No reason to be." Koda shrugged. "Charley'd just bring it back."

"Very impressive," the General said. "I'm sure you find a man like that very useful in . . . whatever it is you do."

"He's handy around the house, too." Koda nodded impatiently. "Thing is, if you don't mind, Mr. General, sir, we'd kinda like to get down to business."

"Yes, certainly." The General nodded. "I believe you've expressed some interest in purchasing a sample of our new product line."

"Actually, we were much more interested in your old product line. Two ounces of coke, to be exact," Sandy Mudd said. "I already told Squeek—"

The General broke into a gentle, quiet chuckle and shook his head. "My dear Ms. Mudd, if by 'coke' you're referring to the illegal drug 'cocaine,' I'm afraid you've been sorely misinformed. Mr. Bylighter should have already explained to you that I'm a perfectly legitimate businessman. I simply don't sell products that are contraband," the General finished, smiling at Bylighter in such a way that even he understood to keep his mouth tightly shut.

"But you do sell . . . products, don't you?" Ben Koda smiled understandingly.

"Of course, that's why I'm here." The General shrugged. "As you know, the competition in our business is rather cutthroat . . ." the grey-haired dope dealer went on, watching their hands now because he couldn't quite make out expressions in the flickering light from the two park lamps, the distant hotels and the headlights of the occasionally passing cars.

Ben's hands remained rock-steady in his lap, but the General thought he saw the fingers of Sandy Mudd's right hand twitch, just as the apparent hearing-aid (actually a very efficient receiver) began to transmit the sound of a very concerned voice into his ear.

Three of the concealed spotters, whom the terrified hotel clerk had unknowingly almost trampled in his haste to get the hell out of the park, let him go because they all had more important concerns . . . such as reporting in to Al Rosenthal, Jimmy Pilgrim's chief security guard, and the General's sniper protection team, respectively.

The fourth spotter—another one of Locotta's men—would have let the clerk go by too, had one of his rapidly churning wingtips not slammed into the extended leg of the concealed gunman, causing the blindly running clerk to fly head-first into a very large and solid tree.

Suddenly finding himself on his hands and knees with a painfully flattened nose that was throbbing and dripping blood, the stunned clerk stared dazedly back at what looked like—a body? He sucked in a deep breath in preparation for what would have been a very loud scream . . . and then flopped limply to the ground when the business end of a sap caught him directly behind his left ear.

The reasonably quiet disposal of the hotel clerk would probably have gone unnoticed, thanks to the distracting sounds of the nearby traffic, had it not been for the man spotting for the General's rifleman up in the hotel—who caught the clerk's stumbling fall in one edge of his night-scope's field of vision. He thought he saw something else, and then began searching the area very carefully when the clerk failed to reappear from behind the clump of bright fluorescent-green bushes.

After readjusting his scope, the spotter finally located one of the clerk's heavy-shoed feet, and the second . . . and a third? Whereupon the General quickly received the half-expected warning over the hearing-aid receiver:

"Better watch your ass, boss. You got company out there."

"Uh—I'm sorry," the General said, shaking his head apologetically, "I seem to have, uh, lost my train of thought."

"We were discussing the cutthroat nature of business in general," Ben said calmly. "Probably gonna get around to talkin' about how pissed-off us business people get when somebody tries to stiff us on a deal."

"Oh yes, certainly." The General nodded, smiling again. "Which is why . . ." He hesitated a moment, staring at Koda with a curiously amused and contemplative expression.

"Ben," he finally said, "we don't know each other well enough to be asking personal questions about each other's affairs, do we?"

"Not well enough to expect straight answers," Koda acknowledged.

"Yes, exactly." The General nodded. "So please understand that when I ask you this, I'm not so much being inquisitive as expressing some of my own concerns."

"Fair enough," Koda nodded. "Shoot."

"All right. You have a certain look about you . . . a bearing, if you will . . . that makes me believe you have a rather recent military background."

"Possible." Koda shrugged.

"Furthermore, you and your friends—and I'm including Sandy here, as well as . . . Charley." The General smiled, remembering the impressive fade-away move, "don't really strike me as the type of, uh, business people who would divert an excessive amount of their inventory for their own personal use."

"Also possible." Koda nodded calmly. "Even probable."

"Which, of course, makes me wonder . . ."

". . . just who we might be." Ben Koda smiled. "Some very serious business-type people who like to be careful around strangers . . . or cops."

"Yes, precisely." The General nodded. "As you may know, it's often very difficult to make the distinction."

"A problem that just might run in both directions?" Koda suggested.

"Uh . . . yes, I suppose that's true." The General nodded thoughtfully. "Any suggestions?"

"I happen to know a little bit about police procedures, for reasons that are none of your business," Koda said slowly, "so perhaps there *is* something I can do to satisfy your curiosity. Take that briefcase over there, for example."

"Yes?"

"It's yours."

"I beg your pardon?"

"It's yours," Koda repeated. "It contains fifty-five hundred dollars, advance payment for something we expect to get in return."

"One of my products."

Koda nodded his head. "You want to, you can just walk over there right now, pick up it up, and take it over to your car."

"And . . . Charley?" the General inquired.

"He'll let it go." Koda shrugged. "I believe the police call it 'front-money.'"

"Interesting," the General said, cocking his starred head in surprise, and then smiling.

"If I were a cop," Koda went on, "I don't believe I'd be allowed to do that, because . . ."

". . . there'd be nothing to prevent me from keeping the money and providing you with a much inferior product, such as cane sugar, in return," the General finished. "You'd have no legal . . . recourse, because we haven't really discussed what it is you want."

"I'd have no recourse at all . . . *if* I were a cop," Ben whispered coldly, the tone of his voice causing a chill to run down Sandy's spine, and nearly causing the silent Bylighter to wet his pants because the seemingly easygoing Ben suddenly sounded very much like someone he feared more than . . .

"As it happens, I'm not," Koda continued in a much gentler tone of voice. "And, to tell you the truth, General, I don't see you as the type who'd want to spend the rest of his life wondering how or where Charley, Sandy and I spend our evenings."

"Yes, I see." The General nodded, whispering softly—almost to himself. He continued to stare at Koda and Mudd for a few more moments. Then, suddenly, he stood up, stepped carefully around Sandy Mudd's crossed legs, walked over to the lamppost, and stood there, looking first down at the briefcase and then back at Ben Koda.

Then, with another slight nod of his head, the ex-military man brought the fingers of his right hand up to the edge of his fatigue cap, smiled once more, reached down, picked up the briefcase, and started walking back toward his car.

The General's sudden, unexpected action caused a great deal of consternation in the minds of many people—in particular, the members of the D.A.'s surveillance team.

"Jesus, he's walking away," the deputy D.A. gasped in disbelief.

Before Hallstead or anyone else in the hotel room could say anything, a whispery, uncertain voice broke in over the pack-set radio. "Sam-five to Sam-one," the voice rasped over the static. "Do we take him?"

The deputy D.A. turned wide-eyed to Hallstead, who was monitoring the transmitter worn by Bylighter.

"Sam-five to Sam-one," the static-filled voice demanded again. "Goddamn-it, whadda we do? He's goin' . . . he's drivin' away *right now!*"

"No," Hallstead shook his head at the agonized prosecutor, "there wasn't an offer or an exchange. We don't have anything yet."

"Shit," the deputy D.A. snarled, bringing the pack-set radio up to his grimacing mouth. "Sam-one to all Sam units. Negative on the take-down. Repeat, *no take-down.* Let him go!"

"Jesus Christ," Wilbur Hallstead moaned, "now what're we—"

"Hold it," the deputy prosecutor said, still staring out the corner of the window with the binoculars. "Take a look out there . . ."

"Oh shit, no . . ." Eugene Bylighter started to whine in the darkness, watching as the General got into his car, started the engine, and pulled away from the curb, ". . . what's he doin'?"

"Shut up," Ben Koda snarled, coming up to his feet and flexing his hands as he listened intently for any noise, any stray sound that might warn of the stealthy approach of a man like Rainbow.

Koda noted that Sandy Mudd had also come up off the bench, and that her shoulder blades were brushing gently against his tensed back muscles.

The loud metallic sound of a car door opening and closing on the opposite side of the park jarred against Koda's highly sensitized nerve endings.

A shadowy figure with something in its hand stepped away from the second car—the one that had parked across the street between the Clairmont Hotel and the park—and began walking slowly toward the center of the park where Koda had suddenly started forward on an instinctively aggressive intercept course.

The single factor that ultimately saved the cautiously approaching Lennie Orrson in that moment when he and the oncoming Koda crossed paths was the obvious fact—even in the shadow-darkened park—that Lennie Orrson was white.

As it was, the badly startled ounce dealer had only a split second to react—fortunately by freezing in his tracks and dropping his mouth open in shock—to the sudden appearance of the dark-haired figure with the blazing look of pure hatred in his darkened eyes. In that instant, Koda's anger was replaced by a shock of non-recognition that caused him to check the forward lunging motion of his hand just inches from Orrson's wide-open throat.

The two men—one trembling from just-barely contained rage, and the other from fear—stood motionless, face-to-face, for a long moment before Koda stepped back warily.

"I was expecting someone else . . ." Koda rasped half-apologetically, his eyes flickering to the surrounding black-shadowed trees as he remembered Harrington's warning . . .

"Y-you must be the one they call Ben," Orrson said, swallowing in nervous relief as he wondered for a fleeting moment how the General had ever talked him into doing this job. "I was supposed to deliver something to you." He held up the tightly-wrapped, brick-sized package for Koda to see. "I didn't mean . . ."

"Let's go back there." Koda motioned with his head back to the spot where, at that very moment, Sandy was shoving Bylighter back onto one of the metal park benches . . . causing Hallstead and the deputy D.A. to wince as the transmitter gave a sudden electronic squawk, and then miraculously continued to transmit.

"I think there must be some sort of confusion . . ." Orrson began when he, Koda, Mudd and Bylighter were all sitting facing each other in the semicircle of benches.

"The only thing *we're* confused about is what it is we're buying," Sandy said. "We were *expecting* a couple o-z's of coke," she added.

"Actually, you're getting something much better . . ." Orrson tried, and then was immediately interrupted by an angry Ben Koda.

"We went through all that before," Koda growled. "What we want to know is, what the hell is it? Meth? Speedball?"

"No, no," Orrson shook his head, "nothing *that* crude. I'm trying to tell you . . ."

"Well then, *tell us* for Christ's sake!" Hallstead screamed at the radio receiver. He and the deputy D.A. had practically stopped breathing as they hung on to every broken word coming across from the barely functioning transmitter strapped to Bylighter's back, unaware that there were four other observers out there in the blackened park who had carefully moved in close enough to the semicircled group to pick up similar bits of the conversation.

"Look, pal," Sandy was saying, "you can't expect us to pay fifty-five bills for something we've never seen or used before. Nobody does business that way."

"You're welcome to try some." Orrson shrugged, holding the package up in offering.

"In a place like this? Shit!" Koda snorted, shaking his head.

"Look, can't you at least give us an *idea* of what we're buying?" Sandy demanded. "I mean, Jesus, you'd think you guys figured out how to make cannabinol or something," she tried, using the street-slang term for tetrahydrocannabinol, or THC, the active ingredient in marijuana.

"Well, actually, you might say that we did." Orrson smiled.

"You mean this stuff's cannabinol?" Koda demanded, trying to remember what one of the DEA chemists had said at their last in-service training about how difficult it was to make THC synthetically.

"In essence." Orrson nodded.

"But I thought—" Koda started to say.

"—that it was impossible to cook up in a lab?" Orrson asked. "No such thing as impossible. What you got here, my friends," Orrson said expansively, having regained his confidence, "is the genuine stuff, 'cause we got ourselves one *hell* of an alchemist . . ."

"THAT'S IT, WE GOT HIM!" the deputy D.A. screamed, reaching for the pack-set radio.

"But . . . are you sure . . . ?" Wilbur Hallstead said, looking hesitant.

"THC . . . tetrahydrocannabinol." The deputy prosecutor laughed. "Goddamned restricted dangerous drug if I ever heard one."

"Yeah, I know, but he didn't say it was cannabinol." Hallstead said, his forehead furrowed in confusion.

"THC, cannabinol." The deputy prosecutor shrugged, "same goddamned thing." His face flushed with the scent of victory, he brought the small pack-set radio up to his mouth. "Sam-one to all Sam units," he yelled. "Tango-Delta. Repeat, Tango-Delta. Take 'em down!"

As the three surveillance teams dispatched by Locotta, Pilgrim and the General watched with wry amusement, the park across the street from the Clairmont Hotel was suddenly surrounded by a fleet of eight light-bar-flashing patrol units.

Then, as the video cameras continued to hum, a total of fifteen uniformed and plainclothed San Diego sheriff deputies bailed out of the units and moved in with SWAT-type vests, shotguns, and drawn sidearms to help make the arrest for the deputy district attorney— who, along with Hallstead and the two otherwise-useless investigators, had immediately ran for the stairwell in an effort to get in on the action, leaving the little electronic box strapped to Bylighter's back transmitting to an empty room.

As the first three of the converging deputies—which included a very-much-out-of-breath Detective DeLaura—arrived at the middle of the park, they found Ben, Sandy and Lennie Orrson standing very still in the dimly flickering lamplight with their empty hands held high over their heads.

"STAND RIGHT THERE AND DON'T MOVE!" DeLaura screamed, more for the benefit of the other oncoming officers than for Koda, Mudd, and Orrson, who had no intention at all of moving even a finger.

Bylighter chose that inopportune moment to burst out of the shadows, screaming "I GIVE UP!" as he ran toward DeLaura . . . and was almost blown away by five startled deputies—including DeLaura himself, who didn't have enough strength left to strangle the little son of a bitch right there in the park like he wanted to.

"WHAT THE FUCK YOU THINK—!" DeLaura started to scream at Bylighter."

"My money!" Bylighter squeaked shrilly, "you promised . . ."

"Jesus fucking Christ . . ." DeLaura muttered, reaching into his shirt pocket with a shaky hand as he observed six of the uniformed deputies taking the loudly-objecting Koda, Mudd and Orrson into custody.

"Here, you little asshole," DeLaura snarled, throwing the ten fifties at Bylighter. "Hope the hell you enjoy it," he added sarcastically as he turned his back to Bylighter and walked over to take some sort of control of the arrest.

Distracted by the necessity of adding realistic support to the cautiously enacted resistance of Ben Koda and Sandy Mudd, DeLaura never saw Bylighter take off into the darkness toward the Clairmont Hotel. So he had no way of knowing that the youth had taken only a couple of dozen breathlessly lunging strides through alternating patches of diffuse light and absolute blackness when he suddenly found himself clamped in a tight, mouth-covering grip . . .

. . . and then began screaming in silent terror as he stared over his shoulder, wide-eyed, into the savage white eyes of Rainbow, as the edge of the straight-edge razor sliced deep into his neck.

23

"WHAT DO YOU *mean* you don't know what it is?" Sergeant Wilbur Hallstead demanded, glaring at the forensic scientist who sat at her cluttered laboratory bench with a long-suffering expression on her face that suggested she'd heard this sort of thing many times before.

"What I mean, Hallstead," the blond-haired sheriff's criminalist explained patiently, "is that your little half-pound bag of powder here is *not* PCP, or LSD, or cocaine, or heroin or any of the other restricted dangerous drugs on the list. Okay?"

"What if we took it somewhere else, Tracy?" the deputy D.A. suggested with just a trace of bitterness in his voice.

"PD lab's a fifteen-minute drive south of here." The blond-haired girl shrugged. "Won't hurt my feelings any. In fact, if they've got their g.c./mass-spec up today, they might be able to tell you exactly what you *do* have. Not going to matter much, though," she added. "Whatever this stuff is, it *isn't* illegal."

The deputy D.A. closed his eyes and sighed in exasperation. "Well . . . shit," he finally said, backing off a little, "I guess we can always go on the SILO charge."

"You're going 'sales-in-lieu-of' on this stuff?" Tracy Nokes asked, her interest picking up slightly in spite of the fact that she'd been dragged out of bed at three o'clock that morning to analyze this sample.

"Not much else we can do, unless you want to change your mind," the deputy D.A. muttered sullenly.

"So what'd they offer it as?" Tracy asked, not quite ready to give up on this sample just yet. The readings on the instruments were just a little too similar to PCP for her comfort.

"Cannabinol," the deputy D.A. said, trying to sound like an experienced narcotics investigator. "Good old THC."

"Ah—I don't think you're gonna want to hear this," Nokes said quietly, shaking her head.

"What do you mean—"

"You're right, cannabinol *is* a slang term for THC," Tracy Nokes explained gently. "However, it also happens to be the name of a compound you get when tetrahydrocannabinol decomposes. A completely separate and *legal* compound," she added.

The deputy D.A. looked as though he was going to have a seizure right there. "You mean we can't—?"

"Afraid not." Nokes shook her head sympathetically. "Get yourself in real deep trouble if the guy's got a halfway decent attorney."

"That goddamned Bylighter!" the deputy D.A. snarled, turning to Hallstead. "You tell DeLaura I want him to find that little asshole immediately!" he demanded, slamming his fist on a nearby tabletop and storming out of the laboratory, a very discouraged Sergeant Hallstead following close behind.

Tracy Nokes waited until the pair had gone, then went to dial the familiar number of the nearby San Diego Police crime laboratory once again. This time she didn't get a busy signal.

"Lab, Sun-Wang speaking," a cheerful voice answered.

"Hi, Sun-Wang speaking."

"Hey Trace, what's up? Don't tell me you're gonna chicken out on tomorrow night . . . leave me stuck with two dates?"

"Naw, you say he'll keep his hands to himself for a while, I'll trust you." Tracy Nokes laughed. "But that's not why I called. Listen, you got a couple minutes?"

"Sure. Just going through a couple hundred photos, trying to work out some shoe sizes on a bunch of footprints we found at a body-dump." Tina shrugged. "One of them's gotta be a big son of a gun—about a size fifteen boot."

"Jeeze, sounds like Big-Foot-the-Beast."

"Yeah, might be." Tina laughed. "So watcha got?"

"No big deal," Tracy Nokes said. "Just a problem I'm having with some crazy-acting dope we got in this morning."

"Crazy-acting . . . ?" Tina Sun-Wang started to ask, her inquisitive analytical mind suddenly alert.

"Yeah . . . some real weird stuff. Can't ID it. Light tan powder. Screens out real close to PCP, but—"

"Trace," Sun-Wang broke in, "did you get a sloped UV peak around two-thirty-two?"

"Yeah, as a matter of fact—"

"Trace, listen to me," the police criminalist said hurriedly. "Don't go *anywhere*. I'm on my way over there right now."

Down in the interrogation room of the San Diego County Jail, Detective DeLaura and Ben Koda were busy "interrogating" each other with cautiously whispered questions when Sergeant Hallstead and the deputy D.A. entered the room.

"I want to have a little talk with you, Koda . . . or whatever the hell your name is," the deputy D.A. growled, still looking decidedly red-faced after his fruitless conversation in the crime lab.

"Okay," Ben Koda said, glaring right back. "So what're we gonna talk about?"

"I'm thinking about offering you a little deal," the deputy D.A. said, trying to make himself sound thoroughly disgusted by the whole idea. "Letter to the judge, the whole nine yards. All you've got to do is go back out on the street and make a couple buys for Sergeant Hallstead here."

"You interested in knowing what you can do with your little deal?" Koda inquired calmly.

"Listen, you—" the deputy D.A. snarled.

"Yeah, what're you gonna do, hotshot? Tell me a story about how that fucking powder turned out to be THC?" Koda snorted derisively, enjoying the advantage of having already been informed of the preliminary test results by DeLaura, who'd made a quick call to the lab earlier that morning.

"Come on!" Koda shook his head in disgust when the deputy prosecutor remained silent. "You guys know the whole thing was a burn. Probably got that dumb-shit kid to set us up so you could make your stats for the month."

The deputy prosecutor continued to glare at Koda as he tried to figure out another angle. *Any* angle.

"Well, what's it gonna be, Mr. Prosecutor?" Koda asked sarcastically, still worried because DeLaura hadn't heard anything from Charley or Tom Fogarty yet. He had been deliberately taunting the deputy D.A. to block out a series of terrifying images that flickered through his mind. Images of his partner lying face-down in the darkness. Images of a viciously grinning face that matched the maniacal voice wired into Kaaren Mueller's apartment phone. "You gonna charge us with something serious, like contributing to the delinquency of a minor?"

There weren't any other angles, and all four men in the room knew it. Finally, the deputy D.A. accepted the obvious. He didn't have any choice.

"All right, fuck it, let 'em go," he growled at Hallstead.

"Very considerate of you folks," Koda said. "Sure hope you got good insurance coverage for false arrest."

"False arrest, my ass!" the deputy D.A. exploded. "Listen to me, you dope-dealing son of a bitch!" he yelled, pointing a finger at Koda, "we've got all the probable cause we need. All I've gotta do is put your little two-bit friend up on the stand and play a little tape—"

"You talking about Bylighter by any chance?" DeLaura asked, finally fed up with the sound of the deputy D.A.'s irritating voice.

"Of course I'm talking about Bylighter!" the red-faced prosecutor snarled. "Which reminds me—"

"You're gonna have a hard time doin' what you said—puttin' him up on the stand to verify that tape," DeLaura said.

"Not if you get off your ass and get out there and find the little son of a bitch, I won't!" the deputy D.A. practically screamed.

"Don't need to." DeLaura shrugged grimly. "Patrol already found him, about an hour ago . . . face-down in the park across from the Clairmont, with his throat cut ear-to-ear."

The last flickering embers of Eugene Bylighter's life died out on the same evening that the intensive care monitor alarms in Jamie MacKenzie's hospital room went off for the last time.

This sad and morbid coincidence meant absolutely nothing to all but a very few people in San Diego County, two of whom happened to be working in the basement of an isolated home at the edge of the Anza-Borrego Desert (a state park located in the northeastern corner of the county)—using an extensive collection of lists, sketches and Polaroid photographs to build a duplicate of Dr. David Isaac's prototype laboratory—when the phone rang.

After he had checked in on his new two-man, underground lab construction crew, a very self-satisfied Rainbow took a few moments to relay the amusing news regarding MacKenzie and Bylighter to a man who Raynee knew had a similarly morbid sense of humor.

Simon Drobeck, of course, took great delight in relaying the news to Bobby Lockwood.

"Just goes to show what can happen to somebody who starts thinking too much. Bound to get snake-bit." Drobeck giggled maliciously, as he patted the heavy wooden cage of his favorite pet and smiled knowingly at Lockwood, a gesture that just happened to hit Bobby Lockwood the wrong way at a very inopportune time.

It was moments later when Bobby finally made up his mind—without a doubt the easiest decision he had ever made in his life.

"Yeah, no shit!" The curly-haired youth smiled back at the sweating chemist. "Hey, Simon, I been meaning to ask you, didn't you say Pilgrim's gonna be looking for a few more chemists to work all these labs we're building?"

"We'll be needing many more." Drobeck nodded. "Fortunately, we won't be the only people constructing labs. Last I heard, Pilgrim was talking about a minimum of a hundred small franchises in California alone."

"Jesus, you mean like in profit-sharing? Kinda like a Burger King or something?"

"Presumably." Drobeck shrugged. "Actually, it makes a lot of sense when you think about it. Increases the work incentives and spreads the risk. Probably use the computer terminals to pull formulas and orders from a central data base. Why, are you thinking of applying?" The elderly chemist smiled sardonically.

"Nah, with what I know about chemistry, it's a wonder I haven't got us both killed by now." Lockwood grinned, ignoring Drobeck's taunting comment. "'Specially with this rock I got for a hand," he added, holding up his dirt-smeared wrist cast.

"Thing is, though," he went on casually, "I got a friend who used to go to UCSD. Dropped out last year to bum around. Anyway, he called me up the other night, wanting to know if I knew of anybody looking for a warm body. The guy used to be a whiz in chem lab. Think he might have a chance?"

"You're willing to vouch for him, I assume?"

"Trust him as much as I trust you." Lockwood shrugged, grinning and then winking at the raised eyebrows of the apparently amused Drobeck. "Anyway, the guy's gonna be over at the University

Student Center this afternoon. Thought I might go over there and hit him up with the idea if you can spare me for a few hours."

"I can get along fine by myself," Drobeck grunted. "Go ahead, but just make sure you don't tell him too much," he warned. "You think he sounds interested, then let me know and I'll talk to Rainbow. Be nice to have some competent help around here for a change," Drobeck added sarcastically, returning his attention to his careful assembly of the reflux apparatus.

"Yeah, okay." Lockwood nodded, smiling to himself. "I think I'll just do that."

The jailer looked up at the huge wall-mounted clock.

"Ten-thirty on a beautiful, sunny Tuesday morning," he said pleasantly as he finished filling out the property release form. "Nice time to be getting out of this place."

"Definitely gonna brighten up *my* day." Ben Koda nodded agreeably, perfectly willing to be congenial.

"Don't suppose you'd know when they're gonna kick my, uh, girlfriend loose?" he asked, signing the release form.

"Let's see, that would be Sandy Mudd, right?"

"Yeah, that's her."

"Well, assuming that she doesn't threaten to take apart any more of our female-type detention officers, I'd say in about ten minutes." The jailer chuckled.

"Uh, she didn't hurt anybody in there, did she?" Koda asked, suddenly concerned that his partner might have earned herself a couple of much more serious charges, and at the same time grinning at the thought of an indignant Sandy Mudd being strip-searched by one of the not easily intimidated female jailers.

"Naw, just got her feathers ruffled up a bit." The cheerful jailer shook his head. "You don't mind my saying so, that gal must be a real handful at home." The jailer winked as he separated the multilayered form and gave Koda his copy.

It was readily apparent to the relieved agent that the morning shift at the county jail had a completely different opinion of prisoner KODA comma BENJAMIN. Koda guessed it had something to do with being released on an "insufficient-cause-to-hold" writ, which probably didn't happen all that often around the county jail. Either that or they hired a completely different type of jailer to work the day shift.

"Sure as hell can't argue with you 'bout *that*." Koda nodded his head in unfeigned amusement. "Guess if I was smart, I'd just let her stay here a while till she calms down."

"No, thanks," the jailer chuckled as he made a few appropriate notations in his jail log. "Way I figure it, the only matron around here who could handle that girlfriend of yours, one-on-one, went off duty at six this morning."

Koda grinned as he slipped his wallet into his back pocket and then sat down to put on his tennis shoes, his fingers brushing across the deep gouge in the right heel that had been made when the surging dark water had driven him feet-forward against the barnacle-encrusted rock . . .

"Anything else I've gotta do here?" he asked, standing up and looking through the wire-mesh screen at the still pleasantly smiling jailer.

"Just walk over to that door. . . ." The jailer shook his head cheerfully, reaching down and pressing a recessed button, causing the huge metal door at Koda's back to give off a loud "CLACK," ". . . and try to have a nice day."

After walking out, Ben Koda spent two minutes making a very careful check of how many people in the immediate area seemed unduly interested in his whereabouts.

Then, satisfied with his count, Koda sat down, leaned against an ancient, scruffy palm tree and closed his eyes, enjoying the penetrating warmth of the sun's rays against his still-painful bruises, as he waited patiently for the nearby exit door for the female section of the SDSO Jail to make the familiar "CLACK!" sound . . .

. . . which it finally did after another ten or so minutes.

Feeling far more relaxed and worry-free than he had in a very long time, Ben remained sitting with his eyes closed and his back against the gently rustling palm tree until he suddenly became aware that the soothing rays of the sun had been blocked out.

He opened his eyes and looked up at Sandy Mudd, whose flashing eyes, tensed jaw, and tightly-clenched fists betrayed an almost overpowering urge to tear into something—or someone.

"You were going to leave me in there until I *calmed down*?!" she demanded incredulously.

"Hi, jailbait," Koda said pleasantly as he levered himself up on his feet. "Hear tell you caused your keepers a little trouble last night."

"That goddamned bulldyke *bitch*!" Sandy Mudd snarled, ready to unleash her pent-up emotions in an outburst of highly uncharacteristic cussing, when she suddenly realized that her head was being

gently held in two very strong hands as Ben Koda bent forward slightly
and gave her a very firm and unexpected kiss . . .

. . . an action that caused Sandy's eyes to blink wide-open in
shock. Then, without really meaning to, she found herself wrapping
her arms tightly around Ben's lean, muscular back as she felt her own
body yielding in what started out as an awkward embrace . . . and
very rapidly became something else entirely . . .

. . . until they finally came apart, still touching each other's
arms, Ben trying not to think about the enticing warmth of her firmly
soft body, and Sandy just standing there in disbelief.

"What . . . ?" she started to ask.

"Yeah, I guess you probably wouldn't have liked being strip-
searched by one of them lady turnkeys," Koda said, a very strange look
appearing in his dark eyes as he shook his head slowly in apparent
amusement.

"You son of a bitch!" Sandy snarled, finally finding a release-
mechanism for all of her frustrations as she drove her clenched fist
deep into Koda's unsuspecting solar plexus, putting every ounce of her
considerable strength into a blow that sent both of them tumbling to
the ground into a wrestling, thrashing, laughing and screaming pile of
muscular arms and legs . . . and ended up with Koda flat on his back,
his forearms braced against Mudd's straining armpits and shoulders as
she hesitated in her determined effort to strangle her still-laughing
fellow-agent.

"You're turning out . . . to be one hell . . . of a role-player,
partner," Koda gasped as he tried to catch his breath, uncomfortably
aware of the rhythmically expanding pressure of Mudd's firm breasts
against his inner forearms.

Sandy's watering eyes flickered for a moment in hurt confusion.
"G-Goddamn you, Ben Koda," she said in a shaky, choked whisper,
"who said I was acting?"

"No theatrical talents, huh? Well, I hate to break it to you like
this . . ." Koda said as he slowly lowered his arms until her still-
heaving upper body was resting gently but firmly against his chest . . .

". . . but I wasn't either."

. . . which resulted in a more lingering kiss this time that neither one of them wanted to stop. Especially Koda, who was finding it
increasingly difficult to ignore the radiating warmth from Sandy
Mudd's muscular legs and hips that were pressed tight against his own.

"Trouble is, though," Koda said as they stopped kissing long
enough to take deep breaths, "there's a whole bunch of people watch-

ing us right now who aren't just out getting their daily jollies," suddenly reminding Sandy that they were lying on the grass in a public park, right next to the county jail.

"Huh-uh, don't look around," Koda whispered, gently restraining the movement of his partner's head with his hands.

"Oh—Jesus," Sandy whispered, still caught up in a swirl of conflicting emotions that very definitely included frustration. "What're we supposed to do now?"

"Well, now that we've pretty much confirmed our boyfriend-girlfriend act to everybody's satisfaction," Ben Koda said, fighting against his emotions to keep his voice calm and relaxed, "there's probably not a whole lot more we *can* do out here without getting ourselves rearrested for indecent something-or-another."

"But . . .?"

"And, seeing how one of those voyeurs out there happens to be Charley," Koda whispered, giving Mudd one more brief but very satisfying kiss before gently rolling her over onto the grass and then helping her up to her feet, "I figure we oughta take ourselves about a two- or three-block walk, and then get ready to hitch a ride before that giggling son of a bitch forgets he's supposed to be out here picking us up."

Back in the secure quiet of his Palm Springs vacation home, Jake Locotta and Joe Tassio sat back watching carefully as Al Rosenthal played back his surveillance video tape on a high-resolution monitor.

The bright, fluorescent green figures on the screen moved through their paces, recreating Eugene Bylighter's nervous entry into the park, his contact with Koda, Mudd and Shannon, the arrival and departure of the General, and the subsequent arrival of Lennie Orrson leading up to the arrest.

"So when were they released?" Locotta asked after Rosenthal shut off the monitor, and then stopped and rewound the tape while Tassio went over to turn on the lights.

"Ten-thirty this morning," Rosenthal said.

"Could be a twist," Joe Tassio suggested in a low growl.

"Or a confirmation." Locotta nodded contemplatively. "And the kid . . . what's his name? Bylighter? The one we saw run out of the picture after receiving the money . . . ?"

"Didn't figure him to be significant." Rosenthal shrugged. "Told the guys to concentrate on the arrest. Cops found him in some bushes about halfway between the benches and the street. Single cut across the throat, real deep."

"Rainbow . . ." Locotta whispered, a slight smile appearing on his otherwise grim face.

"Who the hell else?" Tassio growled.

"Makes sense." Locotta nodded. "They use a throwaway to make a trial run, to confirm the stuff's legal . . ." he shook his head quietly, ". . . and then cut loose their connections. Nice. *Real* nice," he whispered, his eyes narrowed with controlled anger. "I recognized Orrson. So tell me about those other three, Rosey. The girl, the guy and the spade. Who are they?"

"Probably just some people looking to make a buy, happened to be handy." Rosenthal shrugged. "I ran a copy of the tape past some of our inside people to check 'em out. Nobody's seen any of them around before. Don't show up in our fed, state or local files either. Way they got treated when they were booked, I'd say they're probably not heat. Little too realistic," Rosenthal smiled.

"Never did catch the big spade, did they?" Locotta commented.

"Disappeared." Tassio shrugged. "Figure that big boy's still running."

"Yeah, I guess he probably is." Locotta nodded, distracted by the knowledge that he'd have to deal with the game-players in his southern district—*whoever* they were—*very* quickly. It was a bad time for word to get out that Jake Locotta might be losing control of his newly consolidated organization. A *very* bad time.

"Ah, Jake . . ."

"Which is exactly what *we're* gonna be doing if we don't get this thing settled *fast*," Locotta went on, and then looked up at Rosenthal. "What is it now, Rosey?" he rasped softly. "What've we got in dope?"

"Eighty-one percent," Al Rosenthal said quietly. "Damn near everything we've got that's liquid."

"And the rest of them are just waiting out there," Locotta growled. "Waiting like fucking sharks to chew us apart, soon as they think we got a problem."

"Dope's dangerous, Jake," Rosenthal reminded unnecessarily. "You know how a lot of the guys feel about . . ."

"Fuck 'em," Locotta snarled. "They think it's too dangerous, they can sit on the sidelines. I'm not letting that much money slide through my territory without taking a piece. People who get in trouble're the ones who play games when they oughta be taking care a' business."

"You want 'em hit?" Tassio asked calmly.

Locotta remained silent for a few moments, his eyes seemingly unfocused. "Not yet," he finally whispered, his voice cold and distant. "Not till I know exactly what kind of game they're running down here." He looked up at his two trusted lieutenants. "Put the word out. Anybody who associates with Pilgrim or Rainbow or the General. Tell 'em Jake Locotta wants some information . . . and he wants it *now!*"

As Tracy Nokes watched carefully, Tina Sun-Wang injected a microscopic extract of Kaaren Mueller's blood into the gas chromatograph . . . sending it through seventy-five feet of temperature-controlled, whisker-thin glass tubing to the detector at the other end. As expected, the two major contaminants in Meuller's blood—which had traveled at slightly different speeds, and thus gradually separated during the long trip through the micro-thin tubing—produced two distinctive peaks on the chart paper.

"That's it." Sun-Wang nodded, stepping aside so that her San Diego sheriff's counterpart could get at the multigauged instrument with *her* sample.

As Tina, and one of the PD homicide detectives she'd talked into coming along with her, watched closely over Tracy Nokes's shoulder, the SO criminalist injected a diluted solution of Hallstead's powder into the instrument.

This time, the pen on the slowly moving chart paper only produced one peak, but, as Tina Sun-Wang had predicted, its relative location on the chart confirmed that the main component in Hallstead's powder traveled thru the thin glass tubing at precisely the same speed as one of the contaminants in the PD homicide-victim's blood.

In other words, they were very possibly the same compound.

A pair of matching peaks on a GC chart weren't conclusive enough, but forty-five minutes later, two matching thin-layer spot patterns narrowed the odds considerably. The glazed-eyed homicide detective went out to get a cup of coffee as the freshly inspired criminalists continued working.

Another hour later, feeling absolutely certain now but still forcing themselves be conservative, the two forensic scientists laid two highly discriminatory infrared charts over each other . . . and immediately observed an almost perfect match of thirty-seven major peaks on the two-foot-wide strips of chart paper.

Bingo.

Meaning that at 12:30 that afternoon, Tina Sun-Wang and Tracy Nokes *still* didn't know the chemical name of the drug in Sergeant Wilbur Hallstead's half-ounce bag of powder, but whatever it *was*, it was unquestionably one of the two drugs that had somehow found their way into the raped, slashed and abandoned body of a still-unidentified young woman found at the base of the Torrey Pines cliffs eight days ago.

They explained as much to a suddenly very interested police homicide detective, who immediately ran to a nearby phone to call one of his SO homicide buddies.

"Bill, this is Frank. Yeah, I'm still out at your lab. Listen, you better get over here. Yeah, they made a match. Yeah, I know . . . a real mind-blower. Hey, listen, maybe you better get hold of your narc sergeant . . . what's his name? Yeah, Hallstead. Good ol' Wilbur. Yeah, why don't you try to get him down here too, if you can. I figure at least one a' you guys oughta be *real* interested in this shit."

Detective Martin DeLaura was halfway out of his desk chair—figuring he might just as well drive over to the isolated crime lab with Hallstead as stay in his office and worry about the crock of shit he and his buddy Ben Koda were into up to their necks—when the phone at his desk rang.

"Yeah, DeLaura," the frustrated detective sighed.

"Got a live one for ya, DeLaura," the watch commander said cheerfully. "Wants to give up all his evil ways and turn every dealer in South San Diego."

"Why don't you tell him to go fuck himself instead," Martin DeLaura suggested, reaching into his desk drawer and fumbling around for the aspirin bottle.

"Thought I'd let you tell him." The helpful lieutenant chuckled. "Give you people a chance to do some honest public relations work. Earn all that overtime pay for a change. He's hangin'-by on four-six." Click.

DeLaura glared at the silently humming phone for a moment, then downed three buffered aspirin with the cold, bitter dregs in his coffee cup, and punched the glowing button on his phone marked "46."

"DeLaura," the unenthusiastic detective grunted.

"Uh—are you a narc?" the muffled voice asked.

"Nah, I'm the fuckin' janitor," DeLaura growled. "You always stuff a roll of toilet paper in your mouth before you talk on the phone?"

"Oh—" the muffled voice said, and then, much clearer: "Uh, that better?"

"Yeah, much," DeLaura nodded. "Okay, so I'm a narc. What'd you want t' talk about?"

"Uh—" The voice on the other end took in a deep breath and then let it out in a long sigh. "I . . . uh, guess I wanna turn a lab."

"You *guess* you want to turn a lab," DeLaura repeated slowly. "I don't suppose you've got a name?"

"Uh—Bobby."

"Got a last name too, Bobby?" DeLaura inquired with forced patience.

"Uh—yeah."

"Okay, Bobby," DeLaura went on, his patience dwindling rapidly, "maybe you could tell me what kind of lab we're talking about."

"Uh—it's a dope lab."

"A dope lab. That's good, Bobby." DeLaura nodded, his eyes still closed. "Tell you the truth, I was kinda hoping it was gonna be a dope lab. Now maybe—"

"Uh, listen—" Bobby Lockwood said nervously, "I—uh, really don't want to talk about this over the phone, okay?"

"Yeah—sure," DeLaura said, becoming mildly interested as he detected the genuine nervousness in "Bobby's" voice. "You wanna meet somewhere, talk about this lab?"

"Yeah, I really do. Listen, I, uh, I know you probably think this is some kind of game, but I'm really serious. You ever hear of a guy named Jamie MacKenzie?"

"I've heard the name once or twice," DeLaura said. "So what?"

"You know how he died?"

"Yeah, the stupid son of a bitch jumped out a window after he got bit by one of his pet snakes," DeLaura said. "So . . . ?"

"So Jamie never owned a snake in his life," Lockwood said. "I know for a fact he was scared to death of the things."

"Yeah, well, so am I. Big fucking deal."

"Okay," Lockwood said, "what if I told you that the guys who put that snake in Jamie's room were the same people who're dealing this new analog-dope out on the street?"

"You're shittin' me," DeLaura growled, sitting up sharply in his chair, suddenly very interested now.

"No, no way," Lockwood said.

"Jesus . . ." the narcotics detective whispered.

"Yeah . . . well, now you know how serious I am. Listen, can you meet me—uh, at the Scripps Aquarium on University?"

"What time?"

"In about an hour. I'll be in a blue Datsun."

"License number?" DeLaura asked, scribbling in his tattered notebook.

"Uh—one-cee-gee-bee, uh, two-seven-nine."

"I'll be there, kid," DeLaura growled, hanging up the phone and then reaching in his desk drawer for his shoulder-holstered .357.

24

As DELAURA RAN down the stairs to the parking lot, Sergeant Hall-stead and two very excited sheriff and police homicide investigators were busy in the sheriff's crime lab coming up with the fascinating possibility that a curious dope-burn by a well-known San Diego pound-dealer just might be linked to the shredded remains of a John Doe who had been dismembered by an estimated eight sticks of dynamite—in an apartment rented by a beautiful redheaded woman named Kaaren Mueller, and on the same night that a beautiful Jane Doe redhead had been left to die at the base of the Torrey Pines cliffs.

The only problem was that it didn't make any sense, because no one could come up with a logical reason for three people—counting the ill-fated Bylighter—to be murdered over some as-yet-unidentified powder that was perfectly legal to possess.

As a result, Tracy Nokes and Tina Sun-Wang were suddenly very busy trying to figure out the chemical structure of the unknown compound, using a multi-peaked infrared spectrophotometer chart that didn't match up with any of the known charts in their computer data base . . . which meant they'd have to derive the structure piece by piece, using complex mathematical analysis. Their scribbled calculations had already begun to fill the surrounding desk tops.

By the time the tired, muddy CSI team that had spent the last four hours in the park across from the Clairmont Hotel—working Bylighter's death scene—finally staggered back into the forensic lab, their arms loaded down with search equipment, evidence bags and plaster casts, they found every table and countertop covered with notes, chart paper, case reports, scene photographs and half-empty coffee cups.

"Jesus Christ, Tracy," one of the crime scene technicians groaned, standing in the middle of the examination room with a sagging cardboard box labeled "CAST" in both hands and a brown paper evidence bag under each trembling arm, "can't you clear us any space around here?"

"Oh yeah, I'm sorry, sure." The weary-eyed criminalist nodded as she and Tina quickly got up to help the incoming lab crew. "Here, let me grab that box—" she said, and then almost sank to her knees from the sudden, unexpected weight.

"My God, how much plaster did you use for this thing?" Tracy Nokes demanded, quickly setting the sagging box gently down on the nearest table.

"Whole can." The white-and-brown-faced scene investigator grinned tiredly. "Biggest footprint I've ever worked. Gotta be at least a size-fifteen boot," he added, shaking his head . . .

"What did you say?"

. . . and suddenly found himself being yanked around by the arm and staring into the widened eyes and open mouth of criminalist Tina Sun-Wang.

Bobby Lockwood had been sitting in the front seat of his small blue Datsun for almost twenty minutes, feeling very nervous and exposed in the public parking lot of the Scripps Aquarium building— which was located halfway down a long winding sea cliff road that led to the exclusive Southern California beach city of La Jolla, just north of San Diego—when he saw a man in a blue windbreaker walk out of the building and then up to the driver's side of his car.

"You Bobby?" the man growled.

"Uh, yeah. You . . .?"

"Detective Martin DeLaura. Why don't you park around back? Meet me over at the picnic bench behind those trees."

"Okay, but . . ." Lockwood started to say, glancing around nervously.

"Don't worry about it, kid," DeLaura growled reassuringly. "I watched you come in. Nobody tailed you. See you over there," he finished, and then walked away toward the side of the building.

Four minutes later, a still-nervous Bobby Lockwood was showing a handful of Polaroid photographs to the now extremely interested narcotics detective.

"This the lab where they're making those analog drugs?" DeLaura asked, wanting confirmation before he went any further.

"Yeah, one of 'em."

"There's more than one?"

Lockwood nodded. "At least two that I know of. Supposed to be a whole lot more being built, maybe a hundred eventually."

"Jesus." DeLaura shook his head. "So where's this one located at?" he asked as he shuffled through the photographs.

"Uhh, it's near the Anza-Borrego desert . . ." Lockwood said, figuring it wouldn't make any difference that the photos were of the mountain lab. The setups were virtually identical, and having been blindfolded going in, he didn't know where the mountain lab was located anyway. ". . . but I'd rather not say exactly where just yet . . ."

"Jesus Christ, Bobby!" DeLaura started in, and then immediately calmed down. "Okay, I understand what you're saying. No problem, we'll do it your way. But listen, I need to know something . . . and it's very important. This stuff they're making—do you know if any of it's illegal?"

"Uh, I guess I'm not really sure." Lockwood shrugged. "Tell you the truth, I don't know what *any* of the stuff is we're making. All I do is help the chemist. See, the thing is," Lockwood went on hurriedly, afraid that DeLaura might lose interest, "I thought maybe I could take somebody in who knows . . ."

"You can take somebody into this place?" DeLaura asked, startled. He hadn't been expecting that kind of opportunity.

"Yeah, sure—I mean, I think so." Lockwood explained to DeLaura how Pilgrim and Raynee and Drobeck were supposed to be looking for more chemists, and the offer he'd made . . .

"Jimmy Pilgrim and Rainbow," DeLaura said, shaking his head as he stared at Lockwood. "You're running with some heavy-duty people, kid."

"Yeah, tell me about it." Lockwood nodded, licking his lips nervously.

"So what do *you* plan to get out of all this," DeLaura asked pointedly.

Bobby tried to explain, starting in with how he'd helped to set up Jamie MacKenzie and ending with a description of Simon Drobeck and the snakes, the hit against his delivery team, and his final realization that his role in the drug business had gotten far more serious than he'd ever intended.

"It's not much of a game any more," Lockwood whispered, staring out over the Pacific Ocean. "Way things are going, I know if I'm ever gonna get out, I gotta do it now. Thing is, though, I figure I kinda owe something to Jamie." He took a deep breath. "So that's what I'm doing here talkin' with you . . . ," he said, bringing his head up and looking DeLaura straight in the eye, ". . . trying to see if I can do something to make it all balance out."

"You thought about the protection you're gonna need after this all goes down?" DeLaura asked.

"I—d-don't think I'll need it." Lockwood shook his head. "Soon as I get one of you guys in, I'm taking the first plane heading to Alaska. Once I get up around Anchorage, where I know some people, I'll be all right. Lotta places up there where a guy can get lost for a few years."

"Up to you, kid," DeLaura shrugged as he stood up. "Now all I gotta do is find myself a volunteer."

"You two been having fun out there?"

Bart Harrington asked the question casually after Koda and Mudd had entered the Mission Bay Hotel room, sitting down on the bed across from Harrington, Fogarty and Charley Shannon. Sandy Mudd had unconsciously placed herself so that her knee brushed against Ben Koda's leg, an action that didn't go unnoticed in the roomful of men like Harrington who were trained to be observant of small details.

Fortunately for the two late-arriving agents, only Charley possessed the truly incriminating knowledge, having earlier advised the startled pair that they had exactly two hours to take a nap or lie out on the beach or whatever. That way he could sneak down to the beach and check out the volleyball action for a while before going up to the room and telling Fogarty they were back.

"People just gettin' outta jail always need little time t' themselves, t' kinda sort things out." Charley had shrugged. "Jes' make sure you're both back here by one-thirty," he added.

True to his word, Shannon had met the relaxed and smiling agents back at the rented car at precisely one-thirty that Tuesday afternoon.

"Had a wonderful time," Ben Koda snorted as he shook his head, having to work at maintaining a casual poker face and hoping that Mudd was capable of doing the same—which, to her own amazement, she was. "'Course the room service didn't exactly rate up there with this place," he added, glancing around at the opulent splendor of the newly rented command center.

"Told you he's gettin' soft," Charley drawled from his sprawled position in one of the huge stuffed chairs. "Man lets himself get thrown in jail by a' couple dozen a' them sheriff deputies, then he starts complainin' 'bout the food. Next thing you know, he's gonna be wantin' overtime pay," Shannon shook his head sadly.

"So what's lard-ass been doin' with himself besides worryin' the shit outta me?" Koda asked Fogarty.

"We've all been busy around here," Fogarty commented drily. "Even Charley. I'll let Bart fill you in."

"While you and Sandy were making a ruckus out there in the park," Harrington began as he poked at his pipe bowl, "Charley and I managed to track our friend the General back to what we *think* is his residence, which happens to be a house two doors down the street from where he pretends to live."

"You wanna run that by me once more?" Ben asked.

"I didn't follow either." Sandy shook her head.

"As best we can tell, the General drives his car into the garage of one house, goes inside, and then—some way or another—ends up in a house down the street about two minutes later without ever going outside," Harrington explained. "Discovered his game when Charley finally showed up and activated that little transmitter Sandy put in the money briefcase. Kinda hard to pinpoint a man in a house when he's not there any more."

"A tunnel between the first and the third house?" Ben Koda asked.

"At least that," Harrington nodded. "Ran a quick title search this morning and found out that all three of the ocean-side houses, *and* the three across the street, are owned by the same 'investment' company. More'n likely the man's got a bunch of tunnels under there."

"Nice." Koda nodded. "So now we've gotta figure the General can probably rabbit out of any one of at least six holes."

"Exactly." Fogarty nodded. "And which also suggests that Pilgrim and Raynee may have a similar arrangement."

"Too bad you couldn't have tagged that fuckin' Rainbow instead," Koda muttered.

"Couldn't get close enough to him," Shannon growled, "but Ah found somethin' else kinda interestin'. Remember them two cars out there on the bluffs?"

"Yeah." Koda nodded, his eyes hopeful.

"Motherfucker took off in one a' them cars, couple blocks from the park. Same plate."

"All *right*," Koda whispered, his eyes gleaming in barely repressed anticipation.

"Think Ah saw him cut down Bylighter too," Charley Shannon went on. "Too gawddamned bad . . ." he added savagely.

"He was almost certainly armed, and you weren't," Fogarty said, obviously having argued this point earlier. "And even if you could have gotten close enough, and put him down, you'd have screwed up the operation. Kid just ran outta luck—way it goes."

"Little son of a bitch never *had* much luck to begin with," Ben Koda muttered. "So what's on tap?"

"In a couple of hours or so, Bart's going to be taking the boat down the coast, making it look like he's running scared after hearing about you two being arrested. Figure that'll nail down your credentials as amateur dealers."

"And put us down another agent, which means you're probably savin' the best part for last," Koda commented.

"That's about it." Fogarty shrugged. "Based on everything we know about Jimmy Pilgrim's operation right now, which isn't much," the DEA supervisor added glumly, "I have to agree with Bart. There's only one way to work this operation."

"Which is . . .?" Sandy Mudd asked suspiciously.

"Follow up on what little we've got, and increase the pressure," Fogarty said, reaching into his suitcase and handing his three agents their weapons.

"Increase the pressure, huh?" Sandy whispered, looking down at the small but still-lethal Walther automatic that she'd never fired in fear or anger.

"So when do we go in?" Koda asked, slipping the .45 inside the back waistband of his jeans.

Tom Fogarty stared at Koda for a few moments, and then told himself that it was a hell of a time to start worrying about the dreamy, distant expression that seemed to flicker across Sandy Mudd's eyes every couple of minutes.

"Far as I'm concerned," he said, "right now's as good a time as any."

Jake Locotta listened silently as Rosenthal finished reading through his notes, summarizing the wealth of hard and soft intelligence that had started pouring into his phone bank almost immediately after it became widely known to the San Diego underworld that Jake Locotta wanted information.

"So where does all this put us, Rosey?" Locotta glowered, sinking back into his chair and reaching for one of his cigars.

"I think it's time we stepped in," Rosenthal said. "Lotta talk on the street about this new 'Rainbow-Vision' dope the General's supposed to be coming out with this week."

"Rainbow-Vision?" Locotta snorted. "No shit?"

"That's what they're calling it," Joe Tassio said, nodding his head in shared amusement.

"That goddamned Raynee." Locotta shook his head slowly. "Any man'd dress like that, I guess . . ."

"Jake, this sorta thing can get outta control real easy," Al warned. "Word is, this Rainbow-Vision's supposed to be some kind a' fuckin' dynamite. According to LaQue, some of the pound-dealers up north are having trouble getting their people to take full loads of coke . . . claimin' everybody wants to try some of this new Rainbow-Vision crap they're hearin' about down south. Lotta people saying they know somebody who's tried it."

"Yeah, fuckin' dumb-shit people, try anything long as somebody folds it inna bindle. So how bad's this shit hurtin' us?" Locotta growled.

"Little early to tell about receipts yet." Rosenthal shrugged. "But the way it's looking, I'd say we're gonna be down about four points by the end of the month."

"*Four-percent!*" Locotta almost spat out his cigar as he came up in his chair, his eyes bulging open. "You telling me—?"

"And that's a *conservative* four, Jake," Rosenthal emphasized. "Could go as high as five. You ask me, I think we'd better do something before we start catching some serious heat," the aged accountant-adviser warned.

"Yeah, I hear ya." Jake Locotta nodded as he settled back into his chair, his eyes glassy with controlled rage. "What you're telling me, we might just as well start at the source."

"Tin star?" Joe Tassio asked.

"Yeah," Locotta growled viciously. "Do it."

It took a traffic-experienced deputy sheriff less than ten minutes to get Tina Sun-Wang clear across town to the San Diego Police crime lab. There, she and Paul Reinhart and the deputy hurriedly gathered up all of her scene notes, photographs and casts of the Torrey Pines Jane Doe case . . . and then raced back to the sheriff's lab.

It took another hour-and-a-half for Sun-Wang, Reinhart, Tracy Nokes, Hallstead, the original CSI team, and five additional uniformed deputies to go back to the park across from the Clairmont Hotel and cautiously search the area where the buy took place until they found exactly what they were looking for: three more of the very distinctive size-fifteen bootprints, and a tennis shoe print with an equally distinctive gash in the right heel.

From then on, it all went much faster. The unified lab team began working the photographs and casts of the shoeprints, while the PD and SO detectives conducted a very thorough interrogation of the jailer who had booked Koda, Orrson and Mudd, the deputy D.A., his two investigators, and Sergeant Hallstead . . . in an attempt to determine exactly *who* had been wearing *what* out in the park across the street from the Clairmont Hotel during the buy-bust yesterday evening.

Thus, when a smiling Martin DeLaura finally drove back into the police parking lot and ran all the way up to the narcotics office, he found an *extremely* agitated Sergeant Hallstead sitting at his desk and yelling at someone on the telephone . . . something about an arrest warrant that was being issued on a bunch of people they'd just let walk—on the charges of raping and murdering a beautiful, redheaded young woman named Kaaren Mueller.

25

BEING A CREATURE of many self-satisfying habits, the General rarely allowed his scheduled work hours to interfere with his enjoyment of pure, sensory pleasures—which, in addition to drinking, golf and sex, also happened to include hazy West Coast sunsets.

On this particular Tuesday evening, the cloud-strewn sky and the low-lying haze had combined to produce an absolutely stunning spectacle of red and orange hues that ranged from the burnt ambers at the horizon to the fireglow brilliance of the semitransparent clouds. In all, it was quite possibly the most beautiful sunset of the year.

Abandoning his computer terminal and its comparatively pale screen glow, the General hurried out onto his deck, intent on enjoying the final moments of the nightly transition as the flame-colored radiance in the sky began to darken in its dying shift toward blackness.

He was still leaning against the waist-high railing, standing next to one of his bodyguards, gazing out across the fiery, reflective sheen of the calm ocean, when the vaguely familiar voice jarred against his senses.

"Kinda pretty, isn't it?"

"What—!" the General gasped, whirling around at the same time that his bodyguard began to reach—much too late—for a holstered pistol.

"Don't do it," Ben Koda warned, motioning the guard's hand back with the loaded-and-cocked .45 automatic. "Put 'em over your head. Right now!"

As the man obediently brought his hands up in the air, Koda moved across the redwood planks and quickly disarmed the careless bodyguard.

"You *do* remember us, don't you, General . . . ?" Koda asked as he tossed the guard's snub-nosed revolver out over the deck railing, hearing it drop into the dense brush below, as Sandy Mudd quickly frisked the General, keeping her smaller pistol tight against her hip and away from any lunging hands, ". . . the people you didn't want to screw-over, 'cause you'd never know when they might show up on your deck porch?"

"Listen, son, you don't know—" the General tried again as he found himself being directed toward the circle of deck chairs, along with his chagrined and nervous bodyguard.

"Tell you what I *do* know, General," Koda said as he and Mudd sat with their backs to the muffled roar of the ocean and their weapons resting on their laps, facing the back of the General's expansive wood and glass home and the two frightened men. "I know you walked away with fifty-five hundred dollars of our money, and I know we didn't end up with anything in return—if you don't count a fuckin' arrest record."

"I'm—sorry about the incident with the police," the General said shakily, starting to breathe easier now that he realized the pair wanted to talk. "Please understand, there is no way I could anticipate everything that happened out there last night. I—"

"You trying to tell us that *you* got set up?"

"That's *precisely* what I'm telling you," the General nodded. "It seems that the boy, Bylighter, had been turned by the police. We suspected that might be a possibility," he shrugged, "so . . ."

"So you worked it out where *you'd* get the money and *we'd* get busted. That what you're telling us?" Sandy Mudd demanded, finding it very easy to lapse into her role again.

"I'm trying to tell you that the money you lost is irrelevant," the General insisted in a cautiously firm voice. "You were being tested, and the test got out of control. I can easily replace the money right now, if you wish, but I'm afraid the other problems you, uh—" he looked around, and then—remembering Charley Shannon's curious

behavior in the park the previous night—nodded in sudden understanding, "—three are facing right now are far more serious."

"If you're trying to scare us, General, you're wasting your
time," Koda interrupted, nodding meaningfully at the bodyguard who
was sitting with both of his hands resting in open view on the arms of
the deck chair.

"I was referring to your *legal* problems," the General said, annoyed at the apparent failure of his entire security team. The other
guard should have already—

"Legal problems, my ass," Ben Koda growled. "The cops cut us
loose because the dope was bogus. What the hell'd you *think* they
were gonna charge us with?"

"I'm aware that the possession and sale charges were dropped."
The General nodded. "I was referring to the arrest warrant that I believe has just been issued for all three of you . . . on two counts of
murder—three, if you count the boy, Bylighter."

"WHAT!" Koda and Mudd reacted in unison.

"The warrant mentions a young woman named Kaaren Mueller,
and a John Doe" the General was starting to explain when they all
heard a rustle of feet at the far side of the house . . . and then a surprised, muffled yell that was suddenly cut off by the horrible crack-
sound of neck vertebrae being snapped as Charley Shannon's loud
voice shattered the night air . . .

"INCOMING!"

Ben had already started to dive out of the deck chair when he
realized that Sandy was still sitting upright, staring in shocked disbelief at the General—who, along with his bodyguard, had turned his
head in the direction of a pair of rapidly running feet, expecting to see
the missing guard . . .

Ignoring his screaming survival instincts, Ben twisted back and
dove for his unresponding partner, grabbing at her shoulders just as he
caught a glimpse of a shadow figure silhouetted against the bright
background of the study window. A shadow figure that suddenly hesitated upon seeing four figures on the deck instead of the expected two.

Unable to do anything else because his .45 was pressed flat
against Sandy's tensed back, Koda twisted his entire body violently,
sending both himself and Mudd crashing to the solid redwood deck
just as everything began exploding into shards and splinters above
their heads.

Even as his left shoulder and hip struck hard against the wood
deck, Ben was shoving Mudd into the corner of the deck and twisting
himself over sideways . . . sweeping his right hand over in a tight arc

and instinctively triggering a deafening .45 round, one-handed, at the oncoming figure who seemed to be holding some sort of black cylinder at waist level.

Then, before Koda could recover from the eardrum-piercing noise, muzzle-flash, and recoil of the .45—and sight-in on the backward-spinning shadow figure once again, this time with a two-handed grip—the limp, blood-spurting body of the General's security guard fell across the shattered table and dropped heavily across Koda's extended arms and still-smoking pistol.

As Koda snarled and fought his way up to his feet, and then charged forward across the wooden deck with the still-twitching, foul-smelling body of the guard held up tight against his chest as a shield, Sandy Mudd was still flat on her stomach, frantically searching through the bloody, sharp pieces of glass and stoneware and wood splinters and other unidentifiable debris in the semidarkness for the small 9mm Walther that had been knocked out of her grasp by the fall.

Finally spotting the grip of the small handgun sticking out from under a darkly stained fatigue cap bearing a single shiny star, Mudd grabbed for the weapon, her ears still ringing from the sharp muzzle blast of Koda's .45 . . . and then at the same instant, saw—instead of heard—movement out of the corner of her eye. As she turned her head to look, a wrist-thick cylindrical object—the long silencer barrel of a rapid-firing Ingram submachine gun—swept in under the lower cross-boards, an inch above deck level.

Realizing in that horrible moment that she would never reach the Walther in time, Sandy desperately shoved her body up and away from the deck, and then lunged for the threatening gun barrel just as it came around in her direction.

Barely able to catch the top end of the heavy cylinder with the palm of her fully extended hand, the panicked Mudd managed to shove the rough-finished barrel under her chest just as the black-hooded figure triggered a short burst, sending a dozen 9mm slugs streaking across the splattered deck in a muffled roar of gunfire as a dozen hot, expended casings spewed out of the weapon, ricocheting around Mudd's wincing face in the space of a heartbeat.

Numbed with fear, and fighting on survival instincts alone, Sandy frantically dropped her body across the terrifying automatic weapon, trying to keep her grip on the barrel-silencer . . . and then cried out in a moment of sickening horror as the cursing black-hooded figure yanked the weapon out of her hands.

Hopelessly exposed and vulnerable out on the open deck, she tensed against the expected agony of violent death, and so had no idea what was happening when the hooded head was suddenly slammed forward into the solid four-by-four railing post by a huge black hand.

The impact sounds of nose cartilage and teeth shattering against solid wood were masked by Charley Shannon's gutteral snarl of rage as he swiftly drew back his hand and then twisted his powerful upper body at the hips, driving his tight-fisted hand into the lower spine of the stunned killer. The impact severed the man's spinal cord in two places—five knuckles apart—with the shearing edges of violently dislocated vertebrae. The hooded figure dropped like a rag doll to the sloping ground in front of the raised deck.

"Easy, girl," Shannon whispered urgently as he pulled himself up over the railing, a cocked .45 automatic extended in his left hand.

"Ben . . . where is he?" Sandy Mudd tried to whisper, trembling with shock as she tried again to reach for the Walther . . . and found that she could barely keep herself up on her hands and knees.

"Jes' stay down . . . he's okay. Saw him go in the house. Pretty sure there was only four a' them. Ah got two, an' Ah think Ben . . ." Shannon said, tensing as he saw Koda's crouched figure running quickly toward them across the deck.

"You two okay?" Ben rasped, his blood-smeared face and arms glistening strangely as he knelt down by the still-trembling Mudd.

"We're fine," Charley growled. "Jes' gonna have t' change our shorts is all. Anybody else still around?"

"One of those fucking Ingrams finished the guy I shot." Koda shook his head. "Blood an' brains all over the place. Saw another one run across the street . . . hopped in a car and took off. Nobody else in the house. So what the hell's going on around here?" he demanded, as he looked around at the shadow-streaked carnage.

"Don't know." Shannon shook his head, searching the surrounding darkness too for any sign of movement. "Saw 'em comin' in through the side gate, right when they took out the General's other bodyguard. Bastards split up 'fore I could warn you up here."

"Jesus, they must have a goddamned war going over this analog shit," Koda whispered.

"That or the General's got himself a bunch of mean-ass enemies," Shannon grunted. The men stared at each other in sudden realization, and then turned to see Sandy Mudd crawl unsteadily across the broken shards of glass to the twisted form of the pound-dealer.

"Not any more, he doesn't," Sandy Mudd called out quietly, brushing her cut and bleeding fingers across a pair of unmoving eyelids—about the only part of the General's bloody, shattered head and upper chest that hadn't been struck by the first burst of high-velocity jacketed bullets.

"Ah, shit . . ." Ben Koda closed his eyes in weary frustration, realizing that all of their efforts to penetrate Jimmy Pilgrim's operation had been effectively canceled out by the violent deaths of Bylighter and the General. Then he remembered what he had seen in the house. . . .

"Listen," Koda said as Sandy crawled back to where he and Shannon were still kneeling on the deck, "either of you hear anything else out here—like upset neighbors, police sirens, anything like that?"

"Never hear them silenced Ingrams outside a' fifty feet," Shannon shrugged. "All them surf noises down there, ain't likely anybody'd pick up on that one gunshot neither. Probably jes' figure it was a car backfirin'."

"Hope the hell you're right," Koda said as he walked over and pulled the General's limp body up by the armpits.

"What the hell you plannin' on doin'?" Shannon growled.

"Gonna get these bodies out of sight, inside the house," Koda grunted as he started dragging the General toward the sliding glass door. "Something in there Sandy's gotta see."

At 7:15 that Tuesday evening, Jake Locotta was sitting out on his Palm Springs deck when Al Rosenthal slid open the glass door and came out on the deck.

"Tell me something nice, Rosey," Locotta growled, even though he knew from the expression on his adviser's face that it wouldn't be that way.

"Just got word from Joe," Rosenthal whispered in his gruff, raspy voice as he sat down next to Locotta. "General's dead."

Locotta slowly and quietly nodded his head, his eyes deathly cold. "All right, now we can—"

"—but we lost three of the guys we sent in," Rosenthal finished.

Locotta's eyes widened and flickered over at his aged accountant. "Shit," he muttered. "Joe recover 'em?"

"No," Rosenthal rasped, shaking his head. "Couldn't get to 'em. Remember those three who tried to make the buy off the General in the park?"

"Yeah, the ones the cops picked up, right?"

"And kicked loose this morning," Rosenthal nodded. "Apparently they were there at the General's place. Joe doesn't know what the hell they were *doing* there, but they took out three of the four he sent in—first thirty seconds—like a couple a' pros. According to Tassio, he'd have had a fuckin' war out there if he'd tried to go back in."

"Okay, doesn't matter," Locotta nodded. "Long as we put a stop to that goddamned Pilgrim."

"That's just it, Jake," Rosenthal sighed tiredly. "I'm not sure we did. Word's out that every one of Jimmy's ounce dealers just got in their first load of that new Rainbow-Vision. Fact is, it's supposed to be out on the street this evening."

"Son of a bitch," Locotta whispered, glaring out into the darkness. "Maybe we're overreacting to all this shit, Rosey," he went on more calmly. "Maybe it won't sell. Ever think of that?"

"As of six o'clock this evening, we're looking to be *down* seven points on coke orders for the month. It's gonna sell, Jake," the aged accountant rasped, shaking his head. "Seven fucking percent. Never seen anything—"

"You get Tassio back on the phone!" Locotta snarled. "Tell him I wanna know where this stuff's coming from! The place, the people, the works. I wanna know all that; then I want 'em put outta business. Tell him, anything he needs . . . whatever it takes . . . he's got it. You tell him that, Rosey, and you tell him one more thing . . ."

"Yeah, what's that?"

"Pilgrim and Rainbow. I want *them* too!"

Thirty-five miles south of Palm Springs at the edge of a wilderness area famed for its beautiful and treacherous desert landscape, two unlikely chemists struggled in their sweat-soaked clothes to complete Pilgrim's latest order for twenty-five more pounds of the B-16 "Rainbow-Vision" analog.

"You get a chance to talk with your friend?" Simon Drobeck asked, looking thoroughly exhausted as he sat heavily on one of the lab stools and mopped at his dripping face.

"Yeah, I think he's real interested. Wants to talk to somebody." Bobby Lockwood nodded, closing his eyes and wishing Drobeck would hurry up so they could finish and get the hell out of this place before Jimmy Pilgrim called in another order for the B-16 analog. He didn't think he could handle *another* thirty-six-hour session. His head was still throbbing from all that ether.

"When?" Drobeck asked. Their three-day marathon in the Anza-Borrego lab, working frantically to put out the two twenty-five-pound batches, had just about done them both in.

"Told him I'd get him together with somebody this coming Friday," Lockwood said. "That okay?"

"Fine." Drobeck nodded. "The sooner the better."

"So what happened to all those other labs you said they're building?" Lockwood asked. "Can't some of those people help us out with this stuff? I mean, Jesus—"

"Pilgrim doesn't want to go into full production on this analog until he's sure about the market," Drobeck explained. "Apparently something went wrong with the initial testing. Anyway, if the sales of B-16 go as they expect, then he'll start opening up a few of the labs for franchise. Save the rest for the next analogs."

"And in the meantime. . . ?" Lockwood asked, knowing what he was going to hear.

"In the meantime, you and I do what we're told," Drobeck muttered firmly. "Speaking of which, did you remember to pick up that coke we took back from the dealers? The stuff we're supposed to stockpile?"

"In the trunk of the car." Lockwood nodded tiredly. "Twenty-two bricks. Want me to put 'em somewhere?"

"Trunk of my car," Drobeck grunted. "I'll transfer them up to the mountain lab tomorrow."

"Want me to take them up there?" Lockwood asked hopefully, remembering that wherever that lab was, the high mountain air had been wonderfully cool. Not like this desert shit, he thought morosely. Besides, if he could get Drobeck to tell him where the prototype lab was located, he'd really have something to offer DeLaura.

Drobeck shook his head. "I'm going up there anyway," he said firmly. "Besides, I've got some work for you to do down here."

"Oh yeah, what's that?" Lockwood asked suspiciously.

"Rainbow called this morning while you were out," Drobeck said. "Said they've already distributed the first batch of the B-Sixteen, and he wants us to start on another twenty-five pounds, right away."

By 7:15 that evening, Detective DeLaura had spent almost two hours in the office of his frantic supervisor, listening to Hallstead and the livid deputy D.A. scream at each other over a speaker-phone.

DeLaura tried several times to say something that might cool the two confused and angry men down, but it was hopeless. In fact, it wasn't until the two highly frustrated conspirators started to repeat themselves that DeLaura was finally able to escape . . . by suggesting that he probably ought to contact some of his informants—see if any of them had a lead on the three murder suspects who had thoroughly embarrassed the two politically motivated lawmen.

Taking Hallstead's momentary silence for consent, DeLaura

hurried out and ran for the parking lot. Fifteen minutes later, he was announcing himself at the back door of the video-protected sheriff's crime lab.

DeLaura figured he had a reasonable chance of catching one of the SO criminalists working late, but he hadn't expected to see ten white-coated sheriff and visiting SDPD criminalists working feverishly to cross-match evidence on twenty-odd cases that involved toxicology and powder samples from homicides, suicides, overdoses and drug-arrests just now being correlated with a single unidentified drug compound.

Except that, according to the two forensic scientists who excitedly tried to explain it all to a dumbfounded Martin DeLaura, it wasn't unidentified any longer.

"It's a thiopene analog," Tracy Nokes said happily, her smile belying the fatigue in her eyes. "Very similar in structure to PCP. Ah, what'd you say the chemical name was, Tina?" She turned to her police lab counterpart.

"Just a second. One-one-two-thienyl-cyclohexyl-piperidine," Tina Sun-Wang said, referring to one of her notes. "Which is really bizarre, because the synthesis . . ."

After a few more minutes of blank-eyed nodding and smiling and congratulating, DeLaura managed to catch the attention of the supervisor of the sheriff's lab, who was involved in an animated conversation with Paul Reinhart. Trying to blank out the surrounding conversations—which were mostly scientific gibberish to DeLaura anyway—the narcotics detective quickly explained his problem.

"Jeeze, I don't know, Marty." The sheriff's lab director shook his head. "I've got everybody tied up on these cases right now. Besides, you know, it'd be kinda dangerous for any of us to do that sort of thing in this area."

"Yeah, we've got the same problem," Reinhart added sympathetically. "I mean we'd really like to help, especially if you've found the lab putting this stuff out. But the thing is, I'm not sure any of us could get away with playing that role. Be real easy for one of the dopers to recognize us, since we're always out testifying against them in court."

"Yeah, I guess you're—" DeLaura started to say glumly when one of the surrounding white-coated figures suddenly came forward.

"Uh, excuse me," Tina Sun-Wang said, "I know it's probably none of my business . . . but, I don't think anybody'd recognize me, 'cause I've never testified in court against anyone at all."

26

THE UNFINISHED message on the General's computer screen read:

TO: RAINBOW
FROM: GENERAL
SUBJECT: CLAIRMONT PARK SALE

BE ADVISED . . . ALL SUBJECTS ARRESTED DUR-
ING SALE OF THIOPENE ANALOG HAVE BEEN RE-
LEASED FOR LACK OF EVIDENCE . . . APPARENTLY
ANALOG THEORY WORKS . . . ALSO BE ADVISED:
JUSTICE SOURCE INDICATES MURDER WARRANTS
ISSUED FOR ALL THREE SUBJECTS WHO TRIED TO
MAKE BUY . . . RELEVANT INFORMATION TO FOL-
LOW:

"My God," Sandy Mudd whispered, shaking her head as she
stood in front of the glowing screen with Ben Koda and Charley Shan-

---

non at her side, scanning the message as her mind churned with the possibilities.

"Don't worry 'bout it," Shannon said, his own eyes narrowing as he read the infuriating words, "they ain't gonna—"

"No, you don't understand." Mudd shook her head as she cautiously sat down in front of the computer terminal. "I think we can get in."

"What . . .?" Ben had gone over to the den window to pull the drapes closed and check the patio area again. Startled, he quickly turned away from the window, the cocked .45 still in his blood-smeared hand, and stared at Mudd.

"Their computer system," Sandy said, her eyes flashing around the den room, searching for the manual that had to be around . . . somewhere. She slid open the desk drawer under the terminal, then smiled as she pulled out a slick-covered, spiral-bound manual, and immediately began flipping the pages.

"What the hell are you talking about?" Koda demanded.

"The General and Rainbow. They're using these computers to message-switch across telephone lines," Mudd explained. "Gotta figure they're probably using 'em to keep track of a lot of other stuff too. You know, like dealer names, drop-points, money records. Maybe even the labs . . ."

"All that stuff's in *this* here machine?" Charley asked skeptically.

"No, I'm sure it's not." Mudd shook her head. "This is just a remote terminal. The main system—with the big memory bank—is somewhere else. Maybe even in another state, no way to tell. But it doesn't matter as long as all the terminals are connected to telephone lines. They've probably got one for every pound-dealer, at least. That way, all the dealers'd have to do is log into the memory bank with their passwords. They'd have access to all the data they'd need to run their operation. Even better, they could always erase everything in about a second if someone tried to bust in on 'em."

"And you're saying you can get into their records through this thing?" Koda asked, beginning to understand the true significance of what he'd found.

"That's just it, I think we're *already* in," Mudd whispered, her eyes gleaming with excitement as she finally found what she was looking for in the manual: the chapter on operational commands.

"See, that's always the problem with computers," Mudd tried to explain as she quickly scanned the summary list of commands. "To get into the main file systems, you have to log in with the right access code and password. Otherwise, you'll just bounce out—or maybe even crash the system—which is something I could do real easily if I screw up," she half-mumbled as her eyes swept down the page.

"But it looks like the General's already logged in," she added, finally looking up from the manual at Koda. "He must have been getting ready to send Rainbow that message when he got distracted or—"

"Meaning *we* can get at their records, *right now?*" Koda asked hopefully, not really believing it was going to be that easy.

"I think so . . . maybe." Sandy nodded. "As long as I don't do something wrong . . ." Mudd allowed her trembling fingers to hover over the keyboard as she started to enter in the command to call up the main menu, hesitating because she knew how easily she could crash the system by typing in the wrong command. If it crashed, that was it. She'd never get back in, because she didn't know the access code and the General's password.

But if her suspicions were correct . . .

If the security system they were using allowed the dealers to select a new personal password whenever they wanted . . .

Mudd keyed in the five-letter command listed in the manual, and then held her breath as she sent the coded command into the computer processor. In the blink of an eye, the words "MAIN MENU" appeared on the screen, immediately followed by a list of available options . . . one of which was: "CHANGE PASSWORD."

Sandy closed her eyes and sighed in momentary relief. Then she selected the "CHANGE PASSWORD" option, scanned the resulting screen display twice to be absolutely certain, and then carefully typed in the word "GENERAL."

"That's it." She nodded, taking in and releasing a deep breath. "Their access code into the main system was—and still is—'ALCHEMY.' The General wrote it in his manual . . ." Mudd pointed to the neatly penciled word in the margin of the operating commands section, ". . . probably so he wouldn't forget. Can't tell what his personal password was—it's programmed not to show up on the screen— so I just changed it to 'GENERAL' . . . something easy to remember."

"So what's all that mean in English?" Koda asked.

"Means I can get into the system any time I want now." Mudd grinned happily. "Doesn't matter if I crash it. All I have to do is reload the program, type in 'ALCHEMY' and 'GENERAL,' and we're right back in. So let's see what we can find . . ."

Going back to the "MAIN MENU," Sandy began searching the subsystems, one by one . . . and immediately discovered what she'd half-expected.

"It's all in there," she whispered, her lips pursed in frustration as she nodded her head at the screen. "Name lists of all their gram, ounce and pound dealers. Scheduled pickup and drop dates. Bank accounts. Addresses. Phone numbers. Labs. Even something called 'analog formulas.' Probably the instructions for making their new dope."

"Jesus Christ . . . you mean they keep all that stuff in a computer where anybody can get at it?" Koda asked incredulously.

"Actually it's probably safer in the computer than on paper." Mudd shrugged. "We can read all the menu lists, but the way they've got it protected, the only data we can actually *get at* is the General's. Names and addresses of his dealers, things like that. All the heavy stuff, like the labs, files for the other pound dealers, things like that, are protected with higher-level passwords. Probably Pilgrim's or Rainbow's."

"Hey, Sandy, can you change Pilgrim's or Rainbow's password, like you did the General's?" Charley Shannon asked, beginning to understand . . .

"Sure, I *could*, but I'd need their current password first, to get into their file."

"Shit," Charley muttered.

"Lot of other things we *can* do, though," Mudd said. "Watch." As a demonstration, she called up the listing of dealer names for the General's San Diego area. The screen immediately displayed the first twenty-four names and phone numbers in alphabetical order.

"Jesus, I gotta call Fogarty, let him know about this," Koda whispered, awed by the mind-boggling possibilities of the electronic device. "Listen, Sandy, can you print all the General's stuff out on paper?"

"Once I figure out the right commands." Mudd nodded, turning on the dot-matrix printer and then checking the stack of fanfold paper. "Should be able to print out anything I can get at with the General's password. Want me to start now?"

"Yeah, go ahead," Koda said. "Anything you can get at easily within the next fifteen or twenty minutes. While you're doing that, I'm gonna call Fogarty. Charley, see if you can find some mailing envelopes around here, and some stamps . . . and keep an eye on those goddamned doors."

"Gotcha."

Koda had already started out of the room when Sandy Mudd called out.

"Ben, wait a minute! I—I think there's something else we might be able to do."

Ten minutes later, Koda was talking hurriedly to Fogarty on the upstairs phone, filling him in on the assault, the General's death and the miraculous find of the logged-in computer terminal.

"Beautiful," Fogarty whispered. "Goddamnit, it's about time we got a break. So what about this 'alchemist' character? The guy who's making all this analog shit? Sandy find anything on *him* in that computer?"

"If his name's in there, it's probably in one of those protected areas." Koda tried to explain, as best he could, the problem of the higher-level security passwords.

"Shit," Fogarty sighed. "Hey, wait a minute! What about trying to connect into one of our computers? Ask Sandy if—"

"She's already thought of that," Koda said. "Apparently there's some kind of scrambler hard-wired into the General's computer. Say's she can't do anything about it without her tools. I told her to forget it. Figure'd you wouldn't want to risk making a drop."

"Yeah, you're right. Probably people staked out all over that place by now. Okay, don't worry about the protected stuff. Just pull what you can, and then get the hell out of there before somebody—"

"Tom," Koda interrupted. "Listen . . . I think we can get in to Pilgrim."

Fogarty was silent for a moment. "What're you talking about? You just told me—"

"Yeah, I *know*, but just listen for a minute . . ." Koda began to explain the idea that Sandy Mudd had spent the last ten minutes defending with seemingly irrefutable logic.

"I don't like it," Fogarty said.

"I don't either," Koda admitted, "but I think she's right."

"You know what'll happen if she pulls it off, and then they get hold of her?" Fogarty reminded Ben.

"That's about *all* I've been thinking about for the past ten minutes," Koda grunted. "That's why we'd use a split password. Have to have all of us that way."

Fogarty considered his remaining options. There weren't may left. "How long will it take?" he finally asked.

"She figures about two hours to write the program. Three at the outside."

"You think they'll leave you alone out there that long?"

"Only one way we're gonna find out," Koda shrugged.

"And you *really* think she can pull it off?" Forgarty asked, wanting to be absolutely sure.

"Yeah, I do."

Fogarty hesitated. "The thing is, Ben, I'm getting a hell of a lot of pressure from the director to track down that alchemist son of a bitch who's making all this analog shit. Intelligence just picked up word that something called 'Rainbow-Vision'—probably one of Pilgrim's new analogs—is supposed to be hitting the streets in Southern California this evening. Supposed to be coming outta the General's area."

"Jesus, Locotta's probably going ape-shit about now," Koda shook his head. "No wonder the General got hit. Probably going after Pilgrim and Rainbow too."

"Exactly . . . and you people are liable to end up right in the middle of it," Fogarty warned. "You try this plan of yours and you're liable to find yourselves protecting Pilgrim and Rainbow from Locotta while Sandy's trying to locate this alchemist bastard."

This time it was Koda's turn to be silent for a few moments. "Wonderful," he finally whispered. "So what about those warrants?"

"I can't order you to take that kind of risk," Fogarty said. "All it'd take is one traffic-stop by some trigger-happy rookie . . ." He left the rest unsaid. "But if we notify the SO and PD—"

"Yeah, we know. Soon as those warrants get pulled, we might as well pin our badges on." Koda nodded. "Listen, we've already talked it over. Far as we're concerned, you can hold off on that notification for a while."

"You sure about that?"

"Sure as we're ever gonna be." Koda chuckled with uneasy amusement. "Besides," he added, "the way things're going right now, a couple of murder warrants are probably gonna be the least of our problems."

"I don't know." Detective DeLaura shook his head. "I can see about twenty different ways this whole thing could go to shit on us real fast."

He'd been sitting in his office with Paul Reinhart and Tina Sun-Wang for over an hour, discussing and arguing the innumerable options and problems involved in putting a rookie criminalist in on a major underground lab network. Especially one being run by men like Jimmy Pilgrim and Lafayette Beaumont Raynee. If anything, DeLaura was even less convinced than when they'd started.

And besides, he knew something that no one else in the room—or in the entire sheriff's department, for that matter—knew: that Pilgrim and Rainbow had already sadistically murdered two law enforcement officers and wouldn't hesitate for a moment to kill another.

"Suppose I—" Tina Sun-Wang tried again, her enthusiasm for the project undiminished by DeLaura's concerns.

"Look, it's bad enough that the kid's supposed to be bringing in a *guy*," DeLaura interrupted. "We can probably work *that* out . . . say you're a friend of the friend, or something like that. But the thing is, it's not gonna do us any good just to get you into that Anza-Borrego lab and get probable-cause for a search warrant. What we need is an ID on that asshole alchemist. And the only way you're ever gonna get close to him is work your way up . . . which means you've gotta convince those bastards that you're one hell of a dope chemist. You really think you can do that?" DeLaura demanded.

Tina Sun-Wang was silent for a moment, thinking about how little she really knew about dope chemistry in an underground lab. But then her mind flashed back on the pale, anguished faces at the two autopsies she'd recently attended—those of a beautiful Jane Doe redhead and a little Mexican girl named Theresa.

"Yes," Tina Sun-Wang nodded her head firmly, "I know I can."

At 10:35 that Tuesday evening, Sandy Mudd finally looked up from the General's computer terminal and nodded her head.

"It's ready," she said to Ben and Charley. "I've made two trial runs with test passwords. The program ran fine each time."

"So what does that mean?" Ben Koda asked, uncomfortably aware that he and Charley and Sandy were about to penetrate a major underworld operation . . . with their only backup consisting of blind faith in a machine. He didn't much care for that idea.

"Means that if nobody turns this computer off after we leave, and the phone links don't go down, and about twenty other things don't go wrong, we just *might* pull it off," Mudd replied, staring straight into Koda's dark, worried eyes. "In other words, a piece of cake," she grinned tiredly.

"Shit, can't ask for better odds than that," Shannon grunted. "So whadda we do next?"

Sandy got up from the terminal and pointed at the empty chair. "You go first, Charley," she said. "Type in a word—any word you want—as long as it's not more than eight characters. Just don't let either of us see it," she reminded, joining Ben over at the far side of the room as Shannon laboriously typed in his secret password.

"Okay, now what?" he asked, turned around in the chair.

"Hit the return key," Mudd said. "Lower right hand corner." Shannon did so and then got up from the chair as the screen went blank.

Mudd then turned to Koda, knowing that he was the one who would have to make the final decision—go or no-go—within the next few minutes. "Your turn, partner," she said with forced cheerfulness. "Pick a good one."

At 10:45 Tuesday evening, while Charley Shannon was cautiously working his way along the cliffside darkness toward a distant neighborhood mailbox, the following message was being printed out through the computer in Lafayette Beaumont Raynee's underground office:

TO: RAINBOW
FROM: GENERAL
SUBJECT: CLAIRMONT PARK SALE

BE ADVISED . . . ALL SUBJECTS ARRESTED DUR-ING SALE OF THIOPENE ANALOG HAVE BEEN RE-LEASED FOR LACK OF EVIDENCE . . . APPARENTLY ANALOG THEORY WORKS . . . ALSO BE ADVISED: JUSTICE SOURCE INDICATES MURDER WARRANTS HAVE BEEN ISSUED FOR ALL THREE SUBJECTS WHO TRIED TO MAKE BUY: KODA, BEN . . . SHAN-NON, CHARLEY . . . MUDD, SANDY . . . SOURCE IN-DICATES WARRANT MAY INVOLVE FATAL ASSAULT ON POLICE OFFICERS . . . RECRUITMENT PROS-PECTS? . . . END

Then, at precisely 12:15 Wednesday morning, exactly ninety minutes after the modified version of the General's last message to Rainbow went out over the modem-connected telephone line, the second message was transmitted:

TO: RAINBOW
FROM: KODA, SHANNON, MUDD
SUBJECT: ALERT

THE GENERAL'S DEAD . . . WE WANT TO TALK
WITH YOU . . ."

27

AT 1:30 WEDNESDAY morning, an hour after receiving the shocking computer message, Lafayette Beaumont Raynee and his catlike bodyguard moved cautiously up onto the General's ocean-view deck. As they did so, Raynee's backup team—his three ex-mercenary dope distribution guards—ran in crouched, zigzag patterns to predetermined, triangulated positions surrounding the street, yard and hillside.

The bodies of the General, his bodyguards, and Locotta's assassins were no longer in sight, but Raynee could see where six sets of drag marks had merged into one thick, bloody streak that led in through the sliding-glass door to the General's living room.

Once his backups were in place, Raynee slipped two heavy-bladed throwing knives into the palms of his hands, then nodded his black, bushy head at Roy Schultzheimer, who was pressed tight against the outside wall next to the open glass door with a folding-stock pump shotgun.

"Now," Raynee rasped, and then quickly followed the lunging Schultzheimer in through the glass doorway.

Ben, Sandy and Charley were sitting on the General's sofa, their empty hands in clear view—their handguns and the three Ingram submachine guns all out on the coffee table (unloaded, because neither Ben or Charley fully trusted themselves to ignore their survival instincts)—when Schultzheimer and Rainbow burst into the room.

In those first deadly-quiet moments, Rainbow's sweeping eyes took in the three unmoving figures on the couch, the bullet-filled magazines next to the unloaded weapons on the coffee table, and the six pale, torn, and distinctly odorous bodies lying side by side on the General's beige carpet in the middle of a thick, glossy puddle of rapidly congealing blood.

Seeing Rainbow for the first time in person, both Ben and Charley immediately realized that their agonized decision not to leave themselves the option of a loaded weapon—preferably one of the Ingrams—within arm's reach had been the right one.

Standing framed by the doorway, in the full glory of his multicolored wardrobe, Raynee's glaring eyes, the gleaming white teeth, the bushy black hair, the outstretched hands with the long, clawlike knives . . . all were fused into a tensed, steel-spring body that seemed to yearn for release.

Definitely the right decision, because given the chance—even the slightest chance—Koda and Shannon both *knew* that they would have gone for their weapons, understanding that they had no choice but to destroy the ruthless madman who stood before them.

Raynee was the first to speak. The contrast between his look of feral awareness and the unexpected gentleness of his soothing words jarred against Koda's and Shannon's nerves.

"Been wantin' t' meet you people face-up for a *long* time," he whispered, smiling as he carefully put the two throwing knives down next to the unloaded firearms. Roy Schultzheimer remained standing by the door, scanning the room as he held the shotgun up and ready.

Charley could feel Sandy's leg muscles tense up against his own. "Easy," he said softly, slowly shifting his eyes between the deadly calm menace in Raynee's eyes and the easy, relaxed readiness of Schultzheimer. His hand brushed soothingly against the girl's shoulder, ready to throw her aside and make a grab for one of the Ingrams—and one of the loaded magazines, if it came to that . . .

. . . and hoping like hell it wouldn't, because now that he'd seen Raynee in the flesh—finally sensed the cruel malevolence of the street warrior—Charley finally understood what Tom Fogarty had known and feared all along: that he and Ben might not be capable of dealing with Rainbow after all.

"Heard about you too," Koda replied with icy calmness. For reasons he couldn't begin to understand, the vengeance-seeking entity in the back of his mind seemed to be soothed by the physical presence of the madman it fully intended to destroy.

"You people do all this?" Raynee asked.

"Some of it." Koda nodded, staring into Raynee's coldly dark eyes. "Three with the hoods. Interrupted a conversation we were having with the General . . . about some money he owes us."

"That right? How come the General owes you money?" Raynee asked, not interested in the answer—he already knew that—but rather in Koda himself, or something about him.

Something that he could sense . . .

"Long story." Koda shrugged, feeling the intensity of the street dealer's probing eyes. "Boils down to the fact that we paid the man for something we didn't get. And now that we got ourselves into a little trouble—thanks to the General—we need the money to make a move."

"What kinda trouble you talkin' 'bout?" Rainbow asked.

Koda paused, staring contemplatively at Raynee's dancing black eyes.

"Has to do with a little misunderstanding with the law around here," he finally said. "Got the impression they aren't real interested in hearing our side of the story, so we're planning on moving outta town for a while. Trouble is, we got a problem with transportation."

"Man with the boat took off on you?" Raynee suggested, smiling as he noted the varied expressions of apparent surprise on the three faces.

"Maybe." Koda nodded cautiously.

"That why you wanted to talk with me?" Raynee pressed on.

"Something like that." Koda nodded. "Figured you might—"

"So how'd you get into the computer?" Raynee interrupted.

"Sandy here's worked with computers before." Koda shrugged. "Spotted a couple of teletype messages on the printer. She played with the General's computer a little while, and then came up with your name on some kinda 'mailbox' list, which I guess doesn't say much for your security system. Anyway, since we'd already lost out with the General, I figured what the hell," Koda shrugged.

"That a fact, girl?" Raynee said, turning his gaze over to the paled face of Sandy, who was sitting—visibly tense and nervous—between the two men.

She nodded wordlessly.

"You broke into our system, jes' like that?" the drug dealer demanded.

Mudd nodded silently again.

"You scared a' me, girl?"

"Yes." Sandy Mudd whispered, somehow finding the nerve to stare directly into Raynee's crazed eyes.

"Thass good." Raynee suddenly smiled. "Sounds like maybe you got more brains'n these dudes here."

"Listen, you may be fucking crazy . . . like they all say," Ben Koda said calmly, "but right now, our other choices don't look so hot either."

Raynee seemed to like that answer. He nodded and just sat there, apparently lost in thought for several long seconds.

"How much money we talkin' 'bout?" he finally asked.

"Fifty-five hundred's what we gave the General. That . . . and whatever this mess is worth," Koda said, nodding over at the blood-soaked bodies.

"You figure Ah owe you for them three?" Raynee asked curiously.

"What the General was telling us before those assholes showed up sounded like they'd probably be out looking for you next." Koda shrugged. "Figure we might have saved you some trouble."

"Might have at that." Raynee nodded thoughtfully. "Maybe Ah oughta give you folks a chance to finish earning that money, plus a whole lot more. Whadda ya think 'bout that?"

"Workin' 'round *here*, in San Diego?" Charley Shannon growled.

"Thass right." Raynee nodded. "Whas' the matter, don' you like that idea?"

"Sounds like a dumb-ass thing t' do, ya ask me," Shannon said.

"Yeah, I'm not sure . . ." Koda started in when Raynee interrupted again.

"Ah know all 'bout your *problem* with the po-lice." He smiled. "Ain't gonna matter none, far as Ah'm concerned . . . long's you can keep your eyes open, an' don' mind doin' little more a' this kinda work," he nodded over at the six bodies.

Koda looked over at Shannon—who hesitated for a long moment and then shrugged agreeably—and then at Sandy, who nodded with considerably less enthusiasm.

"Okay, long as you know the situation. So when do we start?" Koda shrugged.

Raynee snorted in apparent amusement as he scooped up the knives in one hand, stood up, and then walked over to the General's sprawled and deflated body. "Looks to me like you folks done already started."

By 2:30 Wednesday morning, it was estimated that at least fifty thousand young men and women between the ages of sixteen and twenty-five had purchased and tried one of the bright, rainbow-patterned, quarter-gram bindles of the B-16 analog . . . the new drug the street dealers were calling Rainbow-Vision.

It was a marketing man's dream, the word-of-mouth feedback to virtually every one of Jimmy Pilgrim's seventy-five ounce and five hundred-odd, gram dealers coming back as either "incredible," or "mind-blowing" or—more often than not—just plain "fucking *unbelievable!*"

And the word was spreading like a windswept brush fire.

It didn't take long for the local telephone companies to figure out that something big was going on, either, especially when people started tying up the main trunk lines feeding out of San Diego, Riverside and San Bernardino Counties. And it wasn't just users eagerly calling up their friends to describe the wonderfully chromatic rush of the new powder. It was also about five hundred gram dealers hurriedly reporting in to their ounce distributors with demands for more of the Rainbow-Vision.

Lots more.

In fact, in all of Southern California, there was only one known negative report on the B-16 analog, and that came from Raggedy Ann and Raggedy Annie, who along with their lovesick buddy, William Benson Sandcastle III, were busy calling every one of Jimmy Pilgrim's dealers that they knew to complain shrilly that the new stuff wasn't the *Power*-Rainbow that all three of them had been waiting for so desperately.

It took Roy Schultzheimer almost an hour to drive circuituously to Raynee's underground office, which was securely hidden—now out of absolute necessity—from Jake Locotta's searching enforcers. Jimmy Pilgrim's three ex-mercenary dope guards followed closely behind in a separate car.

From Sandy Mudd's perspective—sitting in the back of the gaudy van with Rainbow, Ben and Charley—it seemed easily the most terrifying hour of her entire life. Far more so than her recent encounter with Locotta's hooded assassins. Unlike Ben and Charley—who knew better than to dwell on all of the possibilities that were now completely out of their control—Mudd had never really learned to deal with fear of the unknown.

Had they been able to talk openly among themselves, Koda might have explained that working "undercover" was very much like jumping out of a helicopter at night into dark ocean currents, and being caught up in an uncontrollable rush toward some unknown shore, having no idea what might be waiting beneath the surface or at the end of the ride.

When the van finally pulled to a stop, and the back door was opened, Koda, Shannon and Mudd found themselves in an underground garage.

Schultzheimer led the way into a concealed stairwell, through a long underground tunnel, and finally into Raynee's cavernous office . . . immediately followed by Koda, Mudd, Shannon and two of the guards. Raynee and the chief of the military-like protection team had already disappeared through another connecting door to the garage.

As they all filed into the dark, echoing room, Sandy Mudd recognized the cagelike array of metal and electronic pulse detectors, and gave silent thanks to Fogarty for insisting that the three agents go in clean. Her belt with the incriminating transmitter imbedded in the buckle would never have made it past Raynee's security screen.

They all stood silently in the darkness until Roy Schultzheimer turned on the light switches, giving Koda, Shannon and Mudd their first look at Raynee's blade-studded habitat.

"Jesus," Koda whispered, blinking at the glistening edges of the wall-mounted battle-axes and swords and knives . . .

"Man likes blades." Schultzheimer grinned as he came up beside the three agents. "Likes the ladies too," he added with a snickering grin as he brought the back of his hand up alongside Sandy Mudd's shirt.

"Watch yourself, man," Charley Shannon growled a warning . . . and then tried to jerk away—too late—from the slashing, backhanded blow that was literally too quick to be seen. The impact of Roy's calloused knuckles snapped Shannon's head around in a spray of blood from his split lower lip.

"YOU MUTHAH . . .!"

Sandy Mudd's scream was masked by Shannon's roar of outrage as he swung his massive right fist at the bodyguard's smirking face (a blow that, had it landed, might have torn Schultzheimer's curly blond head loose from his neck), and then staggered forward into the nearby wall as the catlike Schultzheimer sidestepped the vicious swing, slammed a fist-thrust into Shannon's nose . . . and then a solid side-kick into his ribcage . . . before dancing back out onto the expansive wrestling mat like a playful tomcat.

Before the stunned and infuriated Shannon could come back off the wall to go after Schultzheimer, Ben Koda moved between his part-ner and the mat . . . and then advanced toward the grinning, pale-eyed bodyguard.

"He told you to test us . . . that what this is all about?" Koda demanded, noting that the two guards hadn't even bothered to bring their Uzis up.

"Could be." The still-grinning Schultzheimer nodded, in-stinctively evaluating Koda's carelessly open approach and his clenched fist. "You figure it's your turn?"

"I'm figuring it's about time we set some ground rules if we're gonna work together around here," Koda said coldly, starting forward in a boxer's stance to throw a sharp left jab—

—and then—at the last second—twisting back and away from Schultzheimer's hand-strike, catching the fist with both hands, wrist-locking the startled martial arts expert to his knees, then deliberately bringing his tennis-shoed right foot around in a solid, snapping, round kick—square into Roy Schultzheimer's handsome face.

To the amazement of everyone in the room except the two guards, Schultzheimer seemed to absorb the impact of the punishing blow without serious effect. He tumbled over backward and then came up to his feet with a grin on his bloodied face, as though he'd finally found somebody he could play with on an equal basis.

Realizing at that moment that he was almost certainly out-matched by Schultzheimer, Koda dropped into the classic defensive stance he'd practiced hour after hour at his grandfather's *dojo*, waiting for the expected attack.

—and then relaxed gratefully when Raynee burst into the un-derground room and came stomping out onto the mat.

"Ah, told you t' *test* em, not try t' kill 'em," Raynee snarled, shoving his still bloodily grinning bodyguard out of the way.

"You people havin' fun?" he demanded, glaring first at the smoldering Shannon and then at Koda.

"That's what you hired us for, isn't it," Koda snapped back, knowing instinctively that this was no time to back down.

"Yeah, that's right, Ah guess Ah did." Raynee suddenly grinned. "An' Ah ain't never tagged ol' Roy like that neither, so maybe you people gonna work out okay after all. Fact is, you'd better . . ." Raynee went on, his eyes glittering dangerously as he held up a broken fossilized ivory figurine in his sinewy black hand, ". . . 'cause it looks like ol' Jake Locotta's boys jes' got done trashin' mah place."

At that moment, the head of Jimmy Pilgrim's protection team stuck his head in through the back door to the underground office.

"It's going down," he called out to Raynee. "Locotta's people're running wild out there. Picking some of our gram dealers up off the streets right now."

Raynee's face contorted. "Looks like there's gonna be some serious shit goin' on 'round here 'fore long," he whispered. "Might be a while 'fore you an' Roy can go back t' playin' with each other. Gonna have any problems handlin' that?"

"Not's far as I'm concerned." Koda shrugged.

Raynee's eyes flickered over to Shannon.

"Ah can wait," the burly agent answered with a nodding growl.

"Thas' good, bro'." Raynee nodded, slapping Shannon's reluctantly extended palm. "Kinda lookin' forward t' seein' you two boys workin' out with Roy here . . . see if mah man's really as good's he thinks he is," Raynee said, winking at Schultzheimer, who was licking the blood off his smashed but still grinning lips.

"Meanwhile, why don' you give these folks a littl' tour a' the place?" Raynee nodded at his undaunted bodyguard, then immediately shook his head as Sandy Mudd turned to follow Koda and Shannon.

"Not you, littl' lady," Raynee grunted, turning his glittering eyes on Mudd. "*You* get yourself ovah *there*," he said, pointing at the terminal at the far end of his office. "Want you t' show me jes' *'xactly* how you busted in t' mah security system."

28

BY 3:45 WEDNESDAY morning, Jake Locotta was working on his fifth cup of strong black coffee as Al Rosenthal briefed Jake on the unprecedented events taking place within his Southern California territory.

"It's as bad as I've ever seen it," Rosenthal rasped. "Everybody's askin' for some a' this Rainbow-Vision shit. And you remember that seven percent I was tellin' you about. Well, you can forget it, 'cause the last check I made—'bout a half hour ago—we were down twenty-two percent! Can you fuckin' *believe* that?" the animated accountant demanded. "Twenty-two fuckin' points. I'm tellin' ya, Jake, we got ourselves one hell of a *problem*."

"It's more'n just a problem, Rosey," Locotta said, his voice laced with smoldering rage. "This shit's gettin' fucking *serious*. I just got a call from Mario in Jersey. Word's already spread to the East Coast. New York, Boston, Miami, you name it. Said he even got a call from Sanchez down in Colombia, wanting to know what the hell's going on out here."

Rosenthal winced and shook his head.

"Where the hell's Tassio?" Locotta growled, sweeping the empty coffee cup off the table. "Goddamn it. I told him to get me—" then hesitated as he heard a car pull up into the driveway outside.

Moments later, Joe Tassio came hurrying into Locotta's enclosed patio.

"Well?" Locotta demanded.

"Boys down in San Diego might a' hit some pay dirt," Tassio said, pausing to catch his breath. "They're coming in off the chopper right now. Be here in a few minutes."

"Pilgrim?" Locotta's eyes glistened with anticipation.

Tassio shook his head. "Nah, still drawin' a blank on that son of a bitch. One of our teams think they mighta spotted Rainbow's van in the Del Mar area, though. Could 'a been heading back to his house. Got the whole area staked out, just in case. Want me to send 'em back in again, check it out?"

"Hold off," Locotta grunted. "If Rainbow's in the area, then Pilgrim's gonna be around somewhere too—that, or he's fuckin' dead. Either way, I don't really give a shit. Right now, I'm a hell of a lot more interested finding that fuckin' lab where they're making this Rainbow-Vision crap, and shutting it *down*. And that includes their goddamned chemist. What'd you say they call him?"

"Just 'Alchemist,'" Tassio shrugged. "That's all we've got so far. No name."

"Maybe if we brought Rainbow in, Jake," Al Rosenthal suggested. "Get him to talk . . ."

"Shit, you could hang that goddamned Rainbow by the balls for a week and he still wouldn't talk," Tassio growled. "Waste a' time. We're better off trying t' tag the bastard . . ."

"Then you'd goddamned well *better* tag him!" Locotta shouted, slamming his fist on the breakfast table. "You tag Rainbow, and you find Jimmy Pilgrim, and you find out where the hell those bastards are making this stuff!"

"If Pilgrim and Rainbow're gonna keep on dealing this new powder, then they've gotta contact their lab sometime," Rosenthal said soothingly. "And when they do—"

"We'll shut 'em down," Joe Tassio nodded impatiently. "But I'm tellin' ya, Jake, you'd better hear what these girls—"

Just then a burst of outraged feminine cursing split the morning air, immediately followed by a resounding slap—and then silence.

Moments later, the scared yet defiant and still struggling figures of Raggedy Annie and Raggedy Ann were dragged into Locotta's patio by four of Joe Tassio's enforcers.

"All right," Tassio growled. "I want you to tell Mr. Locotta here *exactly* what you've been telling everybody else on the street about that *Power*-Rainbow."

* * *

By four o'clock that morning, Sandy had grown sufficiently confident in her role-playing to feel almost at ease as she explained to Rainbow how his computer system could be better protected against unauthorized users. Against people such as herself, she wanted to add.

"It's not that the programmers who set up your system didn't do a good job," Mudd said, as she tried to describe the pitfalls of computer data protection to Raynee—who was clearly out of his depth, but extremely interested, nonetheless. "It's just that they could have made it a lot better. I mean, I really *shouldn't* have been able to get into the General's records, like I did just now."

"Yeah, Ah ain't arguin' *that* none," Raynee nodded, not at all pleased by the sight of the General's monthly balance sheet glowing on the screen before his eyes. "But what was that you was sayin' 'bout how you could mess up our whole fuckin' system?"

"Oh yeah, sure," Mudd nodded, nervously aware that the moment she'd been dreading had finally arrived. "That's because the computers you guys bought have something called a 'SANJO' program imbedded into the operating system."

"A San-Joe program? What the hell you talkin' 'bout, woman?"

"It's like a tool kit they put into computers," Mudd lied. "The programmers use it to design the specific menu functions for the buyer, but they're supposed to take it out when they're finished."

"An' they didn't?"

"Apparently not," Mudd shrugged. "Here, look—" she quickly typed in the commands that would—she hoped!—call up her hurriedly written program from the General's computer, praying that no one had turned off his machine, or . . .

The computer screen in front of Raynee and Mudd flickered, and then the words "SANJO PROGRAM ACTIVATED" flashed on the screen.

"See, there it is," Mudd nodded at the screen, forcing herself not to laugh aloud with pure relief at the sight of her bogus program. "Now, watch." She typed in three more command strings, then stood up and walked away from the computer.

"What you doin', girl?" Raynee demanded, suddenly alert.

"I'm just demonstrating what I told you," Sandy Mudd said. "I walked over here so I couldn't see you use your password. Now try to log into the system."

"Whaddaya mean, *try*? You sayin' Ah can't . . .?"

"Go ahead, try it." Mudd said, forcing herself to smile confidently.

Raynee glared suspiciously at Mudd for a moment, then looked down at the keyboard and carefully typed in his password with one finger.

The screen immediately flashed the words: "INCORRECT PASSWORD."

"What!" Raynee snarled, his terrifying eyes boring in on Mudd's tensed face. "What'd you do t' this thing, girl?"

"Nothing, I just used 'SANJO' to mess up your security system," Mudd shrugged, feeling her knees weakening. "You want it back the way it was, just enter in the words 'STOP SANJO'."

After glaring at Mudd again, Raynee slowly typed in the nine letters and then hit the return key.

"Now try logging in again," Mudd directed.

This time Raynee's face broke into a relieved smile as the computer obediently offered up the menu of his personal set of highly protected files. For a few uneasy moments, Raynee had been concerned that he'd made a very dangerous mistake in allowing the girl access to the terminal.

"Maybe you're pretty damn good after all, woman," Raynee nodded.

"Actually, I can probably do better," Mudd forced the words out through her constricted throat.

"Say what?" Raynee cocked his black-Afroed head.

"I'll show you," Mudd said. "First turn the computer off . . . so you cancel out your password."

Raynee did so.

"Okay," she took a deep breath, "for example, you've probably got some protected files in the main memory that only you and your boss are supposed to see. Give me a for-instance. A file that the General couldn't get at with his password."

"All dealer names," Raynee shrugged, watching the girl closely. "Pilgrim said only him and me can see all the names. Pound dealers can only see their own. You sayin' that ain't true neither?"

"Watch." Sandy walked back to the terminal and quickly keyed in a series of commands, one of which invisibly searched out and utilized Raynee's high-level password that had been captured and retained by Sandy's waiting SANJO program. Then she stepped away from the terminal again.

"Okay," she said, "I've typed in the commands. All you have to do is hit the return key."

Raynee did so, and suddenly the words "MASTER DEALER LIST" appeared on the screen, followed by twenty alphabetized names. Sandy walked up and depressed the scroll key, deliberately keeping her eyes averted from the screen by staring at Raynee's shocked expression as the computer obediently scrolled through the entire list of six hundred and forty-three names.

"Ah'll be gawddamned," Raynee shook his head. He stared up at Mudd with an expression of stark malice—sending a wave of cold fear up her spine—as everything suddenly seemed to click into place within Raynee's streetwise mind. "Think you're pretty clever, don't ya, girl?" he whispered, his voice deadly cold.

"Why, just because I can get at all your records?" Sandy asked, thinking that her diaphragm had suddenly become paralyzed.

"Thass right," Raynee rasped, his eyes seeming to pierce into Mudd's skull. "Use that San-Joe program any time you want . . ."

"Yeah, I guess I *could*, but you're forgetting something," Mudd said, fighting the panic that was threatening to overwhelm her thought processes. Somehow, she still had to type two more words into her SANJO program.

"Yeah, whass' that?"

"One, we work for you now," she said, "and two, I can cancel SANJO out any time you want."

"That right?" Raynee said suspiciously.

"Sure, all I have to do is—" she started to reach for the keyboard, and suddenly found her wrists clamped tightly in Raynee's sinewy hands.

"You tell me, an' *Ah'll* do it," Raynee whispered, releasing Mudd's wrists, but still effectively controlling her with his hard eyes.

"Just type 'ERASE SANJO,'" Mudd whispered, distantly aware that her hands were beginning to tremble with helpless fear. Ben and Charley were somewhere else in the underground complex with Schultzheimer and the protection team, leaving her very much alone with Raynee. If anything went wrong now . . .

"E-r-a-s-e S-a-n-j-o," Raynee muttered to himself as he carefully typed in each letter.

"And the return key," Sandy Mudd whispered, feeling relief as Raynee hit the final key which set the most devastating function of her hastily devised SANJO program into place, and at the same time—completely unknown to Mudd—drastically altered the security mechanisms of Jimmy Pilgrim's expensively programmed computer.

However, as Sandy had planned, there were no outward indications of the damage—intentional or otherwise—caused by SANJO. Raynee's terminal screen simply flashed up the falsely reassuring words: "SANJO PROGRAM ERASED FROM MEMORY."

"Ah'll be goddamned," Raynee shook his head once again, a wide grin appearing across his evil-looking face. "Ah think Ah jes' found mahself mah own lady alchemist."

Uncharacteristically displaying far more brains than guts upon finding herself sprawled across Jake Locotta's patio, Raggedy Annie didn't hestate to spill anything and everything she even *thought* she knew about the Power-Rainbow . . .

. . . while Locotta and Rosenthal listened in growing shock, horror, and disbelief as the butch-girl vividly described the "trips" she and Raggedy Ann and Wee-Willie had taken on the Power-Rain-bow.

As Raggedy Annie continued to babble about everyone she could think of who'd had *anything* to do with the Power-Rainbow, Joe Tassio sent his men off to track down the one living person who—according to Raggedy Annie—was the most likely link to the source of the fabled new drug.

It didn't take them long to find her.

At 5:50 Wednesday morning, one of Joe Tassio's highly professional gunmen transferred that one person (an incredibly beautiful young woman, he thought, if you didn't count the single swollen black eye) out of a helicopter, dumping the bound, gagged and semi-conscious Skylight at Locotta's feet on the living room floor, and handing the mob boss a folder paper bindle with some scribbling on the outside.

"Found that in her purse," the youthful enforcer said respectfully.

"A-Seventeen?" Locotta read out loud. "What the. . . ?"

"THAT'S IT!" Raggedy Annie lunged to her feet from the far side of the room. "THAT'S THE POWER-RAINBOW! I TOLD YOU. . . !" she started screeching, and then went down hard under the slashing hand of Joe Tassio.

"So this is it, Rosey," Locotta whispered as he carefully unfolded the small paper bindle and then stared silently at the thin, compressed sheet of white crystalline powder. Then Rosenthal shrugged his shoulders, wet his index finger with the tip of his blotchy tongue, gently dipped his finger into the powder, and brought it back up to his dry lips.

For a few long moments, Jake Locotta's living room was deathly silent as everyone stared at the aged accountant.

Then . . .

"Jesus . . ." Al Rosenthal whispered, his ancient, runny eyes opening wide.

"What is it?" Locotta demanded, glaring at the unfocused eyes of his trusted adviser. "Rosey, what the hell're you seeing?"

"Colors," Al Rosenthal whispered. "Lots of colors, Jake. You . . . you can feel them . . . almost like . . ." Rosenthal's voice drifted off as his red-veined eyes locked in on the terrified face of Raggedy Ann.

"Come here, girl. You want some?" Rosenthal asked.

"Yes . . . please," she whispered as Rosenthal slowly dipped a bony finger into the powder and then extended it over to her opened mouth.

As Locotta and Tassio watched with disbelief, the street girl licked every grain of the white powder off Rosenthal's finger, and then slowly wrapped herself in tight against the accountant's legs with gratitude, looking for all the world like an overly affectionate kitten.

Then, before Locotta, or Tassio could say anything, another figure bolted past her guard and scrambled down next to Al Rosenthal's chair.

"Please," Raggedy Annie whispered desperately. "Please, mister, can . . . can I have some too?"

"How long's he been in there," Locotta asked, staring at the closed bedroom door behind which his once-impotent adviser and the two street urchins were still noisily occupied.

"Forty-five minutes," Joe Tassio said with disbelief. "Want me t' go check on him?"

Locotta remained silent, staring down at the opened bindle of white powder in his hand. "I don't fuckin' believe it," he rasped, shaking his head slowly. "I—"

"Jake—?"

"Huh—? Uh, no—no, leave him alone." The mob boss shook his head distractedly, trying to decide if he really believed what he was seeing and hearing with his own eyes and ears.

"Fuck it, I gotta find out for myself," he finally muttered. Locotta dipped a finger into the bindle of Power-Rainbow and brought some of the sticky crystals up to his own mouth.

At 6:45 Wednesday morning, a thoroughly unnerved Tassio decided he couldn't wait any longer. Barging in through the door of Locotta's bedroom, Tassio ignored the intertwined sleeping forms of the two absolutely mouth-watering women—Skylight and Locotta's violet-eyed blond companion—and began shaking his sweaty and snoring boss.

"Jake, *goddamn it!* Come on, wake up!"

Locotta finally came around. Less than an hour after testing the Power-Rainbow out on himself, the West Coast mob boss was physically, mentally, and emotionally drained. Even when he finally opened his eyes, he wasn't really there.

"Wha—no—no more," he mumbled, blurry-eyed and sated—and then came wide awake as his head recoiled from the powerful slap of Joe Tassio's open-palmed hand.

"What the hell," Locotta snarled. Then his eyes cleared and he saw the intertwined figures, and remembered—

"Oh Jesus," Jake Locotta whispered weakly. "Where—Joe, get Al in here. Gotta tell him—"

"Al's dead, Jake." Joe Tassio shook his head. "Heart attack, I guess . . ." his voice trailed off.

Locotta stared up at Tassio numbly for a moment, and then nodded his head in understanding. "Help me outta here, Joe," he finally whispered, allowing Tassio to help him get dressed and into the kitchen, where he gratefully began to sip at a reviving cup of hot coffee.

"Jesus, Jake, we thought you'd had it," Joe Tassio said. "After we found Al like that . . ."

"It's not a poison." Locotta shook his head. "That stuff really works. God-*damn* does it work. Tellin' ya, I never felt anything like it in my whole fucking life."

"Jake," Tassio whispered, "—the organization. If word about this stuff gets out—"

"Yeah—yeah, I know." Locotta rasped. "What'd you do with those two hookers?"

"You mean the Rag twins?" Tassio asked carefully. "We've got 'em locked away. You want . . . ?"

"Yeah, bury 'em . . . deep." Locotta nodded. "The last fuckin' thing we need right now is to have those two out on the street flapping their jaws about this stuff."

"What about . . .?" Tassio gestured with his head at Locotta's closed bedroom door.

Jake Locotta's eyes widened in anguish as he remembered the incredibly, brilliantly . . . chromatic . . . emotions that had bound the three of them together on the wide bed. For a long moment, the mob boss hesitated, feeling himself being torn by irresistible—and totally opposing—desires. But ultimately, the instinct for survival was too deeply ingrained. He nodded his head.

"Them too."

A deeply shaken Jake Locotta then sat quietly sipping at his coffee with trembling hands as Joe Tassio first made a phone call.

"Tell me something, Joe," Locotta rasped. "If that fuckin' Pilgrim's the one who came up with this Power-Rainbow aphrodisiac shit, then why the hell isn't he dealing it, right now, 'stead of this Rainbow-Vision? According t' what that Annie broad said, it's nowhere near as good."

"I don't know, Jake." Tassio shrugged, having no idea what his boss was talking about. "Maybe he's just holding it back—letting people get used to switching over from coke—before he hits 'em with the hot stuff."

"Tell you what," Locotta said seriously, finally starting to regain control over his badly twisted emotions, "that ever happens, the Organization can fucking *forget* about dealing grass an' coke an' heroin."

"Jesus," Joe Tassio shuddered.

"And you know why?" Locotta whispered. "'Cause whoever ends up with this Power-Rainbow shit, they're gonna *be* the fucking dope market, period, 'cause nobody's gonna *want* anything else."

Locotta couldn't go on, knowing that he and Joe Tassio would never see it happen. Long before that day arrived, they'd be held fully responsible for the collapse of a multibillion-dollar business, unless they somehow managed to come up with this Power-Rainbow themselves.

Which was exactly what they were *going* to do, regardless of what it took, because both men *knew* what "fully responsible" meant. They had put their share of shallowly buried bodies under newly rising buildings and freeways. More than their share.

"Joe, we gotta *find* that fuckin' alchemist," Locotta said fervently. "I'm tellin' ya, whatever it takes . . ."

"But—"

"One million dollars," Locotta said, licking his dry lips. "Cash. Put the word out on the street. Anybody who finds the chemist who made this stuff. Put a dozen tags on Rainbow too if you gotta, but goddamnit, *find* that alchemist bastard!"

"You want him dead?" Tassio asked.

Locotta shook his head. "Shit no, *alive*," he said with emphasis. "He's gonna give us the formulas for these analogs if we gotta take his brain apart piece by piece, 'cause I'm tellin' ya, Joe . . . we wanna walk away from all this, we gotta have that Power-Rainbow!"

29

IT WASN'T UNTIL Sandy Mudd tried to call up one of the protected files in Jimmy Pilgrim's computer at 7:30 Wednesday morning, searching for some reference to Pilgrim's chemist, that she discovered the damage she'd inadvertently caused with her illicit SANJO program.

Waiting until she was finally alone—except for the one guard on the other side of the underground office—Mudd used Raynee's embedded password to call up the highly protected MASTER LIST OF PASSWORDS file, hoping to find the name of Pilgrim's elusive chemist in what she fully expected would be a very lengthy list . . .

. . . and then stared blankly—first in bewildered confusion, and finally in slowly dawning horror—at the single password-name combination that appeared on the screen.

Raynee's password.

Mudd immediately realized that somehow in writing the SANJO program she'd instructed the computer to erase the remainder of the master password list. The computer was now indicating that it would accept only Raynee's password as valid, which meant . . .

Jesus, she thought numbly. She'd just shut down Jimmy Pilgrim's entire communications network.

Sandy was still staring at the almost-empty screen, wondering how she could possibly have made such a horrendous programming error, when Ben Koda came in and walked over to her at the computer terminal.

"You find that bastard yet?" he asked quietly, rubbing Mudd's neck affectionately, and then immediately came alert as he felt the tension in her muscles and saw the shocked expression in her eyes.

"Ben, I think I—" she started to whisper, and then quickly shifted over into a technical description of her "new" security system for Pilgrim's computer as Raynee, Schultzheimer, Shannon, and the three guards came in and gathered around the computer terminal at Raynee's direction.

"Okay, girl." Raynee grinned, "want you t' show these folks here—"

"WHAT THE HELL'S GOING ON AROUND HERE?" a loud voice demanded from the far side of the room.

The eight people around the computer—including Raynee—jerked their heads around as the bearded man with the horn-rimmed glasses and three-piece suit walked into the room.

"Hey, man, what you doin' here?" Raynee grinned widely. "Ah thought you said we wasn't gonna—"

"I got your message about the General," Pilgrim growled. "Tried to get back to you a little while ago, but I couldn't get through on message-switching," he added as he walked across the extensive mat. "Goddamned computer's on the—"

Pilgrim's eyes suddenly became icy-black orbs as they focused on Koda, Shannon and Mudd. *"Who the hell are these people?"* he whispered in barely contained fury.

"Hey, man it's okay. Computer's workin' fine," Raynee laughed. "Fact is, we jes' been fixin' it up."

"YOU—WHAT?"

"Hey, man, it's cool," Raynee said uneasily. "These folks be righteous. They's the ones what did in them three dudes hit the General." Raynee gave Pilgrim a quick rundown of the action at the General's house.

"So you let them in *here?*" Pilgrim whispered increduously.

"Ah'm tellin' you, man, they's cool," Raynee insisted. "Ben, Charley an' Sandy, they *all* got murder-one warrants out on their asses, on account a' dumpin' a' pig . . ."

Pieces of intelligence that he had been gleaning from his varied sources during the last forty-eight hours suddenly began to fall into place within Jimmy Pilgrim's coldly analytical mind. "Ben Koda and Charley Shannon . . . ?" he started to ask, his eyes widening in disbelief.

"Yeah, thass right." Raynee nodded, visibly amazed. "How'd you know—?"

"Cop killers, my ass!" Jimmy exploded. "They're the ones who got made at Torrey Pines where you dumped that Kaaren broad. Boot and shoe prints . . ." Pilgrim's eyes flicked down to Charley Shannon's large boots and Ben Koda's torn tennis shoes, and then back up when he suddenly realized that Sandy Mudd was typing furiously on the computer terminal.

Exploding with rage, Pilgrim lunged across the floor at Mudd—just as she finished typing the words "LOAD SANJO II" and frantically hit the return key. His clenched fist caught her sharply across the jaw and sent her crashing against the wall, unconscious.

Pilgrim started to turn—to scream out his anger at Raynee—and then grunted and dropped to his knees in agonized shock as Koda drove a solid front-kick into his groin . . . just as Shannon's back-sweeping forearm sent Raynee and the computer terminal crashing to the floor, a shower of glass exploding from the video tube.

In the brief chaos that followed, Roy Schultzheimer let out an explosive *ki-yi* scream as he slammed his fist just beneath Koda's right ear before Ben could follow up the groin kick with a lethal sword-hand thrust to Pilgrim's exposed throat.

Koda collapsed to the floor. Shannon spun and started after Schultzheimer, his black, bearded face masked with raging fury—

"HOLD IT OR AH'LL CUT HER!" Raynee yelled, and Shannon turned to see the bloodied, furious killer holding a straight razor up tight against Sandy Mudd's throat . . . just as a vicious, flying side-kick by Schultzheimer sent Shannon staggering to the floor next to his unconscious partner.

On the wall-mounted blackboard in his office, a very animated David Isaac and Nichole Faysonnt were comparing the structures of the three most prominent analogs tested to date—the thiopene, the B-16 and the A-17—and trying to reach some conclusion as to the most probable reaction sites of the molecules.

The phone rang. It was Isaac's secretary, advising him that his eight A.M. appointment was fifteen minutes early and waiting outside.

"Thank you, Michelle. Send her in, please," Isaac said, and then turned to Nichole as he hung up the phone. "Why don't you go ahead and start setting up for the A-Eighteen synthesis," Isaac said to his warmly smiling lover. "I don't think this will take long."

"You're anxious too, aren't you," the bright-eyed girl smiled as she picked up her red-cloth-covered lab notebook and disappeared around the corner.

"What we accomplish today may prove to be historic." Isaac whispered to himself, thinking that if the A-18 analog turned out to be even a slight enhancement of the wondrously sensual 17 . . .

Then he looked up as his visitor knocked at his door.

"Ah yes," Isaac nodded, walking around his desk and extending his hand. "Miss . . . uh?"

"Sun-Wang. Tina Sun-Wang," the young woman said. "I was one of Dr. Bacon's graduate students last year."

"Yes, of course. You mentioned that last night," Isaac nodded, motioning for Sun-Wang to take a seat as he returned to his desk chair. "I'm sorry, but I'm a bit distracted. We've been having some unexpected . . . uh, success with our research lately."

"Congratulations," Sun-Wang smiled politely. "I hope I'm not disturbing—"

"No, no," Isaac shook his head, thoroughly enjoying the euphoric sense of purpose and well-being that had been one of the delightful side effects (in addition to his regained virility) of his unintended ingestion of the B-17 analog. "You're not disturbing anything at all. But, uh, perhaps if you could go into a little more detail as to how I might be able to help you?" Isaac added pleasantly. "You were a bit vague . . ."

"Yes, I know." Tina Sun-Wang nodded, feeling slightly embarrassed as she reached into her purse. "I'm sorry I couldn't tell you more over the phone, but . . ." she said as she laid the leather badge-holder and five Polaroid photographs out on Isaac's desk, "but you see, this project I'm working on is considered very confidential, so I couldn't—Dr. Isaac, is something wrong?"

Tina Sun-Wang suddenly realized that Professor David Isaac's face had turned deathly pale.

"Where . . . did you get these?" Isaac asked as he reached out to pick up the polaroid photographs, his widened eyes switching back and forth between the shockingly clear photographs of the Eagle Mountain lab and the San Diego Police criminalist's badge.

"That's what I wanted to talk to you about," Sun-Wang said. "You see, I've just recently hired on with the San Diego Police Department . . . in their crime lab . . . and I've sort of volunteered to go into an underground lab, in the role of a dope chemist."

"You're working for the Police Department . . ." Isaac re-peated, seemingly unable to believe his eyes *or* his ears.

"Yes, I know it sounds a bit crazy." Sun-Wang shrugged apolo-getically, "but since I know very little about making illicit drugs, I asked them if I could come over here and talk with you . . . thinking that perhaps you could—"

"—teach you to make illegal drugs?" Isaac whispered in-credulously.

"Oh, no." Sun-Wang grinned self-consciously, still far too inex-perienced in law enforcement matters to recognize the expression on Isaac's face for what it was. "Not exactly, anyway. I mean that'd be great, but mostly I just need to learn a few tricks—you know, magic stuff—so I can look the part. I remembered you were always giving talks on alchemy in your undergraduate classes, so I thought maybe you could teach me—"

"To be an alchemist?" Isaac whispered weakly.

"Yes, I suppose that's about it." Sun-Wang nodded uneasily, wondering what she had said or done to cause Isaac to become so upset all of a sudden.

"And this is the, ah, underground lab you intend to go into?" the stunned professor asked.

"I suppose." Sun-Wang shrugged. "Actually, to tell you the truth, we don't really know for sure. The person who's gonna take me in—vouch for me . . ." she smiled self-consciously again, ". . . gave us the photographs, but he hasn't said where the lab is yet. I'm supposed to go out there with him this Friday, day after tomorrow—assuming that I can get ready in time," she added.

"So you don't even know where this lab is, then?" Isaac asked, wanting to be absolutely sure.

"No, we don't." Tina Sun-Wang shook her head. "The detective in charge of the case says it's typical for a, ah, snitch not to say where we're going. As I understand it, that way he still has something to bargain with."

"I—see," Isaac said, feeling his heart pounding loudly.

"Actually, we don't even know for sure that this *is* a dope lab," Sun-Wang went on. "That's why I brought the photographs. I thought perhaps you could give me an idea of what they might be making."

"Fascinating," Isaac said, nodded his head slowly as he picked up the photographs and made a show of examining them closely, while his mind churned, trying to reason it all out. Then, after a few more moments, he put them down and looked up at Sun-Wang.

"I don't think I can tell you what's being made in this lab," he said numbly, his voice seeming unnaturally loud in his ears. "I don't see anything unusual about the setup, but I suppose we can come up with a few, ah, magic tricks to help you look the part of an—underground chemist."

"Wonderful," Sun-Wang started to say—

"However," Isaac went on, "before I can do something like this, I'll have to get approval from the department chairman." He rose from his chair.

"Uh, excuse me, professor," Tina Sun-Wang said, suddenly very uncertain, "but I'm not sure you can do that."

"Oh, why is that?" Isaac asked, his stunned mind coming alert.

"This operation—you see, I guess it's supposed to be kept secret. I mean, they let me come out here and talk with you 'cause I told them you were highly thought of at the university, but—"

"I see." Isaac nodded, unable to accept the ridiculous possibility that all of this was just some sort of horribly ironic coincidence. "Uh, perhaps if I simply alluded to the, ah, nature of the problem, without going into any specifics?"

"I suppose—I guess that'd be all right." Sun-Wang shrugged, still a little uncertain.

"Fine." Isaac nodded hurriedly, reaching up to his bookshelf and taking down a well-used textbook. "Then perhaps if you glanced through this while I get things worked out with the university—uh, perhaps you'd like some coffee while you're waiting? I can have my assistant bring you a cup. Sugar or cream?"

"Black'd be fine." Sun-Wang nodded, startled by the friendly treatment she was receiving.

"Maria," Isaac called out through his doorway, "could you please bring our young friend here a cup of coffee?" Isaac waited for the acknowledgment of Nichole Faysonnt, and then turned to Sun-Wang. "Please don't go away, I'll be back in just a very few minutes," he smiled, and then disappeared through the doorway.

In the locked confines of his private laboratory, Professor Isaac spent five long, nerve-rattling minutes trying unsuccessfully to log into Jimmy Pilgrim's message-switching system.

Then, as he watched the cryptic words "INCORRECT ACCESS CODE" flash up on the screen once again, he heard a gentle knock at the locked door.

"Yes, who is it?" Isaac demanded, trying desperately to calm himself down—and to *think*—

"It's me."

Isaac hurried over and opened the door, motioning for Nichole to hurry inside before he closed and locked the door again.

"What's the matter?" Nichole Faysonnt asked.

"Police," Isaac whispered, even though his office—where Tina Sun-Wang was presumably still sitting—was a good thirty feet across the main lab from the locked door.

"What?" Nichole's mouth dropped open.

"Sun-Wang," Isaac said. "One of Allen Bacon's grad students last year. Now she works for the San Diego Police Department." Isaac hurriedly described his startling conversation with the newly-hired forensic scientist.

"My God," Nichole whispered. "I mean, it has to be a trap, doesn't it?"

"I think so." Isaac nodded.

"Then what—?"

"I don't know," Isaac admitted, shaking his head, "but we've got to do something very quickly."

Jimmy Pilgrim was painfully standing beside Raynee's desk in the underground office, his furious eyes fixed on the two still-unconscious bodies (Raynee and Schultzheimer being occupied in searching the handcuffed, semiconscious Shannon) when the phone rang.

"Who?" Pilgrim demanded, glaring down at Raynee.

"Don't know." Raynee looked up and shrugged. "Like you said, nobody's supposed t' be callin' in here any more since we got them computers."

"Get them out of here," Pilgrim directed.

Pilgrim let the phone ring four more times, before finally picking it up.

"Hello?" he growled.

"This is Isaac." The nervous professor spoke hurriedly. "I—"

"What are you *doing*, calling here?" Pilgrim furiously demanded. "I *told* you to use the computer if you—"

"Goddamn it, I tried," Isaac whispered insistently, trying to keep his voice low, "but I couldn't log in. Somebody must have changed my password."

"WHAT?" Pilgrim practically screamed. "What do you *mean*—?" and then he remembered the girl typing frantically at the terminal just before it had been destroyed. And what had Raynee said? Something about them working to "fix" the computer before—

"God-*damn*—" Jimmy Pilgrim began to rage when Isaac's next

words suddenly jarred at his mind. "What did you say?" he shouted, and then listened in growing horror as the professor described the sudden, incomprehensible appearance of Tina Sun-Wang.

"You're *sure* they don't know where the lab is?" Jimmy Pilgrim demanded when Isaac had finished, trying to think who else—besides Raynee, Schultzheimer, Drobeck, and his highly trusted three-man guard team—knew the location of the Eagle Mountain prototype lab.

No one. Which meant it couldn't be the mountain lab that the police were focused on, Pilgrim decided. And the first of his one hundred planned franchise labs wouldn't be ready until at least Saturday. Which left . . .

"I . . . I don't think so," Isaac finally answered. "The girl said something about being taken out to the lab this Friday though. Some—snitch, I think she said, is supposed to take her in."

. . . Anza-Borrego, and Bobby Lockwood, Pilgrim nodded, smiling coldly to himself as the pieces fell together, remembering now how Lockwood had reacted to the news of Jamie MacKenzie's punishment. And now that MacKenzie had died . . .

Of course.

In a curious way, Jimmy Pilgrim was almost proud of how the youth had apparently decided to take his revenge. Offering to take a police chemist into one of Jimmy Pilgrim's labs was an impressively calculated act of defiance . . . which just might work out very nicely, Pilgrim thought, now that he needed another decoy to keep Locotta occupied for two or three days.

Unfortunately, sacrificing the Anza-Borrego lab would probably mean the loss of Drobeck too, Pilgrim realized, but that was a minor problem. It was much more important that Locotta find his "alchemist" . . . or at least *think* that he had.

Then Pilgrim remembered the twenty-two one-pound bricks of cocaine he'd taken back from the pound dealers in a two-for-one exchange for the Rainbow-Vision analog. The ones he'd ordered Drobeck to store in the Eagle Mountain hideaway.

"Rainbow," Pilgrim called, covering the mouthpiece of the phone with his hand, "get hold of Drobeck . . . *right now*. Tell him to cancel delivery on that coke to the mountain. Tell him to stay down at the Borrego lab and help with the analogs."

"What if he's already gone?"

"He won't be." Pilgrim shook his head. "Son of a bitch hates to get up early.

"Okay," Pilgrim grunted at Isaac after removing his hand from the mouthpiece, "I'll take care of it. Now what's this I'm hearing about some A-seventeen powder being some kind of aphrodisiac? What do you know about that?"

"The Seventeen analog? That was one of the first two I sent you. Remember, that one and the thiopene," Isaac said. "You people tested it . . . said it wasn't any good."

"Yes . . . I remember," Pilgrim growled, remembering in fact that it had been Bylighter who had first handled the vials of the new analogs . . . and how they'd lost critical production days during the confusion over the initial testing. So that now, instead of having a stockpile of the B-16 Rainbow-Vision on hand to carry out the first phase of his devious game, Pilgrim was having to push everything, taking risks just at the time when Jake and his headhunters were on the streets, searching with growing desperation for Pilgrim's rogue team . . . and for his alchemist.

Especially his alchemist.

But once he had those hundred franchised labs in place, and the batches of analogs cooking, Pilgrim reminded himself, it would be too late. If Jake Locotta wanted to remain in the dope business, he'd have to come to Jimmy Pilgrim . . . just like all the others. Because Jimmy would be the only one with access to Dr. David Isaac and his wondrous analogs. And it was going to stay that way, even if *he* had to be the one to destroy the creative source of the long-dreamed-of chemicals.

It would all be a matter of timing, Pilgrim knew, and he didn't have much time left. Things were happening much too quickly, especially the unexpected things that he simply couldn't have anticipated, no matter how carefully he'd planned the game.

For a brief moment, Jimmy Pilgrim regretted having given Raynee the go-ahead to eliminate the wretched little gofer—their first planned decoy—if only because now he wanted to experience the pleasure of ripping Bylighter's throat out with his bare hands for costing him all that valuable time.

Now he had to deal with the awesome possibility that this A-17 analog—the one they'd had in their hands ten days ago—just *might* be the "alchemist's dream" they'd been waiting for.

"The cookbook for the A-seventeen . . . is it available now?" Pilgrim demanded.

"The procedure's in the computer." Isaac hedged. "But I can't . . ."

"We're going to fix the computer," Pilgrim snarled. "I mean right *now*. What about your notes?"

"You told us to destroy—"

"I *know* what I *told* you to do," Pilgrim whispered menacingly. "I'm asking you—"

"We've got a lab notebook that I keep locked up," Isaac admitted. "The procedure's in there."

"Good," Pilgrim said, closing his eyes for a moment to clear his mind, refusing to allow himself to lose control now. "Can you get out of there, right now, without her getting suspicious?"

"Uh—I suppose, but—"

"I want to see you up at that lab, as soon as you can possibly get there," Pilgrim growled, deciding that it was definitely time to take Dr. David Isaac out of circulation. "And make *sure* you bring that notebook with you," he added emphatically.

"B-but I thought you said—it'd be too dangerous for us to meet?" Isaac stammered.

"Do you still want the rest of the Maria documents?" Pilgrim asked.

"What?"

"You meet me up there with that notebook, the rest of the pages are yours. It's a two-and-a-half hour drive. You'd better get going," he whispered coldly.

Jimmy Pilgrim slammed the phone down, made two quick outside calls to set his decoy-trap in motion, and then turned to Raynee.

"You and Roy stay here," he ordered. "Find out who those jokers *are*, and then hook up one of the spare terminals. I'll patch in from the mountain lab, soon as I get that little bitch to tell me what she did to the computer."

Then, motioning for his three Uzi-bearing guards to follow, Pilgrim went into the back office, grabbed the still-unconscious Sandy Mudd by the front of her shirt and dragged her toward the door to the underground garage, yelling over his shoulder, "And don't forget, keep Drobeck at that Borrego lab!"

Professor David Isaac turned to Nichole and said, "He wants me to meet him up at Eagle Mountain and bring the A-seventeen procedure. Say's he'll give us the rest of the Maria documents in exchange for your notebook."

Nichole Faysonnt looked at the red-cloth notebook in her hands, staring at the label where her name had been crossed out . . . and replaced by the name that Isaac called her now.

Maria.

"That means he doesn't think he needs you any more," she whispered. "He'll—kill you if you go up there."

"You're right," Isaac nodded. "But what he doesn't realize is that I don't need *him* any more either." Isaac put his hands on either side of the girl's face and then kissed her gently. "Why would I want Maria's lab notebook . . . when I have Maria herself, right here?" He kissed her again and they held each other tightly for a moment, both lost in their own analog-enhanced illusions.

"Then what . . . ?" Nichole finally asked.

"Collect everything we'll need to produce Eighteen that we can't buy without attracting attention," Isaac said, reaching up to a nearby shelf and starting to put small vials of expensive chemicals into his worn briefcase.

"Then you're not—?"

Isaac shook his head. "There's only one thing we *can* do if we're going to survive . . . and continue with our work." He looked back at Nichole—the young graduate student who had somehow truly become his fantasized Maria. "We have to run."

Jake Locotta was drinking coffee in his kitchen that Wednesday morning, determinedly ignoring the sounds made by Joe Tassio's men as they transferred the four sheet-wrapped bodies into the trunks of two vehicles. Then the phone rang.

Tassio answered it, listened for a moment, and then looked up at Locotta with a wide, malicious smile on his face. "Looks like that million got some people's attention," he said. "We just got a tip on Jimmy Pilgrim's lab."

Tina Sun-Wang had been sitting in Dr. David Isaac's office for almost fifteen minutes before she got bored with the extremely "dry" textbook and started looking around the professor's book-and-paper-filled office.

Seeing very little that appeared to be interesting, Sun-Wang stared at the complex chemical structures drawn on the blackboard behind her chair. Deciding to see how much she still remembered about chemical nomenclature, she started to code out the first of the multiringed compounds . . .

. . . and got as far as "one-one-two-thienyl-cyclohexyl-" when the alarm bells started.

Tina sat there feeling her upper spine and hands start to tingle—as she went back over the nomenclature again, convinced that she must have made a mistake because . . .

"One-one-two-thienyl-cyclohexyl . . . piperidine, oh, God," she whispered to herself.

Tina stared at the incomprehensible blackboard for another thirty seconds before she stood up and walked over to the doorway entrance to the main lab. The girl—what was her name, Maria?—was nowhere in sight.

Then, not believing that all of this was really happening, Sun-Wang grabbed for the telephone book next to Isaac's desk, quickly located the number for the San Diego Sheriff's Department and dialed the number on Isaac's phone with trembling fingers.

"Detective Martin DeLaura, and please hurry. This is an emergency," she whispered when the desk officer answered.

It took exactly twenty-three seconds for Sergeant Wilbur Hallstead to pick up DeLaura's phone. Sun-Wang knew that because she counted every one by the slowly-sweeping second hand on the wall clock over Isaac's desk as she listened nervously for the sound of approaching footsteps.

"Hallstead."

"This is Tina Sun-Wang, from the San Diego Police Department. I have to talk to Detective DeLaura immediately."

"Say, aren't you the one from the PD lab who's—"

"Yes, that's right. Listen, please, I—"

"DeLaura left here a little while ago," Hallstead said. "He said he was going out to U.C.S.D. to meet you somewhere."

"Oh no—listen, can you get him on the radio?"

"I imagine so," Hallstead shrugged. "Is it serious?"

"Yes, I think so," Sun-Wang nodded nervously. "If you can, tell him I'm in Dr. David Isaac's office, at the main chemistry building, third floor, and that he'd better hurry. There's something crazy going on around here . . . and I think I may have done something terribly wrong."

A tired, sweaty Bobby Lockwood hurried down the stairs into the basement of the Anza-Borrego lab and picked up the phone just as it began to ring for the fourth time.

"Yeah," he said, and then came alert immediately as he recognized the enraged voice of Rainbow.

"Where you been?" Raynee demanded. "Ah been tryin' t' call you."

"I, uh, just went outside for a few minutes," Lockwood said hurriedly. "Trying to get some air. These chemicals . . ."

"Drobeck," Raynee spat. "Where is he? I wanna talk t' him."

"Uh, he left here early this morning . . . couple hours ago," Lockwood said. "Said he was goin' up to the mountain."

"He take them bricks with him?"

"Yeah, sure." Lockwood nodded. "He said you told him—"

"Shit!" Raynee snarled. "Listen t' me, you *stay* in that lab where Ah can get hold a' you. The Pilgrim an' me, we're gonna be comin' down there, checkin' on that next batch this afternoon." Then he slammed down the phone.

Bobby Lockwood stood thoughtfully in the sandy, ether-soaked confines of the underground lab for a few moments. Whether it was the edge to Raynee's voice, or the fumes, or the realization that he was playing a horribly dangerous game, Lockwood didn't know, but somewhere in his mind, a small, nervous voice was telling him to get his butt in gear.

He put down the phone, walked outside in the warm morning sun, got into his car, and began driving very fast out on the main road in the direction of the Palm Springs airport, about ninety winding desert miles away—very intent on putting himself on the first plane heading anywhere in the direction of Anchorage, Alaska.

Lockwood had decided that it was probably a very good time to start paying attention to some of his late father's useful advice, and take a very sharp turn away from the directed pathway of his life, preferably as quickly as he could get his feet in motion.

He almost made it.

30

IN SETTING HIS decoy-trap for Locotta's men, Jimmy Pilgrim made three perfectly reasonable assumptions:

One, that the tipped presence of Simon Drobeck, Bobby Lockwood and an in-production batch of the Rainbow-Vision at the Anza-Borrego lab would draw the attention of Jake Locotta and Joe Tassio.

Two, that the promised arrival of himself and Rainbow at the desert lab this afternoon—to check on that latest batch of Rainbow-Vision—would be enough to keep Locotta in place for a couple of hours, regardless of what Drobeck might be forced to reveal about the Eagle Mountain lab.

And three, that the presence of twenty-two pound-bricks of cocaine in the Borrego lab, when the San Diego County sheriff's deputies arrived to check out their latest anonymous tip, would make things extremely difficult for Locotta . . . at least for two or three days, which was all the time that Pilgrim needed.

But it didn't quite work out that way.

Spotting Bobby Lockwood's rapidly departing vehicle from the

air, Locotta abandoned his surveillance of the cinder-block home and
directed his helicopter pilot to run the fleeing vehicle off the road,
while Tassio's jeeps and sedans immediately converged on Pilgrim's
reported lab.

Ten minutes later, a terrified Bobby Lockwood found himself
tied to a chair in the basement of the Anza-Borrego lab, frantically
telling Jake everything he knew about the analogs, Simon Drobeck,
the "alchemist" who had apparently designed the prototype lab that
was "somewhere up in some mountains, about a three-hour drive from
San Diego," and Jimmy Pilgrim's planned inspection of the desert lab.
At the same time, Joe Tassio used the lab phone to check in on the
small army of men who were still sweeping the southern half of California for Jimmy Pilgrim and Rainbow.

Jake Locotta was just about ready to assure himself—with some
carefully applied pain—that the tearfully cooperative youth really
didn't know where Pilgrim's mountain lab was located, when Joe Tassio
yelled excitedly from across the basement.

"Jake, they spotted Pilgrim!"

"Where?" Locotta demanded, abandoning the as-yet-
unharmed Lockwood and hurrying over to the wall phone.

"Just a second," Tassio shook his head, listening . . . and then
turned to Locotta with a wide, malicious smile on his craggy face.
"Palomar Airport, near Oceanside. Pilot, three bodyguards and a girl
with him. He took off in a chopper about a half hour ago, heading
northeast. We got a plane up over him now."

Locotta's eyes gleamed with barely repressed rage and anticipation. "Get some people to take this place apart, brick by brick," he
said, smiling at his chief enforcer. "You and me, we're gonna handle
this fuckin' tag, *personal!*"

Thus, by the time that the late-arriving San Diego sheriff's
deputies—accompanied by Paul Reinhart—finally swarmed over the
Anza-Borrego lab in response to Jimmy Pilgrim's anonymously called-
in tip, they found very little of actual interest . . . other than some
residue in a disassembled pile of dirty lab glassware, five professionally
silent mob enforcers who quickly surrendered, and a desperately
grateful youth named Bobby Lockwood—whom the otherwise distracted gunmen hadn't gotten around to yet.

The physical effort involved in moving the twenty-two pound-
bricks of cocaine into the living room of the Eagle Mountain cabin
didn't appeal to Simon Drobeck in the least. Among other things, it
involved walking back and forth from the car to the cabin seven sepa-

rate times before Drobeck got the last of the plastic-wrapped packages inside.

It was the type of job that Drobeck would normally have assigned to Bobby Lockwood without a second thought. However, aside from the security problems (which the obese chemist might well have ignored anyway), today was a very special day for Drobeck.

Today was his birthday . . . and the morning that he'd purposely set aside to play in the Eagle Mountain laboratory all by himself. Although that wasn't quite accurate, because Drobeck wasn't going to be *all* by himself.

On the eighth trip from the car, Simon Drobeck brought in his glistening python wrapped protectively around his waist and shoulder. There was still one thing that could ruin his birthday celebration, Drobeck reminded himself as he switched on the lights and entered the basement, unmindful of the strong ether odors that permeated the air. It was entirely possible that the elusive kangaroo rat had found a way out of the underground laboratory. Drobeck had carefully plugged up two access holes he'd found in one of the window frames and the door, but still . . .

Then, as Drobeck shut the door and slipped his treasured pet down to the cool concrete floor, he heard the scurrying of tiny feet in a pile of shredded paper scraps . . . and smiled in anticipatory pleasure.

Drobeck had intended to amuse himself by playing with the new computer terminal while his hungry pet began its slithering hunt, but he quickly discovered that the computer no longer recognized his assigned password as being valid.

Distracted, and insulated in the tightly secured basement lab, Drobeck never heard the whumping sounds of the flared rotor blades. Instead, confused and slightly irritated by the unexpected problem, Drobeck almost missed the event that he had waited for—even dreamt about—for so long.

Sensing the tension in the air, Drobeck slowly turned in his chair just as the python deliberately brought its head and neck back into the characteristic S-shaped position as it inched forward, its eyes fixed on the furry, white, long-tailed rodent that had stopped to concentrate on its own new-found interest: the tasty insulation on the yards of wiring installed by Professor David Isaac.

As Simon Drobeck took a slow deep breath, and then held it expectantly, the thick-bodied reticulated python made yet another millimeter adjustment in its tensed position . . . then lunged forward, the snake's blurring head snapping tightly over the tiny, distracted mammal.

In the span of an eye-blink, four things happened virtually simultaneously:

The tiny kangaroo rat, realizing at the very last what was about to happen, tried to open its mouth to squeal in protest, and then had its sharp teeth driven deep into the insulated wire by the sudden compression of the snake's merciless jaws.

The subsequent twisting motion of the python's heavy recoiling body caused the small rodent's teeth to snap several of the thin copper strands within the insulated cable . . .

. . . which, due to the intimate contact being made between the "hot" wire of the vacuum pump and the teeth of the hunted and hunter, caused one hundred and thirteen volts to surge through the nervous tissue of the two grossly dissimilar animals . . .

. . . and which also—because the kangaroo rat had long since chewed through the ground wire so carefully installed by Isaac many days earlier—created a brief spark that ignited the low-lying ether fumes . . .

. . . just as Jimmy Pilgrim's three guards kicked in the door to the basement lab, and just as Drobeck took in a last, deeply satisfied breath of air, that for a very brief moment felt like liquid fire pouring into his lungs, the basement windows exploded outward in a roar of searing flame.

Ben Koda drifted up into the hazy range of semi-consciousness, wondering why someone seemed to be trying very hard to kick his limp body across a concrete floor.

"Come on . . . thass it, wake up," Charley Shannon hissed, nudging at his partner once again with one of his size-fifteen boots.

"Where . . ." Koda whispered weakly, grabbing his aching head as he became vaguely aware that—wherever they were—it really *was* pitch dark.

He tried to lift his head up off the cold concrete, but decided to put it right back down where it belonged before he threw up. Somewhere in his unfocused mind, the word "concussion" was whispered as he tried to remember how and why . . . and then did.

"Sandy," Koda rasped, fighting back the waves of nausea that seemed to originate deep in his stomach. "Where is she . . ."

"Pilgrim took her," Shannon growled in the darkness. "Heard him say he was going up to some lab. Gonna make her tell him how to fix his computer back up."

Ben moved his head slowly—trying to determine how badly he was hurt—and finally decided that it was mostly bruised muscles and nerves. Nothing seemed to be broken or cut. He was trying not to think about Sandy . . . and Pilgrim . . . and Rainbow.

"Where the hell are we?" Koda finally asked, after taking in several deep breaths.

"Room next to Raynee's office," Shannon muttered. "Threw us in here a few minutes ago. Crazy-ass motherfucker laughin' 'bout it the whole time, too."

"You okay?"

"Got mah hands cuffed behind mah back," Shannon growled. "Otherwise Ah'm . . ."

"You dudes havin' fun in there?" the tinny voice rasped through the recessed wall speaker over their heads.

"Why don't you come in here and find out, asshole," Ben Koda muttered loudly, figuring that Raynee would probably have the room wired.

"Don't know as Ah'm gonna do *that*." Raynee laughed. "But Ah jes' *might* think 'bout lettin' you boys outta that room, soon's you start tellin' me all 'bout yourselves."

"You know any good reason why we don't want to be in here, outside of the obvious?" Koda whispered to his partner.

"No, but Ah'll bet ya *he's* got one." Shannon's eyes scanned the darkness when he suddenly saw a small, distant yellow spot that seemed to be . . . rising up?

"Been a long time since Charley and I've been scared of the dark, shit-head," Koda called out, his head slightly less fuzzy now that he'd begun to move it around a little.

"That a fact?" Raynee snickered as he and Schultzheimer watched the two men on the TV monitor connected to an infrared-filtered video camera inside the room. A similarly filtered bulb in the ceiling provided all of the necessary light for the remote surveillance system.

"Guess maybe Ah oughta jes' turn them lights back on then, huh?" Raynee continued over the microphone. "'Course, if'n Ah did that, you jes' might figure you liked it better when it was dark," he chuckled. "'xample now, you see them yellow spots ovah there?"

"Left side," Shannon muttered.

"Yeah, I see them," Koda acknowledged. "Looks like some kind of halloween . . . SHIT!"

The light switch that Raynee hit with his hand caused the room in which Koda and Shannon were sitting to be suddenly filled with a dim blue light; more than enough illumination for the two agents and the sixteen-foot king cobra to suddenly see each other. The huge snake reared a good five feet off the floor, flaring its hood in a hissed warning less than twenty feet away from Ben and Charley, who immediately leaped up and backed against a wall, as far away from the snake as they could possibly get.

"Like Ah said, anytime you boys'd like t' come outta there, you jes' start talkin'." Raynee chuckled, watching the two men slide further along the wall as the snake began to move forward, aggressively intent on defending its territory.

"We told you who we were, you crazy-ass son of a bitch!" Koda yelled at the now-visible camera as he and Charley kept moving, trying to keep from being cornered by the slowly weaving, slowly stalking reptile in a room that was suddenly much too small.

"Okay, *that* the way you gonna be . . ."

Jimmy Pilgrim had designed the game room—and the game— that Raynee's Rainbow-personality enjoyed so much. In fact, Pilgrim had insisted on being the one to initiate the game . . . by sitting in the dark room for a full hour, and thereby impressing the holy shit out of Raynee, who watched the fearsome reptile on the video monitor slither past Jimmy Pilgrim's unmoving legs five separate times during that hour . . . not knowing (as Pilgrim certainly did) that cobras lacked the heat-sensing organs of their distant pit viper relatives.

". . . maybe Ah'll jes' find out how scared a' the dark you boys really are." Raynee chuckled as he flicked the switch again, causing everything in the room to suddenly disappear into a sea of black. Everything, that is, except the pair of angry yellow eyes hovering now in midair and then moving closer . . .

The sound of Schultzheimer loading his shotgun distracted Raynee for a moment, so he didn't see Koda suddenly drop down to his knees in front of his partner—who was still straining to get his arms free from behind his back.

"Watch the eyes, and don't move!" Koda whispered as he worked desperately with his numbed fingers. "Tell me when it gets close."

"Shit, it's already *close*," Shannon said shakily. "Whatever you got in mind, you better *hurry*."

"How far?" Koda asked, trying not to listen to the rustling sounds of the snake's thick body as it slithered across the rough concrete floor.

"It's gettin' *close*, man. *Real* close." Charley Shannon whispered, feeling as though he was being hypnotized by the swaying movements of the fiercely gleaming yellow discs that were growing larger . . . becoming more sharply defined . . .

"Now Ah *know* you're not praying' down there . . ." Raynee's laughing voice echoed through the room as he tried to pan the camera down . . . while the equally amused Schultzheimer put his shotgun down against the desk, moving in closer for a better view of the video screen.

"Lift your foot up, NOW!" Koda yelled, and sprang to his feet, swinging around and thrusting his boot-covered hand out at the gleaming eyes as they lunged forward with a guttural, hiss-like expulsion of air from the snake's wide-open mouth.

Ben felt the solid impact all the way down his arm as the massive king cobra struck at the boot-sole in the darkness. At that same instant Shannon let out a bellowing roar that almost completely masked the metallic tearing sounds of handcuffs being wrenched apart.

Hovering on the edge of total panic, and acting before he had a chance to think about what he was doing—because he knew he didn't dare stop to think about it—Koda grabbed out at a patch of blackness just below a savagely gleaming yellow eye . . . and suddenly found himself thrashing around on the concrete floor, desperately clutching the thick, swollen, twisting neck of the unbelievably strong sixteen-foot snake with both hands as he fought to keep the furiously searching mouth—with its deadly fangs—away from any part of his body.

"What the hell . . . ?" Raynee yelled. He was still staring at the thrashing green body on the monitor, when the wall in front of him suddenly exploded in a flying spray of plaster and ancient weapons as Shannon came tearing through the two-by-four studs and plasterboard with a look of maniacal rage in his eyes.

Before either Raynee or Schultzheimer could react, the screaming Shannon threw a jagged two-foot chunk of solid two-by-four like a boomerang, catching Raynee square across the face. The impact sent the street dealer tumbling over the top of his desk in a cursing pile of flailing arms and legs.

Momentarily shocked into immobility by the sight of the oncoming Shannon, Schultzheimer started for his shotgun, realized he'd never reach it in time, and then came up out of the chair in an aggressive stance just as Shannon lunged forward with the rest of the splintered stud held high in both hands.

Screaming in rage, Shannon swung the six-foot length of two-by-four down like an ax—viciously shattering it against Schultzheimer's instinctively upraised arm—and then dove across the desk after the falling martial arts-trained killer.

Raynee came staggering up to his feet on the far side of the desk with blood flowing freely from his mouth and nose, and a throw-ing knife upraised in his right hand. At that moment a wide-eyed Koda stumbled through the hole in the wall with the head-end of the hiss-ing, thrashing cobra still clutched tightly in his hands.

Ben Koda and Raynee saw each other at the same instant, Koda twisting to the floor amid the thrashing coils of the cobra just as Raynee's arm blurred forward, sending the heavy-bladed knife thud-ding deep into the wall just barely above Koda's head.

Raynee started to reach for another knife, but he heard and then saw Roy's thick neck crack and snap loudly under the relentless pressure of Charley Shannon's arms. Snarling, Raynee grabbed the medieval battle-ax off the nearby wall, just as Koda managed to scram-ble to his feet with sixteen thrashing feet of enraged king cobra twist-ing and coiling around his hands.

Raynee never saw him coming.

Raynee's mouth peeled back in a blood-crazed grin, as he brought the gleaming, wide-bladed ax up over his shoulder with his right hand—aiming for Charley Shannon's wide, exposed back. He was starting into his throw just as Koda lunged forward with a savage snarl and heaved the furiously hissing snake, head-first, at the street killer.

Raynee heard the cobra coming even before he turned to look, threw up his left arm instinctively, and then screamed in horror as the snake's wide-scaled head clamped down tightly over his wrist, burying the poisonous fangs deep.

Then, before either Charley or Ben could react, Raynee threw his arm across the desk-top . . . and drove the sharp, rounded edge of the ancient fighting ax down through his own lower arm, just above the cobra's flattened head. Emitting first an agonized scream, then a horrible grunt of pain and shock, Raynee dropped the ax and imme-diately clamped his right hand tightly around the cleanly severed wrist that had started pumping bright arterial blood across the jagged ends of the now-exposed white forearm bones.

Rainbow stood wide-eyed with his bleeding wrist pressed tight against his now-blood-soaked shirt, a look of murderous insanity on his blood-smeared face as he stared down at his clawed black hand being twisted about in the frenzied jaws of the cobra. Then the underground office was rocked by a concussive blast as Charley Shannon triggered an explosive charge of buckshot from Roy's shotgun that shredded both the head of the still-biting snake and Raynee's severed hand.

In the ear-ringing silence that followed Raynee stared at the murderous expression in Shannon's eyes, and made a screaming, lunging dive at Koda with a straight razor that had suddenly appeared in his right hand, only to fall headlong when his foot slipped on the bloody floor.

Numbed by the shock, the pain, and the full expectation of imminent death, Raynee staggered to his feet again, a horribly agonizing task because he had to drop the razor in order to keep his right hand clutched tightly around his rapidly bleeding wrist. Wobbling on his shock-weakened legs, he watched helplessly as Shannon racked the expended casing out of the shotgun and chambered a second round into the smoking weapon that was now deliberately aimed at his groin.

Charley didn't understand at all when Koda yelled, "No . . . don't kill him!"

"Why?" Shannon demanded, his thick finger already tightening on the trigger.

"'Cause we're gonna need the son of a bitch to get Sandy back," Koda growled as he kicked aside the still-thrashing remains of the cobra and reached down for Raynee's blood-splattered desk phone.

31

At 9:05 wednesday morning, a very preoccupied Detective DeLaura drove into the parking lot next to the main chemistry building on the U.C.S.D. campus, and had just pulled in next to a battered VW bug when he noticed two people in white lab coats—a man in his early thirties and a much younger woman—running in his direction.

Distracted by a number of interconnected problems, which included the unknown whereabouts of his longtime buddy Ben Koda, the now-occurring raid on a lab out in Anza-Borrego, and the seemingly panicked call from Tina Sun-Wang that the dispatcher had briefly summarized over the radio, DeLaura did something that he normally wouldn't have done . . . except that he happened to be distracted, concerned, and very much in a hurry.

Intending only to stop the running pair and ask for quick directions to Dr. David Isaac's lab, DeLaura stepped away from the detective unit, reached into his jacket pocket, pulled out the leather billfold with his gold police shield, and held it out in front of the oncoming

382

young woman—just as he spotted another distant figure who looked very much like Tina Sun-Wang come running out of the nearby building . . .

. . . whereupon DeLaura suddenly found himself being physically attacked by a hysterically screaming Nichole Faysonnt as Isaac dropped his briefcase in the middle of the parking lot and stood there, pale and shaking, with his hands over his head.

Koda was cautiously standing just inside an open garage door two houses down from Raynee's Del Mar residence, with Roy Schultzheimer's shotgun in his hands, as he watched a sedan driven by Tom Fogarty roar into the driveway.

"Where's Charley?" Fogarty demanded as Koda stuck his head in through the open passenger window.

"In the van," Koda said, nodding back at Raynee's black van parked inside the garage.

"Rainbow alive?"

"Last time I looked." Koda shrugged. "But he's not talking. So where we going?"

"U.C.S.D., chemistry building," Fogarty growled. "Get your ass in gear. They're waiting for us."

Koda ran back to the van to confer with Charley for a moment before jumping into Fogarty's sedan, barely managing to shut the door before Tom had the vehicle into reverse and squealing back out of the driveway.

"Any word on Sandy?" Koda asked.

"Sheriff's SWAT team hit the lab at Anza-Borrego a little while ago," Fogarty muttered, keeping his eyes on the twisting road. "Found DeLaura's snitch and a bunch of Locotta's muscle. Looked like they were taking the place apart trying to find something. No sign of Pilgrim or Sandy."

"Shit," Koda snarled. "So what the hell're we going out to U.C.S.D. for?" he demanded, his dark eyes flashing with frustrated anger. "Jesus Christ, Tom, we're running out of fuckin' *time*! Either get one of the techs out here to hook up another terminal to that computer line, so we can offer Pilgrim a straight deal, Sandy for Rainbow, or let Charley and me go out in the desert someplace where we can *talk* to the son of a bitch."

Fogarty ignored Koda's comments for a moment. "I think we've got a third option," he said finally. "DeLaura's out at the university right now. We think he's found Pilgrim's alchemist. . . ."

By the time a singed, dazed but otherwise unhurt Jimmy Pilgrim went back to the helicopter and helped his pilot drag the semiconscious form of Sandy Mudd into the slightly damaged living room of the Eagle Mountain cabin, the fire had pretty much burned itself out.

It was so high and isolated, it was doubtful that anyone else had heard the explosion or seen the flames that burned clean in what remained of the basement laboratory, because, aside from the few bottles of highly flammable solvents, there wasn't much else in the basement that would burn easily. Except, of course, for the clothes and hair and skin on the three grossly dissimilar charred bodies that lay still in the middle of the blackened concrete floor, and the three less-charred bodies of Pilgrim's own guards sprawled in the blast-damaged stairwell.

Having known that smell before, Pilgrim knew what he'd find downstairs, so he really wasn't in a great hurry to go there. Instead, he and the pilot dragged the bound, gagged and struggling Mudd into the living room and threw her onto a chair next to a nice, neat stack of plastic-wrapped bricks. The twenty-two pounds of high-grade cocaine that Simon Drobeck had delivered to the mountain lab.

The presence of the shiny-white pound-bricks, as much as anything else, told Pilgrim how badly the situation had deteriorated in the last few hours. The decoy-trap he'd counted on to give him those extra two days had never fallen into place. All he could do now was to quickly get the altered password to his computer records from Mudd, find the mountain lab's computer terminal, print out the procedure for that incredible A-17 analog . . . and then disappear.

When Pilgrim finally did walk down to the basement, there was little question what actually caused the normally cold and indifferent mob boss to sink into momentary dispair.

Having indifferently stepped around the torn bodies of his three loyal guards—and almost completely ignoring Drobeck's horribly burned body—Pilgrim stood and stared in dismay at the shattered remains of the burned-out computer terminal.

Realizing that the success of his entire operation—his intricate game plan to irrevocably alter and control the sale of illicit drugs in the United States—was now dependent on the timely arrival of a university professor and a laboratory notebook, he could only stare despondently at the blackened remains of his prototype laboratory.

He was still lost in his thoughts when he heard the sound of helicopter rotors. Realizing that his pilot might be having doubts about hanging around the now-dangerous mountain top lab site, Pilgrim ran up the stairs . . . and found himself staring into the cold, murderous eyes of Jake Locotta.

After complaining loudly about the waste of valuable time, Charley Shannon backed Raynee's van into the basement of the U.C.S.D. chemistry building in response to Tom Fogarty's direct order that Raynee's severed wrist receive some sort of medical treatment.

It wasn't that Fogarty really *cared* whether Rainbow—the man who had viciously murdered two of his agents—died of infection, a bullet, the gas chamber . . . or by strangulation at Fogarty's own hands, for that matter. He was simply trying to balance, as best he could, his obligations as a federal agent supervisor with his equally unswerving determination to recover another one of his agents—*alive*. And if all that happened to involve a slight delay in the hospitalization of a crazed killer like Rainbow, well, that was just too goddamned bad.

"That man needs a doctor," Isaac whispered as the back of the van was opened and the bloody, moaning figure of Raynee became visible.

"What the man *needs* is a body bag," Shannon muttered darkly, dragging Rainbow into an upright position.

"But . . ." Isaac started to protest, and then felt Tom Fogarty's hand on his arm.

"Why don't you come upstairs to your office with us, Doctor, while we give this man some medical attention," Fogarty suggested, motioning the group toward the elevator. "I think it's about time you and I had a very serious talk."

Koda waited until the elevator door closed behind Isaac, Nichole, DeLaura, Sun-Wang and Fogarty, made one last check to be sure they were alone in the basement, and then nodded at his partner.

"Gonna be doin' this for your own good, shit-head." Charley Shannon grinned as he wrestled the moaning Raynee over to the edge of the van's doorway.

"You muthahf . . ." Raynee started to curse, and was shut off when Shannon clamped his arms around Raynee's chest and mouth. Ben Koda gripped the severed wrist tightly with his left hand, quickly ripped the makeshift tourniquet and bandages off with his right, and then poured an entire bottle of Merthiolate over the bloody, exposed tissue.

Raynee's bulging eyes rolled back into his head as he tried to scream. Then, mercifully, he fainted from the searing pain, making it easier for the agents to quickly use a pair of small tube clamps and the rest of the emergency first aid kit from Isaac's lab to first clamp off the two severed arteries, then securely bandage and tape Raynee's wrist.

The result wasn't exactly professional, but Koda and Shannon figured it would probably keep Raynee from bleeding to death during the next couple of hours. And that, as far as the special agents were concerned, was a hell of a lot more than a man like Raynee had any right to expect.

Dr. David Isaac and Nichole Faysonnt were sitting together in one corner of his office, opposite the others, when Ben Koda walked in.

"He decide to cooperate?" Koda asked Fogarty.

"Not exactly," the agent supervisor growled.

"As I've just reminded your supervisor, we don't have to say anything without a lawyer present," Isaac said, his reviving confidence shaken by the sight of Koda's blood-spattered shirt and jeans. "If you'll just read us our rights . . ."

"You happen to be a lawyer too, Dr. Isaac?" Koda inquired politely.

"I know my rights." Isaac shook his head insistently. "And I *do* know for a fact that we haven't done anything illegal. Every chemical we've made is perfectly . . ."

". . . deadly?" Koda suggested. "Maybe you'd like us to show you a list of all the people who've died recently on account of your 'legal' chemicals? Fact is, thanks to you, we've got bodies scattered all over Southern California—including a couple federal agent friends of ours," he added coldly.

"But we didn't—you can't charge us for something we had no control over!" Isaac insisted vehemently. "Besides, you can't prove—"

"Actually," Tina Sun-Wang broke in, "there's a good chance that we *can* match the drugs in the bodies right back to your lab." She was still trying to adjust to her drastically altered mental image of Isaac, and she had no idea if what she had just said was really possible, but she figured—correctly—that Isaac wouldn't know either.

"I doubt that—ah, I think I want my lawyer now," Isaac said uneasily, suddenly unnerved by the realization that he and Nichole might be charged with murder.

"For what?" Koda asked.

"Since we're under arrest, we have the absolute right—" Isaac started in when Fogarty interrupted.

"Dr. Isaac, has anyone here actually placed you or your girlfriend under arrest?"

"What? Ah—no," Isaac admitted, suddenly puzzled. "But you—"

"Dr. Isaac," Tom Fogarty said patiently, "so far, all I've done is tell you a hypothetical story about some very vicious criminals who are now actively killing each other over some new kinds of drug analogs. One of them happens to be in that van downstairs. You are *not* under arrest, nor are we preventing you from going anywhere. As a matter of fact, you have every right to insist that we leave your office, right now."

"What. . . ?" Isaac's eyes widened with disbelief.

"You see, in fact, you're absolutely correct," Fogarty smiled coldly. "There really *isn't* much we can charge you with right now, or at least not much that we could actually make stick . . . unless maybe Tina here can really match those drugs of yours back to some bodies," he added thoughtfully.

"But—"

"But," Fogarty went on, his voice turning icy, "those people we've been talking about—the ones who've been killing each other right and left for the past few days over your *perfectly legal* drugs— have got one of our agents. Kidnapped her. We think they took her to a lab up in the mountains somewhere around here. As it happens, it's probably a lab you helped build."

Fogarty hesitated for a moment, conscious of Ben Koda's presence in the room, and then went on.

"Right now, we're figuring she's still alive, because they think she's got something they want awful bad. But when they find out she doesn't have it any more, they're very likely going to kill her. And there's not a whole lot we can do about it without your help."

Fogarty stared straight into Isaac's frightened eyes. "Care to make a guess as to what it is they want?"

"I don't have to—" Isaac started to insist once more, when Ben interrupted.

"Anybody bother to tell you there's a million-dollar contract out on your head?" Koda asked Isaac.

"What . . .?" Isaac blinked.

"One million dollars in cash, if you're brought in alive," Fogarty nodded pleasantly. "Payable upon delivery by Mr. Jake Locotta, Syndicate boss for Southern California. We understand he's not real happy about seeing his multibillion-dollar business in cocaine and heroin go down the drain—thanks to Jimmy Pilgrim and some guy they call the Alchemist. Kinda makes you wonder why Locotta wants you alive, doesn't it?"

"A million dollars?" Nichole whispered, her eyes and mouth

agape.   "My God, that must be why Pilgrim wants us up there—"

"What?" Fogarty's eyebrows came up.

"Nichole," Isaac warned, "don't—"

"Jimmy Pilgrim," Nichole blurted out, shaking her head tearfully. "We're supposed to meet him at the mountain lab this morning. He—he told us—insisted that we bring the procedure to make the A-Seventeen analog—the most potent one so far," she whispered. "We're supposed to be leaving, right now. But we're afraid, because we know—"

"Isaac—" Fogarty started in, and the professor shook his head wildly.

"No, you don't understand—we *can't* help you! They'll—"

"Isaac," Koda whispered menacingly. "We might not be able to charge you with any of the dope, but I'll promise you something. If Sandy dies up there—because of you—I'm gonna personally dust every fuckin' inch of that lab until I find one of your fingerprints."

"But—" Isaac shook his head helplessly.

"And if it turns out I can't make you an accessory to murder," Koda went on, his voice icy cold, "then I'll promise you something else. Doesn't matter *where* you try to go, I'm gonna make goddamn *sure* Locotta knows how to find you."

Koda, Shannon, Sun-Wang, Isaac and Nichole had been talking together for almost fifteen minutes—mostly in quiet tones, waiting for Tom Fogarty to finish making the hurried arrangements—when Isaac's office phone rang.

It was Pilgrim, demanding to know why Isaac hadn't left yet.

"We got delayed. We're leaving right now," Isaac said, watching Ben Koda's slowly nodding head as he reminded Pilgrim that it would take him about two and a half hours to get there. Yes, they were bringing the notebook, Isaac reassured Pilgrim. And yes, they'd hurry. Then he hung up the phone.

Fogarty came into Isaac's office and nodded his head. Everything was ready. It was time to go.

Then Ben turned to Isaac and growled, "You're getting a chance to walk away from all this shit you started, professor. All I can say is, you damn well better hope and pray we can pull it off."

32

"HE'LL BE HERE," Pilgrim whispered grimly as his eyes met those of Jake Locotta for perhaps the fifth time during the first hour that they all sat in the living room . . . waiting.

"Yeah, he better be," Locotta rasped, matching Jimmy Pilgrim's cold expression for a moment before looking at the bloody and semiconscious form of Sandy Mudd on the floor.

Pilgrim had made his life-hanging appeal to Locotta—arguing that he had a hundred labs almost ready to begin making the new analogs, that only by working together could they get an analog production and delivery system going in time to stave off the rest of the enraged Syndicate, and that all they needed now was the cookbook. Pilgrim had also tried to regain some leverage by making a brief, explosive attempt to beat the computer-code information out of the stubbornly silent Mudd . . .

. . . and failed miserably.

Outraged and frustrated by Mudd's mumbled insistence that she didn't know the new codes, Pilgrim worked much too quickly, continuing to beat the defiant young woman with mindless savagery even after she lost consciousness. He only stopped after Locotta threatened to let Tassio and his two grim-faced enforcers take their traitorous associate apart, starting at his knees.

It wasn't any feeling of compassion that had motivated Locotta's calling a halt to Pilgrim's crude interrogation. In fact, considering the rapidly deteriorating situation, Jake Locotta figured he might have to start working on the girl himself—if that was what it was going to take to get his hands on the A-17 analog.

No, the idea of torturing—or even killing—the young woman hadn't concerned Locotta in the least. What had bothered Jake was that his cold, vicious subordinate seemed to be enjoying himself as he slashed his open hand back and forth across her bruised and bleeding face.

Locotta hadn't liked *that* at all, because as far as he was concerned, Jimmy Pilgrim's days for enjoying the sordid pleasures of his criminal life-style had just about come to an end.

In the interval of the next hour and a half, two sedans carrying five more of Jake Locotta's professional gunmen arrived at the Eagle Mountain location, parking their vehicles next to Jimmy Pilgrim's silent helicopter on the dead-end road in front of the cabin.

Locotta's own chopper was already back up in the air, hovering at a distance with two of his assault-rifle-armed bodyguards watching the winding roads for the first sign of Isaac—and anyone else.

With two up in the helicopter, and five shotgun- and Uzi-armed men—excluding himself and Tassio—on the ground, Jake Locotta was fully confident that he could deal with any remnants of Jimmy Pilgrim's final game plan.

Now it was just a matter of waiting. . . .

They had been sitting in the living room of the Eagle Mountain cabin for exactly two hours and forty-five minutes, when the warning came over the scrambled pack-set radio in Joe Tassio's hand.

"Guy and a broad in an old VW, coming up the road," the static-blurred voice announced.

"Okay," Pilgrim nodded, "the son of a bitch's coming. Now we—"

"Another vehicle right behind them," the radio-voice continued. "Black van—"

"That's gotta be Raynee," Pilgrim rasped. "He's the only other one who—"

Locotta motioned to Tassio, "Check it out."

"Can you see who's in the van?" Tassio asked, keying his radio.

"Some nigger," the radio crackled. "Can't see anybody else. Okay to let him up?"

Locotta nodded his head.

"Yeah, let him come up," Tassio ordered the chopper crew. "But anybody pops outta that van with a gun, you waste 'em."

"Ten-four," the radio crackled once more, and then remained silent as Tassio motioned for his five armed gunmen to take their predetermined positions around the interior of the cabin.

Locotta, Tassio, and Pilgrim all heard the VW bug coming up the driveway. Pilgrim was the first to a window. He looked out and immediately recognized Dr. David Isaac sitting nervously behind the wheel of the battered VW.

"He's here," Pilgrim started to growl. Then he stood transfixed at the window as Isaac made a quick U-turn in the driveway in front of the cabin, and quickly accelerated back down the driveway and onto the road.

"What the hell?" Pilgrim snarled, lunging for the door. He stopped, his hand still holding the knob of the open door, as he saw the familiar, blood-splattered figure walking up the steps with a small red notebook held loosely in one hand.

"Hi, Pilgrim," Ben Koda said calmly, only his purple-bruised face and his dark, glittering eyes hinting at the depths of his tightly controlled fury as he came up to the door. "You gonna invite me in?"

"Joe," the radio crackled again. "Van's stopped and turned around, about a hundred yards down the road . . . looks like they just dumped a body out the back door."

"What—where's Rainbow?" Pilgrim blurted out, and then his bearded face contorted—first in disbelief and then in rage—as he suddenly realized the significance of Koda's blood-stained shirt and jeans.

"Sounds t' me like he's layin' out there on the road. . . ." Koda shrugged, shouldering his way past Pilgrim to the middle of the living room, his eyes taking in the unexpected presence of Jake Locotta, and Joe Tassio, and the five serious-faced enforcers whose weapons were now pointing at him.

"He's probably gonna live, if he doesn't die of heatstroke out there," Koda went on matter-of-factly as he walked across the room toward Mudd with his hands carefully in sight.

Koda saw Sandy's horribly swollen, bruised and blood-smeared face. Fighting the emotional surge of relief and fury that threatened to unleash the vengeance-maddened entity in his mind, Koda knelt down and carefully removed the blood-soaked gag from Sandy's battered mouth. She tried to smile, and then had to lay her head back against the couch, too badly hurt and exhausted to move or talk.

"It's okay," Koda whispered, and then winked reassuringly before standing back up and turning to face Pilgrim and the other men in the room.

"Figure a man gets himself snake-bit, decides to cut off his own hand, not a whole lot you can do about it," Koda forced a tight-jawed smile. "Know what I mean?"

"Who the HELL—?" Jake Locotta started to snarl, and then his eyes flickered in recognition. "You're the guy in the park," he said much more softly. "You and this broad here, and the—"

"Nigger?" Koda asked, shaking his head. "You people got yourselves a real problem with this racial crap. No wonder you can't get your shit together."

"Listen, you son of a bitch . . ." Locotta growled, in no mood at all to take any crap from some street-level dope dealer. He was still trying to figure out what the hell was going on.

"The thing ol' Pilgrim here never did understand," Koda went on, ignoring Locotta, "is that Charley, Sandy and me, we were just out trying to make ourselves a living." As he continued to stare into Pilgrim's deadly cold eyes, Koda's mind suddenly flashed up the images of Sandy's brutally ravaged face and Kaaren Mueller's wrists and ankles . . . and he had to force them out before the entity screaming in the back of his mind could claw its way out.

"That's something you might not have to worry about much longer," Joe Tassio suggested menacingly, as he waited obediently for Locotta's signal, his eyes flickering over at his five alert enforcers— three of whom were carefully watching Koda and Mudd and Pilgrim while the other two watched the windows.

Ben Koda turned his head to stare curiously at Tassio. "You're not the one who worked her over, are you?" he finally said.

Joe Tassio blinked, his eyebrows narrowing in momentary confusion, because this man appeared to be much too calm and self-assured.

"Joe, the back of that van's filled with sandbags," the static-filled voice blurted out over Tassio's radio, the whumping sounds of the helicopter rotors loudly audible in the background. "Looks like at least one guy in the back—probably the driver—with a rifle."

Tassio's eyes widened in sudden understanding.

"Naw, I didn't think so," Koda said mostly to himself, shaking his head as he watched the hulking Tassio move quickly over to the window with a pair of binoculars. "Don't look like the type."

Jimmy Pilgrim couldn't control himself any longer. "Where the hell's Isaac—" he snarled, starting to move forward toward Koda . . . and then halting when one of Locotta's gunmen stepped forward with a shotgun.

Koda looked down to Jake Locotta's smooth, unbruised knuckles, ignoring Pilgrim now. "Same with you, sport," he said to the tensed mob chief, "and since your playmates here probably had better things to do, that just about narrows it down to our asshole friend," Koda whispered coldly, turning to face Pilgrim. "Trouble is," he held up the notebook in his right hand, "him and me, we still got a deal to work out."

In uncontainable fury, Pilgrim lunged toward Koda, his face contorted with murderous rage. Then he jerked to a stop as Locotta's protective enforcer loudly chambered a round into the short-barreled shotgun.

"He's definitely got somebody else out there, Jake," Tassio called out. "Looks like that nigger friend a' his."

"The professor had to go somewhere kinda sudden-like, so he asked me to drop this off," Koda went on conversationally. "Looks like just a plain old lab notebook. Has somebody's name on it, though. Nichole something-or-another. Except that name's crossed out. Now it just says 'Maria.' Guess that must mean something to you, huh?" he asked, looking straight into Pilgrim's eyes.

"Give me that," Pilgrim rasped, ignoring the shotgun as he reached . . .

"Uh-uh, we didn't drive all the way up here just to *give* you something." Koda shook his head, tossing the notebook past Pilgrim's outstretched hand to Locotta—who fielded it awkwardly, as Pilgrim's eyes, hands and body followed the trajectory of the precious notebook that meant *everything* now to almost everyone in the cabin.

Locotta quickly waved off the bodyguard who was about to splatter Pilgrim and began thumbing through the gridded, light green pages.

"What you're lookin' for starts on page eighteen," Koda suggested. "Something about how to go about making some kind of analog. Number A-Seventeen . . . that the one?"

"There, that's it!" Pilgrim blurted out. "A-Seventeen. That's the one that Raggedy Annie bitch was yelling about!"

"I'm really glad to hear that." Koda smiled. "'Cause like I said,

Charley and me, we didn't drive up all this way just to *give* you people something. Fact of the matter is, we're planning on *selling* you something."

Pilgrim's face twisted into a spasm of anger. He shook his head, seemingly speechless. He started for Koda again, mindlessly frustrated by the fact that he needed more time. He was having to think on his feet now, knowing he didn't have enough time to set up the games that would make the girl want to talk and talk and talk, until—

"HOLD IT!" Locotta yelled, finally starting to put the pieces together.

Pilgrim hesitated in midstride, and then turned on Locotta. "We *have* it!" he hissed, his mouth twisting in rage as his clawed hand pointed back at the waiting Koda. "*Why* . . . ?"

"Your friend out there," Locotta growled at Koda, ignoring Pilgrim's rabid gesturing. "This Charley. You figure he's gonna help you get back what we already got?" Locotta's voice was rough, tired and expectant. He'd been in this business far too long not to know that there had to be something else.

"I don't think you understand," Ben Koda said. "I'm not offering to sell *that* . . ." he gestured at the notebook in Locotta's hand. "Like you said, you've already got it. What I'm offering is a couple more pages—twenty and twenty-one, to be exact."

Both Locotta and Pilgrim scrabbled at the notebook . . . and then stared back up at Koda as they discovered the torn edges of the missing pages—the last two pages of the A-17 synthesis procedure.

"That nigger . . ." Tassio growled, coming back to stare over Jake Locotta's shoulder.

"That's right, Charley-the-Nigger." Koda nodded serenely. "Right out there in the road, 'bout a hundred yards or so. Go on out there and call him that if you want to. He's got those pages . . . and a couple other things too."

"I'll go . . ." Joe Tassio snarled, starting for the door when Koda interrupted.

"You go out there like that and the first thing he's gonna do is burn those pieces of paper. Then he's gonna put you—and anybody else who comes out that door—on the ground with a couple three-oh-eight rounds. An' sometime after *that*, he's gonna be comin' in here after Sandy, mostly 'cause he's kinda fond of her."

Koda went on, when no one said anything, "Charley's really a nice gentle guy, if you don't count all the people he's had to hurt lately. 'Course he's probably not gonna be real happy when he sees her lookin' like that," he added pointedly.

"We don't *need* those pages," Pilgrim growled savagely, his eyes boring into Koda's. "The whole procedure's in the computer. All we need to do is get the password out of that little bitch . . ." He started for Mudd, and Koda stepped in his way as two Uzis and a shotgun centered on Pilgrim's chest.

"She hasn't got it, Pilgrim," Koda whispered quietly, his hands twitching as he forced his mind to clamp down hard on the raging entity.

"Bullshit! I'm telling you, Jake, she's the one who changed all the passwords!" Jimmy Pilgrim almost screamed at Locotta.

"No, you don't understand." Koda shook his head. "She got at the passwords. Charley and me are the ones who put in the new ones. Had her turn her head while we did it too. So what I'm telling you people is she can't give it to you, even if she wanted to, because she *hasn't got it*.

"We do," he added calmly.

"And if you figure on trying to get it out of us," Koda went on, smiling at Pilgrim, "you're a little fuckin' late, 'cause Charley and I had Isaac erase the memory banks of your computer from his lab about three hours ago. And since he's long gone by now, the only way you people are ever gonna get your hands on that A-Seventeen analog is to deal with the one source you got left."

"We don't even know he's *got* those pages," Pilgrim whispered hoarsely.

"Send your buddy out there with the book." Koda shrugged, nodding at Tassio. "Stripped to the waist and unarmed. Charley'll let him match up the torn edges. Don't think there's any way we could fake something like that."

The silence in the room lasted almost fifteen seconds.

"Whaddaya want for 'em," Locotta rasped.

"Tell you the truth, what I'd really like is about ten minutes alone with Jimmy-the-Freak here," Koda said easily, "but the fact is I'm willing to settle for Sandy . . ."

"That's *all* . . .?" a disbelieving Jimmy Pilgrim blurted out before he could help himself.

"You got a deal," Locotta growled.

". . . and maybe a pound or so of Jimmy Pilgrim's coke over there," Koda nodded at the pile of plastic-wrapped packages sitting by the stone fireplace. "We'll even throw in that fuckin' Rainbow as a bonus, seeing's how we're not gonna need him any more."

"What?!" Locotta rasped.

"It's like we've been trying to tell you people all along," Koda explained. "Me and my friends, all we wanted to do was buy a couple ounces of coke and go out sailing. But you guys just *had* to make it difficult."

"All you want's the broad and a pound of *coke*?" Locotta asked incredulously. "You guys have any *idea* what that seventeen-shit can *do*?"

"Supposed to be some sort of hotshot aphrodisiac," Koda shrugged. "Don't mean much to Charley or me. He's horny all the time anyway, and I've got my lady friend over here," Koda added, winking down at Sandy, who had been struggling to come up to a sitting position when Koda's offhand comment caused her puffy eyes to blink open, and her bleeding, swollen lips to flicker into a painful grin.

Locotta handed the notebook to Tassio. "Go on out there and check it out," he growled, continuing to stare at Ben Koda as Tassio stripped off his shirt—revealing a chestful of thick, corded muscles covered with a mat of grey hair—and then stepped cautiously outside the door with the notebook in one hand.

They all waited for almost two minutes without speaking, the silence in the room broken only by the echoing roar of the slowly circling helicopter.

"You sure you only want one?" Locotta finally asked. "Whole pile of them things sitting there. Don't mean shit to me," he shrugged. And, in fact, Jake Locotta really didn't care one way or the other. But he was determined to find out what was behind this seemingly suicidal young man.

"One'll do us just fine." Koda shook his head. " 'Long as it comes from Pilgrim. We're not greedy, we just want what he owes us."

"Get him one," Locotta growled at Pilgrim. "Now."

Pilgrim walked over and picked up one of the pound-bricks of cocaine just as Joe Tassio came back into the cabin with the loose-limbed form of Raynee over his shoulder. After dumping the semi-conscious street dealer to the floor indifferently—Raynee's black, Afroed head striking the floor with a loud thunk—Tassio walked over to his boss, who looked up questioningly.

"Pages match," Tassio muttered.

"And?" Locotta demanded.

"Man looks like he's by himself." Tassio shrugged. "We got enough people to take him, but he won't go easy."

Locotta nodded as if confirming something he'd already suspected. "Well Mr. . . . . ?"

"Ben'll do fine," Koda said. "And your friend there's mostly right, except I don't think they can do it . . . and a whole lotta people around here are gonna die if they try. So how about that coke?" he reminded.

Locotta hesitated, then turned to Pilgrim. "Give it to him," he growled.

Pilgrim moved forward as if he were in a dream, giving the plastic-wrapped package over to a grinning Ben Koda with a hand that trembled with rage and hatred. From all outward signs, the so-far outmaneuvered game player looked as if he was about to have a seizure.

Koda accepted the package, nodded pleasantly at Pilgrim, then slowly and carefully removed one of Rainbow's thick-bladed throwing knives from his back pocket, using one sharp edge to cut a small slit in the tightly compressed brick. A few small chunks of a distinctly odorous, chunky white powder spilled out onto the floor.

"Okay," Koda nodded at Locotta as he walked over to the couch and used Rainbow's knife again to cut the bindings away from Sandy Mudd's wrists and legs—under the watchful eyes of Locotta's enforcers—before slipping it back into his hip pocket. "You ready to make the switch?"

Jake Locotta nodded silently.

"How about you, jailbait? You ready to go?" Koda asked Mudd, bending down and gently helping her to her feet.

"Ben, they're not going to let you . . ." she tried to whisper through her swollen lips.

"It's okay, partner," Koda whispered, finding it necessary to shove the entity back once more because she'd been hurt so bad . . . and because the knife and Pilgrim were so close to his twitching hand. But he *knew* he couldn't lose control now, not if he wanted to get her out of the mountain cabin alive.

"Oh yeah, one more thing," Koda said, turning to Locotta. "That chopper . . . put it away somewhere."

"What . . . ?" Tassio's eyes widened.

"Keep it in the air, but move it over to the other side of the mountain. Once I walk out there, I don't want to see that thing, just hear it. It shows up while we're making the switch, Charley starts burning paper."

Joe Tassio started to protest, but Locotta shook his head . . . and Tassio reluctantly brought the radio up to his mouth and gave the order.

Koda waited until he heard the rotor blades drifting away. "Now that we've got that settled, gentlemen," he smiled, "I think it's time we all went outside."

As Charley Shannon watched carefully from his sandbagged position, Pilgrim, Koda, Mudd, Locotta, Tassio, and four of the armed enforcers all walked slowly out into the middle of the driveway—leaving one of the Uzi-armed gunmen, Pilgrim's pilot and Raynee inside—and then came to a halt about fifteen yards from the road, in front of the two empty sedans and Pilgrim's silent helicopter.

From their position, the men, except Koda—who was concentrating on supporting his severely injured partner—could all see the makeshift, sandbag bunker inside the open back doors of the black van that was parked about a hundred yards down the road. There was no visible sign of Shannon, just the end of a steady rifle barrel pointing in their direction.

It was ghostly silent this high up, Ben Koda realized. The only other sounds in the high, pine-rustling mountain air were the distant, rumbling sounds of a helicopter off flying somewhere in the low-lying clouds that surrounded the mountaintop.

Almost hating to break the silence, Koda turned to Tassio, still supporting Sandy with one arm.

"What's gonna happen," he said, "is you're gonna walk Sandy here down the road and help set her in the passenger seat of that van, real nice and gentle-like."

Tassio glanced over at Mudd's bruised face.

"Yeah, Charley's not gonna be too happy," Koda acknowledged, "but he won't do anything," he added reassuringly. "Then, when she's all settled in, he's gonna give you those pages. You might as well get started. It's a long walk."

It took the still barechested Joe Tassio almost five minutes to make those hundred yards, gingerly walking beside the wobbly, determined girl the first thirty or so yards, then having to quickly catch her and carry her the rest of the way when her legs finally buckled.

As he got to the opened back doors of the van, Tassio discovered he didn't want to look into the fiercely glaring eyes of Charley Shannon—who appeared to want nothing more than to toss aside the scoped assault rifle and come over the sandbag barricade after Tassio with his huge bare hands.

But he didn't.

Instead, Shannon motioned Tassio around to the passenger side of the van with a cocked .45, watched as he gently secured the semiconscious Mudd into the front seat . . . and then wordlessly handed over the two notebook pages. As Tassio turned back toward the cabin, Charley Shannon shut and locked the passenger-side door, set the .45

on the driver's seat, and quickly scrambled back between the seats to his spotting position behind the sandbags . . . and the rifle.

Joe Tassio walked back at a deliberately slow pace, the two torn pages clutched in his slightly shaky hand, ultimately relieved—and secretly amazed—when he didn't feel a .308 bullet tear into his broad back. He handed the pages to Locotta.

"You satisfied?" Locotta growled at Koda, staring at him with the look of an exceedingly irritated and vicious man who was about to indulge himself in some long-delayed amusement.

"Couple more things." Koda shrugged, causing Locotta's eyebrows to rise. The dark-haired agent slowly reached behind his back and pulled a tiny radio transmitter out of the shirt-covered waistband of his jeans.

"First of all, you able to hear all that, Charley?" Koda asked in a normal tone of voice. All eight men turned to look down the road . . . and saw Charley Shannon's thick arm wave through the driver's side window as the van started up and began to move slowly down the road.

"Good." Koda nodded, noting that one of Locotta's enforcers had already started edging over toward one of the parked sedans. "Okay, Charley, why don't we give these folks a little demonstration of what's gonna happen, any of them start thinking about followin' you two down that road.

"See, Charley and I've gotten so we just don't hardly trust people any more," Koda explained, turning his back to the road and savoring the wide-eyed shock and confusion on the seven faces—especially Pilgrim's. He ignored the shotgun and the two Uzi submachine guns that were now pointed at his midsection.

"Kinda figured you people might get the idea to welsh on the deal after you got hold of those pages, so . . ."

At that moment, Ben Koda heard a car door slam behind his back. He spun back around . . . and stared down the long asphalt road as the wobbly figure of Sandy Mudd came staggering away from the sharply braking van with Charley Shannon's .45 in her hand.

"SANDY, GODDAMNIT . . . !" Koda started to yell.

His words were drowned out in a sudden, reverberating roar of churning rotor blades as a black-painted helicopter dropped out of the clouds and came thundering in low over the top of the stopped van.

At the instant the helicopter passed over Mudd, a long-barreled, nose-mounted chain gun cut loose with a burplike chatter, sending a hundred and fifty armor-piercing, 30mm projectiles streaking into the asphalt roadway with an earsplitting roar . . . throwing chunks of asphalt, shredded car and helicopter parts, and flaming gasoline twenty feet into the air in front of the standing men as the Apache attack helicopter roared by and then banked around sharply.

"HERBY . . . ONE-EIGHTY!" Ben Koda screamed, spotting Locotta's helicopter as it burst through the cloud cover behind the Apache, the barrels of two assault rifles sticking out of the open side door.

Koda yelled hoarsely once more—this time more of a "rebel yell"—as Herby Dawson spun the massive gunship in midair, judged angle and speed instinctively, and then obliterated the swooping Bell Ranger in a billowing mass of flame and metal with a nose-leading, three-hundred-and-sixty-rounds-per-second burst from the Apache's two side-pylon-mounted, six-barreled Mini-guns.

In the relative silence that followed, the scream from the cabin doorway, and the single gunshot from Mudd's .45, sounded almost like children at play.

But as Ben Koda turned to look in horror, he saw Lafayette Beaumont Raynee standing poised in the doorway with a crazy grin on his bloodied face and an Uzi—once belonging to Tassio—clutched in his single hand.

In that instant, Raynee's eyes focused on Koda with murderous intent, but a second .45 slug from Mudd's shaky hand tore splinters out of the doorframe next to Raynee's head, and the sadistic killer realized how he could hurt Ben Koda even more . . .

"SANDY . . . CHARLEY, DROP HIM!" Koda screamed—too far away to do anything other than watch helplessly—as Raynee sprinted madly across the yard and dove behind a thick pine tree that absorbed Sandy Mudd's shakily aimed third shot . . . and then two much-too-high .308 rifle rounds, because Mudd was standing almost directly between the tree-protected Raynee and Charley Shannon, who was already scrambling out of the sandbagged van.

Laughing with glee, Rainbow swung the stubby-barreled Uzi around the tree to bear on the hopelessly exposed Mudd . . .

"HERBY!"

. . . and then disappeared in a vectoring eruption of dirt, grass, blood, cloth, tissue and white pine as the whirling barrels of the Apache's Mini-gun pods sent two converging streams of machine gun bullets up the lawn and into the tree trunk.

The Apache came around like a dancing dragonfly to hover out over the cliff, its lethal weaponry—the still-smoking 30mm cannon and the six-barreled Mini-guns—now facing the Eagle Mountain cabin and the scattered array of now-visibly-unarmed men.

In the moment of wind-rustling silence that followed the final, deadly roar of the Apache's gun pods, a far less violent but equally shattering event took place on the driveway in front of the isolated Eagle Mountain cabin.

In making his desperate dive to the ground in those terrifying moments when the 30mm tank-stopping rounds ripped into the gas tanks of the cars and helicopter, Jake Locotta had lost his tight grip on the two torn pages out of the Maria notebook.

As he lay there now, sprawled out on the asphalt driveway and trembling from the violent display of pure firepower, Locotta, and the still-standing Jimmy Pilgrim, watched in helpless horror as the gusting mountain winds caught up the torn pages and sent them fluttering toward the flaming remains of Locotta's vehicles . . . each page bursting into a brief puff of flame and smoke before drifting away as powdered ash.

At that moment, something in the expressions of Jake Locotta and Jimmy Pilgrim seemed to die.

"Herby, you see this asshole still standing up here in front of me?" Ben Koda whispered hoarsely, the transmitter held loosely in his hand as he stared straight into Pilgrim's crazed eyes from a distance of about fifteen feet. "Man's name is Jimmy Pilgrim, the son of a bitch game player Charley and I been tellin' you about.

"Tell you what," Koda went on, a thin smile forming beneath his ragged mustache, "if he's not down on the ground with the rest of these bastards in about three seconds, why don't you see if you can put him there. Don't worry 'bout how many pieces."

Ben Koda heard the sudden change in pitch of the rotor blades behind his back as the Apache came around suddenly in a crablike movement . . . and then Pilgrim was scrambling down to the asphalt between Locotta and Tassio.

"Now that we've got your attention," Koda said, staring down at the seven sprawled men whose eyes were fixed on the noisily hovering black helicopter, "on behalf of Freddy Sanjanovitch and Kaaren Mueller and Sandy and Charley and a whole bunch of other Federal-type agents like myself . . ." Koda hesitated as he knelt down, slipped the DEA Special Agent badge out of his sock, and then held it out in front of Locotta, Pilgrim and Tassio.

". . . you assholes are all under arrest for assault, kidnapping, murder, and . . . oh yeah, *especially* for the illicit sale of a restricted dangerous drug. . . ."

"Like we tried t' tell Fogarty, Muddy-girl . . ." Charley Shannon grinned and winked as he came up to the teary-eyed Mudd and carefully removed the still-smoking .45 from her shaky hands—just as the first of the helicopters bearing teams of San Diego-based DEA agents began landing in front of the cabin—". . . it jes' couldn't be all *that* hard t' buy a pound a' coke off a little ol' dope dealer like Jimmy Pilgrim."

EPILOGUE

THE PENETRATION and dismemberment of Jimmy Pilgrim's San Diego-based drug-dealing empire by Tom Fogarty's DEA Task Force team generated a wave of repercussions that were ultimately felt clear across the North and South American continents.

At first, the damage seemed containable. The Syndicate council met and made the initial determination that Jake Locotta was not to be held *fully* responsible . . . yet. He would be given an opportunity to clean up the mess in San Diego, mostly because none of the other Syndicate chiefs wanted any part of that poisoned territory.

As such, Locotta and Tassio were allowed to make their bail. And, in the parlance of their organized crime peers, they hit the street running.

Given the choice, Jake Locotta would have much preferred to extract his revenge in small pieces—starting out by allowing Jimmy Pilgrim to sweat out every minute of his trial. But Locotta didn't have that option, because he didn't have that much time. He'd been given a finite number of days in which to bring his hemorrhaged territory back

under control. And to Jake Locotta, control meant one simple word.
Fear.

So Jimmy Pilgrim was given only a few brief moments to experience all of the horrifying terror he had once inflicted upon almost everyone in his path before the suffocating fumes of lighter fluid became a billowing fire that turned his cell into a blackened pit of rictus-faced death.

Word of Pilgrim's inevitable fate spread quickly, but as Locotta and Tassio secretly feared, it was all too little . . . and much too late. The initial fifty pounds of Rainbow-Vision, Jimmy Pilgrim's legacy to his street dealers, had long since had its intended effect.

It all came down to the irrepressible fact that the B-16 analog—while far less potent than the fabled Power-Rainbow—was definitely more enticing than cocaine. And then too, of course, it was still perfectly legal to possess.

Michael Theiss, Pilgrim's money man, disappeared off his yacht somewhere in the Bahamas two days later, after being persuaded to reveal the exact locations of the seven completed and the ninety-three planned analog labs being financed by his investment group. Accordingly, one by one, these remnants of Jimmy Pilgrim's intricate game plan also disappeared under the guise of accident and betrayal. But still it wasn't enough.

By the time the first of Pilgrim's planned franchise labs went up in flames at the hand of a professional arsonist, five chemists had independently determined the molecular structure of Rainbow-Vision . . . and immediately worked out synthesis methods for replenishing their dwindling stocks. Within a week, fresh supplies of the B-16 analog were back out on the streets, but this time its distribution was no longer restricted to Southern California.

There were still some rumors going around to the effect that Rainbow-Vision wasn't really the *good* stuff, but with the sudden, inexplicable disappearance of William Benson Sandcastle III these rumors gradually died out for lack of verification. But by then, of course, it was much too late.

The market for Colombian-grown cocaine base hit bottom two weeks later. Which, coincidentally, was the morning that a wandering prospector discovered the bodies of Jake Locotta and Joe Tassio—both with hands bound behind their backs and a single bullet hole in their foreheads—face down in a Mojave Desert arroyo . . .

. . . that happened to be about sixty miles due west of a camping spot on the Colorado River where Hazel Fogarty was cooking breakfast for five special agents of a DEA Task Force team, who were enjoying a well-deserved break from their efforts to document their case in report form while there was still someone left to prosecute.

"So whaddaya think?" Charley Shannon asked Sandy, gazing out over the glassy river water as he leaned back in his precariously creaking folding chair.

"You mean Isaac? I still don't think you should've let him go," Mudd said cautiously through her still-tender but rapidly healing jaw. "He's just going to cause us trouble. . . ."

"Naw, don't worry none 'bout that professor," Shannon grunted. "We'll get ourselves another shot at that boy, soon's he sticks his head up. Ah was talkin' 'bout our crazy-ass partner out there," he said, nodding out at the scene on the river edge where Ben Koda was balanced on one foot with his other ski-fastened leg held high in the air.

"Oh, him?" Sandy grinned innocently, shielding her eyes with her hand as she stared out from her lounge chair at the lanky silhouetted figure of Koda—who wobbled precariously as Bart Harrington swung *Spirit of Seventy-Six* upstream. Mudd then laughed with only a little bit of pain as she watched Tom Fogarty almost fall out of the stern of the boat as he worked frantically to untangle the sky rope.

"I don't know, Charley." Sandy finally shrugged, the peaceful serenity of their surroundings visibly reflected in her eyes. "Guess I haven't figured all that out yet. Important thing is, though," she turned to her trusted friend with a dimpled grin on her purple-bruised face, "does he know how to ski?"

"Not's good as me," Charley Shannon shook his head firmly, and then yelled out with the full force of his powerful lungs . . .

"HIT IT!"

. . . blissfully unaware that in a small hidden laboratory many miles east of the Big Bend playground, the Creator and his faithful alchemist Maria silently held the gold-tinged mother liquid of the A-18 analog in their skillful yet trembling hands, impatient for their ancient research to begin once again.